SECRETS AND SHADOWS

SECRETS AND SHADOWS

A NOVEL

ROBERTA SILMAN

CAMPDEN HILL BOOKS

For information, address the publisher:

Campden Hill Books
317 Blue Hill Road
Great Barrington, MA 01230

www.robertasilman.com

ISBN: 978-1-64008-902-0 (hc)
ISBN: 978-1-64008-900-6 (pbk)
ebook: ISBN 978-1-64008-901-3
Library of Congress Control Number: 2017913574

First Edition

Book design by Rita Lascaro
Typeset in Stone Serif
Manufactured in the United States of America
Printed by Puritan Press, Hollis, New Hampshire on acid-free paper

"The worst survived, that is, the fittest; the best all died.

—PRIMO LEVI, "THE DROWNED AND THE SAVED"

"Only the brave know how to forgive . . . .
A coward never forgave; it is not in his nature."

—LAURENCE STERNE, *SERMONS*, VOLUME 1, NUMBER 12

For Bob

PART I

1

"EVE?" His voice is raspy.

"Paul?"

"Is this a bad time?"

"No. This is a fine time." Eve's heart is pounding, but she is determined to remain calm. The silence deepens.

"Did Claudia call?"

"Yes." Eve waits for his usual dry, crisp tones.

Instead, his voice is subdued, troubled, unrecognizable, exactly as their daughter Claudia described. "It's so odd, this happening on the same day as *Kristallnacht,* the coincidence is remarkable. Eerie. I guess that's partly why I'm calling, I . . . wanted to talk to you . . . "

Eve stiffens.

"I was wondering . . . " His voice trails off to a whisper.

He sounds so uncertain, so disheartened. For a second a feeling of triumph surges through her at this unexpected switch in their roles, then concern kicks in. "Paul, are you all right?" This is so unlike his recent self, since their divorce he has been terse, business-like, even when she has tried to talk about the children.

"I'm not sure," he says, and she can see him in her mind's eye, leaning forward as he always did when he needed to think. She waits, realizing that Claudia was right to be concerned. Now he says, "I think I'm just stunned." That makes sense, they all are, and Berlin was a huge part of his life. "Look, Eve, I know this comes from nowhere, and I have no right to ask it, but I was wondering . . . I wonder if you might come with me . . .

to Berlin." His voice is so low she can hardly hear him, but his relief at getting out the question is unmistakable.

Can you hear such relief at long distance? Eve wouldn't have thought it possible. She stares at the phone, once more imagining his furrowed brow and tense forward position. But she knows enough not to respond. This is too important—this complicated proud man, after five years of being apart, finally asking for her help. This proud man who was her husband for 23 years, who is the father of her children, who caused her such pain finally calling her.

So she says, quietly, "We're all stunned."

Again silence. Then he says, "I'm not sure why, but I need to go back, and I'd like you to come with me." His voice is stronger now, not so plaintive, more reminiscent of the voice she tries at all costs to avoid, that brusque voice that has been his since they parted.

"Yes," he repeats more firmly. "I'd like you to come with me."

Hearing it Eve suddenly feels fear, what she felt so often in the last few years of their marriage. And, like a reflex she cannot control, the fear turns to anger—as if all the rage she's repressed for so long is suddenly erupting. Without any warning she feels like a human volcano. She manages to tamp down her unexpected rage before she speaks.

"Eve, did you hear me?"

"Of course I heard you." Her voice is cold. "But this is ridiculous. Bizarre. You calling me now, after all those years when you couldn't wait to get off the phone whenever I called you." Her eyes are filling, and she pauses to wipe away a tear.

Before she can collect herself, he says, "I can see why you might feel that way, but can't you let me explain?"

"Now I'm not sure." She feels herself sitting straighter. "For the last five years, since the divorce came through, you've never let me explain. You've hardly had a minute for me. Even when there were things we needed to discuss. So why now?"

Then, before he can reply, "What about all your fancy girl-friends, what about this Anna woman Claudia mentioned?"

Eve's voice grows higher. He hates it when she gets shrill. So does she. Girding herself for the click of the phone, she holds the receiver away from her ear.

Another long silence. Finally he asks, "Are you finished?" Finished? Why she hasn't even begun!

But she says, "Yes."

Now Paul's voice sounds eager, young. She hasn't heard such verve in his voice for years. "I know we're divorced, but as a friend, my friend. Couldn't you . . . come, as a friend?"

Has he gone crazy? He has more friends than anyone she knows. Paul can't walk down Fifth Avenue without meeting twenty people who consider him their friend, it's family legend.

"I'm not your friend, Paul, I'm your wife, or was, for 23 years. But I'm not your wife anymore, and if you want a friend, call Ian or one of your other buddies from Yale, or one of your pals from the office." There! Make him angry and get rid of him. What she's always done when she's had enough. Yet in her heart she knows it is a cowardly ploy.

"You have every right to be angry, and maybe I have no right to ask. After all I put you through. But I can't go alone, and when I realized I had to go back to Berlin . . ." his voice dwindles to a whisper.

"Why now?" Eve repeats.

"A number of reasons, complicated, and connected to The Wall coming down. If you come, maybe I can make you understand why things went so wrong. I thought maybe we could walk and talk . . ."

"Now you want to talk? What about all those years when I wanted to talk?"

"I know it seems absurd, and I know how hard my silence was for you, Eve, but I'm telling you the truth, and I thought maybe you would help me."

Again he pauses. "I guess it's too much to ask. Though it wouldn't take long . . . I'm sorry I even asked, try to forgive me." Is he asking forgiveness for this call, or for everything else? His voice sounds so weary, and she wishes she had held her temper. But before she can form the question, there's the click of the telephone, and he is gone.

Shocked that he has retreated so quickly, Eve stares at the receiver in her hand. He wasn't the one who usually ran. For a few seconds she isn't sure if their conversation really happened. Can she have imagined it? But no, it is true: Paul, her husband Paul has called.

*   *   *

Slowly, against the noise of the busy signal of the phone which she leaves off the hook because she needs to gather her wits, Eve resorts to an old habit to calm herself; she goes over everything that happened this afternoon and evening up to now.

After lunch she went to her garden to plant the last of her bulbs. Before setting to her task she stood for a few minutes, taking in the gorgeous November light, the most beautiful of all, she'd always thought, as if it knew its days were numbered. As she watched the sun's stubborn sheen turn the surface of Lambert's Cove to a length of shimmering silk, she was struck—as she was so often, in every season—by its reckless radiance in this small corner of the world, throwing its light here there and everywhere so that you hardly knew where to look first.

Then as she knelt and worked the friable soil, she remembered a quotation she had read in her twenties: "A man carries two lives within him: the life he dreams and the life he lives; and only rarely—the young would hang themselves if anybody ever told them how rarely—do the two converge." As always, she was struck by its irony. When she first read it, she had been sure she would live the life she dreamed, for she had just married Paul. Now, at almost fifty, she was alone, surrounded by this wild opalescent glow, living a life she had carefully carved out for herself that had nothing to do with Paul or Manhattan or even, if she was completely truthful, their three children who were now grown. And not even able to remember who had written it.

But November afternoons were always shorter than she remembered. Before long a chilly grayness threw itself over the Cove as sinuously as a blanket might cling to the curve of a thigh. She finally conceded to herself that the planting would have to wait until morning. In the encroaching dark she gathered her tools, dragged the bulbs back into the shed, and shivered a little as she entered the back door, glad to be warm. After changing her clothes, she lay down on her bed for a nap before dinner. A perfectly ordinary November day on Martha's Vineyard. Until the ringing of the telephone.

"Mom!" Claudia's voice was urgent. Eve sat up, it was after seven. "Mom, you need to put on the television, they're tearing down the Berlin Wall. It's unbelievable, it's coming down so fast it looks like *papier mâché*." Eve ran downstairs to put on the TV and picked up the extension, then watched the crowds moving, as insistent as waves slapping the shore in a storm—rushing, searching, embracing, crying. One wrenching scene after another, and everyone carrying a piece of the wall, artifacts that would surely appreciate in value, an announcer was now saying.

"Isn't it amazing?" Claudia's voice quivered with excitement. She was their youngest, on a fellowship at the Sorbonne. And before Eve could reply, "I called Dad, he's stunned, absolutely stunned. So many of his old haunts, the cafe he loved so much, his old school, the synagogue, all of them right there. He can hardly speak, doesn't even sound like himself."

A twinge of hurt, like a scab pulled off too quickly, rose for a moment in Eve's chest. Of course Claudia had telephoned her father first. But surely their most exuberant child was exaggerating. Paul could always find something to say, that was part of his enormous charm.

Then a voice in Eve's head: But not about Berlin. You waited for years, and after a while you stopped asking, or even waiting.

"I'm worried, Mom. Maybe you could call him?" Claudia's voice was suddenly small.

"We've hardly spoken since the divorce."

"I know. But he sounded so strange."

"I'm sure he's fine." Then, brightly, "Didn't you tell me he had someone new?"

"Yes, her name is Anna. It came up because I wanted to make sure they didn't come to Paris when you plan to." Hearing that had made Eve immensely sad. Children having to maneuver so their parents didn't pass on the stairs. How had they come to such an awful place?

"Well, maybe he can talk about this to her," Eve said as firmly as she could.

"Maybe. And maybe they'll go to Berlin," Claudia said, the lilt in her voice returning. "How I wish I could. But I have a huge paper on Balzac and Zola due at the beginning of December." Finally Eve could hear a shred of guilt. Foolishly, Eve had let Claudia know she was disappointed that Claudia wasn't coming home for Thanksgiving. Then, evenly, "How are you, Mom?"

Eve straightened. "Fine, and so good to hear your voice, and so amazing, this news. The world is topsy-turvy."

"No enemy, no Cold War." Claudia giggled. "What will the spies do, the KGB . . . oh, my God, what will John Le Carre do?" Laughing so warmly, so intimately with her child, Eve forgot for a moment how far away she really was.

"It's incredible, but I must go, I'm exhausted, and have an early class tomorrow. History in the making, is there anything better? I love you." As suddenly as she'd crashed into Eve's day, she was gone.

And now, the phone still twanging its busy signal, Eve can feel a pang run through her. How she misses the kids sometimes—their bulk in her line of sight, at the table, in the doorway of her bedroom saying goodnight. So many years, so many daily habits, and then they are adults and gone. Sometimes she can hardly remember all the books before bed, the sore throats, the childhood diseases; often it is a shadowy mist, then a dream, or a moment like this when it will spring to life, as vivid as it once was.

And tonight, Paul. Her husband who was born in Berlin. And who is Anna? Is she just another in a string of beautiful, sexy women or someone important to Paul? Last, and most intriguing, will this propel him to go to Germany? Not likely. Whenever anyone talked about visiting Germany, Paul's face would always latch closed.

You can't call Paul. You'd be crazy. So stop wondering.

Then the phone again, this time her father. "Isn't this amazing?" he asked, but before she could answer, "Have you spoken to Paul?"

"No, but Claudia has."

"How is he?"

"Fine, I guess. Why don't you call him?" After the divorce Eve had thought her parents would stay in touch with Paul, but they hadn't seen him, except occasionally, at the synagogue where they all belonged.

"Maybe." Soon he admitted he wanted to go back to watching the news.

Within the next hour Eve spoke to Eric and Jeremy, her twin boys and Sarah, Jeremy's wife, her parents again, her Aunt Blanche, her special Vineyard friend, Max, and her old friend, Deborah. With each phone call she felt more and more isolated. A wave of dizziness finally reminded her she hadn't eaten since lunch. It was almost nine. She made a sandwich and planted herself in front of the TV, watching the newscasters tell the same story over and over.

Accompanying it, like part of a fugue, she heard Claudia talking about Paul, then her father's concern for him, then Max's excitement. But she kept returning to Paul. She had been sensible and refused Claudia's request to call him. Episode ended.

Yet when the telephone next rang, there he was.

Asking her to go with him to Berlin. It was unbelievable. Now, after her children were on their way in the world—Jeremy practicing law and married to Sarah, Eric, in a good job with an investment banking firm, Claudia at the Sorbonne—after she had learned she could live quite comfortably and certainly more peacefully without him, Paul had re-entered her life. And she, who prized civility above all, had behaved badly.

Eve could feel a blush rising from her neck. She had thought all she wanted was to live her tidy life. But after hearing his voice, hearing that plaintive, almost childish, "it wouldn't take long," part of her also longed to hear what else he had to say.

Slowly she put the telephone back in its cradle, somehow feeling stronger now that she had gone over in her mind how she had come to this place. And she knew the episode was far from ended. What would she do? She wasn't sure. She needed time.

But as she put the receiver back into its cradle, she was assailed by a rush of emotion, a rush of memory so sudden and insistent she could do nothing but give in to it . . .

I loved Paul Bertram, whom I married when I was twenty-one and he thirty-one, with all my heart: The way indulgent parents love a cherished, difficult child, beset by doubts, yet determined to make everything right. That was because the whole truth about him was too painful to grasp—maybe impossible to grasp—for we met in the fall of 1960, when America was still in a fervor of hope that evil could be erased, that peace and fraternity would prevail.

By then the Second World War had become distant, surreal, romantic, alive only in novels and movies, which weren't true, anyway. The reality of what had happened in Europe took almost two decades to seep into the consciousness of a generation which had been protected from the horrors of not only the war, but what came to be known as The Holocaust. Of course there were people who had experienced it firsthand, who could tell of terrible pain and anguish. But they didn't, they couldn't. It was too new, too raw. And even if they had wanted to tell their stories, no one wanted to listen. For more than two decades people wore blinders—Jews, Gentiles, everyone—and strove only for a future where the United States would be the most powerful country in the world, where its citizens would be free and have a fair chance.

Although my family were Zionists and knew about the Nuremberg trials and displaced persons and refugees flocking to Israel, they didn't talk about the concentration camps during the war, or for a long time after it. What could one say when faced by images of naked corpses stacked like wood? Of people who were living skeletons? Such things were unspeakable; people didn't talk about calculated exterminations, terror or murder to college girls like Eve. Besides, now they had new worries: Joe McCarthy and his henchmen, the Rosenbergs, Korea, the Cold War, problems in a place called Indochina. By 1960 the Second World War was long over, thank God, done with.

As soon as we fell in love, I knew that Paul's German childhood was very different from my American one, but I hardly thought about it. It had happened so long ago, and when you met him, you had no clue that he had ever lived anywhere but the United States. His past was stripped of all meaning, and all that mattered now was the present.

It is a golden autumn twilight, maybe our fourth date, and he is walking towards me. Never have I known such intensity, the feeling that every cell in my body is at attention, stretching towards him and him, alone. So this is love! Exactly as I suspected when I sensed him running after me that day in the Public Garden.

Now he sees me and we are rushing towards each other and I feel his body against mine. As he steps back for a moment, his piercing blue eyes are taking in my features, my hair, the neckline of my dress. Then his supple fingers gently push a lock behind my ear. Saying, with that innocent gesture, you are mine. You will always belong to me.

After that day I lost any talent for seeing objective truth. I saw only what I wanted to see or what Paul wanted me to see: the solid, handsome person who would take risks, who would reach the cutting edge of his profession, yet who exuded an amazing serenity, and an authenticity that drew people to him, that made others trust and respect him. A man whose name people knew. A man filled with the desire for knowledge and success, who read voraciously, who was proud of his Ivy League education, whose religion was museums, concerts and opera, who excelled at tennis. A tall strong man who was gentle when he touched me, who was always considerate of my needs, and who was so American there was no trace in his speech, bearing or outlook of his German birth in 1930 in the luxurious bedroom where his father and grandfather had also been born.

"What do you mean, he's not American-born?" My mother's eyes grew wide. "He could be an ad for Brooks Brothers, he doesn't even look Jewish with that fair coloring. And no hint of an accent." Her voice escalated between fear and disbelief.

"He was born in Berlin, they were merchants, diamonds, I think, but they didn't get out in time, so he and his family spent most of the war there, and at the end of 1944 were found by an Allied reconnaissance mission. They were sent to England and in 1946 they came to New Jersey. He finished Yale in three years, went to Harvard for law school, and he's lived in Boston ever since." That was all Paul had told me, all I thought I needed to know.

"Were they hidden? How did they live, who helped them, Jews didn't just live in Berlin unless they had contacts? Could they have been collaborators?" My father's shrewd glance frightened me. "You can't just marry someone we don't know anything about, come to think of it, I have read about Jews who were hidden, but we're not even sure any of this is true, are we . . . ?" His voice trailed off, unsure, ashamed, for he was not a man given to ranting.

"Now, tell me again, about his parents." My father patted his face. "And when we can meet them." How determined he was to be reasonable, and how much he loved me. More than I could suspect then. But one look into his eyes and I could see how unhappy he was. He didn't even like Paul's looks, murmuring, "You'll have blue-eyed children." What had been so unusual—that my brown-eyed, dark-haired parents had produced a red-haired, blue-eyed child so pale that I glowed in the dark—seemed a crime now that I had found Paul.

We were married on a sparkling August day in 1961. Paul's parents seemed dazed. My father thought that had to do with the Berlin Wall, which was going up at that very moment, but the Bergers (they had kept their name) had left Berlin far behind. What my father saw were parents dazzled and perplexed by their handsome, formidable son who stood a head taller than his father—by his education, achievements, and not least by his uncanny ability to become more Yankee than Yankee, as easily as a chameleon changes colors in the sun. How did they feel when he changed his name? It had happened before we met, but must have caused them pain.

And now they were perplexed by me: this fair woman with red hair and long limbs who looked as if she had come over on the Mayflower, yet who was Jewish and whose family looked Jewish. The mutant. And maybe offended by my family, who, despite their good intentions, were walking on eggs, afraid to ask questions because, if the truth were known, they didn't really want answers. Although they found Paul charming and intelligent, they had qualms about my marriage, even after they had learned more—that the Bergers had lived hidden in Berlin until the end of 1944 and somehow escaped to Sweden and then London before coming to the States.

But their qualms didn't stop me; the truth was that I simply could not imagine not being married to him.

Paul didn't lie about his past although, with time, he became an accomplished liar about other things. He basically evaded all questions about his past, perhaps not wanting to overwhelm me, or maybe not wanting to overwhelm himself. Or maybe he thought that just as the curdled clouds and jagged lightning of a summer storm give way to the clearest light, his European past would recede and yield to a marvelous marriage.

He was right, for a time.

But it didn't last. When Claudia was ready for kindergarten and I needed her birth certificate, I found a piece of onionskin in the file marked "Important," a paper tattered with folding and unfolding, that confirmed that Paul, his sister Berthe, and his parents, Frieda and Gunther Berger, had been found in a barn about a hundred miles from Berlin, not far from the village where they'd once had a summer place. Fleeing the Nazis, living by their wits, sheltered by farmers. By then there wasn't a spare crust of bread, a spare egg or potato. The country was on its knees, and even if you had cash, like the bundle folded into Frieda's bra, or jewels, hidden in the heels of her shoes, you couldn't get food.

It was written by the reconnaissance mission dropped behind enemy lines. Two Americans and one Englishman, amazed to find an intact family, the first in their experience. I nodded as I read; I knew all this. But then:

They seemed surprised to be alive, they had so completely prepared themselves to die they were in shock when they realized they had been rescued. At first they were reluctant to come with us. The son was the most difficult. His English is the best, he's very intelligent, but he's utterly despondent, hardly speaks. The parents and sister are more hopeful, but are very worried about him, which is why it is imperative they be removed from here as soon as possible.

I read the letter again, trying to control the shudder rushing through me. Such a mournful word, despondent, like a stone sinking into a pond. The leather file had a key, but I'd looked in it before, when I needed the twins' birth certificates and Claudia was a baby and my life seemed full to bursting. When I was convinced I knew all there was to know about this capable, exciting, sometimes puzzling man. The occasional raised hand or black look was an aberration; so was the odd silence, the slam of a drawer, the sharp turn of a heel. What importance did such things have after we had made such beautiful love, proof of which was my nightgown balled on the floor or turned inside out on my body? They were simply a passing mood, apprehension about a case, help problems at the office.

Then I was young enough and strong enough to convince myself that love could overcome everything, that whatever was broken or injured could in some way be made whole. There is nothing like love, or youth, to warp your vision.

Madly in love. How apt that phrase is. Mad with love. Out of my mind with love. Mesmerized, transfixed, immobilized by love . . .

2

"WHY NOW?" Eve had asked. Perfectly logical, Paul thought as he made himself two scrambled eggs and a scotch on the rocks with a dash of lime. What he always drank when he was bushed.

As he tried to reconstruct their conversation, he kept hearing her curious, innocent question, and the timbre of her voice awakened all the longing he had tried so hard to suppress during these last five years without her. How he yearned to be in the same room with her, to see her lovely tranquil face, even the frown that would bloom above her eyes as she took in what he was telling her.

They had had only the telephone. Still, that was better than nothing.

What he should have told her was this: As I watched those frantic people, I realized that I was as vulnerable as that Wall, that all the defenses I had so carefully constructed in order to live here, as an American, as your husband, as the children's father, were as fragile as that Wall. That those defenses were no more than a web of evasions and lies I had created because I thought I could erase the past. And that now, as I saw the city of my childhood becoming a whole again, I realized I could no longer live this way. That I had to face what had happened, not only to us, but to me when I was a child, hidden in Berlin.

If he had been utterly honest, would she have understood? Agreed to come? He wasn't sure. He had been so secretive for so long. Never had he willingly revealed anything about his past, even after they had been stunned by Stanley Kramer's movie

"Judgment at Nuremburg" which came out only a few months after their marriage. Nor had he gone back to Germany in the 70s, when people were beginning to travel there. And in the mid-80s, at the time of their divorce, he had been contemptuous of those survivors who went back to their villages as guests of a repentant German government.

So, "Why now?"

He was a fool to have called her. He wasn't thinking straight.

He hadn't even bothered to tell her the truth about this afternoon. Eve thought Claudia had given him this startling news, but he had actually heard about it at the office when someone stuck his head in his door and said, casually, "The Germans are destroying the Berlin Wall." At that Paul rushed into the conference room to join at least a dozen other colleagues in front of the TV, all of them transfixed by the thousands of East Berliners flooding the checkpoints in the Wall and demanding entry into West Berlin.

The announcers were beside themselves with excitement, barking constantly how astonishing this was, then panning over the exhilarated crowds. It was only a matter of time before the soldiers would succumb, open the checkpoints and give way to the relentless rush of people. And now, before their eyes, East Berliners and West Berliners had begun to hack at the Wall. Soon a divided Germany would become one.

Paul sat there, stunned and silent, until one of his older partners said, "My God, Paul, you look like you've seen a ghost."

Paul looked up, slowly loosening his tie. His movements were those of an obedient child. His hands were clammy and he tried to speak, but there was no way he could explain. How could he tell anyone that the prospect of The Wall coming down had loosened emotions in him he didn't know he still had?

So he simply allowed himself to be led into the Mens Room by an older colleague who had known him too long and too well to ask any questions. An older colleague who was the only one still in the firm who could recall that Paul had been born in Berlin, and when Paul finally met his gaze, he said, "I'll wait outside. When you're ready, I'll walk you home."

Now Paul sat with a tray and again watched the madness of the mob at Checkpoint Charlie, again heard the announcers ask, over and over again: Why had this flimsy wall lasted so long? Why had it exerted such power? Was it that we all—Russia and the Western bloc—needed to play cops and robbers after the War? And what would happen now that it had been destroyed on November 9, 1989, the 51st anniversary of *Kristallnacht*?

History, that restless traveler, had taken a shocking turn, he realized as he sipped his drink. And at this moment History was staring him in the face, as close as it had ever been.

While afternoon darkened into purplish dusk Paul watched the city of his birth flit before him: the streets he had walked as a child, the gardens he had loved and never dreamed he would ever leave, the synagogue, the huge sprawling Grunewald, the shop where his father and grandfather made their livings, even the neighborhood where he had committed the most despicable of acts.

Finally, in the midst of this amazing tumult, he had begun to think more clearly than he had in years: He admitted to himself that he was no longer a man who lived by his wits, who was nourished by those abstract concepts: hope and the future. At almost sixty, his past was intruding on his present and his very existence had become a stagnating lie. When Eve had divorced him almost five years ago, he had felt utterly alone, depressed for the first time since he had landed on these shores. And since then he had been running, as he had once run in Berlin, for his life.

After Claudia asked only a few hours ago, "Dad, can you believe this?" he knew he had to tell the truth. But to whom? Certainly not to her, for how can you place such an impossible burden on a child? Anna? No, she was too vain, too impatient.

This journey required compassion, generosity, patience. Then Eve loomed in his mind, the woman he had married on the weekend the Berlin Wall was being built. Another stunning coincidence, he realized.

All afternoon she haunted him, just as she had haunted his dreams those first few months after they'd separated—erotic, clotted dreams that left him exhausted at dawn. If he could bring Eve to Berlin, if he could walk with her through the city and tell her all that had happened to him there, perhaps she could finally understand that he was the trouble, not she, and why their marriage, so dazzling at the beginning, had faded into a grayness that was more depressing than either of them could ever have imagined.

But Eve was on Martha's Vineyard. They had hardly spoken since Jeremy's wedding last spring.

The prospect of returning to Berlin frightened him, and when he considered it again, Paul could feel his shoulders crumple. After all these years could he face what had happened there? Reveal the betrayals? Untangle the many threads and, finally, wrench free from the web of secrets and shadows that had become his life?

Seeing those East Berliners suddenly wrenched free, he had been filled with jealousy. They had shaken off the bonds that had limited them for a generation. But he? He was still imprisoned behind a shell of his own making. An escutcheon-like armor, which had thickened as he grew more and more afraid. Of his own happiness. How could you be afraid of happiness? he had asked himself again and again. There was no answer.

He had heard stories of survivors who told their children stories about the camps, the hiding, the atrocities. Although he knew he could never do that, he had wanted to share everything with Eve, to tell her why he had fallen so completely in love with her at first sight, to tell her why, within the circle of her love he felt safe. Yet he never could, and when the past threatened to overwhelm him, he had turned on her.

On himself.

On everyone he truly loved.

Now he could see them at their happiest: A still-warm September day and the five of them meandering into the Museum of Modern Art as if it was their second home, the children—the twins were twelve and Claudia was ten—streaking from them towards Picasso's sculpture of a goat, giggling with pleasure as they circled it, loving each detail, as delighted as if they had come upon an old friend.

"Look at those kids," someone said, "see what a good time they're having."

Paul could feel his heart swell with pride as the children waved, then took off for their favorite paintings—Starry Night, Monet's Water Lilies, Rousseau's Sleeping Tiger—gulping in the colors and shapes with so much pleasure on their faces that it hurt to look at them. After about an hour of looking, they all met for lunch in the garden and all he could see was the sunlight dappling the children as they darted among the beautiful Maillol and Cezanne and Matisse statues. Feeling, as they lingered over their coffee and occasionally admonished the kids for their exuberance, that invisible thread of desire for Eve grow ever and ever tauter until they went home and made dinner, watched "Love Boat" and, after the children were fast asleep, made love deep into the night. Never had he been more content. He could taste it.

Then, though, came the doubts, creeping wherever he turned. Surely he didn't deserve such profound pleasure, not after what he had witnessed, after what he had done. Before coming to this country he had been tainted by all kinds of evil, evil so despicable that no one could ever know about it. So instead of taking himself in hand and doing the hard work of telling the truth, he kept it all inside and began to self-destruct. He didn't understand it then, but now he knew it was no coincidence that three months after that unforgettable day at the museum, Frankie had entered their life.

Could he finally confess all this to Eve? He didn't know, but it was worth a try. Did he dare? He had to dare. She was the only one who might understand. So he had gathered all the strength he had and called her.

But, as he had feared, it was too much to ask.

3

DAMN HIM! How dare he crash into her life like this? As she sat there, looking like a normal woman watching a unique moment in history, Eve had the sensation of being torn apart. Her body was filled with anguish, an anguish she thought she had put behind her forever. And now, finally the tears that had welled in her throat since she heard that first, hesitant "Eve" came streaming down her face onto her lips and hands and clothes.

Eve didn't know how long she sat there weeping. For what they had had, for what they had lost? Or for what they might have again? She didn't know. These thoughts hadn't crossed her mind since she held that divorce agreement in her hand in the winter of 1985. At last she was free, she had told herself, finished with Paul forever.

Yet she was wrong. He had called, and in a flash she felt she had returned to her old life. Once more there was hanging between them not only the three children, but that overwhelming binding love.

How can such a strong, binding love die? It didn't seem possible, and there were times when Eve was as puzzled as her children and her parents and her friends. And it had taken a very long time. For years she had resigned herself to whatever he dished out. But when he had become cruel, she left.

End of story. Not so different from a lot of stories in New York in the early 80s, Eve reminded herself now that the tears were abating. She poured herself a Scotch and sank into the sofa and concentrated on the faces halfway around the world that looked as dumbfounded as she felt. How could something that had had such power over the world for so long crumble as quickly as a child's pile of blocks? No one could have predicted this. During the weekend of her marriage Eve's father had sat riveted to the TV, watching this wall go up. And now 28 years later, it was being destroyed so swiftly the newscasters could hardly keep up with it.

Still, it lasted longer than your marriage.

Eve jumped up and walked to her bulletin board, then stared at a photo she had clipped a few weeks before—a mother who planned to return to East Germany was saying goodbye through the fence of the West German Embassy in Prague to her teenage daughter who had been given permission to emigrate west. Their hands clasped the bars of the fence and their foreheads touched, though you could see only their profiles and closed eyes. Would they find each other? And wasn't it strange that she had cut out this picture so recently?

More important, how did you say goodbye to a child you might not see again? Eve could not imagine it.

And now, her children's father, the man she had loved so passionately when those children were young, wanted her help. No, put it out of your mind. How many times had you tried to help in the past, only to be rebuffed? No, you can't put yourself through any of that again, Eve told herself. It was after 10. Finally, she turned off the television. Sleep was out of the question, but she couldn't watch anymore.

Slowly Eve tidied the kitchen, then walked upstairs to her desk and spread out the chapter she had been working on earlier. Soon after her divorce a friend had asked her to copy-edit a book, and she had discovered she loved the work and the financial independence that came with it, so now she did it almost full-time. This new novel was about the Middle Ages, as sad as *Kristin Lavransdatter*, though, mercifully, not as long, and written with the same authority she and Paul had loved in Undset and Mary Renault and Bryher. *The King Must Die*, *The Last of the Wine*, *Coin of Carthage*.

As she sat there, sharpening a pencil, her mind circled back to those cherished times when his beautiful voice seemed to be re-shaping those old myths, when the five of them would sit bundled before a fire in their little Cape Cod in Menemsha while the wood crackled and hissed because it was too green, while they fought to keep their eyes open, not wanting to miss a word. Then, later, when the house was quiet, making love before the dying fire while the lush prose echoed in their ears.

But that was then.

*   *   *

She didn't do more than put some papers into piles, busywork, really, but it allowed her to let her mind rest a little. If only she could retreat into the forgetfulness of sleep, but it was no use. She could feel the tears rising again in her throat. Finally she understood why, especially at the end, Paul had buried himself in work, it was the most wonderful escape in the world.

If he wanted a friend to go to Berlin, why didn't he ask one of his partners? Or this Anna woman?

He doesn't want them, he wants you. He needs you.

Was it possible—her self-sufficient, capable, brilliant Paul? He had lived his life entirely alone, it sometimes seemed, especially towards the end. So of course she had gotten angry at him, just as she had when he had offered a convenient lie or when he'd been too busy to talk to her after they divorced. Why hadn't he remarried, he'd had almost five years.

"If either of you had fallen madly in love with someone else, then all this would be understandable," Claudia had flung at her before going to Paris. "It's crazy, both of you still alone," she had added, trying to get a rise out of her mother. But Eve had retreated into silence. There were things you couldn't tell anyone, certainly not a daughter. Moreover, she'd resolved never to turn the children against Paul.

Besides, they wouldn't have believed her. Paul had been an

exemplary father, never so much as raising his voice. And always so interested in what they thought. How his blue eyes would deepen when Eric or Jeremy wanted his attention, even for something as silly as a joke. It had sometimes made her heart ache to see how much pleasure he took in those small moments. And how much they loved his interest in them. Even when they were older and he lied, they forgave him, probably taking their cues from her. Yet no memory of Claudia's teenage years could ignore those Saturdays when the twins were on dates or in college and Paul was simply not there. Didn't Claudia wonder where he was, or was Paul's absence a relief for her, too?

So many questions. That the kids should have asked, that she should have asked? Did they know about his silent rages? His infidelities? Had they been hearing gossip for years? Did they blame her for tolerating an intolerable situation? Pity her? Think she was too passive, too timid? A masochist? Questions crowded her brain: questions she had stifled for so long that forming them now made her blush, humiliated.

This time, though, Paul had not lied, but had asked for her understanding. Perhaps not just for his need to go to Berlin, but for everything else, as well? She wasn't sure.

But she was sure of one thing. In his voice was a tenderness she had thought she would never hear again. It reminded her of those precious months before they married, when he would look at her with such need and trace the line of her collarbone as gently as if touching the top of an infant's head. If anyone had asked her, she would have said Paul could never be as vulnerable as he had sounded tonight. No, not the man whose glances became so furtive, whose features became so mask-like, whose face looked twisted and cruel by the time they parted. A man who had changed so much she hardly recognized him. A man from whom she wanted only to flee.

Still, the voice she heard tonight belonged to the man she had once loved.

Like a body risen from the dead.

*   *   *

She had to get out into the air. She pulled on her warm winter jacket and gloves and a hat and went out, hoping that the bracing cold and huge night sky would give her the equanimity eluding her. A light frost coated the hushed dunes, the gritty sand gleamed in the moonlight, and the waves were growing high. The roar of the surf drowned out any other sounds. Here it felt as if nothing of importance were happening anywhere, including Berlin. Wasn't that why she'd come here to live—to feel this serene indifference?

"People who gravitate to islands need a ring of water around them," Paul used to say when they began to rent houses on the Vineyard. "We're all outsiders, in some profound way, that's why this place is filled with such interesting folk." Perhaps he was right, for it was that ring of water she'd longed for when she told her Aunt Blanche about this piece of land overlooking Lambert's Cove.

It was the only place she could imagine living, the only place where she wouldn't feel hemmed in by her mistakes. And once settled here, Eve knew she had done the right thing. Instead of feeling lonely as everyone had feared, she had become more connected to the natural world. Morning after morning, dusk after dusk she would watch the sea flow into the sky and the sky flow into the sea and think, Here there are no limits, here I can live in a blessedness of my own making.

Yet now the real world had intruded—the world of society, civilization, politics. Eve stopped and looked up. Orion was rising in the wintry sky, the same Orion rising over New York, over Berlin, over Paris, the same constellation her children always found first: The hunter and his three-star belt.

She began to walk again, her mind racing with scenes of such harrowing reality that it took her a few moments to fix on the one that hurt the most, the one she had worked so hard to push down that it now took several minutes to cohere in her mind . . .

I was 35 years old and for my birthday we were redecorating the apartment. A logical thing to do now that the kids were past finger-painting the walls, and Paul's career was taking off. Logical or not, it was what I wanted, but no decorator, no cookie-cutter Park Avenue apartment for me. Still, where to buy furniture, rugs, lamps, especially with such a discerning husband?

I turned to a neighbor whose family had lived in New York for generations, whose dinner parties were like something out of Edith Wharton. She sent me to a long drink of water, a one-time model turned decorator, named Frankie Bidwell. First, though, Frankie had to get to know the Bertrams. So Frankie and Paul and I spent a string of Saturdays at the zoo, the Botanical Garden, museums; then, after the kids were tucked away, we ate leisurely dinners and sometimes went to the opera or a play or a concert—once a revival of "Beat the Devil" that made us laugh until we hurt. Wonderful evenings, etched forever in my mind. Frankie was charming, gutsy, smart, and slowly she guided us through showrooms and antique houses and auctions.

After several months we had a living room we loved, then a dining room, a simpler room filled with Shaker furniture that was an interesting foil to the elaborate inlaid desk, the camel back Belter sofa, the Chinese lamps, the little bibelots Paul saw as signs of home. But he was so delighted by each biscuit box, each small ivory, each piece of Steuben that I didn't have the heart to say no. So the living room and foyer became Paul's and the dining room mine. "That's a sensible arrangement," Frankie agreed, trilling her captivating laugh.

And now it is a magical June evening and touches of the long sunset spill over the edges of the windows in a striking blend of amethyst and apricot. Frankie and two other couples are here for dinner. Feeling utterly marvelous, I sit at the head of the table and even though our guests are discussing the Vietnam War, there is a lightness in their voices. It is 1975 and it is ending. At last.

My eyes meet Paul's, expecting to see an expansive calm in his eyes. He loves nothing better than to sit at the other end of the table playing the gracious host. Instead, he is frowning and groping in his pockets for a cigarette. A giggle begins to spill from me. He didn't believe me when I announced I was getting rid of every last cigarette after he promised to give up smoking.

But now he will see I wasn't kidding. I will not help him, and now I excuse myself to oversee the moving of the samovar into the living room where coffee will be served. There's new help in the kitchen, and I want to be sure they are careful with the huge silver affair Paul and Frankie found one Saturday when the kids and I were bedded down with flu. As I am helping a sweet Irish woman find the best place for the unwieldy, steaming monster, I spy Paul rustling around in the foyer, frantically searching for a cigarette. I resist the temptation to call out to him and remember how he said, only last night, "It's easy for you, you've never smoked, but it's awful, that wanting a cigarette. I hate it and wish I could stop." He looked so frustrated I put my arms around him, filled with love for him, yet determined to help him lick this addiction.

Now I watch him go to the drawers in the end tables, then, after the maid goes back to the kitchen, I step behind the damask drapes where the kids love to play hide and seek. Thrilled with my little ruse, protected by drapes that were once my mother's and that match our furniture like a charm, until I see Paul groping in Frankie's pocketbook for a cigarette.

All at once my face and neck feel scalded, as if the hot coffee is pouring all over me, through me, into every crevice of my body. Of course! He and Frankie are lovers. His remoteness in bed has nothing to do with him trying to stop smoking. They have been lovers since winter, when I could feel him drifting from me, like a boat escaping its mooring. My knees buckle, and I grab the drapes. A sound rises in my throat, but I suppress it, because if I let it out it will be a scream. So I wait until Paul finds Frankie's Kents and takes a drag from the cigarette, letting the smoke go deep into his lungs. I watch his body, which I thought I knew so well, relax with the pleasure of it.

Then he returns to the dining room, and finally, as if coming from the kitchen, I, too, return to the table. For the rest of the evening I hear an ugly hiss in my head, an accusing hiss, as if it were I who has sinned, I who has caused harm. Is that punishment for my stupidity?

My naivete? The scalding sensation comes and goes, yet I stay calm. Until everyone is gone, Frankie last, of course. When I confront him, Paul stares, speechless. When I ask him whether there is a female equivalent in the English language for cuckold, he drops his eyes, and after that it is as if there is a permanent scrim between us. We never discuss it again, not even after all the times the kids ask, irritably, where Aunt Frankie has gone. . . .

For months afterwards Eve hardly knew what she did. She could recall only a terrible sadness, a kind of teetering at the edge of her life, then a weary acceptance that this was her life. She and Paul were bound together by all sorts of things, not least the children. She believed him when he promised never to see Frankie again, and although there were long periods when he was faithful, there were also times when he was not. Somehow she always knew, and she would begin to feel as if a fish hook were lodged in her throat and once went to the hospital when she couldn't swallow. With time Eve learned to live her own life and keep her distance. The more aloof she grew, the more enraged, the crueler Paul became.

Now Eve was aware of her sneakers crunching against the pebbles as she walked. How can a memory stay so strong, so painful?

And why did she continue to blame herself after she realized what was happening. Why would she stand before the mirror searching her face and body for clues that might tell her why he wasn't home. She wasn't as smart as he was, but then, few people were. And she wasn't aging badly: her red hair growing lighter, masking the few strands of gray, her skin clear, her body straight, still good legs, though she had less bosom than when she was young and some stretch marks from the babies and that slight dimpling in her thighs which meant she didn't exercise enough.

Occasionally men eyed her; once Paul's friend Ian came on to her when he was slightly pickled, saying, "While the rest of us get older you get younger, Eve, darling Eve. Why don't we run off together?" She simply shrugged. Ian had already been married three times. Another time a young man sidled up to her in London, claiming to be from Philadelphia, as if that gave him license, and invited her to lunch.

How pathetic she'd been: An able-bodied, intelligent, pretty woman who had brought up three terrific kids, ticking off her good points, trying to figure out why her husband hardly came near her any more. Once she caught on, after the episode with Frankie, she knew exactly whom he saw and when and where. Yet after a while she didn't even listen to his elaborate fabrications. For they weren't about anything that mattered—the women he saw, the evenings spent in fancy restaurants when he swore he was at work, the weekends he was supposed to be away and was bedded down in some seedy borrowed apartment.

What mattered were the secrets buried deep in his being, secrets that drove him to irrational, occasionally violent behavior, and perceptible only by that flicker of fear which had settled way back in his eyes about twelve years into their marriage. A flicker so fleeting you would wonder if you'd really seen it, but which sometimes gathered an intensity you could not ignore. By the time she recognized that it was fear, Paul had learned to mask it with such sarcasm and irony she convinced herself she couldn't dig deeper.

She should have, but she didn't. When she finally realized how miserable they both were, they had been married for 23 years. It was time for her to leave. They would have to manage without each other.

She stared into the blackness of the cove, the line where the water stopped and the star-filled sky began. In the still night only the steady lapping sound of the water curling towards shore could be heard. Then, almost in a whisper, Eve again heard that tentative "It wouldn't take long."

As if this trip were some dreaded process you had to explain to a child, like the appendectomy he once explained to Claudia in the blinding light of an emergency room. Holding a frightened five year old in his arms and telling her that after the stomach ache she had so stoically endured, she had to have an operation. "They will give you an anesthetic, which will make you numb so you won't feel anything," he began. Precise. Patient. Never mentioning sleep, because anesthesia is not sleep, but "the closest thing to death," her father once told them.

Eve was terrified that day, yet she could still remember the rush of love and respect she felt for Paul. The memory tugged at her, filling her with longing to see him. Then she wondered, what's happening to me? One moment I'm seething with anger at him, another minute yearning to talk to him. And what about all those humiliations? Yes, there were those, but there were other things, too. Things she needed to clear up, things she'd never understood. So much that was left hanging because she had never insisted on knowing the whole story.

People thought of her as brave because she finally left Paul, but that wasn't bravery. It was common sense, the instinct for survival. Her ability to live alone, to survive the long winters on Martha's Vineyard came from a stubborn patience, a stoicism which was simply part of her character and which may have contributed to the failure of the marriage, she now realized.

Whatever it was, it was a far cry from courage.

*   *   *

Eve's hands trembled as she dialed. It was almost twelve but he was a night owl. Now, though, his voice was furred with sleep. "I'm sorry, Paul, did I wake you?"

"No, yes, I don't know, I must have dozed." So wary and so weary. Where was her warrior husband now, the man she always thought of as Alexander the Great?

"I'll go. If you want me to come, I'll go with you," she said. How easy it was, she thought as the words came out. Then, though, the silence between them stretched, almost unbearably, breaking at last into a jumble of words spilling simultaneously from both of them.

Paul said, "I'll call you back with flight times, it won't be easy, but I can probably pull some strings. They say the airlines are putting on more planes. Maybe we can leave by Monday."

Suddenly apprehension replaced relief. Surely he didn't expect them to sleep in the same room? Before she could think how to ask, he broke in, "We can stay at the Crown Prince, near the Grunewald, not as noisy as the Kempinski, but elegant. I'll get two rooms."

"Fine, Paul." He invariably went for the best and biggest, while she preferred small. She should have thanked him but was so relieved at having her own room, she could think of nothing else. After a pause she recovered. "I'll need a little time to tie up some things, but I can probably fly from here to New York on Saturday."

"You can stay here if you like," he replied quickly, "the guest room's . . . hell, you know what it's like, nothing's changed."

"No, I'll stay with Blanche."

"Of course, whatever you think." Her fingers tingled with nervousness. Then he added, gently, "Take as much time as you need." So benign she almost confessed that what she'd been wearing these last five years wouldn't do for traveling with him. But that was not his affair any more. Some of their worst moments had been while shopping, he and the sales people in collusion, she often felt, especially since he lusted after some elusive chic, something between Rita Hayworth in "Gilda" and Greer Garson in "Madame Curie." "There, she has it!" he'd say, enthralled by Alida Valli or Catherine Deneuve or Anouk Aimee. As if discovering gold.

Why was it so important? She never wanted Paul to look like anyone but himself. Isn't that what love is? But why didn't she have the guts to refuse when he insisted on shopping with her? She once bought a green chiffon dress by herself, and his face always lit up when he saw her in it. Why hadn't she done that more often?

Oh, God, what have I done? Eve wondered as they said

goodbye. Her mind was a tangle, she had no idea what was ahead, but a promise is a promise, she reminded herself.

And although she felt a chill of fright once again surge through her, she knew the die was cast.

She couldn't renege now.

4

PAUL WAS SHAKING by the time he put down the phone, and his mouth felt unbelievably parched. Of course sleep was gone. He could hardly believe it. Wide awake, his first thought was to call someone. No one but the children, who had called in the course of the evening, knew that he was thinking about going to Berlin. Besides, they were all either asleep or on their way to bed.

Then he considered calling his sister Berthe who was a night owl just like him. Yet to what end? Berthe thought he had shared everything with her during those years when they were hidden and then wandering in the countryside, but the truth was that he hadn't. Besides, Berthe had been more successful than he in putting the past aside. She would have no patience for any of this, and she surely didn't want to hear more about his failed marriage, for which she always blamed him.

The only person who had a faint clue of all that had happened to him was his father, Gunther, whom Paul had adored, but who seemed to have made a silent pact with his son as soon as their plane lifted into the fog above Sweden at the end of 1944.

"It is over, Paulie," he had told the boy as they headed for England. "We have a chance for a new life." After that he never talked to Paul about their life in Berlin—about the large home, about the comforts they had enjoyed, or about the tribulations they had suffered, especially at the end.

As his father polished his English, which he learned as a child in one of Berlin's best Jewish primary schools, Gunther simultaneously cast off his past. Yet he clung to his name.

"It will be so complicated, our son having one name and Berthe and us having another," Frieda had pleaded with him when Paul announced his intention of changing his name to "Bertram."

"So it will be complicated," Gunther replied. "I was born Gunther Berger and I will die Gunther Berger." Throughout all the mortifications he endured in this new country, America, where people didn't trust them at first, where people didn't really want to have much to do with them, Gunther had maintained his dignity, running his hardware store as efficiently as he had run the famous Berger's Jewels on the Kurfurstendamm.

But why was he obsessing about his father? Gunther was dead, thankfully before Paul's divorce, of a massive heart attack while he was locking the door of the hardware store on a Wednesday evening, the eve of his 82nd birthday.

And his mother was dead, too. So that left Berthe who had clung to her maiden name Berger with a fierce pride until she married Zachary Goldstein, whose unmistakably Jewish name she took with equally fierce pride. Who didn't really have a clue about all that had happened to him, and would surely berate him now. He could hear the asperity in her voice as she would say, "I can't believe you had the gall to ask her, Paulie. But I'm not surprised that she is going. She has more compassion than almost anyone I know."

Once in bed, he dozed, and daydreamed . . .

He is walking across the Public Garden on a beautiful, still warm October day, and he can feel the lift of a breeze through the still green leaves, and there she is, exactly as he remembers her. Her tall, sharply angled body is hurrying just as she used to hurry around the garden and into the vast fields, and he can feel himself starting to run, bumping against Bostonians rushing with their briefcases under their arms, or meandering behind strollers or chatting with friends, to catch up to her. Panting, "Pardon me, excuse me," as he weaves through the crowd, his heart hammering as he grows nearer.

It is just as she said it would be that day when she led him into the music room of that huge schloss *"... soon this madness will be over... and one day soon we will be able to live like human beings again and walk without fear in Berlin and Dresden and Munich. Because there are people who believe in good, not evil." And then her voice singing into his ear, as beautifully as the music she played on the piano, "Who knows, Paul, maybe you and I will meet someday, on Unter den Linden, or near the Tiergarten."*

Alix, the woman who saved their lives, who was determined to balance the Nazi evil with her own acts of individual goodness. Here, in front of him, not in Europe, but in Boston, wearing a fawn colored skirt wide enough to accommodate her long stride, and a white starched shirt whose sleeves were rolled up to show the exquisite line of her lovely forearms. How can it be? Paul thinks as he runs, and when he reaches her side, he sees that it cannot be.

Of course this beautiful woman is not Alix, but someone who looks so like her it is uncanny, unnerving. Her tall, loose-limbed build, her way of walking with her body slightly turned, her mass of reddish hair pulled from her face with a shiny gray ribbon which is almost the same color as her slate eyes. Deep blue-gray eyes that seem so wise although she is clearly so young. A mere college girl, he realizes as he comes closer.

Paul wants to put his hands on her shoulders and stop her so he can take a longer look, so he can convince himself that this young woman is a stranger, someone he's never seen before, and certainly not a reincarnation of someone he loved almost twenty years ago in another country.

But she senses his presence next to her and looks at him with startled amusement in her eyes. Slowly her elegant light eyebrows lift, and she asks, in a breathless whisper he will never forget, "Do we know each other?"

He should have told her right then—about Alix and the schloss *and the brutality of the Nazis. But of course he doesn't. How can you assault a stranger with those facts? Facts that are entirely irrelevant to this moment. For he is falling in love, at first sight, exactly as all the movies of this amazingly optimistic country say you can. Besides, how can you tell someone you have just met that, suddenly, for the first time since you last saw Alix, you feel safe? He would have scared her to death and never seen her again.*

So Paul says, "No. But I thought you were someone I once knew. The resemblance is eerie, striking. I'm sorry." By now they have stopped and stepped off the path and out of the rush of oncoming people. Slowly they introduce themselves, then walk to the Boston Public Library where she is determined to find the material she needs about Elizabeth Bowen, because she is writing a paper for her English course at Wellesley on Bowen's novel, The Death of the Heart, *which was published in 1938, and the library at her college is woefully inadequate in material about the modern British writers.*

"'The death of the heart which leads to all sins.'" Paul suddenly tells this young woman whose name is Eve. "It's in the machzor . . . *"*

She stares.

"The Jewish prayer book," he tells her.

"I know what a machzor *is," she says, and he can feel his heart beginning to explode. She frowns and shakes her head. "I don't remember it, but I'll take your word for it." Then she stops and smiles at him with the sly humor he will learn to love, "But how could that wonderful Irish writer know a phrase from the* machzor?*"*

They laugh and float together to the library where they chat for a few moments. Then she disappears and he goes on to his office. But in his pocket is a slip of paper on which she has written her name and address and telephone number.

Years later they regaled the children with that simple tale of their meeting, and once they stood on the very spot where Paul caught up with Eve. They were visiting Boston for the bicentennial celebrations to walk The Freedom Trail. Of course there was no mention of Alix or why she had meant so much to him or why their mother's fantastic resemblance to her had played such an important part in their courtship and eventual marriage. How could he tell his children about Alix when he had never even told Eve?

As he thought about that simple fact, Paul was shocked. How could he have been so silent for so many years? How could he have lived a dual existence for so very long? It seemed incredible to him now.

No mention of *The Death of the Heart*, either, Paul realized, because at that time he and Eve were still unbelievably happy, still intensely in love, and the mysterious relevance of that book and its unforgettable title to their future could not be imagined by either of them.

5

GROWING UP Eve had been called "wholesome," but after she met Paul she had learned that she was pretty, maybe even beautiful. It happened the first time she went to his office.

He was on the telephone, looking out over the Public Garden, and when his secretary beckoned her to go in, his voice was husky with emotion: "She reminds me of Deborah Kerr, the same dignified beauty, the exact coloring. Gorgeous red hair, with a coppery sheen, like the hay with the light spangling it when we went to visit Nona and Papa . . ." His voice faded, then rose, "And later, at the summer house, the last summer . . ."

Eve coughed to signal her arrival. He turned and after he hung up, said, "I was telling my sister Berthe about you, how you remind me of our childhood." She expected him to go on, words tumbling from his mouth, but he fell silent. Yet his eyes told her everything: intense blue eyes, as clear as bits of brilliant sky, clearer than she ever saw them again, and filled with promise. Of truth, happiness, intimacy? Eve could never sort it out. Perhaps it was what she wanted to believe, what he wanted to believe, maybe what Paul thought he could *will*.

But he said no more that day, just came close and gathered her hair in his hands. His touch was electrifying and sparked desire and pride. Who wouldn't be proud? From that moment she'd gained a confidence she had never felt before.

And now? She peered into the mirror the next morning, her face cheerful and clear. She couldn't remember who had said, "At fifty you get the face you deserve," but here was her pleasant face, open and unafraid, the tension lines she'd had in her early forties smoothed by time, by the knowledge that dawn might bring loneliness, but peace, too. And that gives one a different kind of assurance.

Then she thought of all she had to do before she left: Plant the bulbs. Batten the house down for winter. Max. Her neighbor, Dozie. Her Aunt Blanche. Quickly she dressed and went downstairs. Would she tell Max where she was going, with whom? She wasn't sure.

First, Dozie. The old woman was close to ninety, and they had met her 25 years ago when they were searching for their first rental. Unable to resist a bookstore anywhere, they'd stopped. "Like Bertram in *Mansfield Park*?" Dozie asked.

"And Trollope's Bertrams," Paul replied.

"There's a Bertram in Scott, too. Are you Scottish or English?"

"Neither," Paul said, "I was born Paul Berger." Eve was surprised. This was information he rarely shared. On hearing it, Dozie was so stunned she almost fainted. Yet once she recovered Dozie became one of Paul's fans. "Such an impressive man, such a well-shaped head, no one would ever know his background, he looks so American." Such a bigot, the kids couldn't stand her. Still, Dozie loved books, and for that Eve and Paul had overlooked everything.

Downstairs Eve scooped up a blooming African violet. Dozie was always easier if you had a present in hand, although it was years since Eve had been in her house. Whenever she delivered groceries she stood at the door while Dozie groveled in her ancient handbag. This time, though, Dozie said, "Come in, come in," her dress flapping around her frail frame like clothes not quite fastened to a paper doll.

Eve could hardly believe her eyes. Dozie used to begin the day by wiping the leaves of her house plants and rearranging flowers and grasses, then stacking magazines and newspapers and books into tidy piles. Her house often held a combined tang of ammonia, furniture polish, wax. Yet now there were only heaps of clutter, a veil of grime clinging to everything, and a vague, rank smell. Eve began to breathe through her mouth.

"Can you put it here?" Dozie gestured, then murmured, sheepishly, "I'll get a dust rag." While Eve waited, she looked at the bookshelves, awestruck, as always, by their number and quality. Here and there were autographed photos of Charlie Chaplin, Hemingway, Kenneth Tynan, Jack Nicholson, Laurence Olivier, Faulkner, Graham Greene, Peter Quennell. Then Eve stepped closer. Could it be? Yes, here was a photo of Paul, twenty-three years ago. She'd taken that snapshot when she was pregnant with Claudia. How happy he looked!

How had Dozie gotten this photo? It had not been here when they were friends, and now it made her uneasy: Her young Paul, the Paul she'd loved so intensely, here in Dozie's bookcase. It was creepy, like some latter day Dorian Gray, and for a second she considered asking about it. But Dozie was a notorious liar, especially as she aged. When she returned, Eve said she was going away and left as quickly as she could.

Who would have dreamed Dozie would have a photo of Paul? And why had she gone over there at all? Because the old woman's daughters live far away and she has no one, and if not for her you wouldn't have this house, Eve reminded herself. When she and Paul separated, he kept the Manhattan apartment, and Eve resolved to settle on the Vineyard. At that time Dozie was selling this piece of land and was delighted when Eve inquired about it and eventually bought it. But when she learned about the divorce she was wild.

"This is Theodosia Earlham, you tricked me!"

"I don't think so, Dozie. I wanted to buy land, you had some to sell. End of story."

"You never mentioned the divorce. But what a fool you are, such an exemplary man, such wonderful instincts, so brilliant, you must be losing your mind," Dozie screeched.

"Perhaps I am, but you and Paul can correspond, and when you come to New York I'm sure he'll take you to lunch."

"Never mind what I do, that's none of your business any more. And I'm no longer Dozie to you, if you need to address me in future, I am Mrs. Earlham!"

So Mrs. Earlham it was when they met in town, or even when Eve delivered the groceries. Yet Eve had heard from more than one person that Dozie was glad they were neighbors. "You're never mean," she had once told Eve, "and so many others are, including me." Besides, Eve would never forget Dozie appearing one day with a Keats in her hand. "A little gift," she said.

That summer Paul fell in love with Keats, reciting those beautiful lines as they walked the beach, the lilac twilight deepening around them, their toddler twins growing heavier with each step. After the children were in bed, they would nurse their Scotches on the porch, and talk about those poems, as happy as they would ever be, under a field of stars blooming over Menemsha.

*　　*　　*

As Eve walked around the house, fastening the storm windows, checking the doors, she remembered how indignant the children were when she told them her plan to move here. "What do you know about houses? Builders, architects, plumbers, electricians, gardeners? You've lived in an apartment all your life," they'd said as if all those rented houses counted for nothing.

To which she'd replied, "I'll learn whatever I need to know." And she had, never admitting how demanding it was to care for this beautiful house which she had planned with an architect friend and which she loved more than she ever imagined she could love an inanimate thing. And never really confronting what was hidden in the children's dismay at her decision to live on the Vineyard: Are you still going to be the mother we know, or are you going to turn into some hippie divorcee? How can love disappear? Why did you leave our father? Where is the love you told us about when we were little?

Eve's parents were no less dismayed, and her brother and sister were not surprised, but too involved in their own lives to help. Only her Aunt Blanche, her mother's younger sister, had come to her rescue.

"I know you didn't ask, but you shouldn't have to think about money now. You'll simply have to have your inheritance before I die, and if I live too long and need help at the end, you'll have to take me in." Her voice as clear and firm as the ping of rainwater on a metal roof. "Build a house, before it is too late." Never asking, why Martha's Vineyard, won't there be too many memories, how on earth will you manage in winter?

Childless, rich, widowed, Blanche had never disappointed Eve. Nor had she judged Eve, not even when Eve ran to Blanche's apartment in a raincoat thrown over her bathrobe, her slippers flapping as she raced down Park Avenue, as frantic as someone fleeing a burning house. The last day of her marriage—the day she had finally understood she had to leave Paul.

*   *   *

After she had packed and made arrangements to fly to New York on Saturday, Eve watered the plants. Putting two orchids on a deep windowsill she watched the sun's rays scatter shards of purple onto the white walls catching a facet of glass here, a grain of wood there. At first people had asked, "When are you going to furnish?" but she ignored them and soon they were praising her insistence on simplicity. "Spare and elegant," Max sometimes said. Once he added, "Just like you," making her blush.

Finally Eve picked up the phone. In the last two years they had taken trips, talked endlessly, occasionally slept together. But never had Eve felt with Max what she had felt so often with Paul—that her body was a burgeoning spring, with always more to give. Only once, in India, after a Mercedes truck came barreling toward them on the Grand Trunk Road, did Max say, amazed, "I don't want to die, I thought I wouldn't mind, but

I don't, and it's not my kids, or my work, it's you, Eve." He'd hugged her, but nothing after that.

Most important about their patchy intimacy was the easy talk she'd never really had with Paul, and had missed before she knew how to describe it. And which gave her a confidence she didn't know she had. Max had also expanded her world. She would never forget visiting the birthplace of the math genius, Ramanujan, the train plunging through miles of green dotted by the brightly colored saris of the women as they worked, looking like birds about to soar overhead. A glorious world, a world, truly, without end. Still, that was a year ago, and their closeness dissipated after their return.

At the sound of her voice, Max asked, "Where shall we eat?"

"I'm afraid I can't make it."

"Is everything okay?"

"Blanche fell and hurt her leg and needs help." How easily she lied, how despicable.

"Then of course you must go," he said with a small sigh.

"I'll be gone at least a week, but back for Thanksgiving. I'm expecting you."

"I'll be there, and we have a date for New Year's Eve, you do remember we're supposed to be in Boston?" Eve was surprised; Max didn't usually look so far ahead. But this new decade was the last of the century, and within a week afterward, her big birthday.

Later she finished editing the book, wrapped it for mailing (she would do that from New York) and finalized arrangements with Blanche. Then she went to a small safe at the back of her closet and slipped her wedding ring onto her finger and put it in a zippered pocket in her handbag: She would wear it when they traveled. It was so much easier. Sick of the bellboys and concierges searching her fingers, she had bought a thin gold band when she was with Max in Delhi. Just before they left she had given it to a porter who'd been especially kind. He tried to protest. "Pawn it," she said. The man's eyes had widened with surprise and delight.

Before bed Eve called her closest friend on the Vineyard, Gwen. Although Gwen knew all there was to know about her, she had decided not to tell Gwen where she was going. But Gwen was a political junkie and wanted to talk about Berlin. Finally Eve was able to break in, "I'm going to Manhattan to pig out at the museums and do some theater." Remembering her lie to Max, she added, "Blanche has hurt her leg and needs help. Since I'm not going to be with my parents for Thanksgiving, this is also a good time, before winter closes in." Lying so easily again. Was she afraid the trip would be a colossal disaster? Even if it was, it was probably better not to tell Gwen now.

Instead she asked Gwen if she could look in on Dozie when she was gone. Groaning, Gwen agreed.

6

SUN POURED from a brilliant blue sky. As soon as Eve got into the cab, she realized she'd forgotten to get something for Blanche who had a birthday soon. She'd stop at the Metropolitan Museum gift shop if the cabbie was willing to wait. When he agreed she leaned back.

Whenever she returned to New York it always took Eve time to get used to the concrete, the dirt, the noise. But that was only the surface. What about the violence, the homelessness, the sick, AIDS? Had she been a coward, leaving when she did? Yet one more middle-aged woman making sandwiches in a shelter would hardly matter. And each time she came back, Eve was struck by how dark the city had become. Knife-like buildings cutting off the light, streets like tunnels, shadows everywhere. Only at the edge of Central Park were people with their faces turned to the sun, like satellite dishes in a meadow.

At the museum she tilted her head. "The Waltz of the Flowers." Eve's step quickened. As she neared the south fountain she saw a cluster of people watching a man with a life-sized doll which he hugged as he floated, exquisitely, joyously, in wide arcs. Swirling as if he had all the time and space in the world, as if the plaza were a ballroom at Versailles or the Piazza San Marco where she and Paul danced on their honeymoon.

Close by was an old-fashioned victrola, perched on a table, and attached to it two speakers. The doll had flowing blonde hair and a picture-book face, and she wore a green taffeta New Look dress nipped at the waist over a crinoline. You could glimpse slim ankles above four inch stiletto heels. When the music stopped the man put the doll down and changed the record and bent over to fix a shoelace. Eve drew closer.

Now strains of "The Blue Danube" lifted into the air while the man gave a formal bow. A silvery sigh rose from the crowd. He was fair, with thin sandy hair, not young, but not old. Forty, maybe fifty. Slight, and oddly elegant in his black pants and suspenders and plaid shirt and solid tie. He gave a shy smile, then bent once more. Eve saw what she had missed until now. The doll's rigid ankles were attached to his with what looked like pony tail holders. Quickly he tightened them. That done, he gathered his partner to him, and slowly they began to glide, his face breaking into sheer rapture. Eve had a flash of recognition that she'd seen him before, about a year before she left New York. Her suspicions were confirmed when someone said, "He used to be here a lot, then he disappeared for a few years, but now he's back again."

Of course! It was the day she and Paul walked from their first visit to their lawyer for their divorce. They had watched the man gravely, and here he was, again, dancing his heart out with the doll of his dreams. When he stopped, the crowd sighed with regret, then clapped and Eve joined the surge towards him as they dropped bills and coins into the case of his victrola.

"Isn't he wonderful?" "Fabulous, he should be in show business." "I think he once was." "I heard he was a ballet dancer, with Balanchine." Then more clapping as the man began to whirl, as swift as a top, again. His pleasure was what you might see in a bridegroom. No, more like her parents' faces when they celebrated their 50th soon after she and Paul separated. Almost levitating through "The Anniversary Waltz," undeniably linked—something I will never have, Eve had thought that day.

Yet here she was, about to meet Paul. What had been altruistic and principled on the Vineyard suddenly seemed insane, and scary.

"Your problem is your staunch belief that everything can be fixed," Paul had told her near the end. He was right: She had based her life on the premise that to love with all your heart and leave the rest to destiny were all you needed to live a decent life. She still thought so, though her own history proved her wrong.

So why was she getting involved again? Think only about that happy man and his doll, surely that's a good omen, Eve told herself, then hurried inside and bought a blue bowl for Blanche. Her aunt loved colored glass.

*   *   *

"Berlin?" Blanche's eyebrows lifted in alarm.

"He called and asked if I would go with him and I said yes." Eve paused to let her aunt take it in. "We have a flight Monday night." When Eve talked about going to India with Max, Blanche had said, "Go!" Now silence.

"Are you sure you want to do this? You seemed so relieved when you left him and got settled on the Vineyard. It could be like disturbing a hornet's nest."

"I was relieved. And when I met old acquaintants I was amused to see how dumbfounded they were. That I was still standing although I had left the famous Paul Bertram. You know what the gossips said: 'I never understood that marriage. He was too smart for her.' 'I've heard he lives a very fast life now. We just saw him at the opera with a stunning woman.' 'Doesn't surprise me, he always had an eye, even when they were married, it was a nightmare.' " Blanche winced.

"Or something like this," Eve continued, " 'Wasn't he a poor boy who made a fortune at his law firm? That Park Avenue spread cost a pretty piece of change, French antiques, Persian rugs, a basket collection of museum quality . . . and so smart, had *Daedalus* in the john . . . ' "

Finally Blanche giggled. "It was all those high-brow magazines in the john that did Jack in. You know, you're a marvelous mimic, for years we thought you might become an actress."

But Eve wasn't finished, "And what about the ones who said,

'In the early years you could almost smell the attraction ... You don't say, never would have thought so, she's always seemed a bit cool, and not much flair.' Or the ones who said, later, 'she's utterly clueless.'"

"Don't, Evie, why are you making yourself miserable? Don't do this," Blanche said.

"Okay, I'll stop," Eve said. "But when you're depressed and not at all clueless, it's sometimes easier to appear dumb."

At that Blanche interrupted sharply, "You've never been dumb."

Eve stared for a moment. "All those people reminded me of kids singing rounds, and I heard every variation, so did you and Mom and Dad. Occasionally the kids were carriers, though they didn't realize it. But when they were, I felt an undercurrent of blame."

"That's ridiculous. The children were just upset that people were talking, They were old enough to sense things, but they couldn't have blamed you. Besides, Paul wasn't discreet, which always surprised me. Claudia once saw him with Frankie," Blanche said, her face flushing with embarrassment.

"I know. Berthe and Zach saw them, too." Eve would have liked to tell her aunt how Paul's sister had called her, horrified. But she refrained. Still, the memory of their conversation still made her ears burn with shame. She never knew what upset Berthe more: that Paul was unfaithful or that she knew about it and did nothing.

"But why did it go bad? That's the real question, isn't it?" Eve asked her aunt.

"No one knows why a marriage goes bad except the people in it."

"Sometimes you don't know what's wrong until it's been wrong for so long that you can't do anything about it," Eve began. "For the first couple of years we were happy. Marvelously happy. Then after the children came, three kids in five years, things became a bit more difficult. I got nannies and sitters, and finally the kids went to school. But after a while it didn't matter how much we went out. It was never enough. And no matter how many successes he had at the firm, it wasn't enough. He wanted to do more, be the best, be seen everywhere. So after a while it was easier to stay at home and let him go. But I also knew this didn't have to do only with the kids, or us." Eve looked up, as if to ask, Can you take it, but Blanche was unruffled.

"Often wonderful sex would be followed by a silence that lasted for days. When I realized it was becoming a pattern and wanted to talk, he'd say, 'It's not your fault, you're a terrific mother, a terrific woman, don't make it worse than it is.' Or he'd get angry and ask, 'You have marvelous kids, enough money, a beautiful home, what more do you want?'

"He was so unpredictable. Things would improve for months, and then he would be running again, running for his life, chased by demons. I would ask questions, but they made him angrier. And abusive. And, at the end, nastier than I could have ever predicted. I was living with a stranger and had to leave. But I never identified those mysterious demons."

"Do you know more about them now?"

"I think so. I always knew they had to do with his past, but I stupidly thought you could ignore the past. I was afraid to probe and became too passive. I went into therapy, but one therapist thought I was a malcontent, a spoiled brat, the other called me 'paranoid.' I should have found a third, but by then I was exhausted and tried to go it alone. By the time I fled, I was a crazy person. You remember."

"How could I forget?" Blanche said sadly. Her eyes met Eve's. "Is it possible he's a man without a soul? I knew one once, when I was very young."

Eve stared. It had never occurred to her that Blanche had known any men besides Jack.

"People with no center," Blanche continued, "like a mutant apple without a core, or the first seedless grapes. Not a very good analogy, even a little weird."

"No, it's fine, good, in fact. I wouldn't say he has no soul, I'd say it's barricaded so well that no one can touch it, or even find it, maybe not even him."

"Assuming that you're right, how can you help him?"

"I'm not sure, but it's worth a try. There were so many things I didn't understand."

Blanche nodded. "Neither did the rest of us. We were all bowled over when you brought him home, he was so in love with you. Then things went downhill . . . it was horrible, watching you grow apart. He became a different person."

It was Eve's turn to nod. "I should have been smarter . . . no, smart had nothing to do with it. When Claudia went off to college, I was terrified at the thought of the two of us alone, so I ran." Eve flushed and lowered her eyes.

"But you had to save yourself. Everyone knew that. And you look so much better now, sometimes your eyes are as gay as when you were a girl," Blanche broke in.

"I'm not a girl and never will be again, Blanche. I had a husband and three kids, and now that husband seems to need me. Our marriage was such a mess at the end, just dwindling into nothing, but now I've got a second chance." Her voice had tapered to a whisper. She looked at her aunt, tears filming her eyes.

Blanche's gaze deepened with respect. Eve loved those eyes, the same satiny brown eyes of her mother and Claudia. "Do you still love him?"

"I don't know, after Jeremy's wedding I hated him. Days, even weeks, go by when I scarcely think about him. But when I heard Paul's young voice . . . I just don't know." Eve could feel her color rising again. She longed to tell Blanche about the man and his doll, and how she saw herself and Paul tied together. But the man and doll didn't seem real when she saw them, how could she make them real now?

"Then you must go, you'll never forgive yourself if you don't. Even if it is a hornet's nest."

*　　*　　*

On Sunday morning Eve hurried up Park Avenue to her parents' apartment house. They, too, deserved the truth. After lunch with her parents, she and Blanche were going shopping.

How different her errand today was from the day almost 30 years ago when she had also come home unexpectedly, to tell them about Paul—the week before Christmas 1959, during her junior year in college, the most important errand of her life. Hurrying...

For now she, who had never had a boyfriend and who had watched almost all her friends from high school and college get engaged, was planning to marry one of Boston's most eligible bachelors, a man whose name everyone knew, a highly respected young lawyer, an outstanding, remarkably intelligent person. Emerging from the station she stared at couples walking with their arms around each other. But she was no longer wistful, for suddenly, she, too, knew what it felt like to be held in someone's arms. And that day New York welcomed her with unexpected tenderness. Christmas carols wound around her as she walked past festooned doorways and light poles, past store windows twinkling with story-book characters, past faces shining with anticipation and joy.

What an innocent world that was, the streets so clean, the people so polite, so friendly, hunched slightly against the cold as they checked off their last-minute chores, then quickened their pace as they sensed snow coming in the feathery air. It was a city that had no way of knowing how much it would change, just as lush, rolling farmland had no way of knowing it would become a battlefield or death camp. Although New York would be utterly different in a generation, nothing could mar its majesty, its splendid hotels glistening near Central Park, its glittering new glass structures that enhanced the elegance of the Empire State and Chrysler Buildings.

Eve took deep breaths, savoring the tangy smell of roasting chestnuts, then bent backwards to take in the magnificent tree at Rockefeller Center. Around her enchanted children, drugged with cold, tugged on grown-up hands. How well she remembered her Aunt Blanche and her mother skirting knots of people until they found a safe place for her and her brother and sister. A holiday ritual they all feared and loved.

Eve stopped, captivated by the skaters. One woman, not young, all in red, carried an enormous silver fox muff. While the others fell away, she moved, dreamily, beguilingly, as if waltzing across the Aral Sea. Soon people began to clap, yet Eve didn't linger. Nor did she suspect that Paul would come and skate at this very rink all through their marriage.

Soon long basting stitches of snow were hemming a soupy sky to the wet sidewalks as she floated uptown. She caught the flakes on her tongue, listening for the inevitable hush, while the chestnut vendors packed up, and the religious slipped in and out of the many churches. How exhilarating, how radiant it was!

Her father's eyes brimmed with pleasure at the sight of her. And then she was embraced not only by her parents, but also by Blanche and Jack. Eve's mother's family lived within blocks of each other, and when she and Paul moved to New York right after their marriage, they would live in this neighborhood, too. But Eve didn't know that then, no, all she knew was her happiness, and theirs, as well. Their smiles when she described Paul, how they'd met, what he did, his family in New Jersey where his father owned a hardware store.

Eve offered nothing that day about his birth and childhood, not because she wanted to evade, but because it didn't seem important. When you're happy only the present matters. That's also true of unhappiness, but Eve had no thoughts of unhappiness then. Nor did she understand how the present spirals into the past, just as the past reaches into the future, so it is all one, coalescing into the moment you are in.

*   *   *

Later Eve consoled herself that they appeared old before she told them. Each time she visited everything seemed lighter, especially their eyes, those brilliant, blazing eyes now fading, like the stones on the Cove bleached and buffeted by wind, sun, sea. Yet their white hair was thick, their backs straight, their minds clear. And the table set precisely with fine linen and porcelain and silver, like the British in India. This apartment was still a microcosmic vestige of the city she had loved so much. Here all was unchanged, except the people.

Eve waited until they finished their egg salad sandwiches, then took the last sip of the strong coffee they drank only until 2 p.m. "I'm leaving for Berlin with Paul tomorrow night."

Her mother stared, her hearing was going. Eve moistened her lips, about to begin again, but her mother said, "I heard you, I'm just speechless." Her father was imperturbable. Was there any way you could surprise a man who had practiced medicine for sixty years?

She turned back to her mother. "Aren't you going to say anything?"

"What's there to say? You're not asking, you're telling."

How belligerent her mother sounded. Eve had been their most placid, studious child, their potential "bluestocking." How relieved they were when she married. Yet watching her marriage had not been easy for them, and they were relieved once more when she left Paul, proud of her for standing up for herself, for they were too astute not to sense something of her situation. But her independence these last five years seemed to scare them a little. In vain Eve searched her father's eyes for a trace of encouragement.

"Do you understand why Paul feels he has to go," she asked.

"Perfectly. What's not so clear is why you have to go with him."

"I'm going as a friend, an old friend."

"I haven't noticed much friendship between you these last years," her mother blurted.

"He certainly wasn't very friendly at Jeremy's wedding," her father added. Eve nodded. Seeing their unhappy faces, she felt herself flush with anger at Paul.

"You're both right, and I'm sorry, Paul was so awful that day, and I should have done something about it. But he wasn't awful on the phone, and there are things about his past, things that created difficulties between us . . . So I've decided to go."

Part of her, deep down, hoped they might ask, "What things?" as she had hoped years ago. But they weren't able to ask then, and they couldn't ask now. She had long ago learned there were some things you had to tough out on your own. And, in a way, their refusal to get involved had given her the freedom to divorce Paul. And the freedom to go with him now.

So she was relieved when her mother put her palms on the edge of the table, gave a little push, and rose.

"Here, Ma, let me help you with the dishes."

"No, talk to your father, he's filled to the brim with the Wall, and I'm sick of it." Then her hand on Eve's wrist, weighted with concern. "Oh, Evie, I hope you know what you're doing."

Eve and her father walked, arms linked, into the cozy den. "Remember what Francois Mauriac said after the Wall went up?" he said. "'I like Germany so much that I want there to be two of them.'" Of course that led to his asking about Claudia and her year at the Sorbonne and what Eve thought she might do next, and the other kids, whom her parents had seen last week.

Then he turned to her, "Do the boys know you're going with Paul?"

"I'm calling them this afternoon."

He nodded and said, "Please let me know the details of your flight." Since Paul and she had divorced, her father had resumed his role as patriarch.

Eve wanted to say, "Dad, I'm middle-aged," but she couldn't. Somehow that would emphasize their age, the last thing they needed, especially since she had dropped this new worry in their lap. So she did her best to concentrate while her father talked about what David Dinkins as Mayor would mean for New York, and how good it was that race was less of an issue now.

When it was time to leave, Eve hugged them, saying, "I'll be back before you know it," trying to ignore their helpless shrugs. As she left Eve was filled with a nameless sorrow, a sense of foreboding as vague as the fog over Lambert's Cove, and as mystifying. Did it have to do with their age? Or was it her own fear she saw mirrored in her mother's eyes?

Then Eve realized she hadn't called her college friend, Deborah who had lived in Seattle. They'd spoken after the destruction of The Wall, and she'd intended to call her after Paul's call, but hadn't. How many times had she telephoned Deborah that first year on the Vineyard? She had dreaded her phone bill, her weakness made visible. But slowly she stood on her own. She used to test herself: How many times could she play Patsy Cline's "Sweet Dreams" before starting to cry?

Now she thought: I'll tell her after I've returned, when I have something to tell.

*　　*　　*

Blanche was determined to go to Saks, but after about two hours she looked deathly pale. "Let's go home, Blanche, this isn't important," Eve said.

Her aunt shook her head. "I'm fine, and we've done very well, with the pants suit and blouse and those tops. But you need a dress. I know just the place." Eve insisted on taking a cab, and there, happily, was an elegant gray dress embroidered with *soutache*.

"Perfect for traveling, dress it up or down," the saleslady urged, then produced a red and black damask shawl. "With this and red shoes you can go anywhere." Eve winked at Blanche.

Only whores wore red shoes, or Moira Shearer. An old family joke. But Blanche was nodding.

"I don't usually wear red, with my hair."

"But you wear the pin with the garnets all the time, that's red," Blanche said.

"That pin was Frieda's, she wore it all the time, too," Eve said shyly.

"I know, she loved you very much. And it's beautiful." Blanche's voice was gentle.

The saleslady sensed an opening. "That myth about redheads not wearing red is an ancient taboo." She draped the shawl. "There!" Eve looked in the mirror. She was right.

An hour later while Eve was spreading everything they'd bought on the bed, Blanche hurried in and thrust a Bergdorf box at Eve. In it were a soft wool bathrobe and a nightgown of the smoothest silk. "Oh, Blanche, they must have cost the world!"

"You're still so young, with lots more living to do," Blanche said.

"I'm going to be fifty in January."

"I know. I remember it well, a miserable icy day. Grandma and I had to call two cab companies, we were afraid you'd be born in the lobby, and the doorman kept saying, 'Second children come fast.'" Family legends, they never failed to comfort, thought Eve.

Blanche straightened. "You have a whole life ahead of you. Aunt Eva, for whom you were named, lived to 96." As Eve thanked her aunt for the extravagant gift, she remembered that Blanche had made her bridal shower so many years ago. And now?

Suddenly Blanche said, "And now we're going out to eat." Eve stared. She'd looked forward to shucking her shoes and eating in front of the TV, which she and the kids used to do when Paul wasn't home. What Blanche did when she was low. But now her aunt's back was ramrod straight as she cut the tags off the pants suit. "You've got to break in these clothes. It's down the street, country French. My treat."

"Oh, Blanche, do we have to?"

"Yes, we have to. It'll be quiet as a tomb."

*   *   *

The snug restaurant was decorated in shades of cinnamon and blue. Blanche lifted her glass. Suddenly Eve felt better. Maybe it was the feel of the fine blouse against her skin. Because Paul put so much stock in good clothes she'd never trusted their magic, but she could be wrong. And such good food, and a congenial buzz.

"Surprising, on a Sunday night," Blanche murmured. "I guess word gets around." But then, after a pause, "Oh, dear." When Eve looked up, her aunt was a ghostly white.

"What's the matter?" Eve rose in alarm.

"I'm fine, sit down. Paul's just walked in, with a woman. He's coming over . . . Oh, hello, Paul, how are you?" Graciously Blanche extended her hand.

And there he was, alone, tall and slim, exactly as Eve imagined him, except that his sandy hair was now a dusky silver. But the shape of his head was the same, and there was a small dent in his hair from his hat. He'd always loved hats, she called it his "Third Man obsession," but he looked older than he had at Jeremy's wedding, and his tie was loosened, giving him a limp aspect, like the cyclamens Gwen brought from the library for Eve to revive. He also didn't seem so eager to impress, so determined to stand out.

Eve rose, glad for the millionth time that she was tall. "Hello, Paul," she said, then leaned towards him and brushed his cheek, aware of the fragrance of his shaving lotion.

"Why, Evie, you look wonderful."

"Thank you. Would you like to sit down? This saves us a telephone call."

"No, I'm with someone, I worked late." He tilted his head towards a small woman at the bar. "Isn't this place heaven?" Eve was puzzled, he'd always preferred flashier places. "And I don't have the arrangements with me. Can I call you later?" His voice was soft when he turned to ask Blanche how she was getting along. Eve could hardly believe her ears. Or her eyes now that she saw the deep lines around his mouth, the crows' feet flaring from his eyes. Or the eyes themselves—not steely and stern, more like the water of Lambert's cove when spring arrived, more blue than gray, the subtlest harbinger of warmth and summer. Questioning, uncertain. Even Blanche looked mystified.

"the voice of your eyes is deeper than all the roses" Eve remembered, then,

> your slightest look easily will unclose me /
> though I have closed myself as fingers, /
> you open always petal by petal myself as Spring opens /
> (touching skilfully, mysteriously) her first rose.

How easily the lines from e.e. cummings came back. She had never understood what they meant, she still didn't, but she knew they evoked physical longing. All at once she pictured Paul and that woman in a shadowy room fumbling with buttons, snaps, straps against the rustling surging sounds of passion being slaked, and in her nostrils, yes she could swear it—the sour-sweet stench of sex. What do they do? The same things she and Paul did? New things?

He was waiting for an answer. "Later is fine, Paul, we'll be up until eleven," she said. Then he hurried towards the woman whose dark red nails were drumming impatiently on the bar.

Blanche sighed happily. "You were so poised, marvelous, really." She giggled. Why that's Claudia's giggle, Eve realized, then smiled. If Blanche only knew. She would think her stark raving mad if Eve told her what she'd imagined. But she knew what it meant: That she was jealous. She'd never cared when she saw lipstick smudging his collars or smelled other women on him when he came to bed, she'd simply crept as far away as she could. And when the busybodies dropped hints, she hadn't given a damn. Now, though, that woman's slender, straight back and black chignon were awakening stabs of envy she hadn't felt since Frankie.

While they were having dessert, Paul and the woman left. The woman was agitated, Paul's back was rigid. Was she furious she wasn't going with him? Did she know he was going? Did he care for her? Or just amusing himself? Oh, how little she still knew about him!

Later, when he called, Paul didn't mention her. Can you be sure she's Anna? Yes, she had to be, there was a connection between them, any fool could see it. Patience, she told herself, and hung up, staring at the Bergdorf box.

Why not? Maybe nightgowns needed to be broken in, too. She cut off the tags. It felt like water on her skin. Slipping on the robe, Eve went to her aunt's room. Blanche was reading. After Eve thanked her again, worry clouded Blanche's eyes. "Oh, Evie, that place is a cauldron, all those old grudges and angers bubbling up. I'm scared for you."

"Don't worry, we'll be fine, Paul is a wonderful traveler, he's been all over the world."

Blanche just shook her head, murmuring, "But this is a new world."

7

EVE FROWNED at the tickets marked First Class. Paul smiled.

"I know it offends you, but it seemed dumb not to be able to sleep a little," he said.

"You hope." Eve shrugged. "I guess that's part of the bargain, stay in a small hotel to please Eve, travel First Class to please Paul." Still, her voice was cheerful. And once they were airborne she patted his arm, a silent acknowledgment that he was right. After they had poked at the food and sipped some Fume Blanc, Eve stretched. How good it felt to have all this room.

Turning to the window she stared into the vast blackness. Though she knew the physics of flight she had never understood it and insisted on their flying separately when the children were growing up. They had looked forward to flying together someday, but had divorced before they could. The last time they flew together was to Italy, on their honeymoon.

She stole a glance at Paul reading *The New York Review of Books*. "It's a wonder you haven't died of boredom from that damn thing by now."

"You're right. A lot of it is pretentious, wrongheaded, smug, like me. But there's usually one fabulous piece, by someone who cares passionately for his subject, and the rest is fodder for parties." He'd never been so truthful before. Was this the same Paul whose conversation during the last months of their marriage was an enfilade of scorn?

What has changed? Eve wondered, searching his face. Aside from the vague, nearly imperceptible fatigue she'd seen last night and the gentler aspect of his eyes, he looked like the man she'd married. A man she'd always been proud to be seen with. Perhaps too proud?

Don't think so much, were Blanche's last words, don't search his face or eyes, don't make comparisons or say too much, just wait, listen. "Learn to listen," her mother used to admonish.

The stewardess began to lower the lights. Eve opened Isherwood's *Goodbye to Berlin* and read for a while, but soon the words were swimming before her eyes. As she turned to her left side where she always slept, her right hand tucked under her lips, she could feel Paul watching her. Within moments, though, a voice burrowed through the darkness.

"Well, I'll be damned! Paul Bertram! Why it's been years, centuries." A tall man with dark slicked-back hair was pumping Paul's hand. "This your new wife? I heard you didn't lose any time beating the bushes, never one to let the grass grow, God, it's been so long." Eve sat up, her hands flying to her mussed hair.

"Kenny Wilkovsky," Paul exclaimed. "Or Kent Wilson?"

The man laughed. "Always Kenny to old buddies." Of course. The man had been a TV interviewer, then an anchor man, but there was a scandal and he'd been fired. Now he said slyly, "Aren't you going to introduce me?" Paul looked confused. Laughter foamed through Eve's chest, but she merely extended her hand in her best Brett Ashley way.

"You'll have to make do with the old wife. I'm Eve Bertram."

"But I heard you were divorced. I am, too, I could have sworn Ian told me you were, and after a devilishly long time."

"We are." Eve smiled, though both men looked embarrassed. "What brings you to Berlin?" she asked, her voice cool.

"The biggest story in the world right now. Best we've had since Nixon's resignation. My people went ahead to do the leg-work, and I'm going for the actual interviews. You know, mothers, daughters, brothers, sisters, spouses who were separated. Heartrending stories for the American public. NBC called me back, what assholes." Then, "How are your folks, Paul?"

"They both died, within the last few years."

"Sorry to hear it. Mine are gone, too. But I sure hope your Mom handed down her recipes. Best cakes I ever ate, *ever.*" A lower voice, "Have you seen Ian?" Before Paul could answer, "I got divorced years ago. No good, ships passing in the night, don't know how people make it to twenty, thirty years, God, a lifetime." Suddenly he was crestfallen.

"Do you have children?" Eve asked.

"Yeah, two boys. Brilliant, one at Harvard, the other at Brown. Totally fucked up, don't know their asses from their elbows, not even sure which sex they like. God, what a mess, children, how do you bring them up?" He paused. "Mine seem so far away sometimes, like we were, that first year. Scared to show what we felt, always hiding something. But we outgrew it, found friends, decided what we wanted to learn. I hoped they'd come around, maybe it was the divorce, they were so young . . .

"You know," he paused, leaning towards them, "there are pockets of darkness in both my sons."

What could they say? Reflexively groping for Paul's hand, then restraining herself, Eve waited, but before they could respond Kenny muttered, "I'm beat," and shuffled away.

"How sad," she started to say. But Paul didn't want to talk about Kenny. His voice was hard. "Damn it, Eve, why are you wearing your wedding ring, you didn't wear it at Jeremy's wedding."

"I didn't wear it then because we're divorced. I wore a ring when I went to India with Max . . . because, because I felt safer, don't ask me why. And I'm wearing it now because we're traveling. I never knew you were friends with Kent, Kenny."

"I wasn't really. We were all in the same freshman college. He was from Ian's home town. When Mom sent me a different cake every week, we'd finish it in one sitting, then look at each other aghast. Filling up our loneliness, I guess. He's kind of pathetic, no?"

"Good looking."

"Always was, but he hasn't had much luck. His first love died, and he married, but it was a disaster. Since then it's been one woman after another. Ian says Kenny and I are searching for something we'll never find. You know Ian was furious about our divorce?" Eve shook her head.

"Livid. He told me, 'Fight for her, she's the best thing that ever happened to you.'"

Eve had always thought Ian and Paul's other close friends considered her spineless, especially after Paul made no secret about seeing other women. Now Paul gazed at her. She stood her ground. Wait. Listen.

"Your not wearing your wedding ring was what set me off at Jeremy's wedding, especially since we were walking him down the aisle. And you, clinging to Max all through the reception, as if he were Christ himself."

"Paul, please," she protested, but he ignored her.

"Claudia told me how angry everyone was, but I was angry, too. With you hanging onto Max, how could we be a family? And fluttering, God, you never stopped moving, all I could think of was the father junco shaking the feeder on the Vineyard."

Eve frowned. She thought only she remembered that bitter Christmas when the father junco had attacked the open bird feeder, scattering seeds onto the frozen snow so the younger ones could feed, as juncos always did, from the ground. So many memories, they became a code when you have been married as long as they were. Bracing herself for more, Eve straightened. But now a curious flatness curtained Paul's eyes; he went back to his reading. It was ironic, this man who had refused to wear a wedding ring—"I hate men wearing jewelry,"—in a rage about hers. Yet it helped explain his behavior the day of the wedding.

So much is invested in symbols like rings. Eve stared at the faint gleam on her left hand, pulled it off and dropped it into her pocket. Separate entities from now on. The man dancing with his doll floated through her mind. With kids you're tied together for life. But the kids are grown and you and Paul are divorced. No ring. Finally she leaned back and pulled the blanket over her shoulders and fell asleep.

*   *   *

Although Paul had gone to Yale without a glance back, his sister Berthe felt more comfortable staying home for college and had gone to Rutgers. She graduated a few days before Paul graduated from Harvard Law School. By then she was a beautiful young woman, with a striking resemblance to their mother. Looking at her Paul sometimes felt he was looking at the elegant young Frieda Berger he had adored during his childhood. But Berthe was bolder than Frieda and had no trouble expressing her opinions.

On the day of his law school graduation, when Paul received more than his fair share of honors, he had expected his parents to be happy, even triumphant. Instead, they seemed more diffident than ever. More bewildered, really, than he had ever seen them, so he drew Berthe aside and asked, "Are Mom and Dad all right? They were so happy at your graduation, but they seem so subdued today."

Her reply was crisp, almost harsh. "They're not Mom and Dad. They're Mamma and Papa, and the truth is they hardly know who you are anymore, Paulie. Neither do I. We're doing the best we can with your new persona, this hail-fellow-well-met person who seems to be the most popular man in the class. Why you seem as Protestant as these Ians and Fritzes and Kevins who are your friends. I know we weren't all that observant when we lived in Berlin, but we never forgot we were Jewish. How could we, after all that happened? But you have. Let's just get through the rest of all these celebrations and go home."

He had wanted to tell Berthe that day how wrong she was—that his best friends, Ian and Fritz were Jewish, but that they didn't think being Jewish was such a big deal. How they had spent hours convincing Paul that the most wonderful thing about being American was that none of that mattered, no one cared what religion you were or what it had cost you. The most important thing was that you were American, the land of the free, the home of the brave—where no one could prevent you from taking advantage of every opportunity you had, where you could date any girl you were attracted to.

"Don't make such a big deal out of religion, Paul," Ian once said. "Here people don't really care that much about it."

But he could almost see Gunther and Frieda breathing a sigh of relief when he told them Eve was Jewish, and the wariness he had felt at his law school graduation slowly dissolved after he brought Eve home. His parents, better than anyone, could see how happy he was, and gradually drew Eve into the family circle with a warmth they rarely showed here in America but that he remembered from their younger days in Berlin.

After the marriage Frieda and Eve began to cook and go to concerts together, and Gunther taught her how to play chess, and there were Sunday afternoons when Paul would close his eyes, listening to the hum from the kitchen, where Frieda and Eve and often Berthe were preparing a meal, and he could feel himself drifting backwards in time, to the large kitchen he still recalled so vividly, and the cherished ease he had felt as a child in that homey room.

Once he caught his father staring at Eve and when he said, "What is it, Papa?" in German, his father answered, "She reminds me of someone, but I can't quite remember who. Something about the way she carries herself." Then he shrugged and smiled. "Not important. She's a wonderful woman, Paul, I'm happy for you."

Paul felt a shiver. His father had seen Alix only once. That afternoon, when his father was unusually relaxed, was an opportunity to talk about that woman Eve resembled, to tell his father what had really happened to her, to confess how much she haunted his thoughts. But when his father looked at him so intensely, he had been paralyzed with fear and confusion. How to begin? Where? And why had he kept all that to himself for so long? Surely he could trust his father. But no, not now, he told himself, why spoil things now?

Later Paul decided he had done the right thing. Indeed, the only thing. He really had no choice but to maintain his silence.

And when Eve produced twin boys Frieda and Gunther behaved as if she had done it all herself, as if Paul had had nothing to do with it. Frieda came to Manhattan and stayed with them for a week to help them. She was impressed by Eve's stamina and her impressive abilities at organizing their now very complicated household. She and Eve's Aunt Blanche became friends during that hectic week, and when she left, Frieda whispered to her son, "You are a lucky boy. And be sure you help as much as you can. She doesn't ask for much and she's quiet, but she's no pushover."

At the time it was a point of pride. But as he had watched Eve field Kenny's awkward question, as he had seen her commanding poise and her genuine delight in the poor bastard's mistake, Paul realized, as he should have long ago, that his mother's praise was also a warning.

*   *   *

Although she looked as if she was sleeping, Eve's mind wouldn't stop racing. Now it fixed on the children and their skepticism when she called to say goodbye.

"Are you sure about this, Mom?" Eric asked.

"Yes, but I don't really expect anyone to understand. We'll call you next weekend from Berlin. I don't know when we'll be home, but surely in time for Thanksgiving."

Jeremy was more direct. "If it turns out to be the wrong decision, come home, Mom. I'll meet you at the airport. Don't do anything you don't want to do." Now married, he was the authority on marriage.

"I'll be fine. I want to go."

"No, Mom, you think you should go. I sure hope you know what you're doing. Sarah sends love. Me, too," he added softly.

Claudia said, "I can't believe this. You and Dad?"

"Me and Dad."

"I'll never understand you two." Eve stiffened, expecting a lecture. Instead she heard a tinge of fear. "I'm not sure I think you should go with Dad," Claudia paused, reversing herself completely from the child who had asked Eve so plaintively to telephone her father. Then she said, more cheerfully, "Be sure to take lots of notes, and maybe you'll come to Paris on the way home?"

"It's awfully close to Thanksgiving, and I'm expecting the usual crowd . . . "

"Oh, Mom, give me a break. Thanksgiving comes every year, but 1989 is the only year the Berlin Wall came down. Besides, Gwen can do it, or Max, let Max cook his macrobiotic, life-prolonging recipes, and you come to Paris." Claudia paused. "I'm sure I can turn up a turkey. I'm going to call Daddy right now." Her voice became bossy. "Maybe the boys and Sarah can come, Thanksgiving in Paris, it could be better than April in Paris. Oh, Mom, it would be so good to see everyone." The catch in Claudia's voice surprised Eve, but before she could answer, her daughter said, "Be careful," and was gone.

It wasn't like Claudia to be so apprehensive. Not Claudia, whose favorite childhood story was about Alexander the Great and his father King Philip and Philip's horse, Bucephalus, who was so wild no one could ride him. One day Alexander asked if he could try. Although Philip was worried that he might get hurt, he decided to teach the boy a lesson. What he didn't know was that Alexander had observed the horse very carefully and realized that Buchephalus was afraid of his own shadow, and that's why he went crazy. So Alexander turned the animal to face the sun and climbed onto him and didn't have a lick of trouble. "And so Alexander taught his father a lesson," Claudia would say as she finished the story.

All children think they're like Alexander—invincible and smart. That captivating story always made Eve wonder even more about Paul as a boy, but although there were photographs scattered around the Berger home, many of them of a smiling, confident youngster who clearly got all the attention he needed, she could never bring herself to ask why there were no pictures of Paul after he was about ten or eleven. Or about that smiling child who looked so cheerful. Somehow she sensed that such questions would be an intrusion.

The Bergers were more formal than her parents, and his father Gunther, always reserved, became more distant as he aged. Even Paul's sister Berthe was no help. If Eve asked an innocent question—about a recipe or a custom—Berthe would clam up and say something like, "The past is past." Or, "I don't really remember." But she was thirteen when they came to America. Surely a 13-year-old has lots of memories of her native country. Still, it was not up to Eve to criticize Berthe's apparent amnesia.

Only Paul's mother Frieda seemed able to conjure up some memories of their life in Germany, and with time Eve knew she could have asked Frieda more questions, but by the time she wanted answers, things between her and Paul had gotten so complicated that she was uncomfortable discussing him with anyone. They would have to work out their differences themselves; it was not fair to involve his parents or sister or friends. Especially his parents, who had lived through more than enough for one lifetime. Besides, the boy in the photos and the exquisite little girl whose brown eyes held so much laughter had nothing to do with the Paul and Berthe she knew.

Now Eve was wide awake. After Gunther died and Frieda got sick, Eve came down from the Vineyard every ten days or so and stayed with Blanche or her parents for weeks at a time, going to the hospital early in the morning and, often, again at night. The fact that she and Paul were divorced seemed irrelevant, Frieda was still her mother-in-law, a beloved presence in her life. The oddest thing was their mutual silent agreement never to discuss Paul. It was as if he were away on an extended business trip.

One evening, just before Eve was about to leave for the night Frieda became very agitated and groped in the drawer of her night table, and took out the silver and garnet pin she had worn almost every day. Clasping Eve's arm, she said, "Such a good girl ... like a daughter, like Ruth, and a fine mother and wife ... but he's so complicated, no one could have done more than you did ... " The syllables fell away, but then she loosened her grip and seemed to gather strength.

"It was our fault, for staying, a terrible mistake. He doesn't mean it, he's afraid, he's been afraid ... since ... " she began, stopping, confused. After a few moments she made one last effort, "Such a brave boy when he was small, like a bright star, or a candle glowing ... " and again that distracted circling of her eyes, all the time stroking Eve's arm with gnarled, swollen fingers, "and I want you to have this," she finished, pressing the pin into Eve's palm.

Returning to her parents' apartment, Eve had thought: Maybe Frieda will talk more and I can sort all this out. But just before dawn the next day, against all predictions, Frieda Berger died.

By now Eve was sitting up again, but when she glanced over at Paul, she could see he was getting sleepy as he read.

Eve never spoke about her last encounter with Frieda. The only person she could have told was Paul, but by then talk with Paul had become a competition in terseness. And Berthe had been devastated by her mother's death, becoming, if anything, more unwilling to talk about the past. Yet those last moments with Frieda became more important over time, burnished in her mind like a beloved poem, or glossy stone whose surface is such a comfort to touch.

Juncos, wedding rings, the kids, Alexander, Frieda. The mind has no mercy. Then she asked herself, What do you know? That the life you so carefully constructed for yourself is not as sturdy as you thought. That you are going to Berlin with Paul because he is haunted by ghosts of the past, and he has to put those ghosts to rest. That this trip won't be easy, and to compound that, you have no idea what he's done since the divorce, what books he's read, what performances he's seen, what cases he's working on. Yet he's still Paul—older, quieter, maybe wiser, certainly friendlier.

Now Paul's eyes were closing and jerking open. She pressed his arm, "Time to give up."

Paul closed his book, saying, "You know, Nabokov thought Isherwood was pure *kitsch,* the worst."

"And it just may be that your adored Nabokov was wrong," she retorted. She hated *Lolita* although she loved some of the other Nabokov books, especially *Speak, Memory.* Paul's eyebrows rose and his gaze deepened.

"You know, his father was a staunch Liberal although he was one of the richest men in Czarist Russia. He edited a famous émigré magazine in Berlin, and on the night of March 28, 1922, he was killed protecting his old political ally, Milyukov, from an assassin's bullet. Threw himself in front of Milyukov who was saved, then went after the assassin but then a second assassin shot him several times. He was 52 years old. The assassin was a right-wing Tsarist named Taboritsky. It happened in the old Philharmonia Hall, in East Germany. We can go visit it, if it's still there. Anyway, in 1936 that same Taboritsky was named second in command of émigré affairs under Hitler. That was too much for Nabokov, and right after he found out about the appointment, he wrote to friends in America asking for a teaching job." Now Paul was alert and his eyes had deepened to a startling purplish glow.

Eve could feel that old melting sensation she always had when he gave her, like a small precious gift, some wonderful piece of miscellany like this. He had a photographic memory, and she had forgotten how much she enjoyed these little tidbits. Or how much her obvious pleasure delighted him when he was able to recall such morsels.

"How can you remember all that, all those names, especially when you're so sleepy?" she wanted to know. "Remarkable," she whispered and reached across and tucked his blanket around him. For a second he lifted his hand to touch hers, then nodded, giving her a crooked smile, too tired to answer. Besides, there was no answer, it was an old saw between them.

"Sleep well," she said softly. Within minutes Paul's breathing was even, relaxed.

She wasn't so lucky. Instead of unwinding into sleep, her brain throbbed with Kenny's mournful "pockets of darkness." Weren't there pockets of darkness in all of us? The blinding black of the theater after the movie has begun and you arrive late, pushing down panic, until aisles, seats, torsos come into focus? Or your mind's calm when you awake, until reality pierces your consciousness, reminding you of your failures and your failed wishes and dreams? Or that place in Paul, so alluring when they made love but that, with time, became something to fear?

PART II

8

THE MOB seemed mad with a buoyant exhilaration. Here was Berlin's famous Tegel airport filled with voices on what seemed a million TV sets asking, over and over again, the same questions he had heard in New York. Yet here the questions seemed more pressing. And the people! Never had he imagined so many people.

Was he crazy? Dragging Eve into this maelstrom? Most of the people in this airport were foreigners wanting to snatch a piece of history. Voyeurs. Totally removed from the real story because this wasn't their country and they had no idea that Berlin had always been different from the rest of Germany: That Berliners were witty and smart and skeptical to the point of cynicism and singularly adept at a unique brand of humor and self-mockery. That they were called "a race apart" because they trusted no one, were utterly independent, totally self-absorbed, and considered themselves above politics. That their refusal to take Hitler seriously was probably what made it possible for their city to become home to the Gestapo and its infamy, creating one of the greatest ironies in modern history. And that a large percentage of those Jews who stayed were too smug to realize what was happening until the SS was in their backyard and the War at their very doorsteps.

It was also the place where Jews like your family knew very well what was happening but waited too long, Paul reminded himself. And that's why you're back.

Once more his glance scanned the airport. The hope now surging around him reminded him of the mood during late

1943, when Berlin was beginning to be pounded by Allied bombs as no city would be attacked in all of the Second World War. The total number of bombings would number over 360, would destroy the ten-mile square center of the city, and would kill or wound a total of 150,000 people.

But for the hidden Jews it was a miracle. Suddenly the earth seemed to shift beneath your feet as you grasped the amazing, wonderful, inescapable truth that Hitler and his Nazis were going to lose the war.

It was mild that Chanukah, a warm wind blowing through their slightly opened attic windows, cleansing their cramped, smelly rooms, billowing the curtains, causing a few loose papers on his father's desk to flutter to the floor. Although the candles of the Menorah flickered madly, they did not go out. "It's a sign, just like the sign to the Maccabees, that soon this madness will be over," Hjalmar insisted. Hjalmar Friedmann, his father's best friend, the Gentile who had saved their lives.

"The Nazis cannot win, such evil cannot triumph, it would be a denial of everything we know as human," he would declare, but Hjalmar died without knowing the extent of the evil, without knowing that by 1945 the very notion of "human" had been utterly changed. Or that, by then, hope and joy seemed to have disappeared from Germany forever.

Yet here, before Paul's eyes were optimism and jubilation, all because of the destruction of the Berlin Wall and all it implied: the end of this long bleak Cold War.

How different this crowd was from the German mob, which grew more and more oppressive as the war dragged on. Composed of earnest, dull Germans, obedient to a fault, and singularly lacking in humor, that mob had been beaten to a pulp after the First World War and were weighed down by the Treaty of Versailles and the failing Weimar Republic. In the 1930s they were regarded as a people in distress, a people whose past was filled with men of genius, but who were not practiced in the ways of democracy as the English and French or Americans were. Who had lost their drive and could not understand the concepts of personal independence and rugged individualism that might help them resist Hitler. Thus, they had seized on his rhetoric and became good Nazis, denying what was happening.

How well Paul remembered all the arguments to justify them. As well as their bleached northern eyes, their vacant stares, even the faintly acrid odor emanating from their bodies when they formed a crowd and stood, shifting from one foot to the other, and watched the marching soldiers, then, later, those same soldiers herding Jews towards the train stations. Suddenly he could even taste that disgusting taste he had known so well—as sharp as anise—as their hysteria grew to exactly the frenzy that Hitler and his henchmen wanted.

Without warning memories flooded his brain, swelling, pressing against him like a fierce, grizzled wave beating at his chest. Nausea rose in his throat.

Plucking Eve's arm, he muttered, "Let's get out of here," then propelled her towards the exit. The air was thick with dust—for everyone seemed to be carrying a piece of the Wall—and the sweet scent of pot.

"Too many people," he explained, breathing deeply until they found a place to sit down. The insanity today was contained in the airport, but the madness he remembered was everywhere, on the streets, in the stations, in the Tiergarten, the Grunewald, at parades on the Ku'damm.

"It's a little like a rock concert," Eve said. If he hadn't been so queasy, he would have laughed. Eve's habit of shrinking things to what she could hold in her mind had alternately amused and exasperated him. He finally concluded that it was a logical extension of her protected American childhood, her blithe innocence, her limited view of the world.

But that was in the past. Now that they were here, he had to make her understand. Somehow he had to make her grasp all that had happened to him, to evoke the slowly descending fog of terror that enveloped their lives while they were hidden, and also the sense of freedom he had when they began to wander—a sense of freedom that was utterly shattered at the end.

Yet how?

And how to justify all those years of running from the past? Paul closed his eyes and saw that folded piece of onionskin, the letter that became their passport to freedom. Because of his fair blond looks he had had the responsibility of carrying it when they were shunted north of Berlin, to Sweden, then to England and, finally, to the States. It became part of his body, tucked into his worn passport case, until one day, about ten years into their marriage, when he placed it in the leather folder with their marriage license and the children's birth certificates. Hoping Eve would find it, and that her questions might lead them both out of the morass their marriage had become.

Hoping in vain. He still didn't know if she had read the letter or not. She never said anything, and he couldn't bring himself to ask. What cowards they both were! That small act became emblematic of all that was wrong in their marriage, yet somehow they stayed together, gradually leading more and more separate lives.

Until she left, and each of them was truly alone.

Now Paul stood up. "Let's go. The faster we get to the hotel, the better I'll feel." He pushed their cart laden with luggage to the queue for a cab. The fresh air was a relief, and when he looked up, he was aware of something else, something besides the fear and the hope and the disgust.

He was home. Here were the sharp lilac skies, the stiff winds that blew in from Scandinavia, the light that looked like skimmed milk when the sun slipped behind a cloud. Or, when the sun shone, the clear air shot through with those gorgeous purplish splashes you get only in latitudes closer to the pole. Never had Paul seen such dusks—warm liquid oranges and reds and yellows and purples bursting into the sky and slowly descending below the horizon. For years he had dreamed of their crimson shimmer. As a boy he'd thought them gloriously beautiful, yet over time they became merely one more thing tinged with blood.

But still, *home*.

*   *   *

"Idiots," the cab driver shouted as he loaded their luggage. "Like kids at a carnival. Screaming about freedom. There is no such thing as freedom. You can be free one day and chained the next. Didn't Prinz-Albrecht-Strasse teach them that?"

Paul started with surprise. Prinz-Albrecht-Strasse was where the Gestapo detained their prisoners. The man was probably 65, with bushy graying hair and a plump face. Were you in Prinz-Albrecht-Strasse? Were you tortured? Did you work there? Paul wanted to ask but said nothing. Besides, all this could be a show to impress the tourists, just as so many Germans had lied to the invading Americans and Russians in the spring of 1945. "If you were all resisters, how did the Nazis imprison and kill so many?" one general asked.

Silence was best.

After making sure they were settled, the driver turned the steering wheel sharply and they swung onto the ring road. "Please, I ask you, speak in English," he said. "To practice. We expect much Americans now that disappeared East Germany. Like something in a tale of fairies. But so much people, pushing, wanting, shrieking. Your hotel is good, a quiet position, away from such circus. Shrieking or screaming, which is better? And do you say fairies or elves?"

Paul and Eve finally exchanged a smile and sat back. "You talk, I don't want to take the chance I might slip into German," Paul whispered. For years Paul had been told he had no trace of German in his speech. Now, though, he was thinking in German, as unexpectedly as he sometimes dreamed in German.

Eve spoke slowly. "Shrieking or screaming, either one. And fairy tale is better than tale of fairies, and fairies are more generally used than elves. When talking about a building, location is better than position."

The driver nodded briskly, then, "Here on business?"

"More or less."

"First time here?"

"Yes."

"Because of the Wall?"

"Partly, other things as well, it's complicated . . . "

"The world is complicated, hard to make sense of. But not as bad as when I was young, then the world was crazy . . ." his voice dwindled and he concentrated on negotiating a turn before launching into a rehearsed talk about the sights in Berlin.

Finally, he cautioned, "Don't try to speak German, too hard, better teach us English, for future. Kennedy, your countryman, is not correct, must be 'Ich bein Berliner.' He said, 'Ich bein ein Berliner,' which means I am a jelly pancake!" He chuckled merrily until they reached the hotel and cheerfully unloaded their baggage.

The concierge's practiced glance sought Eve's hands. Nowadays some women didn't wear wedding rings. But a couple with the same name wanting two rooms?

Eve began to circle the small lobby as Paul signed in. When he was finished, he watched her peer at a series of botanical prints, glance at the people lounging in the easy chairs, finally linger near the window, taking in the small garden, dreary and empty now.

As she stood there, the sun abruptly appeared, and her head was framed by a glow of light glistening on her reddish hair. Fainter now than when she was young, and shorter, but still beautiful, its auburn glints heightened by a few silvery strands. In the short time they'd been together she seemed sturdier, and her face bloomed with the resilience of youth. It was strange, after all she was almost five years older than when they parted, but today she looked younger. She was also slimmer than the day she whirled at him in a panic, clamped her mouth shut and flew out the door. As if to say, we are beyond speech, now I must act. Running out with just a raincoat over her nightgown and robe, and never returned.

None of that fright and anger was visible now. No, before him was an attractive, assured woman who smiled at him and the concierge, a woman who led a deliberately serene existence. "A very independent woman," Claudia had reported with a strange pride.

Was that was what she had been trying to tell him last night when, in reply to his incoherent rambling about her wedding ring, she simply took it off and dropped it into her pocket? Not even deigning to reply.

Now, though, Paul was amazed to see Eve put her hand back into that same pocket and slip on her wedding ring with that same innocent diffidence that had attracted him to her in the first place, but also with a confidence that said: You will never know all there is to know about me.

Her inconsistencies had fascinated him when they were young. Could he ever know her well enough to tell her everything? Did she really want to know? This complicated woman who could recite lines from Keats as easily as she could sing a Patsy Cline song? Or did she prefer the not-knowing, the silence? He hadn't known then and didn't know now. Yet he was still beguiled by her, his wife for more than twenty years.

She has not been your wife for almost five years.

"It's a lovely hotel, a wonderful choice," Eve said as she came closer. The concierge started, then looked from one to the other, and nodded. Brother and sister. A shiver ran up Paul's spine. A Southern motel owner had made that assumption years ago. "We're married," Eve had said, flushing with wild indignation. Can't you see how madly we love each other? her eyes had flashed.

As soon as the concierge handed them separate keys with a pompous, "Miss Eve Bertram, Mr. Paul Bertram," she merely lowered those same gray eyes, then asked for a map. While she inquired about concerts and theater, it was Paul's turn to step away.

When Eve saw the concierge's conclusion, her eyes had filled with shame. The same shame Paul had seen so many times before, as if everything between them was her fault. Always too willing to accept blame, convincing herself when he lost his temper that she had provoked him. Which only made him angrier.

Oh, how often had he wished he could confess that the dark places in their marriage, those black holes, had little to do with her, that their life together was simply another link in an inexorable chain that, over time, had come to have the cruel edge that many inexorable events have. And if he couldn't tell her while they were married, why hadn't he come clean at the end?

Paul guessed that unconsciously he needed to make her suffer. Answers to such questions are often simpler than we expect. Simone Weil was right, evil is contagious.

Again that voice in his head: You were amazed when you fell in love and had that reprieve of the early years, it was her unconditional love that gave you everything you had dreamed of when you left this city for the last time, dreams which had, against all reason, come true. Until you looked back and convinced yourself you didn't deserve such happiness and smashed it all to bits. So you became enraged, even though it was your fault. Refusing to admit your insane need to run away from yourself, letting her think she was not enough for the famous lawyer, sophisticated art lover, brilliant reader, charming raconteur, musical aficionado. What the gossips said. But they were wrong.

Suddenly Paul became more alert, hearing Eve say, "Thank you so much, this all looks wonderful, absolutely wonderful. And so nice that the season is in full swing."

"Don't miss the Philharmonie, it is a jewel," the concierge said, captivated by her enthusiasm. She smiled again, tucked the brochures under her arm and, with their individual keys dangling from their hands, she and Paul walked to the elevator.

As they unlocked their adjacent rooms, Eve said, "Let's just unpack and wash, then have something to eat and a walk. I could do with some exercise." Though her voice was calm, her foot tapped nervously.

"You're sure you're not too tired?" Whenever they flew separately in the early years, they'd meet at the hotel, dive into bed, then nap and eat and walk later.

That was then.

She shook her head. "I am, a little, but if I try to sleep it will be a disaster. Better to wait until I'm dropping from fatigue."

9

THERE ARE PEOPLE who believe that ghosts hover over Normandy, that you can feel their presence as you walk through the long rows of white crosses. Others claim that the earth at Shiloh and Antietam and Gettysburg has a bloody taint, and they say that people don't swim at Anzio because they can still smell death in the water there. Surely, though, evidence of war must comfort returning soldiers or their descendants. Here's where they fought, here's where my father died, here's where my friend went down, here's where we were shelled.

Here was nothing. As he and Eve walked from Halensee Station to his old neighborhood, Berlin looked exactly as Paul remembered: A city intent on minding its own business. He stared, incredulous. This upper-class district called the Eichkamp that had been a backdrop for lunacy and violence and infamy had reverted to stately, cherished homes, tidy gardens, swept stone walks—such obvious signs of civilization that no one could imagine anything terrible happening here.

Yet it had.

The clue was that the people living in these houses and tending these gardens did not in a single trait resemble the prosperous Jews who built these houses and designed these flower beds. Those proud serious folk were long since gone, and the squatters who invaded this area as early as 1941 and 1942 had simply covered up all the signs of their crimes by turning back the clock and living almost the same lives of those people their parents had hounded to their deaths.

As Paul stared at the peaceful sleepy street he could feel his knees wanting to give way. When he leaned against a bus shelter, its plexiglas shell began to move under his weight. Helpless, he started to slide.

"Take deep breaths," Eve urged, propping herself against him.

"I'm sorry," he muttered, angry at himself. The nausea in the airport was nothing compared to this. A shower of sweat dripped from his temples onto his collar. He turned his head, hoping to vomit, but nothing. Eve was pale, the edges of her lips white.

"Paul!" She guided him to a bench. "Paul, what is it?"

His voice caught in his throat. "It looks so harmless," he finally started, "Like any ordinary well-heeled neighborhood. Exactly as it looked when I was eight or nine. Unbelievable, not a single blemish."

"They're good engineers, wonderful mechanics, so organized. They know how to restore, cover things up, get things going again, you've always said that, all those trains running on time . . . "

"I didn't know what to expect, I was so anxious to get here I hardly thought about what I'd find . . . " he faltered and scanned the street again. Some years the trees were bare by now, as brittle as wire sculptures gleaming in the sun. Today leaves still clung to the trees. Earth warming? Or maybe he didn't remember.

And the houses so sturdy, so pleased with themselves. Reclaimed, restored, just as he had once thought he, too, could be restored. But some memories drive deeper with time, and even the vaguer ones linger like some deadly organism that fouls a healthy pond.

How clear it all was, now that he was here, where he had raced with his friends, whooping with pleasure, his book bag thumping his back. Then, later, slithering along these sidewalks under cover of darkness, like a garden snake in the Grunewald, armed with false papers, his heart banging, praying only to reach home with the food he had been sent out to scavenge at the end—on the back steps of the few remaining restaurants, or in the debris not yet cleaned after the incessant bombing.

"Life or death, Paulie, that's what it is now," his father would say at the beginning of 1944. And each time his mouth as dry as paper, his whole being so desiccated by fright that he was sure he could feel his eyeballs moving in their sockets, his breath sliding through his nose and throat, his bones scraping against each other. Each night the city more ravaged and stinking with burning metal and rubber. Later, after the Allies had hammered it to a pulp, the stink was the rotting flesh of those who'd been trapped beneath the debris, or the corpses before their very eyes. Never since had he known such terrible, knee-knocking fright.

Now, though, no fright, only this awful need to begin. Yet, how? If his partners saw him now they'd be speechless. Paul Bertram inarticulate—impossible!

But here he was not Paul Bertram. Here he was Paulie Berger.

Shifting from one foot to another, as if the stiff bristly fabric of his childhood suits were chafing his thighs, he could hear his tutor, Henry Simmons, who prepared him for the college boards by reading the old Rouse translation of *The Iliad* and *The Odyssey*. "The best stories begin *'in media res,'*" that kind man said. He had never told Eve about him, he realized. But if he told her about Henry, he would have had to tell her about so much more.

"My father was the last in a long line of German jewelers," he began . . .

"In the 1920s and 1930s jewelers were not as exalted as lawyers or doctors or engineers or bankers, nor as respected as architects or writers or philosophers or scientists or teachers, yet being a jeweler had its own caché. All of Berlin knew Berger's on the Ku'damm—the German aristocracy who shopped for their wives and daughters, beautifully groomed, well-spoken, cultivated men whose bearing and dignity and diction were like no others, whose ideals and values made Gunther Berger proud to be German. And the wealthy Jews whose wives clustered on the steps of synagogue, the opera, the Philharmonie, eyeing each other and saying, 'Mrs. Hoffman's earrings are from Berger's.' Or 'Rosengarten's daughter got a perfect pear-shaped diamond from Berger's.' Of course. At Berger's there was quality and refinement, above all.

"And then, in the 20s and 30s the Ostjuden, the Eastern European Jews who believed, like Dickens's Wemmick, in 'portable property.' Escapees from the Russian compulsory military service. For proof of jewelry's value they pointed to the Russian aristocracy—intellectuals who now lived in small flats instead of spacious, sprawling estates, and austere old ladies, dressed in black, who existed for years on a ring or bracelet. Yes, jewelry might, in the end, be the best investment of all.

"But suddenly there were others: Men who swaggered over the showcases in black leather and glossy boots, whose very gestures were menacing and arrogant—the new members of the growing National Socialist Party. The Nazis. Hitler's army. At first distinguishable from the German Army, then simply Germany's Army, never needing to rationalize their purchases—rough men who fancied rings and bracelets, who loved all totems of wealth, who hated the Jews but made an exception of Gunther.

"These Nazis knew all about those devices that could melt and twist gold, set stones like diamonds, rubies, sapphires. They had watched Gunther shaping his marvelous confections to adorn not only their wives, but also the women who sang so seductively in the night spots near the Brandenburger Tor. No, they couldn't hurt Gunther. Their honor wouldn't allow it. Besides, what would they do without those bits of cash that Hjalmar slipped into their outstretched hands?

"'And so,' Gunther announced, 'we will stay. We will dig in our heels and wait for this to pass. If we hold our heads high, time will prove me right.'

"How could they move? A walk through the Tiergarten after lunch was as vital as breath, or food. Besides, Gunther had fought—a mere boy—at the end of the First World War. And hadn't he and Hjalmar stood together in June 1922 and watched the outpouring of love for Walter Rathenau after he was murdered? Those were the real German people, the workers who had marched in the hundreds of thousands to protest the senseless death of that great Jewish industrialist and intellectual.

"This hysteria would pass, no one would listen to this raving maniac from the south. All would be well. So Gunther thanked God he was not an academic, or an employee of a large firm, or a professional whose license had to be renewed. Those pitiable men were prey to those disgusting racial laws, but he and his shop were independent. Not as big as Wertheims or KaDeWe, but successful enough. For jewelry seemed a universal need.

"Sometimes he and Hjalmar discussed it over lunch at the Kempinski Café, only a few doors from the shop. Hjalmar agreed with him, and there wasn't a more intelligent, sensitive man than Hjalmar, his designer and dearest friend. It was all poppycock, and this would not last, *could not* last. The man was mad, an idiot with a bee in his bonnet, who got his ideas from that tired *Protocol of the Elders of Zion* brought here years ago by a Russian fanatic. There were idiots everywhere, why even Henry Ford subscribed to its ideas, which was proof you did not have to be poor and hungry to be insane.

"Then came *Kristallnacht*. Although the shop was spared by his Nazi customers, everyone became terrified afterwards. Sometimes Gunther would wake up to Frieda pounding his chest and sobbing, yet afraid to tell him the terror of her dreams. When Gunther broke down one day, Hjalmar contacted his father in Norway. Perhaps the Bergers could go there until it all blew over? No, it was too dangerous, they had waited too long.

"So they decided that the safest place was here. Look at all those foreign correspondents who haunted the Adlon and Eden bars. How could anything happen when so many foreigners wandered freely? And if things got worse, if the screws tightened, they would make a pretense of going like their neighbors, but stay put. Hole up.

"Of course the house could handle it, it was huge. Gunther was the youngest of five, two sisters who had married men from Hamburg and were still there, and two brothers, both killed in the First War, bringing on his parents' premature deaths, Gunther believed. No, no family who had lost two sons for the Fatherland would be persecuted. Besides, it was surrounded by a thick wall, built by Gunther's father after Rathenau's assassination. 'Better not to have everything in the open,' Gunther was told.

"Their Gentile friends, Hjalmar Friedmann, their talented Norwegian-born designer and his German-born wife, Marga, would move in with their daughters, Rose and Grete. After the Bergers appeared to have gone, they would get false papers from the forgers. It would be a lark and last only until the evil winds shifted. One must never knuckle under to evil. The Nazis could not tell them how to live, and above all they must keep their dignity, and not panic like the jittery imbeciles storming the embassies.

"Gunther and Hjalmar worked hard to convince each other, but by the end of 1940 the evil winds had the force of a hurricane. So instead of going to the Kempinski, where they would see Hitler and Goering, they ate at the shop and drew plans for a secret passage to the third floor. By then they had again stood, shoulder to shoulder, in October 1940 when the first Jews were rounded up and deported. Unable to believe their eyes.

"'Where are they going?' their wives wanted to know.

"'To Poland, where they will be safe,' the men replied, the words like rusty metal on their tongues. By New Year's Day 1941 it was time. As long as it could be kept secret, the Bergers would be safe. They would simply disappear, one day soon."

Finally Paul stopped. Eve's face was drawn but there wasn't an ounce of fear in her eyes. So he drew in his breath and went on:

Until that day Paulie Berger has never seen his mother cry. That soft, spring afternoon he realizes he's heard her cry, but could never iden-tify the faint, breathy sounds that ended in a small, almost meow and were followed by his father's gay voice and the ping of the decanter and the tinkle of glasses. Lying in bed he would picture his parents sitting in front of the fireplace, deep in the blue chairs, Papa lightly chiding Mamma, "Don't worry, all will be well, why must you always worry about what doesn't happen?" Such love threaded between the words, like music floating through the air. Unlike their friends who kept the children upstairs with the nursemaids, the Bergers had their children near them, within earshot.

The walls are thick in that house, the finest on the street, made even more spectacular by the addition of the greenhouse after his parents returned from England. The garden, the greenhouse, the port and claret, the English lessons are results of that marvelous trip. And so are the delphinium whose bulls eye blooms fill the tallest vases, and the trees in the orchard that bear the most succulent fruit anyone has ever tasted.

"The ration cards go further," the children are now told, "if we eat together." So they eat all their meals with the Friedmanns. There are other reasons. When they are alone, Mamma's hands sometimes shake so uncontrollably that her wine spills. Watching the stain spread, Paul can feel a tremor in his chest, as if ice water were trickling around his heart.

On the day he finally hears his mother's cries, she is walking up the Kuhler Weg and he has darted from the Grunewald where shiny buds float on the branches and spring bulbs have pushed through the earth. Crocus, Greigi tulips, bluebells, muscari, hyacinth, lavender, violets, Mamma has taught him all those funny-sounding names, and now, as he zigzags, he says them aloud.

He feels as if he is flying. Of course he can fly, at eleven you can do anything, so here he is, flying as easily as the hawks and peacocks and mallards and nightingales and grebes that Tante Hilda calls water chickens. Flying and dreaming, as happy as the thrush, his favorite because it sings such a clear sweet song. Until he almost runs smack into her striped jacket, "Frieda's coat of many colors," Papa calls it. Like Joseph's coat. A lucky coat. It makes Paul smile, for how can you be anything but happy in such colorful clothing?

Today, though, there is a glistening spot on her bosom, and when they collide he feels its wetness and the colors of the jacket are exploding in his head and when he steps back he sees more tears stream down her face and roll into a puddle suspended on the wool of her suit. As she pulls him close he tastes their salty tang, and feels her heart beating as she struggles to catch her breath. For a second the world stops. But soon she's dabbing her eyes and smiling. She takes his hand and they stumble home.

Tante Hilda removes the jacket, patting the wetness with a cloth, and brings Mamma a cup of tea, then puts cocoa and biscuits before Paul. Now Mamma sobs, a squawking sound, drier, rough, like a deep shudder, and her voice is bruised. "The worst thing was not that they wouldn't let me in, but that Gertrud went in without me. 'You know how much I've wanted to see this exhibit,' she said, behaving as if I didn't exist while everyone stared."

All Tante Hilda can do is nod. But, like the old housekeeper, Paul knows that his mother and Gertrud Hanning have gone to exhibits and concerts for years. They have heard Piatagorsky, Menuhin, Milstein, Schnabel. "How could she do that?" his mother says. "I could feel their hatred boring into me like knives when they said, 'Not you, Madam.'"

There is something new in her voice, something Paulie has never heard, something scarier than her crying. At that moment Paul realizes that his mother's good looks, which make Papa so proud, are the difficulty. Oh, everyone knows she couldn't be more different from Aunt Gertrud than Rose Red is from Snow White, they've joked about it for years. But that's why she was stopped by the guards: her dark, velvety eyes, which are brooding when she's troubled, but as radiant as one of Papa's deepest gems when she's happy, and her shining chestnut hair, her full black eyebrows, her golden skin, the trace of down on her upper lip. Traits which have uncannily reappeared in Berthe, traits that say Jewess! Beautiful Jewess!

Who must be taught her place, who cannot come and go as she used to, who does not belong in this city, in this country, in this world. Who would be better off dead, like all the rest of the filthy arrogant Jews who are no better than animals. Phrases he's heard in the streets, phrases he wouldn't dare repeat in this kitchen, now bathed in a lovely lemon glow.

Suddenly the boy understands why he goes to a tutor instead of to Frau Goldschmidt's school, which has moved to England. Not because a tutor is better, as Papa insists, but because no German school will have him. Why he and Berthe have to tell Rose and Grete what they want from the library, suffering silently if Grete (though never Rose) says, "Oh, I forgot, I'll get it next time." Why they celebrate the high holidays in the cellar of a neighbor's house. Why they sleep together in the attic, a large, low-ceilinged, cozy room, now filled with too much breathing and sighing, and Papa's snores. Why what Mamma calls "the absolute necessities" have been moved into the dresser, one drawer for each of them, and why Tante Hilda gets so pale when the doorbell rings. Even why she is now twisting the dishcloth so tightly it looks like a rag.

All his life, when something unpleasant happened, Papa fixed it. Isn't that what Papas are for? Today all that has changed. Although they say nothing, Paul knows that Mamma and Tante Hilda have, without a word, taken him into their conspiracy. The less Papa knows, the better. He and Uncle Hjalmar have enough on their minds, designing the passage to the attic where the children can play to their "hearts' content."

On that spring day in 1941 Frieda Berger was 35 years old. Despite all that he now understood about his mother's place in this city, in this country, and in the world, her son Paul thought she was the loveliest thing he had ever seen.

*   *   *

After he had finished they sat on the bench for a long time. On their way back to the hotel Eve could see how tired Paul was. Impulsively she stopped in front of a café. "Let's go in here," she said. When Paul was telling his story, she had been calm but now all the details assailed her. What must it be like to have to live with so many secrets? She could not imagine. Openness and honesty were as natural to her as breathing. Yet there was no such thing as openness and honesty here. As soon as Paul had learned to speak, he knew that reticence and elusiveness were far more important. By then the Racial Laws had been enacted.

What we learn young, we learn well. Outside of their marriage Paul could be the warmest, easiest, most affable person in the world. Wanting always to please, even people she knew he couldn't stand. "Never burn your bridges," he would say, "you never know when you might need to cross again." How it had bewildered and infuriated her. Especially because within the family he would sometimes hide behind one subterfuge or another. Once she had heard him lie to his father about why he had been incommunicado for a week. (The truth was he had been in northern Spain with Frankie pretending to be on a business trip.) Now she understood where he had learned to be so adept at lying, and also at bowing and scraping. Here one couldn't afford enemies.

When Eve looked up, she saw sweat beading Paul's hairline. His hand trembled slightly as he buttered his roll. She couldn't speak. Soon, though, their eyes met, and he said, "I'm very tired, just as you are, but I'll be all right in a moment."

At least there were no delusions about how hard this was.

Eve nodded. He was a strong man, she'd always known that. It had been, in an odd way, a source of pride. She could remember only one really bad bout of flu he'd had, when he'd read all of Julio Cortazar's novel *Hopscotch* in a weekend. When we marry, she had thought then, we buy into not only the other person's quirks and flaws, but his strengths and virtues. Paul was spare and rangy and had always possessed remarkable reserves of energy.

Eve leaned back. But would she ever have the luxury of forgetting that Paul was reading the Cortazar to please his newest lover, a Spanish instructor at Vassar? That deluded woman came into Manhattan every Tuesday night for about a year. From the slightly rank smell on his clothes Eve knew her down to the last dangling silver earring.

All of them were tall, like her. The only short women in Paul's life were his mother and sister, built like Dresden figurines. "I'm attracted to tall," he'd confessed when Eve had opted for openness and tried to convince him that he was destroying their family with his senseless dallying.

Yet openness had proved as obscene as silence. He had a string of mistresses, each more absurd than the last. And, as she predicted, he tired of the Spanish teacher, as he tired of them all. Leaving only that marathon read.

Sitting opposite him all these years later, Eve thought: A lot can happen in five years. Might these flashes of nausea and sweating be evidence of some physical problem, or was this the price one paid for remembering? Yet how could she ask him when he'd last seen a doctor? After all, it was she who reminded him they were no longer married.

Still, what if he was sick? And what would life be like without Paul?

During those years on the Vineyard, when she thought she was free of him, she had not been truthful with herself. The reality was that she could not imagine life without him.

Eve looked around the café. A few young people were reading newspapers and books. They had lean good bones, but such unisex haircuts and clothes it was hard to distinguish the women from men. "Why would they want to look like that, the women, I mean? It's impossible to find anything that resembles a figure under all that leather," she murmured, "and such terrible hair. Ghastly, especially that maroon."

"It's not maroon, it's burgundy."

Eve shook her head. "Burgundy sounds classy, this is not burgundy, it's maroon," she insisted. At last he chuckled and after taking a few more sips of coffee, he began to look more like himself. They sat in silence for a minute or two.

"And such dykey clothes," she murmured, thinking about Claudia and their daughter-in-law Sarah, who both clung to their long hair as stubbornly as teenagers and who wore simple, softly draped feminine clothes. Like you, she suddenly realized with a shiver of pleasure.

By now they had finished their snack. And not five minutes after they parted at the doors to their rooms, she threw herself onto her bed and fell into a deep sleep.

*   *   *

For a few seconds after she opened her eyes, an unfamiliar panic throbbed through her, but as she scanned the high ceiling, the flicker of the gilded sconces in a scrap of light from the street, the ornate plasterwork around the door jamb, Eve realized she was in Europe. Everything came back in a rush, but instead of being filled with the fatigue she had felt listening to Paul, she was revived by the deep sleep of her nap. Swinging her feet onto the thick carpet, she pushed aside the floral chintz drapes, opened one of the French doors and stood on the tiny balcony.

Lights twinkled merrily in the distance. Below her people were hurrying: Men with newspapers tucked under their arms, women juggling string bags filled to the brim, both sexes with bouquets of flowers, a horde of young on motorcycles, their black leather shining in the light of the street lamps, their hair as out-rageous as what she saw in the café. She wished her Aunt Blanche could see this harmless scene of a city going home for dinner. How worried Blanche had been. But tonight Berlin looked like any European city—indeed, this was exactly what London and Rome and Copenhagen looked like at the end of the day.

At the thought of dinner Eve realized how hungry she was. Just then the phone rang. Before she could ask, Paul volunteered, "I feel lots better."

But Eve had forgotten that this was not just Europe, this was Germany. In the restaurant enthusiastically suggested by the concierge, thick smells of sausage and fat hung heavily in the air. She wanted to gag. Simultaneously, they both ordered omelettes. The waiter's face fell. "But there are so many specialties of the house, veal stew, or pot roast, steak, a nice New York steak," he coaxed in excellent English. They shook their heads.

When their food arrived, the waiter lingered nearby. After he scurried off, Paul lifted his eyebrows and tilted his head toward the next table. Some Australian newsmen were sharing stories.

"I spent the day riding the subway back and forth from the Tiergarten to Alexanderplatz. It's been blocked for more than forty years," one explained. "And let me tell you, the easterners are a lot more human than their western brothers. They have known what's it's like to live *in extremis*, have they ever, while the ones from the west are still so interested in their own skins. What will all this do to the economy, to their comfortable lives? I wish George Marshall could see how smug they are, but now they'll have to take care of their neighbors."

"Not all the westerners are assholes," another said. "The ones I talked to seemed excited, but they were mostly young. And full of fun. One of them, in his cups, I'll admit, kept reciting 'Something there is that doesn't love a wall...' And another chimed in, 'O wall, O sweet and lovely wall...O wall, full often hast thou heard my moans..." All in English, you can bet if this had happened in our country or England or America, no one would be quoting Heine, or Rilke in German." The speaker chuckled.

At that Paul whispered, "The young here have always been interested in English. My tutor used to say everyone's desire to learn English was an unconscious admission that the Nazis could never win."

Listening to other people's conversation reminded Eve of her first months on the Vineyard, when she was so lonely she would go out to eat at The Black Dog just to hear voices while she ate. But after a while eating alone didn't seem such a curse.

How had Paul handled dinner these last five years? Probably ate out. Still, weren't there nights when he wanted, needed to be home? She knew so little about his life and was tempted to ask all sorts of questions, but that was not part of the bargain she'd made. So she concentrated on dessert, more comfort food: sorbet and linzer cookies. "Almost as good as your Mom's, or Blanche's," Eve said, savoring the subtle tastes. "Now tell me, what's on for tomorrow?"

"The house, near the Grunewald." Paul wiped his mouth, and his eyes held hers for a long moment, as if he needed to find courage to begin.

"My parents got an extra lump of money for the house the year before you and I met. Because of the way we were found, my father received compensation for the property in addition to reparations from the German government. That's what I used to start my practice in Boston, what they used to pay off the house. They had sold the jewelry they brought with them to make the down payment on the house and to send us to college. But this extra money gave them the security they needed."

Eve nodded. Paul had told her some of this when he made the decision to move his practice to Manhattan from Boston, right after they decided to marry. But she hadn't understood all of it. Why they were getting extra compensation. And she hadn't felt it was her place to ask.

"It's on Kuhler Weg, if it's still there. We weren't that far from the street this afternoon when I lost steam," Paul continued, giving her a wry smile. So boyish, at that moment he looked like the twins as adolescents, smiling their crooked little smiles to cover up the shock she suspected they felt at the sudden and alarming changes in their bodies. All at once Eve could feel her hand lifting to touch him, but she caught herself. Don't confuse things. Don't touch him. Don't talk. This was his show, she was merely the audience.

Abruptly, though, his face went pale. Quickly she beckoned to the waiter and signed the check while Paul gulped the rest of his coffee. His movements were heavy, his stance slightly stooped when they rose. As they walked from the restaurant, Eve realized that, despite his good looks and youthful lanky build, and despite the fact that they had taken a rest this afternoon, her husband, no, her *former* husband, looked his age.

10

THE NEXT MORNING small gusts of wind pushed aside the vapor of last night's showers like someone clearing his throat. Russet leaves spun and twisted, then floated for a few moments before skittering down to the ground. Eve stood once more on the small terrace in her robe as the sky lightened and the clouds began to break. She knew that Paul would not stop until he reached the end, and she would need all the stamina she could summon. Even in ordinary circumstances he would never give up in the middle. One step at a time, he always told the kids. She could remember smiling when he would encourage them, never realizing how literally he meant it, how painfully he had learned it.

Out of nowhere came the sound of "Un Bel Di" almost buried beneath a Mozart aria. "Cosi," something from "Cosi." The absurd juxtaposition made her smile. Of course. The music conservatory next door, just as the concierge had warned. "The singers are always first," a musician once told her, "and need to start first thing, like the birds. They claim their voices grow stale when the sun starts to go down, which means after 12 noon. I think they believe their larynxes are tied to their diurnal clocks. Whereas a piano," the speaker was a pianist, "grows more mellow as the day progresses."

The music swelled joyously. The sound of such pure pleasure made Eve's heart lift as she went back into the room. Happy to be moving, buoyed by the spurts of music—for she'd left the door open—Eve brushed her teeth and frowned at the puffy, tell-tale pouches under her eyes. "You'll have to do something about those someday," Frankie had told her once when they were standing next to each other in some cruelly lit Ladies Room.

"Do what?" Eve asked, though she knew perfectly well.

"Have them done, taken out, tucked, whatever." Frankie's smile was malicious. Even you, Eve, even you with your red-head's almost perfect skin, will fall prey to the humiliating ravages of age, Frankie's eyes said. Well, she was right. One sleepless night and she looked like Mario Cuomo's sister. Oh, to hell with it. Suddenly Frankie, New York, even the Vineyard, seemed light years away. A little makeup will take care of it, Eve thought, and our being here together is proof we have left the Frankies of our life behind.

*   *   *

The house was huge, larger than she expected, although she'd once seen a photo of it, and now painted ocher, like the houses they'd seen in Helsinki, a color the Finns called "Petersburg yellow."

"For generations it was white, with black trim, and the sharp definition of the black gave it an oddly modern look, a sense of scale," Paul said.

Eve nodded. That's how she remembered the photo. As she searched her brain, she came up with the day she and Paul arrived at Gunther and Frieda's home in New Jersey a few years into their marriage. A grey January day when her in-laws were clearly upset. An official looking envelope had arrived from the German government with a survey of the land that the house stood on, as well as several photos of the front, sides and back of the house with a formal letter stating that the house had been sold by the government which was its rightful owners after the Bergers had received their compensation.

Eve remembered Paul and his parents conversing nervously in German while Frieda, usually busy and cheerful, sat, her beautiful heart-shaped face pale with shock as she peered at each photo, finally shuffling them and binding them with a rubber band, just as she did a pack of cards after she and Gunther had played a few hands of gin. Playing cards seemed to calm Paul's parents; they would often pull out a deck of cards after Sunday lunch and play a few hands while everyone else read the paper. Or Frieda would sometimes play solitaire when the others were talking around her, slowly turning the cards, her elegant fingers flying to match the numbers or the figures, then binding the deck neatly with a rubber band when she was finished. Eve could never figure it out, because the sight of a deck of cards always seemed to agitate Paul.

That day, though, Frieda was far from calm. In her eyes was a hollowness Eve had never seen—an emptiness that seemed to take her to some far off place where no one could intrude. Before she could ask Paul about it when they were riding home, he said, "She always believed that the house saved our lives."

"Do you?"

"I don't know. She seemed so shocked that it had been sold. I guess in her mind it belonged to her, would always belong to her." From his set expression Eve could see that the conversation was over. But she recalled wondering: What is he keeping from you? She simply didn't know how to ask.

Now he was shaking his head as he stepped closer, saying, "It's so different I can hardly believe it. It looks like a big yellow blob. And the wall is gone, with the wall, the house didn't look nearly so big."

Eve concentrated on the details: the soft, off-white trim that emphasized the monumental sweep of this Palladian villa, whose front door was topped by a gracefully curved pediment. And there, intact on the south side, as if Frieda were still tending her plants, was a greenhouse whose glass shimmered in the sun.

"The glass couldn't have survived the war," Paul murmured, "but that's the original frame. Whoever lives here now takes gardening as seriously as my mother did." Masses of blackened dahlias leaned on their stakes like exhausted scarecrows, and clumps of chrysanthemum in shades from rust and burnt orange to salmon pink bloomed gaily at the edge of the border. Behind was a small orchard where rosy apples clung to their branches.

It was the house, though, that caught the eye. Into its imposing elegance you could have put her parents' apartment, Paul's apartment, and Blanche's, too, and still have rooms left over. No wonder they couldn't bring themselves to leave. This is the home your great-grandparents built, where your grandparents and parents lived, where you belong, where your children belong.

"Do you want to ring the bell?" she asked as he stepped closer, but he shook his head and swallowed hard.

"If you look carefully," he finally said, "you can see the outline of the *mezuzah* on the left side of the door frame. It was pretty big, it had been put there by my great-grandfather, when being a Jew was a source of pride. After they removed it, Hjalmar and Papa spent a whole day sanding the spot. They ended up painting the whole side, but they couldn't completely erase the faint indentation of its outline. The people who painted the house later probably didn't even see it, but if you know where to look, you can see a slight shadow." As soon as he pointed it out, Eve saw it. She didn't know whether to be glad or sad that such a vestige remained. She turned to look at Paul, but now he was thinking about something else. He took her arm and steered her up a little hill.

"They picked this piece of land because it was so near the Grunewald, the largest park in Berlin," Paul began, then stood behind her and propelled her a few degrees. Eve gave a gasp of surprise. When she had read about the rambling Berlin parks, particularly this one, she imagined Central Park. But this was wilder than anything in New York City, and vast, more like Harriman Park in the north. Enormous oaks and lindens and maples and horse chestnuts, some still in leaf, bent over the worn, pine-needled paths like beneficent giants. Soaring trees arched above huge, tangled rhododendron and laurel. Before her were acres and acres of untamed nature that had been here since the 19th century, survived the Nazis, the bombing of Berlin, the lust of rapacious developers. How could anyone criticize a city that had preserved such a magnificent stretch of green?

"Berlin is one huge garden," Paul began. "I can't remember who first said it, Henry James or Turgenev . . ." He shrugged. She was surprised. He usually cared about such things.

Eve looked around. Here was the reason all those birds sang so happily in the mornings. It was only a hop and a skip from their hotel to acres of shelter and nourishment and the dense, stifling smell of berries and herbs and fallen leaves starting to decay before winter closed in.

"We came here after nightfall or in the early hours of dawn," he continued, "until the winter of 1943. There were still lots of Jews in Berlin then, more than 15,000 some said, and Hjalmar always carried a huge roll of bills because a little money went a long way if we should be stopped. Before the smarter, more brutal Nazis set up shop, the Gestapo was a joke.

"Of course we stayed away from the Tiergarten or Unter den Linden where some of the Nazis would kill for the fun of it, and we never went to Grosse Hamburger Strasse where the Jewish old age home became a holding place for those being shipped to the camps. But hardly anyone came out this far. So Hjalmar and Gunther and I would walk here. Sometimes Rose and Grete came with us, but at the end, just the 'men of the family,' as Papa would say."

"But weren't you afraid, it's so big, so many places for danger."

"Actually it was easy. Fugitives lived here for days, sometimes weeks in the bad weather. That's when the Nazis stayed inside, they weren't much for exercise despite all of Hitler's crap about a sound body and mind and a vegetarian diet. In the summer it got more dangerous, when they'd bring their girlfriends here and screw them in the shrubbery."

Might it be dangerous now? Unlike Central Park which was usually thronged with people in the late morning, this edge of the Grunewald was deserted as they walked, their steps crunching twigs and leaves. Eve shivered, when, out of the blue, a woman appeared, walking two Doberman Pinschers. They stood back to let her pass. You never saw them any more at home. "Nazi dogs," people called them when she was a child. Some still did. Eve could see why. Their muscled, quivering bodies were ominous, scary. A reflex of fear rose in Eve's throat.

The woman smiled and said something. When she was well out of earshot Paul whispered, "Said they wouldn't hurt a flea." He paused. "That is until she gave them the command to tear us to shreds. That's what they used to say about the guards at Tegel or Prince Albrecht-Strasse. Such nice people, until they were commanded to burn someone with the tips of their cigarettes or pull someone's fingernails out."

Eve stared, startled, then moved towards a stone wall that was as wide as a bench, and they sat down. But instead of talking about their adventures in the Grunewald, or even more about the house which still loomed in the distance, Paul was somewhere else. In seconds his eyes had retreated, the hostility suddenly gone, and instead an almost fearful gentleness crept into his voice.

"I want to tell you about the *Kindertransport,* which began a few weeks after *Kristallnacht,*" he began. "Hjalmar went to see the first train leave, why I never knew. Maybe he wanted to convince my parents to put us on it and wanted to check it out himself. Or maybe he was just curious. But what he told us surely influenced my mother's decision. I'll never forget how, over dessert one night, he began, as if setting the scene for a play:

"The great maw of the Hauptbahnhof was foaming with steam, smoke, breath, while people ran hither and yon, fear spurting from their eyes, clothes dripping from their bursting packages. Mothers pulled forward, encouraging their children, convincing themselves, then they went back, often turning to the frightened maids they had brought along. For what? To bear witness? Or to have arms to fall into after the children were gone?

"No one knew, least of all the conductors and the police now assembled to direct the tide of humanity trying to board these trains that would take the children to the British Isles. Very few men were in the teeming throng, some grandfathers, and some of those black-coated Ostjuden, their haggard brooding faces worn out with the effort of defying their God, for their God had forsaken them, and the children must be saved. At all costs.

"That was what these last weeks had proved; night after night of praying, arguing, demanding, weeping, even screaming and cursing, had led only to this: the one hope of escape being offered, not to the adults, but to their children. It was apparent in the woeful defeated faces of these pious men as they wove dejectedly through the hurrying women.

"The women had no time to indulge themselves in woe or defeat, the last things these children needed. Why does someone want to kill us? they had already asked, and although there was no answer to such a gruesome question, these women, mostly small and dark-haired, said that the answer was to go away for a while until Mama and Papa can join you. For such a charade these women were calling on that hidden source of strength they had known each time they gave birth. So they strode with good cheer, urging their frightened children on, as if this would be the most exciting experience of their young lives.

"The love so apparent in the women's demeanor made the conductors and cleaners and police look away. 'These Jews are shameless,' one man told me, 'so willing to wear their hearts on their sleeves, they don't need those yellow stars, you know they're Jews the minute you see that love spilling from their dark eyes.' It was embarrassing, upsetting, horrible.

"And how, some of those loyal civil servants were asking themselves, just as I was asking myself, How are we going to go home and describe this chaos, the trembling lips, the clutching fingers, the torrent of emotion, and, finally, the hushed voices so intent on whispering, as if they know that when they let go, they will have to scream?

"As they did later, when the trains slid away and the great station was filled with one vast wail of terror that would resonate in the air for weeks, months, years, maybe generations. 'But we are not

*to blame,' they insisted, 'these were orders from the Fuhrer.' Then
rehearsed what they would say when they got home: 'It was you who
wanted him, you good German hausfrauen who voted for him, so
don't blame us, we were simply doing our jobs while you scrubbed
the floors, polished the brass, and counted pfennigs to see us through
another war.'*

"How lucky you were not to see those desperate Jewish women
weakening, flooding the cars at the end with instructions, embraces,
warnings that only further confused the already bewildered, weeping
children. Oh, what a sight it was! No human should have to see this,
no human being should have to witness such raw love, such open
sorrow . . . "

"He simply stopped then, unable to go on. I remember that my
father and mother stared at him as if they didn't know who he was.
We were all frightened. It was terrifying to hear him tell it. He had
always had a penchant for drama, but this didn't need any drama.
The words were enough."

Paul stopped and stared into the distance for a few seconds,
then continued, "After that incident with Gertrud Hanning,
whom my mother never saw again, I became closer to her and
Tante Hilda. The Hannings had been their best friends, and it
took Gunther and Frieda time to come to terms with the simple
fact that they were never going to be in contact again. So Frieda
would confide in Tante, and Tante would talk to me.

"By the time of the *Kindertransport* I knew a lot more about
my mother than I ever had: How hard it was for her to share her
house with the Friedmanns, how she loved Hjalmar whom she
knew well, but how hard it was for her to get used to sharing the
house with Marga. How she hated to hear Marga order Tante
Hilda around, treating her like a servant when we had always
treated her like a member of the family, how petty Marga was
about money, how she scrimped on food, things like that.

"I also knew how my mother had reached the decision to
keep Berthe and me with them, even before that outburst from

Hjalmar. Earlier, when she had begged my father to leave, he refused, telling her about ships turned back or sunk, neighbors and friends lost in the mysterious gaping unknown of the east. At that time she had proposed that they send us to cousins in Switzerland. Again he refused. But when the *Kindertransport* presented itself and was endorsed by the great Rabbi Leo Baeck, Gunther thought it had some merit. By then, though, she had lost her nerve.

"Tante Hilda told me how night after night Mamma prayed for guidance, wanting to convince herself that perhaps Papa was right. This was a real chance to save us children, far surer than Hjalmar's plan to hide, for who knew when that might end, or how? Again and again Mamma read the story of Solomon, recognizing that the real mother was the one willing to give up her child. But she couldn't. She would die. She could not live without the sound of our voices, the touch of our hands, the questions in our eyes.

"Each day she vacillated a hundred times, trying to gain courage from Tante Hilda, who had seen the First War. Frieda missed her parents who had died within a year of each other in the months before *Kristallnacht.* An only child, she had no one except Tante Hilda, who loved her unconditionally, who would abide by her decision, yet never presume to help her make it.

"Besides, how could Tante help when Tante's world had gone topsy-turvy, like something from *Alice in Wonderland?* All Tante could do was hold onto her ritual of countless tasks, knowing that whatever happened she could never leave this family she had loved since she came here as a girl.

"All this unspoken devotion hung in the kitchen as palpably as the spider web suspended so precariously between the ceiling and the top cabinet that had escaped Tante Hilda's dimming sight. Mamma stared at the swaying of the gossamer web, which also fascinated Berthe and me. Anything to escape the agony she felt.

"She began to have dreams of Hjalmar and Gunther digging her grave: Crackpot dreams in which she could feel the earth touching her and two small coffins beside her grave.

"Unspeakable dreams, which she related to Tante Hilda, who drew back in terror, and who told them, in a moment of weakness, to me. And who urged Frieda to tell them to Gunther. After she did, Frieda knew Gunther would not force her to send the children away. He had never forced her to do anything, he wasn't going to start now. They were two hearts as one.

"One morning the ghost of her mother appeared, saying, in a breathless whisper, 'Do not give up the children, all will be well.' That happened just around the time Hjalmar went to the station and reported about it. The two things coming together the way they did finally ended it. Berthe and I would stay.

"Yet in March 1939, on a day scheduled for one of the trains of the *Kindertransport*, she felt a strange compulsion to go. The despised yellow stars called *Judenstern* had been distributed, but my family never wore them. Indeed we came and went as we pleased, but only when it was cool and Mamma could wear a coat and tuck her thick dark hair into a snood. She said, 'Let's be as quick as we can . . .'"

Paulie Berger lets his mother hold his hand as they enter the Hauptbahnhof. *They have come to pick up Tante Hilda's train ticket. Each summer Frieda and the children and Tante Hilda have gone to Frieda's family's country home, a working farm of fifty acres with fresh air and homegrown food and milk as sweet as honey and hay fields and a small stand of forest to romp in from dawn to dusk. Where they still hope to spend part of the coming summer, yet only after Hilda has said it's safe. But it's March. Why now?*

"Tante will rest easier if she knows she has her ticket. You know how crowded the trains get when everyone and his brother are trying to escape the heat," his mother tells him.

He wants to ask, again, why they can't go with Tante Hilda, why they must wait and see, but he knows better. Everything depends on the Nazis, they are the reason the two families live under one roof and why he doesn't go to school any more, but only to the tutor's twice a week, two long days when Papa rushes him out before dawn and picks him up after dark.

Still, why to the station today? Paul wrinkles his nose at the smell. The same smell that fills the air when he and his classmates are marched into the sports hall for group exercise, when the men come in from haying, sometimes when Tante Hilda bends too long over the steaming tubs in the laundry room. But never so strong as now, in this huge domed station whose walls seem to be crying.

Suddenly his mother hugs him closer, he can feel her fingers through his jacket, nervous, frightened, as they make a path to the ticket booth and he searches vainly for faces he knows. Soon eyes noses mouths melt together, and all he can distinguish are the stars: Hundreds, thousands of yellow stars milling, waiting for the train doors to open, stars in a winding line, like a path in a treasure hunt, fluttering each time their wearer moves. Never has he seen such a crowd, this must be what the crowds are like when the Nazis parade through the streets, though never watched by the Jews.

"It's an acknowledgment of their power to go to their parades, and you could get trampled," his father said. Paul nodded. People are trampled all the time. Though they don't know it, he steals the papers they carefully fold and put in the trash, and reads them under his blanket with a flashlight. People getting trampled are usually on page three.

So he submits to his mother's firm grasp, and they hurry through the sea of people, packages banging at their ankles. Everyone is waiting for the Kindertransport. *He's seen the word in the papers and for months he heard it in whispers that go on forever, that never end with the comforting clink of crystal and his father's cheerful* Prosit, *even though there's still a bottle of sherry and some glasses on the far end of the long dresser in their huge attic bedroom. And he's heard about it again from Tante Hilda, when it was possible that he and Berthe might have to go to England. But then Tante told him they would probably stay. And finally he heard Hjalmar describe it.*

Hjalmar wasn't exaggerating. Never has he seen so many people! A surging mass of people that seems to be running to the edge of a cliff, that looks like the endless line of children in the tale of the Pied Piper. He holds his breath until they reach the ticket window.

"What a day you picked, Madam!" the ticket seller booms and wrinkles his nose. "It is the stink of Jews. Even their children stink. But now we will be rid of them." Then the man peers more intently at Mamma, his face suddenly quivering with alarm. It reminds Paul of Tante Hilda's face when the doorbell rings, but unlike her the man has beady eyes. Sly eyes.

Then he spies Paul and smiles. "For a moment I thought you were one of them," the man whispers, "but then I saw the boy, such a fine specimen. How are you, young fellow," his voice blares, then, in sotto voce *to Frieda, "You should not have come today, Madam, whatever made you come today, it's dangerous, and the child, why on earth have you subjected the child to this? Surely, he doesn't need to see this."*

His mother's hand flies to her collar, her nervous gesture Paul knows so well. "I didn't know, if I had known . . . never would I have come," she lies. "But I was nearby, it seemed convenient," she adds as her gloved fingers sweep the ticket and change from the tray. "Danke," she murmurs, and gives the ticket-taker a shy smile and the barest curtsy.

It is over. Thank God. No, not yet. "It's terrible, what they're doing." The ticket taker tilts his head towards the crowd. "No good German mother would do that, imagine sending a child to the English, they're as cold as the fish they eat," he persists. "Imagine sending a child to strangers, like boarding a horse or sending a cow to the Alps in summer. But what can you expect, all Jews care about is money. Still, many's a day when I've wished for their gift."

Paul thinks he is finished, and he can feel his body relax. Too soon. With a stern glance at Mamma, the man demands, "Could you do that, Madam?"

"No," Frieda replies, relieved to speak the truth. "No, I could never do that." Then she pulls Paul to her so hard he can swear he feels her

warm silky skin against him. But it's impossible. There are layers of clothes between them. As if that weren't enough, she puts her arm around him although he's almost as tall as she is. Saying with one small motion: Isn't he a wonderful boy, my son Paul? Isn't he something any mother would be proud of? Paul hates it when she does that. He bows his head, in terror lest his eyes give him away. Mamma knows him so well he sometimes thinks she can read his mind.

Concentrating, he keeps his eyes peeled to the once polished, now muddy floor so she can't suspect what is racing through his mind: That more than anything he would love to escape that frantic wild look which sometimes comes into her eyes. That when he hears his parents' hurried whispers he wishes they weren't so well off, that they didn't have this big house in which they can hide. Because then they might have had to leave for America or Argentina or Cuba. And most of all, that instead of talking to this disgusting ticket-taker, Mamma was rushing with him to the platform onto one of those sleek trains.

Any place would be better than here.

11

PAUL WATCHED EVE walking towards him. Rest and a bath had transformed her. Gone were the purplish circles under her eyes, the almost imperceptible slump of her left shoulder. Dressed in an embroidered gray wool dress and a reddish shawl, she could hold her own against any of the stylish women now gathering for dinner. All of them were European (the hotel was too small to appeal to most Americans) and reminded him so poignantly of the women of his childhood, women who announced: I am entitled to fine clothes, even if my body has shrunk or fallen, I am still beautiful and deserve to look beautiful until the day I die.

He stared at his wife. She had never cared much about clothes, she didn't even seem to know how well they hung on her willowy frame, and many of their shopping sprees had ended in disaster. But here was proof that she had never needed him, she looked marvelous. When their eyes met, he gave a little bow, hoping to mask his pleasure. Eve saw his glance, smiled, almost to herself, and curtsied.

"I never thought I'd see you in red shoes, I thought they were a no-no. And that shawl is stunning." No use trying to back off, she knew him too well.

"So did I, the shoes, I mean..." Eve's eyes flickered with amusement, "until Blanche dragged me to this store on Madison Avenue. I needed some decent things, I didn't want you to be ashamed of me, and after we found the dress and shawl, the saleslady insisted on the shoes, said they would complete the outfit. They were a fortune but they're wonderfully comfortable." She stopped, embarrassed.

"I was never ashamed of you."

In answer she merely shrugged, then started searching in her handbag, finally saying,

"Damn it, I've forgotten my distance glasses, wait here, I'll be back," and was gone.

Finding an empty chair in a corner of the lobby Paul picked up the current *Newsweek*, but he couldn't read. Why had he cared so much for appearances?

How things looked, what others thought never mattered to Eve. That's why his parents loved her, why she drove the snobs in their life, like Dozie, crazy.

And yet in the most profound way she had cared enough to become a buffer between him and the kids, to pretend that all was well. Her fierce pride could not allow her children to know what was happening between them.

How could she think he was ever ashamed of her?

The truth was that after he married her he had finally been able to achieve some sanity, some stability in a life that was moving so fast he was terrified. For a long time she'd been everything he hoped, patient, indomitable and totally unswerving in her devotion to those mischievous children, when so often he longed to escape.

What gave her that almost relentless ability to persevere, he would wonder, never suspecting how things would turn out: How her forbearance would drive him deeper and deeper into secrecy. And how, in defiance of any logic, that same forbearance would become the glue in their marriage, making it last far longer than he had any right to expect.

Even after the children were almost out of the house and things were clearly unraveling, he would never have left. It was she who had finally had enough.

Forever, she said, we are finished *forever*.

Nothing, though, is etched in stone.

When he heard her say, "If you want me to come to Berlin, Paul, I'll go," he had thought: So much for *forever*.

But how to continue? Tonight he might start by telling her that one of the things that triggered the worst memories were the games she was so content to play with the children: Backgammon, Gin, Old Maid and chess. How they brought back the stifling afternoons when he and Berthe and their parents were trying to whittle away the time, trying not to hear the sounds of Marga and her daughters downstairs. Marga fussing with Tante Hilda about the spider webs hanging from the ceilings, berating her for not polishing the silver properly, for doing the laundry her way instead of Marga's way.

Marga had become a martinet about this house which wasn't even hers. Memories of her arguments with Tante Hilda, which Frieda and Gunther tried to drown out with those endless games would surface when Eve brought out those same games a generation later. At the sight of them he would panic, and, in an effort to obliterate the earlier memories, sometimes scream at them. Trying to ignore the children's accusing looks, then their downcast eyes, as if he were some lunatic whose behavior no one could acknowledge—looks which would only elicit images so searing and painful that, before he knew what he was doing, he would be shaking Eve.

So, layered on top of his memories of the war, were pictures of her cringing body, her startled eyes. Eve never fought back. It was as if she knew he was dealing with something too profound and desolate even to understand. In the end they would be left with endless silences during which he would be filled with a crushing shame.

Yet here she was, standing before him again, cheerful, smiling. "I'll never get used to all these glasses, I can't believe you can still read without them," she said, nodding at the magazine which Paul closed as he stood up. Instead of attempting to reply, he concentrated on helping her with her coat. Still wondering, How can I begin? Luckily, Eve was content to look out the window as their cab wound its way to a restaurant in Savigny Platz.

Soon Paul had composed himself enough to point out the famous places, glistening like Baccarat after the rain. Their sheen reflected the neon lights that had come on again now that the Russians were gone. How brilliant they had been when he was young, and how dark these streets were during the war. How forlorn, even before the Allies bombed the city. By then Berlin had closed in on itself, as if ushering a warning that Nazi pride was a sham, like almost everything else. Except their ability to kill. At that they were superb. But he was not going to refer to that now, when they were more relaxed with each other than they'd been since starting this trip.

Then he became alert to something new. But my God, it's been almost five years, of course she has a new perfume, why would she continue to wear the Arpege you bought every Valentine's Day? What else had changed? Paul found himself sneaking glances at her. No, her puckered brow had its familiar look of concentration as she etched the location of each landmark firmly in her mind. Diligence, attention, respect. Habits of a lifetime. What was important to him had always been important to her. Until they divorced. Yet now it was as if they'd never been divorced.

He couldn't have predicted it would be this way when he called her. Then he knew only one thing: that she, better than anyone, could comprehend the significance of this trip. And if she left small clues that she was a little bewildered, he understood that. He was more than slightly bewildered, too.

*　　*　　*

When their eyes met in the cab, he shrugged. Eve let her mind stretch back to another vision that now, finally, made sense to her. They were in Grand Central Station the first year the twins went to camp, plunging through the crowd on a beastly hot day, and suddenly Paul was covered with perspiration, gasping for breath.

"Daddy's sick," Eric called, pulling on her hand. Her handsome slim husband who always seemed indestructible looked about to crumple onto the floor.

"Daddy's sick!" Eric's voice pierced the clamor. Within moments they found a bench, huddling around Paul while he wiped his face.

"Shall I get a doctor?" Eve plucked at his forearm.

"No, I'll be fine, so many people, more than I expected," he said, only confusing her more, but then Eric produced his new canteen, filled for the train ride. Proudly he watched his Daddy gulp the water. The panic subsided, Paul rose, and soon they were greeting friends as if those few moments had been a dream.

But when the kids disappeared onto the train, he grabbed her hand and pulled her onto the stifling platform, his eyes swiveling wildly until he spied the twins waving at them. She stood there knowing there was nothing normal about this, especially after he snapped, "It's their first time away, for God's sake, they must be terrified." She said nothing. As the days passed, he seemed fine, less anxious than she. On Visiting Day he was also fine, though he never came see them off again, even when Claudia went to camp for the first time.

Surely she would have forgotten it forever if she'd not seen it again earlier today: the same sweating, panting, the same spinning eyes.

For a moment she was tempted to refer to it, but they had reached the restaurant, and it was time to get out of the cab.

*   *   *

Once seated, Eve shifted and began to undo the shawl. "I thought it would be like England, but they know how to be comfortable, don't they? I'm always too warm inside." That was when he spied it, no longer hidden under the fold of the shawl, and said, "That's my mother's pin."

Her head shot up, and her tone was defensive. "Yes it is. She gave it to me the last time I went to visit her, the night before she died. You do know I visited her?"

"Of course, the nurse always told us. But Berthe and I must have spent days looking for that pin, after Mamma died. For all I know she may still be looking for it, she was sure that Mamma would give it to her, we never dreamed she had given it to you, especially after the divorce."

He sighed, knowing how foolish he sounded. But damn it, that was their pin, his and Berthe's. "To be honest, we ending up thinking one of the nurses had made off with it. I can't believe this, we made her that pin, with Hjalmar's help."

Eve unfastened the pin and handed it to him. She looked embarrassed, but he couldn't worry about that now. Feeling the weight of the silver ellipse in his palm overwhelmed him.

"I never knew you made it. Of course I was flattered, no one who knew her could forget that this was her favorite piece of jewelry." A pause. "But I never would have taken it if I'd known you or Berthe wanted it."

The whole truth and nothing but the truth. That was Eve. Paul had no reply. All he could do was stare at the pin and think: It was crazy that his mother had given the pin to Eve.

Or was it?

Finally, their eyes locked. "She loved you because you were so accepting, so serene with the children, so happy to have them. She thought Berthe and I were arrogant, too 'wanting,' wanting everything America could offer and not interested enough in family. I lied before. The nurse didn't tell us when you were there, Mamma did. Every time you came. The time you stayed all night when she first went into the hospital. Your devotion was very important to her, especially after Papa died."

"I loved them," Eve said. "They were kind to me, and I couldn't abandon them. They'd been abandoned enough in their life. I didn't know all that they'd gone through, they were such private people, you all were, but you'd have to be deaf, dumb and blind not to know that."

She spoke so simply, so earnestly. And eloquently, Paul realized. There is always eloquence in such obvious honesty. Then he stared again at the pin in his hand.

"When it was no longer safe for us children to go to the shop on the Ku'damm, Hjalmar would bring home scraps, 'findings' he called them, the leftovers after they cut the gems, which they used mostly for clasps. These garnets were the best," he told Eve.

"The night he brought these garnets home we were so thrilled that we took them to the workroom in the basement, and while Hjalmar melted a silver ellipse at the jeweler's bench that had been there for a generation, we made a tree, a star, then an oval of the clear red stones. None was right, so when the silver was ready to receive them we simply placed a cluster here, another clump there. Fully prepared to be disappointed. Instead it was the best we'd done. 'Like clusters of sunset on the cool face of the moon' was how Hjalmar described it. So we gave it to Mamma for her birthday."

"I'm sorry, Paul," Eve began, "I didn't know any of this, but the truth is, I can't give it back. I can still see the look in her eyes when she gave it to me." Eve took the pin from his outstretched palm and fastened it onto her dress.

"She called me 'Ruth.'" Finally a light of triumph spread over her face. At least your mother knew who I was, her gray eyes told him. At that moment it was as if a voice had said, *She's no longer afraid of you, Paul.*

Without that undertow of fear and wariness in her voice that had become almost a reflex in the last half of their marriage, Eve was once more the woman he had fallen in love with.

Suddenly, they were equals again.

How much I have missed her! he thought.

And just as suddenly her presence here in Berlin made sense. From her newfound ease he could see that she was feeling it, too. So he was not surprised when she leaned towards him and said, "But maybe now you should tell me about Hjalmar."

Paul nodded, "Hjalmar, then the Grunewald, because they are so intertwined." All at once, though, they were interrupted by the waiter. Their eyes met, remembering last night's fiasco, and they ordered a real meal.

Soon they were sipping some Riesling and nibbling the bread, totally comfortable not to say a word. A blessed silence, possible only after all those years lived together, Paul realized. Then he took a deep breath and began,

"You'd think I'd remember shadows more than light, we were in hiding after all, but what's most vivid are the times we could get out. I guess that was the difference between Berlin and other places. Berlin was not a city that could become a cage, it was too big, too spread out, its citizens far too independent. That's why it was possible for so many people to hide there. Research after the war told us that there were more than 18,000 Jews in Berlin in the spring of 1943, and several thousand even at the end of the war. So while we felt terribly confined in hiding, we would get out when we could—not to cafés or restaurants, as some of the more daring young people did, but usually to the Grunewald. The whole situation was a perfect Berlin oxymoron, and as odd as it may seem, it's the light I remember . . .

"The hard blue light of winter when there were the purplish, then rosy dawns, and Hjalmar and Papa and I would trudge, glad to fill our lungs with air. The floating lifting light of Grunewald as it began to turn that tender chartreuse green in early spring and you could literally feel your body becoming freer, more limber now that you could shed some of your clothes. Or the long lavender sheen of a summer twilight when the branches reached down to embrace us, and we knew, if we heard voices, we could climb, as fast as monkeys, into their leafy bowers. Then Berthe and Grete and Rose would go, too, because it was cruel to keep anyone inside during those gorgeous, gossamer dusks, when the stone paths were still warm from the sun. But then everyone was out, and it was risky.

"Twice we were almost caught.

"The first was in May 1941, a few days after Rudolf Hess commandeered an airplane and landed on the lawn of the Duke of Hamilton's estate in Scotland. He had come to persuade the Duke, whom he knew, to convince Churchill it was in England's best interest to give in to Germany. To the amazement of that deranged, devoted Nazi, the English took him prisoner.

"Jokes about Hess made the rounds of Berlin. Hjalmar's favorite was: 'Hitler's 1,000 year Reich has now become the 100 year Reich—one zero is gone.' In honor of Hess's blunder Hjalmar decided to have a party. He would grab any chance to relieve the numbing dullness of our isolation with whatever he could give us—dollops of joy in a meal of boredom and fear.

"Although they were German, Hjalmar's parents had left before he was born. His father was a professor in Oslo and Hjalmar had been brought up there and studied architecture, but longed to be an artist, so he convinced his parents to let him attend the Art Institute in Berlin. They agreed only if he would live with his grandmother, because he had a rheumatic heart and they were afraid he would go wild. But they had no idea how expensive Berlin was, and after he arrived, Hjalmar needed to earn pocket money so he found work as a clown in a supper club while attending school. He met Gunther at the Institute, and when Hjalmar fell in love with Marga and after they married, he came to work for the Bergers as their most talented designer.

"Hjalmar was a little taller than Gunther, but had the same receding hairline, the same benign glance and gentle voice. Nothing in his appearance revealed his genius for living, his uncanny ability to create laughter, to turn a harmless sentence into a minefield of puns, to transform a simple stroll through the Grunewald into an amazing exhibition of twists and spins with his double-jointed limbs. He also knew card tricks, word games and magic. He taught us to skate on the Grunewaldsee and the Havel, he set up a croquet court in Frieda's garden, he brought books from the museums after the Jews were outlawed from them, and in no time we could distinguish Cimabue or Masaccio from Da Vinci and Raphael.

"Though only a few years older than Gunther, Hjalmar was like the God we read about in our *Siddur*, our rock and redeemer. Sometimes I would lie in that limbo between sleep and waking and envision Mamma and Papa starting to fall backwards, then caught by Hjalmar. Hjalmar always behind them, propping them up as they faced the awful truth: The Nazis were not some transient aberration. No they were powerful and intent in their goal, which was to kill all the Jews, and Jews meant anyone with a trace of Jewish blood. That's why we were in hiding. But with Hjalmar it was a great adventure.

"'We'll have a grand old time,' Hjalmar had promised. Every night the air was awash with Beethoven, Schubert, Brahms, Mozart, Berlioz and Sibelius. Booming through the house, making Tante Hilda complain she couldn't hear herself think, which was exactly Hjalmar's intention. Music filling our heads so we could forget how frightened we were."

Paul stopped, his eyes growing dark as the memory poured from his mouth...

On that balmy night when the stock and early lilies are casting their most seductive smells, the four grownups sip cognac in the garden. The men are in evening jackets, the women in peach and ecru georgette, and soon they begin to inhale the heady smells, pick a few spent flowers, sway lazily to Strauss waltzes. Then Hjalmar puts on a record of new songs. Slowly, languorously, they dance to "In the Still of the Night," even though dancing has been outlawed by the Third Reich. Their faces are rapt, their bodies tremulous at first, then more certain. Each couple inextricably linked as they move, bending and swirling until clothes and limbs coalesce into an illusion so radiant it may have been a dream. And, like a dream, the scene wobbles and whirls until they drop, spent, into their chairs. Nursing their drinks again, and talking as if the Nazi Party does not exist and Germany is still presided over by the funny-looking Hindenberg.

The children are speechless with delight at seeing their parents so carefree. Can you feel happiness when it is actually happening? Paul has never thought you can. Yet here it is, while the soft, limpid Berlin night deepens around them.

Soon it is time for bed. Still, no one moves. Before long, the lights in the neighborhood begin to go out and the ocher glow of a fat-faced moon becomes even clearer to the naked eye. All at once Hjalmar looks at Gunther with mischief in his eyes. In unison they rise, remove their jackets and whisper to their wives.

"Are you sure?" Frieda asks. But both women know better than to argue, (they have heard all Hjalmar's arguments that the children must not lose heart), and agree, only on the condition that they hold hands to make a human chain, and never let go unless they hear Hjalmar's whistle, which he'd perfected as a clown. So, at almost midnight, there they are, a ragged cavalcade, moving slowly in the Grunewald, consoled by the beguiling redolence of the violet dark, too happy and tired to be afraid.

Suddenly they see a bundle of humanity huddled in the dense shadow of the big beech tree. At once they stand stock still, peering frantically at a small girl and an old man. The old man bars their way, plunging into his story: He and his grandchild left the house a few minutes before the SS came and took away the child's parents and two other children. They are alive because a Gentile neighbor warned them not to go home. He and the child, Rachel, were passed, sometimes together, sometimes alone, from neighbor to neighbor—a few days here, a few days there—but the SS came around more and more frequently.

The neighbors became frightened. By now the weather was warm. One night they were packed into a car and given some food and a large blanket and driven to the Grunewald. "Someone will find you and help you here, we cannot be responsible," he was told. As if they were baby kittens coaxed towards the Neuersee or Grunewaldsee and left to drown. "We've been here for days, eating berries and ferns after our food ran out," he says.

No one seems to breathe. Above them the leaves tremble, and Hjalmar and Gunther exchange glances, then a faint whisper: They can't leave them here, only someone crazed from loneliness and fear would have taken such a chance. How did he know they were not Nazis? No, they cannot abandon them, if they do they will surely die.

Paul strains to hear them talking, and watches the man's pathetic eyes and the little girl's submissive air, her eyes cast down, afraid to meet his curious gaze. Suddenly the man says, "I am a Vogel and can't fly anymore and I was getting ready to die, but now you have come to rescue us and take us back to the nest." Papa gives Hjalmar a helpless shrug. Later they learn that the man was not delirious with hunger. His name is Vogel, and in his relief he was making a pun in an effort to endear himself to them . . .

"Perwe," Hjalmar murmurs, "maybe Perwe, or Poelchau." Names the children have not heard before but will hear again, because these are the men who work under the cover of the Swedish Church to help Jews escape. When Papa nods, Paul knows the old man and the child will be safe. Papa hands Paul the blanket to carry. "Away from your body, lice," he whispers, and as they turn to go home, a bunch of SS come out of nowhere, drunk, singing loudly.

Immediately the air throbs with Hjalmar's whistle. Berthe grabs the little girl and Papa and Paul plunge their hands under the arms of the old man; in seconds they have hauled themselves into the leafy branches of that colossal beech. Breathing as shallowly as they can, exactly as they had rehearsed, while Grete and Rose start hooting and running away, as if scared, and Hjalmar yells at the Nazis for frightening him and his daughters who are out for a stroll. And now Paul is alert to the old man's smell, the foulest, most disgusting smell he has ever known, of sweat and dirt and urine, and something else. Later, he will smell it on himself and know it is fear, but now all he can do is ask himself: Is this the stink of the Jews?

To punish himself for such a thought, Paul forces himself to help Hjalmar and Papa undress the old man and wash him, and finally it is Paul who stands with Tante Hilda over a bonfire to make sure that their clothes and the blanket are burnt to an unrecognizable crisp.

They stay for five days. Tante Hilda wants to keep them longer because their stomachs have shrunk so much they cannot take more than a scrap of bread and a little soup. Hjalmar is firm. "We cannot jeopardize our own safety." That is only part of it. He is also worried that the children will become too attached to Vogel and Rachel, whose shining face and blond ringlets, once they can see what she looks like, bear such a weird resemblance to Shirley Temple.

On the sixth night Hjalmar takes them in his car to the Swedish Church. The plan is to transport them to some sympathetic family in the country because they need time to recover. And then see if they can be gotten out, maybe to Sweden, maybe to Switzerland. Paul never learns where. You can't ask; it is too dangerous. Like others they will see for a short time, old Vogel and Rachel vanish—as quickly as a rabbit or a coin in one of Hjalmar's magic tricks.

*   *   *

"The second time was in the deep cold when kids were found dead at dawn in the Tiergarten, small town kids who came to Berlin to find work but were starving and wretched. So they'd go into the dark wood thinking that here, next to familiar sleeping trees and bushes, they would find comfort. In the morning they would be found, killed by the bitter freeze. And now Jews were dying the same way, often helped along by a Nazi jackboot or fist.

"But that was the Tiergarten. The Grunewald was different— only people who knew it came here, mostly Germans who were slyly taking over the homes of their Jewish employers who had lived nearby. Just until the Jews returned. "Oh, what lies they tell each other," Hjalmar would say when he and Papa were poring over the books of the business, sipping Scotch, pretending things were normal. When they were most in need of cheering up, they went to the Grunewald at dawn."

Papa tickles Paulie on the warmest part of his neck to wake him, and the boy pulls on his scratchy woolen underwear, for hoar frost clouds the window and Paul's breath spirals above him as he rushes, stealthy as a tiger, around his sleeping mother and sister. Downstairs they sneak past Tante Hilda stoking the fire, but she sees them and tries to tamp down the terror in her eyes.

They are going skating. Paulie carries Hjalmar's skates, and as soon as they reach the path Hjalmar begins his cartwheels, and you can see the bizarre trail of his gloved fingerprints, then his feet, then his glove prints. Giggling, Paul's heart overflows with love for this man who refuses by every action to submit to the insanity of the Third Reich, who will risk his life to take a boy skating because he knows that skating is what that boy loves to do.

Paul breathes deeply. How liberating it is to be out, to move his legs in the stinging cold, to see Hjalmar's tricks. So different from the exercises they did in the stale attic air. Soon Paul begins to run, propelling himself as fiercely as a plane. But not a screaming plane that drops bombs and forces them into the moldy cellar where Tante's hands cramp. No, now he is a plane climbing into heaven, into that stretch of endless blue where there are no bombs or worry or fear, war or hiding. That is how free he feels, zooming, until they reach the pond.

On with their skates, worn brown leather with metal runners, an improvement over the ones he tied onto his shoes when he was little, and then they begin carving huge figure eights into the rimed pond and then, by God, Hjalmar is doing cartwheels with his skates on, teetering as he lands, then zinging off into the middle of the pond, trumpeting like an elephant, or ninnying like a horse, or, when he is getting tired, oinking like a pig. As silly, as loosely jointed as Chaplin's little beggar, whom they all adore. After almost an hour, when they are wiping tears of joy from their eyes Paul realizes how frozen his hands and feet are. The whizzing wind is a razor from the east, so he hoists his skates onto his shoulder and announces he will go ahead.

Papa looks up in alarm, but Hjalmar laughs and waves him on, saying, "Go on, perfectly safe, only idiots or fools like us are out in this cold." Again Paul zooms, this time his body damp with sweat and he thinks about the cup of chocolate Tante will hand him. He scuds along the path, skidding a little, finding a rhythm, then, because the sweat that drips from his forehead is blurring his vision, he closes his eyes—running as fast as he can, scarcely touching the ground, when he is stopped by a chest.

A wool covered chest, not a Nazi uniform, thank God, with its hateful skull and crossbones staring down at you, but a stranger bundled into at least two sweaters and now staring at him in utter amazement as Paul rubs his forehead already smarting with bruise. But Paul has no breath, and what about Papa and Uncle Hjalmar, coming up behind him?

When he lifts his head his eyes meet equally brilliant blue ones. "A little early to be skating, isn't it?" The tone of a young Nazi who has no doubt he will someday own the world. Paul has heard it before, when the SS come to the house and are fended off by Tante Hilda, when groups of SS patrol the streets in summer, when they caught him and Hjalmar coming home from his tutor's (the last day he ever went there), demanding to see his papers and Hjalmar faced them down, calling them louts and how dare they talk to a German citizen in such an insolent way?

"Getting my exercise, as you are," Paul replies in a loud, haughty voice, suddenly transformed into his hero, Erich Kastner's Emil. Now he understands Emil's impudence. Bravery is the safest course when you're in the deepest trouble you can possibly be.

"Out alone, at this hour? Pretty young for that."

"Not really. I'm sixteen," Paul lies, louder this time, because he can hear a faint trudging, then desperate, he shouts, "Want to hear how I can whistle?" and puts his fingers into his mouth and makes a sound almost as shrill as Hjalmar's whistle.

"What'd you do that for?"

"Just learned it, pretty good, isn't it?"

"Not bad." The idiot puts his fingers into his mouth and whistles

even louder. "If you're sixteen, I'm forty. How old are you? The truth." His face is a mask and his eyes look funny. Why he's just a boy, maybe not more than seventeen. But so important.

"Thirteen, almost fourteen."

"Where do you live?"

"What's it to you?" Paul tilts his head, but hears nothing.

"Come on, you can't talk to me that way, I may not be in uniform, but I'm in the SS, they just took me, and I can arrest you." He grabs Paul by the shoulders. He's tall, and strong. "Now tell me, where do you live?" He bares his teeth, exactly like a cartoon of a tiger or lion. "Or I'll beat the shit out of you."

Finally Paul looks at his feet, no jackboots, just walking shoes. In a sing-song voice he shouts "Wilmersdorf" and gives the address he knows best, of the Friedmanns' spacious apartment, then wriggles from the young man's grasp. Running as swift as the wind in the direction perpendicular to the one Papa and Hjalmar are walking, Paulie calculates that he can probably reach an abandoned structure that once had something to do with the Berlin waterworks, deep in a stand of pines, and, if he has to, drop the skates. But he realizes they give him the ballast he needs, as if without the skates he will be lifted above the treetops, and though he can hear the young man behind him, he isn't afraid. The Nazis want to kill him, but he will outsmart them all. Paul decides he'll just duck into the trees and, with luck, his pursuer will pass him, and by the time he realizes he is on a wild goose chase and gets back to the main path, Papa and Hjalmar will be home.

Astonished at this miracle of speed he has become, Paulie passes his destination, then makes a quick turn and slips behind a sagging wall. Soon the Nazi comes along, walking very fast and reciting the address Paul has given him, like a nonsense rhyme to keep him going. A true nitwit, probably the only thing he can keep in his head.

Quickly Paul wends his way home, hiding in the evergreen thickets when he hears voices, but he sees only people with their dogs. No tall blond boy. He pulls his hat down and scoots along. The sun is *shining on the snow and ice, a light that makes his heart soar with the thought of: Home! Now, though, the large trees that hang over the wall don't comfort him. And while he is not afraid, he is exhausted and doesn't know what to do with the fist of anger forming in his chest. After he slips into the garden, he stands looking straight into the sky, letting the sun's brilliance make his eyes tear, because only with the release of this anger can he go on.*

When he knocks on the back door he is scooped up amidst tears and gasps of relief and praise at how clever he was to whistle. They think he's crying with relief, too, but his tears come from rage: that a stupid Nazi goes free while they are prisoners.

Soon they are all sitting around the table eating their steaming porridge, talking at once. In the midst of the tumult, Paul sees Hjalmar look at Marga with eyes that beg forgiveness. His heart sinks. Those wonderful escapades—cavorting in the Grunewald, skating at dawn, climbing trees in summer, frolicking in the garden on summer nights—are to be no more.

And something else has shifted. As Marga closes the drawer to the credenza, she seems to say: This is mine. These dishes that sit so proudly on these shelves, this blue and white Haviland handed down to you by your ancestors, these silver Kiddush cups that give the wine a slightly metallic taste, the lace tablecloths used on the Sabbath and holidays, these treasures are no longer truly yours. They are mine. This house and everything in it is becoming mine. I am no longer a guest in your house, now you have become a guest in mine.

How can so much be revealed in a mere push of two hands, in the abruptly haughty stance of this woman he has known since he was born and whose husband he loves as much as he loves his father? Paulie doesn't know, but it is here, in this room.

Now, finally, he feels fear. So much fear that when news comes that the Friedmann apartment in Wilmersdorf has been vandalized, he cannot find the courage to tell anyone how such a disaster happened. Berthe's dark liquid eyes, like deep pools reflecting moonlight, swim in his head. Oh, how smart and brave you are, Paulie! they said that icy morning. Oh, how lucky I am to have such a brother! His chest swelled with pride. Now, though, he is humiliated by his secret shame.

The truth is that he wasn't so brave after all.

12

EVE COULD FEEL the perspiration dampening her clothes and trickling between her breasts. Paul was mopping his face with a handkerchief, and his eyes, those discerning blue eyes which had never left her face as he spoke, were averted. Should they leave? It was clear Paul needed time to be alone, but here was the waiter telling them their food would soon be out. It was also clear that there was no way he could move.

"I'll be back in a minute," Eve said as she slid out of the banquette and made her way through the crowded restaurant. For the first time since arriving here Eve welcomed the clouds of thick, suffocating cigarette smoke that floated everywhere in this city. In the lounge of the Ladies Room Eve thought: Let the tears come. But nothing. Only this awful chill spreading through her body and an incessant hammering in her head . . .

Sometimes, after they had made love and he was still trembling with pleasure or relief or whatever he felt, she wished she could put her arms around him and let him cry so that the shell he had constructed around himself would crack and splinter and finally fall away. It never happened. He would retreat into silence, falling into a deep sleep. Then she felt as empty as a dry well. When she tried to talk about it, Paul stared, then growled that talk took all the mystery out of sex.

And what about the suppressed rage, the remoteness, the occasional violence afterwards? In the beginning such a rude shock, for what young wife wouldn't hope for some oblique reference to the pleasure they had shared? Instead, as the years passed, there was disdain, bordering on contempt, and once a cold slap when she came up behind him and must have frightened him. Another time, after a divine Beethoven piano recital, a brutal shake of her shoulders when she began to discuss the performance.

The slap and shaking were the least of it. With actions you know where you stand. It was the silence that hurt so much.

But still Eve could not confront the truth. For by then she had realized that Paul's silence had little to do with her or their marriage. To reduce it to something she could handle Eve thought of it as a peculiar flaw that surfaced most often at dawn. Yet nothing she could reveal. And on Monday morning when he stood there in his proper three piece suit, the smell of his shaving lotion blunting the odor of coffee, she would be fooled into thinking their weekend had been normal. In place of anger and remoteness were contrition and need. When he kissed her goodbye, Eve would smooth the black velvet collar of his Chesterfield coat and kiss him back, and by the time he left she would be convinced he couldn't help himself, that his behavior was entangled with his past, a past he could not yet share.

Eve waited for years, hoping to hear about his childhood. His memories seemed to begin at the end of 1944 when the family left Germany and lived with a kind elderly couple in England. But then she discovered the letter from the reconnaissance mission who found them and realized that this was suffering of a different order, and that no one who loved him would make him relive such suffering. Besides, wasn't that what he talked to his faithful psychiatrist about? No, all Eve knew was that there was an inexpressible part of his past that had become part of their present. A present she had to endure.

She loved this man when she married him and after more than a decade together she still loved him. Sometimes, when she saw him across a room she would be overcome by intense desire and filled with pride. What a beautiful couple! People would exclaim, What gorgeous children!

Until, without warning, his face would darken with rage and she would retreat. As time passed, the silences grew longer, hours became days. At first as gentle as the beating of insects' wings against a screen, then billowing into something like the clamor of locusts she had once seen in a film about farmers, seeping into every corner of the house. But nothing you could fight, why you could hardly describe it. Sometimes Eve thought of it as sound, other times as dye working its way into cloth, spoiling the very warp and weft. Or sometimes as poison, like chemicals invading the water, or radiation fouling the atmosphere. Yet she did nothing. They stayed married, not because of the children, or their parents, or his work, or their place in the world, but because she could not imagine any other way to live.

Now she saw them tucked under an eiderdown in Switzerland, in the Engadin about ten years into their marriage. A marvelous hiking trip, just the two of them. They would get out early and hike for about five or six hours, come home and shower and make love, then nap. That day was radiant and warm, so they pulled their quilt out onto their terrace, which faced west, and bundled into their warmest clothes and fell asleep, side by side in the aluminum chaises, their hands locked. For years afterward she could feel that invigorating sun and their delight at waking, almost at the same moment, feeling utterly at peace. But now the memory began to gnaw uncomfortably.

The second afternoon Paul extracted his hand from hers, and sat up a little straighter and said, "Now that we are here, not far from my home, maybe it's time . . . " Then he seemed to lose heart, and instead of encouraging him, as she should have, she simply waited, timid and afraid, until he shook his head. At last he murmured, "No, now is not the time, when it's right, I'll know, but now is not the time, now is not the time," like some mantra.

That had been the time. She had let the moment go and soon they were dressing to go out to dinner with some English people they had met, and although there were other naps and chats during that blissful week, there was no real talk.

It was her fault because she had not been strong enough or smart enough or brave enough to seize the moment. That's what all relationships were: the ability to recognize the moment in which to share something that mattered. But to do that you have to be fearless, for you never know what you will find.

Years ago she had heard someone say, "Marriage is a minefield." But what if a marriage is layered, like a palimpsest, on top of a war, which has minefield after minefield? And what if it is your marriage?

Eve rose. Her knees wobbled, but she steadied herself at the sink and slowly repaired her makeup. With the echo of "marriage" still ringing in her ears she found their table. The waiter was tapping his foot. "Ah, here is Madam!" he said, removing the silver covers with a flourish.

Paul reached across the table. "Your hands are ice."

"So are yours. You must feel battered."

"I do. Yet I'm not even sure that what I've told you was the truth." He paused. "I'm not sure you can trust what I've told you. It's a child's memory, all mixed with what the child Paulie knew and what I have done to that memory all these years. So twisted and misshapen that it resembles a tangled ball of wool. So confused I'm not sure what is really true."

Briskly she shook her head, "It's what you have, therefore, it's what you must work with," she reminded him, quoting his own words almost exactly when he was working on a difficult case. "And now, maybe we had better try to eat some of this food, otherwise the waiter will call the food Gestapo to arrest us."

*   *   *

To his amazement, Paul could taste the food. It was good, a spicy goulash, and soon its warmth began to dispel the chill that had settled over him when he finished talking. He had been grateful for some time to collect himself, and all he could think when he watched her pull on her shawl and head for the rest room was: Oh, how well she knows you, how lucky you are. And now she was content to let him eat.

He looked around. So many reminders of his childhood: That smug arrogance of the stocky German men doing their little dance with the waiters, tasting the wine, sending it back, then drinking it with contented sensuality. And those good German *hausfrauen,* they looked so anxious to please, were so submissive to their men. Most had faded blonde looks and were dressed in conservative clothing while a few had dyed, coifed hair and were dressed to the nines. All dripped with gold.

Yet at the next table was an older couple who didn't fit the stereotype. The man was very thin and had a wry, ironic smile and an endearing habit of running his hand through his sparse hair before he spoke. The woman was small and delicate, very pretty, with glowing fair skin set off by her almost white hair, and an excitable way of speaking with her expressive hands that made her seem eternally young. With them was their son. Once they heard Paul and Eve speaking English they made no attempt to keep their voices down. You'd have thought them French if their German weren't so good. And the man's face was familiar.

Now Paul wondered, Did I ever know you? Of course not. He had attended Frau Goldschmidt's school with the other affluent Jewish children, and after Frau emigrated to England, he went to the tutor, a friend of Hjalmar's. How could he know these people who looked so comfortable and spoke perfect German?

"Do you mind if I eavesdrop a bit? It's interesting," he asked Eve when their plates were cleared.

"Not at all." Her glance scanned the restaurant, as if its dark paneling and hooded lighting could yield clues to the complex story now unfolding. And when coffee came she was happy to cradle the cup in her hands and sip a little.

The father and son were arguing about marriage. Paul caught phrases about a way of life, how difficult it was to give up one's culture and habits; soon the mother was assuaging them both. A buffer between her two men. It could be a scene anywhere, it could be him and Eve with Jeremy, but he and Eve and Jeremy had never sat in a restaurant talking about marriage because by then they were no longer a family.

After a while the son was exasperated and the parents were growing pale. "Leave it alone," the mother said, pressing her husband's sleeve. The son stood up. He was a surprise, stockier than his parents, but he had his mother's high cheek-bones, and dark eyes. He finally said, sheepishly, "Can't you see that this is just a generation gap?" The father shook his head sadly.

Even in their turmoil the three of them clearly adored each other. Paul turned away from them filled with a sickening envy. His children no longer adored him. Respected, yes, maybe admired, but they didn't trust him. He wasn't even sure they trusted Eve. You fucked up, their eyes accused him, resenting him for not being able to do one simple thing: Stay married. Did they do that to Eve? He didn't have the nerve to ask, even the question would hurt her, the last thing he wanted to do, especially after she had listened so patiently.

As he watched the threesome leave and turned back to Eve, now slowly sipping her coffee, Paul realized that the smells of the restaurant, so welcoming when they arrived, were beginning to nauseate him. "Do you mind if we go?" he asked. She shook her head, so he called for their check and paid.

*　　*　　*

Outside a sharp wind was blowing. Eve hunched as they walked, pulling her raincoat tighter around her, murmuring how glad she was to have it. He had urged her to bring one really warm thing that night on the phone. Now he took her hand. They had spent more time together in these last two days than they had in the last five years of their marriage. Then all they wanted was to avoid each other—she often asleep when he came home, and after Claudia went to college, he not bothering to come home at all.

On the Ku'damm the wind hit them with an icy slap. How well Paul remembered it. Yet his mind was clearer than it had been since they arrived. Suddenly words tumbled from his mouth and he was telling Eve about Anna, her penchant for gossip, her malicious streak that frightened everyone but amused him. Then he switched to news about the office, his colleagues, their old friends, shows at the Met and MOMA, operas and plays.

"What about books?"

He flushed and stopped to look at her directly. "I found it almost impossible to read at first, but now it's better, I just re-read *Anna Karenina*," he said.

She started to smile. He knew that smile, he'd seen it when they'd first met, when he was doing exactly what he was doing now, trying to impress her. When he'd "sold" himself to her and then to her equally trusting mother and her more skeptical, astute father. When he *snowed* her. Yes, that was the word Ian had used.

"Big-shot lawyer snows girlfriend, and in the bargain is knocking the rest of 'em dead, has those proper Wellesley girls swooning, creaming in their pants," Ian would shout when he returned to their apartment late at night. And instead of socking him for his vulgar comments, Paul retreated to his room, aching with longing, overwhelmed with terror.

What he couldn't tell Ian, whom he trusted above all, was that he fell in love with Eve because she so uncannily resembled someone else. She had the same eyes—not the same color, hers were greenish gray and the other's were brown with a strange purplish tinge—eyes that had faith in the goodness of other people and welcomed the world, eyes from which kisses seemed to spring, he realized later, like those of Proust's grandmother when she looked at her beloved family.

But even more eerie than the similarity of their eyes was the same elegant way of holding their sharply angled bodies. That's what first caught his eye. From a distance Eve could have been Alix, who breathed new life into his family and whose kindness kept them alive. About whom he could never speak, not to Ian, not to the men who found them, not to the old English couple, not to his tutor Henry Simmons. Not to his parents or Berthe or the string of psychiatrists he saw. And never to Eve, with whom he had once hoped he would share everything.

Over time thoughts of Alix receded. With each decade her existence became more fragile. Some days he would wonder: Perhaps I merely dreamed her saying that "this nightmare will end." Because she firmly believed that good would triumph.

Finally it had. Here, so many years later, was the exhilaration she had foretold. Here was a new Germany where some of the values of the past might finally take hold. Deftly Paul propelled Eve into a square where music blared from the bars, where taxis slid to quick stops, then lurched away, where buses hugging the curb groaned under the weight. Since November 9th Berlin had forgotten how to sleep, and more police had been hired to patrol these streets. Weaving carefully among the people, many of whom were drunk, Paul and Eve stopped to look in the store windows. "Nothing but junk," she said, tucking her arm into his.

As they neared the hotel she sighed, "Oh, how lovely." Schubert's Quintet in C, played with enormous verve, drifted from the Conservatory. Paul stiffened. All his life he had heard how special Berliners were, how talented, how civilized. Especially the Russian Jews who had come to Berlin in the 20s: Pavlova, Kandinsky, Horowitz. And the young Piatagorsky escaping Russia by holding his cello over his head and swimming across the Sbruch River. Then finding his way to Berlin's largest concert hall, and after the concert falling asleep in the loge, then playing his cello at dawn when someone heard him and he became a pet of the Berlin musical community.

We Berliners are special, even our refugees are special, our life is the best in the world, his parents had thought. Where did that get them? To a hardware store in New Jersey where people condescended to them because of their accents and few knew how intelligent they really were. While Nazis like Herbert von Karajan and Elisabeth Schwartzkopf plied their trade to enormous public acclaim.

But he didn't want to spoil Eve's pleasure, so he nodded. As they got their keys, Eve said, "I can't believe they're practicing."

"I warned you, Madam." The concierge's eyes were haughty: Here we work long and hard. Eve looked at Paul, hoping for a retort, but Paul had other things on his mind.

While they waited for the elevator he wanted to say, Come into my room tonight, and let's undress slowly as we once used to, then lie next to each other, waiting for our bodies to tell us what to do. But this time we will talk far into the night, what you longed for, what I longed for, too, but which never happened because I couldn't begin, and after a while decided it was best you didn't know.

He couldn't, he was still too frightened. Yet he surprised himself when they reached their doors. As furtively as a teenager, he planted a kiss in her hair, still thick, beautiful hair that held the fragrance of her new perfume. And strangely grateful when she started with astonishment, then ducked her head and slipped into her room for the night.

13

TOWARDS DAWN Eve stirred, her brain a blur. She shut her eyes, and there was a blond boy with fierce blue eyes jigging and jogging as fast as a torn streak of lightning, skidding wildly over the icy paths, his skates banging against shoulder blades that quivered with exhaustion. She sighed. All night long she seemed to have been racing through an enormous stretch of woodland, chased by the same demons that had chased Paul, and now all she wanted was to lie here, still.

Those skating expeditions with his father and Hjalmar were interludes of happiness in a life increasingly bleak and narrow; they were also acts of rebellion that gave Paul something to look forward to, and the morning he described so vividly marked their end. From then on things would only get worse.

She shivered, pulling the comforter around her shoulders. The boy was gone. In his place was the man pressing his lips together, refusing coffee, moving towards the front closet for his skates, stuffing them quickly into a canvas bag and turning on his heel without so much as goodbye.

"I saw Paul skating at Rockefeller Center yesterday morning," a friend would report, "on my way to work. Having a ball, with the rink almost to himself." Or, "Saw your Renaissance man the other morning, doing backward turns and God knows what else, and people were clapping madly, and he didn't even notice," said another. Eve always smiled and nodded. Of course. Marvelous exercise. And why not? Years later when people started jogging and race walking, someone would always mention Paul, into skating and tennis long before the rest of them.

So full of surprises: An athlete with a strong, lean frame, and a sparkling wit, and a razor-sharp intelligence.

The skating was how he calmed himself, maybe how he forgave himself.

She'd always known it had some significance she didn't understand, and once she'd followed him, wearing a shabby corduroy coat she couldn't bear to throw away, and stood at the railing and watched him. He moved as if in a trance, not even hearing the happy applause when he went into a series of backward crossovers that ended in a jump. As if he were a puppet, she had thought then, and now she knew she was right. As if Hjalmar were whispering into his ear.

Afterwards she considered trailing him into the French café flanking the rink where he would have breakfast, but she was afraid. Would he rebuff her, look through her, chastise her for her raggedy coat? She didn't know. But she did know the skating was related to what had happened that morning, when she lazily beckoned him back to bed after he'd shaved and showered, and instead of caressing her as she expected, he'd exploded, saying he had to get to work and she had children to pack off to school, and what the hell was she doing? As if she were some lazy whore who wanted more, as if they hadn't slept together in weeks, when, actually, they had made love like two normal people only hours before.

Well, almost like two normal people. She didn't know how other people made love, the only person she'd ever made love with up to that point was Paul, but even then she suspected that the deep silence which surrounded their lovemaking wasn't normal. How often had she wished they could laugh, giggle, even bicker? Anything but that leaden, suffocating stillness.

A man doesn't make love to you, then turn on his heel and rush out of the house without reason. Why didn't she swallow her pride and persist? But she never could.

The truth was that she had not been honest with herself. She told herself she'd done nothing wrong, but inertia is as bad as doing something wrong. From the time she held that tattered onionskin she knew he had suffered unspeakably, yet she had not been brave enough to get to the heart of it.

She had been as unwilling to face the truth as those fiercely patriotic Jews who insisted they were German and nothing would happen to them, even after *Kristallnacht*. Who stayed in Berlin until it was too late.

Quickly she threw aside the quilt, showered and dressed. Briskly, with what she hoped was an air of casual aplomb, she entered the hotel breakfast room and saw him. As their eyes locked, she saw that something had shifted, not unlike that peculiar shift he had described the night before when he realized that their house was becoming Marga's. Though he looked drawn, his face was less guarded, and his eyes asked: Can you take it? Can you bear all that I have to tell you?

"Hi," she said softly, then, "What are we eating this morning?" Their little charade when they traveled and always ended up ordering toast and orange juice and coffee. As he gave their order, Paul ran the tip of his forefinger around the rim of his shirt collar. It wasn't just children that bind two people to each other, it was also little gestures and habits that you forgot when you were apart but that screamed for your attention when you were together. How did you ignore those?

Paul leaned towards her. "How about the Kathe Kollwitz Museum? We both need a break and the concierge says the municipal authority has done a beautiful job with it."

"I can't believe you're actually suggesting it." Eve searched his eyes. "You don't have to come, you know, you can meet me afterwards."

He shook his head. "Don't be silly, I'm glad to come."

*   *   *

As they made their way along the Ku'damm in a fine raw mist, Eve had to admire Paul's cheerfulness, his genuine smile when she informed him, "Claudia loves Kollwitz, too. She took the drawing of the young mother with her to Paris."

"Like mother, like daughter," he said.

Kollwitz had been their first battleground when Eve took Paul to visit her History of Science professor at Wellesley. Over the man's desk was an original signed Kollwitz drawing of a mother cradling a blurred child in her large blunt arms. "I call it Science Looking Out For the Future of Mankind," he told them.

Paul smiled the way you would at a senile old lady, saying, "Sorry, she's not a favorite of mine." Eve flushed, while her professor said, also smiling, "Not yet, but she will be."

After Eve gave birth to the twins and hung a print of a mother and child in their bedroom, he said, "So heavy-handed, she's either clumsy or unbelievably grim, absolutely no sense of beauty."

But it stayed there for years. Later, she read him lines from a poem about Kollwitz.: "What would happen if one woman told the truth about her life? / The world would split open." He had stared at her and said, "The world would split open if one man told the truth about his life, too. That's not poetry, that's feminist hysteria."

His idea of a great artist was Georg Grosz. "He has imagination, humor, real wisdom. He knows how contradictory the human mind is, that people can be cowardly and brutal at the same time, that evil has many faces besides cruelty: poverty, sleaziness, class-consciousness, hypocrisy, self-delusion, even comedy. It's work that changes the way we look at the world."

"All that may be true," Eve snapped, "but who would want to live with a Grosz in the bedroom?" Even he had to laugh.

After the women's movement embraced Kollwitz, Paul said, "She doesn't have a speck of humor." Or, "Doesn't she know that the 20th century is filled with irony?"

Hearing him, Eve knew he was also scoffing at her. She, too, was earnest, and God knows, at the end she had nothing resembling a sense of humor. Perhaps she'd never had one. No, that wasn't true, once there had been a duet of laughter, then a quartet, and a quintet. Later the laughter was muffled, tricking into an occasional chuckle or a narrow smile .... Yet when Paul wasn't around, she had no trouble making Gwen or Max or Blanche laugh, and once Claudia had described her as smart and funny.

Still, this wasn't about her, it was about Kollwitz. For some artists seemed above judgment. Kollwitz had endured the death of her son, Peter, in the Great War, and the death of her grandson, also Peter, in World War II. As soon as Eve consented to come to Berlin she'd known she had to see her work, and when she mentioned it on the plane Paul had said, brusquely, "Of course," but she never expected him to join her.

Yet here he was.

They turned onto Fasenstrasse, passing the Jewish Community Center, which was on the list of tourist attractions and billed as a living memorial to the Jews of Berlin. Now it was used for meetings, exhibitions, dances, and one wall was engraved with the names of those Berliners who died in the death camps. They decided to visit it and the Jewish Museum later.

At the museum the line to get in spilled into the street and was filled with young people poured into the usual tight jeans. Many also wore expensive leather jackets and had those peculiar unisex haircuts. The older people were wrapped in rain gear, like them, and spoke in subdued tones. The raw drizzle and bleak mist shrouded their faces, giving them a somber cast. That's what a cold rainy day will do, Eve thought, but when she turned to face the entrance she saw that the weather was only part of it. Looming above her was a huge photograph of Kollwitz, awesome, imposing, the quintessence of dignity.

Eve looked at that wise, compassionate face in her beautiful old age, and for the first time since arriving here, she felt she was in the presence of a friend. For, she had to admit, if only to herself, Berlin frightened her. Not only because of what Paul was telling her. No, there was something more, something menacing in the air, in the voices, in the eyes that stared back at her. As if they were saying: Now that the Wall is down, what more will you find out about us? After you defeated us, we became Allies, but you have no right to pry into our lives. And if not to pry, why are you here, what more do you want?

Was it always that way? Did these Berliners become wary after the War or was there always an irrational streak of violence in these people? Was the legendary Berliner pride a cover-up? The old story of the chicken and the egg? Or was it just the reaction of a city besieged by strangers, an understandable resentment that so many East Germans and foreigners were descending upon them?

Paul might have an answer, but now he was concentrating on a flyer. It would have to wait. As he read, he again ran his finger absently around the rim of his shirt collar.

Soon after they were married she noticed a rash on his neck and decided to iron his shirts herself. He was annoyed and insisted she try a string of laundries, but the rash always returned and she'd return to her ironing. She didn't mind, she actually liked to iron. Then Paul came across an item in the newspaper that George Balanchine created his ballets while ironing. This unexpected bit of trivia delighted them both, and in a flash took the onus off doing it. Now he must have that rash again. But of course she didn't ask.

Finally he looked up and said, "She came from Koningsberg. So did Hannah Arendt, and Frieda Fromm-Reichmann." She nodded with a smile. More miscellany, how had she done for so long without it? But now it was time to move through the exhibit: the benign, early drawings of a friend's nude back, the self-portraits, the women in the waiting room of her physician husband, Karl. Then the striking sketches of the workers, the weavers, the rebels, the poor, culminating in the brutal political posters protesting the plight of Germany's hungry children.

As she went from one drawing to another, Eve was astonished by their force, how these compelling figures, not models but ordinary people, pulled you into their world of fright and dread and hunger and resignation. How they seemed to ache with normal yearnings, with the desire to be loved, yet were always alone. In Kollwitz's world there were no clear light interiors, no dogs or furniture, not even the drapery of modest clothing. To see beauty in such simple, hard lives, was not that the finest gift of all?

Finally Eve looked up. Paul was probably finished, bored, maybe inquiring about a place for coffee. Then she saw him ahead, his face troubled. She wove quickly through the crowd. He stood, riveted before "Prisoners Listening to Music." Seeing her, he murmured, "She knew what was coming, she knew what it felt like to be so bereft you had to hang onto each note as if it were life. This could be me, it was me."

Eve shivered and put her hand on his arm. Before she could say anything a bell rang, and there was a rustle of expectation. They stared at each other, puzzled; the concierge had assured them the museum was open all day. "Let me see what's going on," he said. Approaching a guard, he inquired in German.

Until this trip she had almost never heard him speak his native tongue except to his parents and Berthe. Once he'd sung to the twins when they were infants, a haunting lullaby she reproduced for Frieda, who said, "Oh, that's by Korngold about watching a child sleep safe and sound." Frieda stopped, her eyes clouded with confusion.

"We loved his work, but his songs were banned." She hesitated, then shrugged. "Marga used to say I could be arrested for singing that lullaby, so I sang it all the time when we were hiding. My little mutiny. Once you got to know her, you realized Marga was a wonderful woman. But hiding us was too much for her, as the months passed she became small and petty, especially with Tante, and I truly think she went out of her mind with grief at the end. But she was always afraid of the Nazis."

Eve and Frieda must have had that conversation more than two decades ago, yet here it was, intact. Was this what was happening to Paul? Shards of memory he thought buried now surfacing in their entirety? And how did speaking German affect him? As she listened, Eve heard no hesitations, no fumbling. The German rolled from his tongue as easily as water flows in a spring stream. Yet he had never spoken it to her, and he was relieved that her parents knew very little Yiddish. Once, when she suggested they teach German to the kids, he had stared at her as if she were out of her mind.

Now he said, "They're having a reading, a brown bag lunch reading, to commemorate *Kristallnacht.* They do it every year, but because of the Wall, they postponed it."

People were setting up chairs. Eve looked at them, suddenly aware of individual faces. Beyond the tough clothes and the cropped dyed hair, they were kids, like her kids, taking their youth and health absolutely for granted, wholly absorbed in their task. She wanted to stay. She looked at Paul. His face was guarded, yet curious. He said, "Your choice." When she nodded, he gestured towards the back row and they sat down.

Of course the reading was in German. The curator, an older man, gave an introduction, then people raised their hands when they wished to participate. After he gave them the nod they went to the front. There were about a hundred and fifty in the audience, and after each selection a collective sigh. No applause. Just silence. You could feel everyone concentrating.

Yet how could they, in 1989, feel the bewilderment and agony of those who had lived during those terrible years? You could feel the question in the air as people leaned forward, frowning, tense, a few so uncomfortable their faces had become masks.

One girl, around twelve, rose and held up a copy of *I Never Saw Another Butterfly.* Then she showed that unforgettable drawing of a child standing in the red boat and read the poem which was about sailing to Morocco. From early on there were rumors they were going to pack the children off to Morocco or Madagascar, Eve remembered. When she finished, the girl gave a shy curtsy. Did she understand what she had read? Did it matter? What mattered was that someone brought her here.

Others read, then a brief discussion, then another small silence, and soon a young man in a gray sweat suit rose and went to the front of the room. "I'm an American, studying here," he offered, "and I want to read from Paul Celan. I'm Jewish, though none of my family was in the..." he paused, then said firmly, "This may sound arrogant, but the word *Holocaust* is wrong. It comes from the Greek, *holokaustos,* which means 'burnt whole, w h o l e.'" he spelled. "It's all wrong. Nothing about those lives was whole, they were totally broken, their world was torn into pieces."

Hearing his English was such a relief. Eve relaxed and looked at Paul. He loved Celan, had several books with the German on one side and English on the other. But he had never read Celan to her. "Too difficult," he once said, "He's made a new language out of German, almost as if he couldn't bear to write in the language of the Nazis, but in English it doesn't make much sense."

"Celan is an anagram from Ancel," the young man began, "or Anschel, his family name. He was born in Romania, in the Bukovina, and was an only child and lived there until he went to study medicine in France in 1938. Though he didn't stop here, his train actually went through Berlin the day after *Kristallnacht.*" He looked up.

"An odd coincidence. He spent a year in France, then went home where he was forced to remain and attended university. In 1942 the Germans invaded and rounded up Jews every weekend. Some escaped by leaving their homes and being hidden by their Christian friends. One Friday Paul's mother said it was crazy to keep running, that they must accept their fate. But Paul went to their hiding place, sure his parents would follow. They didn't. When he returned home they had been taken away." The young man stopped to take a breath.

"After the war ended he went back to France where he taught German literature and began to write poems. He called them 'messages in a bottle,' and knew they wouldn't be understood. He didn't care. He said writing them was what was important. He committed suicide in 1970, in the Seine. Celan had never recovered from the deaths of his parents, for which he felt responsible, he always felt . . . well, one critic called it 'God-forsaken.'"

"*Gottverlassen,*" the curator interrupted. A ripple of shock shuddered through the room. A terrible word. The American pulled some index cards from his pocket:

ASPEN TREE your leaves glance white into the dark.
My mother's hair was never white.

Dandelion, so green is the Ukraine.
My yellow-haired mother did not come home.

Rain cloud, above the well do you hover?
My quiet mother weeps for everyone.

Round star, you wind the golden loop.
My mother's heart was ripped by lead.

Oaken door, who lifted you off your hinges?
My gentle mother cannot return.

The reader now looked tentatively at the curator whose hand swept the air as if to say, Do what you want, it is all beyond me, it is all beyond any of us, I am no longer in charge. The American said, "One more, which I don't really understand."

ONCE
I heard him,
he was washing the world,
unseen, nightlong,
real.

One and infinite
annihilated,
ied.
Light was. Salvation.

The room was utterly still. Finally the young man said, "When his friends said they didn't understand his poetry, Celan used to tell them, 'Read! Just keep reading. Understanding comes of itself.' Thank you for this reading. Kollwitz was an amazing woman, and Celan was an amazing poet, and well, all this makes me feel very different about . . . " he gestured, palms upward, "about Berlin."

Now the curator was saying thank you, and people were pulling sandwiches and drinks from their bags and backpacks. They had come not only to listen, but also to talk. Eve was gratified to see someone put his arm around the American and draw him into a group.

Paul touched her elbow. "I want to look at some of the drawings again," he said, "I'll be in the other room." Eve nodded, welcoming the opportunity to catch her breath. Watching the eager young people gather into groups, Eve thought of her children. Perhaps they could call them tonight instead of waiting for the weekend. How she suddenly yearned to hear their voices.

Then she heard Blanche saying, "Your eyes look as gay as they did when you were a girl." Why was so much stock put in being blithe, carefree? Innocence was merely a trait, not a virtue. Which the Europeans had long ago left behind. Unlike the Americans, they possessed a visceral knowledge of the evil in the world. You could feel it in the very air. Was it because of all the wars fought on this continent? Eve had no idea, but she had felt it even as a young woman, traveling through France and Italy before she was married. And did such knowledge make you live more truly, more fully?

Almost dizzy with all that was whirling through her mind, Eve stood. Still, she was calmer than she had been when she entered this museum. She looked around, searching for Paul's tweed back. Through the hum of conversation came his voice. It was calling—urgently, frantically—in German. Fear seized her heart.

* * *

Paul was staring at a woman and a little girl, probably her grandchild. Neat gray braids wound around the woman's head and she was wearing a gray flannel suit, a starched snowy blouse with a cameo, black walking shoes. The child, whose hairdo was a replica of the older woman's, had slipped her plaid coat around her shoulders and held her matching hat as if it were as fragile as glass. She couldn't be more than seven.

The woman looked like a hundred middle-aged women Paul had seen since they arrived, but when she turned and grasped the little girl's hand he gasped. She could have been Marga. The same deliberate, heavy walk that made her seem older than she was. Yet when she turned, she was so much younger, and beautiful, exactly like Marga. Paul had once overheard his parents talking about Marga's Nordic good looks, why people always thought she was from Scandinavia even though she had been born in Stuttgart. And here was this woman who had those same looks and who walked exactly like Marga. And the little girl could have been Grete.

Quickly he followed them to the ticket booth, calling, *"Bitte! Bitte!"* They didn't seem to hear him.

Then he stopped. Surely he had gone mad.

This woman couldn't be Grete. It was utterly impossible, and part of the reason he was here, why he had had to return. He turned abruptly and found Eve, and when she asked, "What was all that about?" he couldn't answer. Luckily she didn't question him, and soon they left.

14

THEY WERE TOO TIRED to visit the Jewish Museum on Fasenstrasse. "I really should check in with the office and find out what's doing there," Paul reminded her.

"We can grab some lunch back at the hotel," Eve said.

"I'm not really hungry," Paul murmured, and when they got there, she went by herself into the restaurant and ordered a chicken sandwich. There was no way she could comfort him. This trip had become an obstacle course. Who would dream that they would find themselves listening to those devastating Celan poems? Read by an American college kid?

When she got up to her room, she could hear Paul on the phone, his voice a little louder than it needed to be, as it always was on a trans-Atlantic call. She smiled. Good that he had the office to distract him a little. Then Eve put down her things and went to the closet. Paul had talked about going to a club tonight, one of those clubs that Hjalmar had worked in when he was young. She'd have to wear the gray dress and shawl again. But the shawl was not hanging with the dress. Nor was it in her drawer. She'd been so tired last night and so shocked by that oddly gentle kiss, she couldn't even recall how she'd gotten into bed.

Quickly she searched the room. No shawl. She remembered feeling it against her when she put on her raincoat, but she couldn't remember taking it off when she undressed. It could have slipped from her shoulders. She pictured the happy face of the woman who had sold it to her, yet she wasn't upset. In light of everything else, how could she worry about something as insignificant as a shawl? Still, maybe she should retrace her steps.

Eve knocked on the door of Paul's room. He had loosened his tie, but his notes from the phone call were neat and regular on the yellow legal pad near the phone.

"Anything important?" she asked.

He shook his head. "It can all wait, the younger men in the firm are wonderful, they can take care of everything better than I would like to admit."

She shifted, embarrassed. "I lost my shawl, last night," she blurted. "I think it fell off somewhere between the restaurant and here, maybe where the boutiques are. Maybe you could draw me a map."

He rose and tightened his tie. "Then let's go and find it." She smiled in relief.

As they strolled, Paul told her about his law firm, how one of the young partners was a woman in her forties with four young kids whose husband brought up the children. "It's a different world, Eve, and those kids are really amazing. I admire that family very much, and she's one hell of a lawyer."

Eve was happy to let him talk, she used to love hearing about the firm and the cases, and she knew that was part of the reason Eric had gone into the law.

When they turned into the shopping street, there, hanging on a bunch of umbrellas, was her shawl! Her breath caught. Neatly folded, it had a note pinned to it. Paul read it aloud to her, "This was found on the ground this morning, damp from the rain, but since it is wool it will not be harmed." That was all.

"How amazing," Eve said, "that someone would take the trouble."

"Let's go into the shop," Paul said, "they may know more."

"Ah!" a woman exclaimed. "You are the owner of the shawl?"

Eve nodded. Then Paul said a few sentences in German. The woman answered in English, "We found it when we opened this morning, someone must have passed by early, on their way to work, that's all I know."

Seeing Eve's incredulity, she went on, "People are very honest in this neighborhood, this is a good area, very old, filled with Germans who have lived here for generations, not like Wedding or one of those districts with all the new immigrants. You can't trust anyone there. But here, no one would think of taking such a lovely thing from its rightful owner. I am glad you came back for it."

"Let's see if there's something here to buy, perhaps for Claudia," Eve said.

Paul shook his head. His face was flushed with anger, and he practically pushed her out the door. Outside he muttered, "What a fucking liar she is. They've deluded themselves so thoroughly they actually believe their own lies. This neighborhood was filled with Jews living in houses like ours that had been built by their Jewish ancestors. The place was crawling with proper German Jews, that's why Frau Goldschmidt's Jewish School was a stone's throw away. That woman is totally deluded, so are the rest of them. It's infuriating, and that shopkeeper can go to hell," he said as they hurried away.

*   *   *

Instead of returning to the hotel they walked. "I need to calm down," Paul admitted. Then with a rueful smile, "Obviously." Now, at almost four p.m. they were sitting on a stone bench near the grave of Moses Mendelssohn. The cemetery was in a tiny park a stone's throw from the remains of the Wall. This area was where the eastern European Jews had settled at the turn of the century and was once called "the street of tolerance," Paul told Eve, "because the beautiful Lutheran Baroque church, the Sophienkirche had a cemetery that adjoined this one. And the Neue Synagogue isn't far. It was built in 1859, before the rise of anti-Semitism, the year that Dreyfus was born in Alsace and a year before Herzl's birth in Pest."

Eve nodded. She remembered that he had written his honors thesis in history at Yale on anti-Semitism and knew all about those two men, but she had never delved into his reasons for choosing it as a topic. And she certainly wasn't going to ask such questions now. But Paul seemed to read her mind.

"Ian thought I was crazy doing all that research on Herzl and Dreyfus. He used to tell me, 'It's over, why don't you choose something current, like Russia's hegemony under the Czars and how that affects our situation now?' But they were part of a direct line to all that happened here, even to Celan."

Before he could go on, they were interrupted by a street sweeper who asked them to lift their legs so he could clean beneath their bench. As the man spoke, Paul translated: "So many visitors, who would believe so many foreigners would come to see this? It was just a wall, an ugly wall, not even good workmanship, shoddy builders. They put up the ugliest housing in the world in East Berlin. And now so many people, but to see this?" The man demanded, pointing to the gray stretch of untouched concrete left for posterity.

"Those Communist leaders saved all the good things for themselves and the people had nothing. No better than the Czars. Worse than the Czars. It was a disgrace, a scandal, and now let the rest of the world know about their dirty tricks!" At that he bore down hard on his broom. Leaves and dust began to fly.

Soon he cast his glance in a wider circle. Though it was only mid-afternoon, drag queens of enormous proportions were going to and from work. "This used to be East Berlin's red light district," Paul whispered.

"That's a scandal, too," the street sweeper murmured, but then he gave them a smile and a good-natured shrug, as if to say, How can you obstruct man's most primitive impulses? Who would want to?

He was right. There was something oddly endearing about those outlandish queens, dressed in garish colors, their makeup so thick they appeared to be some fantastic representation of *woman* you encounter only in fairy tales, or Wagner, or dreams.

"That little girl who read the poem reminded me of Grete,

blonde and light-eyed, a perfect little German girl. Rose was more like Hjalmar, she had his dark eyes and hair and his sense of mischief and joy. Grete was Marga's child. But so *stolz,* and sad, as if her soul weighed her down. Hjalmar and Rose hated what Germany had become and were hopeful that it would be destroyed, but Marga and Grete always seemed to yearn for what Marga called 'the old Germany.' Grete was even a member of the *Bund Deutscher Madel,* the female equivalent of the Hitler Youth, and wore a uniform and was allowed to march because it made the family look patriotic. In her heart I truly think Grete wanted to be a good little Nazi girl.

"Tante Hilda called Grete 'the little old lady.' When Berthe and I would get attacks of the giggles, which was really hysteria, I guess, Rose would join in, but Grete would cry and beg us to stop." Paul looked up, his eyes dreamy.

"It was so long ago, a lifetime ago." His voice was more puzzled than bitter. Eve stared at him in surprise. Now the sweeper had brought a hose and was spraying the walkway in the little park and watering the shrubs.

"You're wondering why I'm not angrier as I tell you these stories, aren't you?" he said. "Well, all those visits to the psychiatrists weren't entirely in vain. Anger obscures the truth. The fact is, Eve, I can't afford anger now, although that woman in the shop annoyed the hell out of me. But when I'm talking about the past I have to try to be as objective as I can." He let his gaze rest on the stone wall and the massive old trees whose leaves were still so green and firm and shining.

Suddenly Eve was seized by a need to talk. About a moment so painful she had never confessed it to anyone, not even Blanche. "There is so much cruelty in our lives, and people are sometimes crueler than they realize," she blurted.

"What do you mean?" his voice was sharp, wary.

"Do you remember a day when Claudia was about fourteen, on a class trip to the Metropolitan Museum that took them through Central Park and she saw you and Frankie talking?"

"I'm not sure."

"Well, I am." Eve's voice was harsh. "It was May and very warm and everyone was shedding their jackets and sweaters and Frankie was wearing a sleeveless green sheath and you had taken off your blue blazer and loosened your tie. Claudia was surprised to see you sitting on the grass at the base of a huge tree, it wasn't exactly what she imagined when you went to work every morning, but when she saw you and Frankie, she wasn't quite sure it was Frankie. It had been so long since she'd seen Frankie, but she took a chance and said, 'Hello, Aunt Frankie.' Instead of praising her for her good memory, Frankie pretended she had made a mistake and told Claudia she was your new office colleague. While you sat there and didn't say a word. But Claudia knew she was right and kept persisting, saying she could never forget Aunt Frankie. Finally she fell so far behind the group that her teacher had to call her to catch up." Eve stopped, but only to take a breath.

"After she ran off to catch up with her class, you and Frankie had a good laugh and Frankie dared you to have a cigarette, even though you had stopped smoking years ago, and you sat there, the two of you, dragging on those cigarettes like a pair of teenagers who had convinced some unsuspecting parent that they weren't really having sex."

Paul stared, his face starting to flush.

"Well, what you didn't know was that I was one of the class mothers, and when I saw Claudia approach you, I hung back and stood behind the tree and heard the whole damn exchange, which told me that not only were you still seeing Frankie on the sly, but also, and far more important, that you could be unbelievably cruel.

"When Claudia came home that night, she told me about it. She thought I was up ahead with the rest of the group, and she was still upset. She knew in her heart that it was Frankie but she wanted to believe you. I let her talk and never cleared it up for her because I wasn't ready to leave you and I didn't want her to hate you as much as I did that day. But after we were divorced she told me and Blanche and my parents that she'd once seen you with Frankie, though she could never tell them that you had lied to her. Which I understood completely, because I could never tell anyone either, not even her."

For a moment Eve thought Paul was going to rise and turn on his heel and hurry away. Instead, he sat there, with his hands hanging limply between his knees and swallowed hard and took a deep breath.

"I'm sorry," he said. "I'm truly sorry. It was cruel and unforgivable, and I've never forgotten it either. But I was not seeing Frankie, we had met by chance and everyone was giddy with the heat and when she convinced me to stop and talk, I did. I had not been seeing her for a long time, and I never saw her again after that. And I never had another cigarette," he added.

Eve was amazed by his sincere remorse, and also relieved to have finally spoken up.

Yet she didn't feel any triumph, just sadness, and a weird sense of being cleansed, as if the sweeper had hosed them off, too. They sat there awkwardly, then, when the sweeper returned, moved to another part of the cemetery.

Now the sun was fighting its way through clouds. The thin light glossed the wet, low-slung branches of the shrubs, and the newly watered grass, revealing the letters carved on the moss-covered gravestone. In this walled spot it felt almost warm, the very air alive, stirring with insects and birds.

Eve turned and read the inscription on the gravestone aloud: "Moses Mendelssohn, born in Dessau on September 6, 1729, died in Berlin on January 4, 1786," then Paul translated the plaque on the memorial nearby:

On this spot was founded the first old age home of the Jewish community. In 1942 the Germans used this facility as a collection point for Jewish citizens. Fifty-five thousand Jewish Berliners from infants to the very old were carried off to the KZ-Lager at Auschwitz and Theresienstadt and were murdered there.

DON'T EVER FORGET. DEFEND AGAINST WAR. GUARD THE PEACE.

"Well, they don't seem afraid to tell it like it was, you have to give them that," he admitted, his voice still the whisper it had been when he apologized. As he spoke, though, it grew firmer, "You know, this was one of the most frightening places in the city, coming here was tantamount to suicide, especially at the end. It was where the Catchers would hang out." His voice was low. "But now they keep the place nice and tidy, and whatever happened here, the terrible tortures, the sadistic acts have been reduced to a few lines on a plaque. It's totally crazy."

"No it's not. You can't expect them to commission a sculpture to torture and death, can you?" Eve said. "And would it be better if the place were overgrown and ugly?"

"Ah, the old question," he said, not even trying to keep the bitterness from his voice. "Is it better that the grass grows at Auschwitz and Dachau, or should they have made it a desert or a poured a huge slab of concrete to commemorate what happened?"

Eve shook her head and averted her eyes. Life springs eternal, just like hope. Besides the healthy trees and grass and the trembling air were other signs of life: Stones piled on top of Mendelssohn's grave, which meant that other Jews had come here to pay their respects, to say, we have been here, we remember.

Now, though, Paul had begun again . . .

"To Marga's everlasting dismay Hjalmar called Rose his 'lovely slattern.' He was right, and his wife was always straightening her, pinning up scraps of torn hem, smoothing down wild cowlicks, pestering her to clean herself and her room. To no avail. All Rose cared about were words: What words could do, how they could be woven into phrases and sentences, like jewels in a necklace. Which words had power, which didn't.

"'I will be a poet, like Rilke, or Hölderlin,' she announced, and her mother shuddered, afraid to remind Rose that Hölderlin was mad in his tower for decades. Never catching on that Rose was teasing her.

"When the Friedmanns moved into our house, Rose was in heaven. Here was the best library she'd ever seen. She began to read French seriously, poring over French grammars and novels. By the summer of 1943 she'd discovered Zola and the Dreyfus case. Hjalmar was proud of her intellectual curiosity, her gift with languages, but Marga worried constantly about Rose, and though none of them supported the Nazis—no, God forbid!—it wasn't wise to be too outspoken.

"'You must remember,' Marga said, 'we are not ordinary German citizens, though we represent the true Germany. We cannot take chances. We have to protect the Bergers, there must be not be a trace of suspicion that anyone lives here besides us and Tante Hilda.'

"It drove Rose crazy, her mother announcing the obvious. Why couldn't Marga realize what we knew in our bones: That living with us in hiding had to be a game, a thrilling game, exactly the adventure her father had promised. That talking about the Nazis was not merely useless, but also stupid because it gave them a reality they didn't deserve. Better to live with your head buried in books and learn the languages you would need after the madness was over.

"Didn't the BBC say that soon the Allies would be here? We listened, almost every night, and when Marga reminded her husband it was a crime, he merely laughed and said, 'So is hiding Jews.' And hadn't the Americans just landed in Sicily? Now Mussolini was finished and Marshal Badoglio of Ethiopia was in charge. Soon someone else would be in charge here, too. And meantime Rose had to practice her French so she could talk to the French prisoners of war who were working on the farms, and learn English for later, when the Americans and English arrived. And try to convince her mother to do the same.

"Then Hamburg was bombed.

"We shouldn't have been so shocked. We'd heard about

the leaflets the Allies dropped, warning the women and children to leave, but no one imagined it would be so bad. The Americans bombed during the day, the British at night. No respite. And then the "windows," those metallic strips which were dropped in bundles to confuse the German radar. But worst were the new phosphorous bombs creating waves of fire, gale-force winds of fire that started after the planes were gone and circled the city and were more horrible than anything used before.

"Rivers of fire swept through the streets, snaking into the smallest lanes and alleys, walls of fire that attacked running men, women, children, burning them alive. What some people said was being done in the camps, what the grown-ups never mentioned in front of us children. Now, though, they were too horrified to practice caution. Was this the Allied answer to the camps, an eye for an eye?

"And why Hamburg, a city that had always held itself aloof, a city that thought of itself as more Scandinavian than German? What an irony.

"Even more worrying, there had been no word from Papa's sisters, Sophie and Hannah, whose children had been sent to Manchester on one of the last *Kindertransports* in the summer of 1939. Now only they and their husbands lived in the large house. For years they had written once a week to Hjalmar. After July 3rd not a syllable.

"One stifling evening in August 1943 Tante Hilda was washing up after dinner, Marga and Frieda and we were reading, Papa and Hjalmar were playing chess. It was far too hot to think about going upstairs, and everyone sat, listless, listening to the rhythmic thud of the moving chessmen.

"All at once a sharp rap on the back door. Before Tante Hilda could open it, two men pushed past her and dropped into chairs at the kitchen table. By now she seen more than she ever dreamed she would and didn't scare so easily. Their faces were blackened with coal and they wore blue overalls and shirts, but there was something familiar about one of them, something in the slant of their bones beneath all that grime.

"When they spoke Tante's hand flew to her mouth. Those men in overalls were Gunther's sister Sophie and her husband. Their home had been burned to the ground. The other sister Hannah had stayed because her husband had heart trouble, and they'd been forced into a shelter for Jews, which might mean deportation. Sophie and Ernest got a ride from a Nazi officer they bribed, then walked the last fifty kilometers at night. Their workmen's clothes had been given them by a sympathetic farm family.

"They began to weep, so by the time I saw them, their blackened, tear-stained faces were as smudged as letters caught in the rain. And their bodies seemed small and fragile, buried beneath the bulky work clothes.

"A hodgepodge of crying and questions, nervous, wobbly laughter while Papa and Hjalmar consulted in silence. Then Papa said, 'It's too dangerous for you to stay here for the night, it will be safer at the Swedish Church.' Hjalmar nodded, frowning when Sophie confessed they seemed to have been followed for a time inside the city limits.

"'If that's the case, I must remain here,' Hjalmar said. So Rose and I were dispatched to the Swedish Church for advice from Erik Perwe, the minister who helped Jews escape.

"'Rose can't go alone, she might be stopped because of the curfew, and then God knows what might happen, in this heat all those soldiers do is drink beer, then wander around looking for someone to molest. Two is better than one, and it's not so late that you'll be noticed. Besides, you're both tall for your age, say you're older if you're stopped, you know what to do,' Papa warned, his voice calm, though his eyes were troubled.

"Both he and Hjalmar looked stunned. Hamburg had been their safety valve, now it was destroyed and his sister had come to him in Berlin. The caprices of war. The first of many. And Rose and I were the ones who had to lead them to safety. I knew from Papa's eyes that even he was frightened, but we had no choice . . .

While he was changing into dark clothes his father comes upstairs to his corner of the attic and sits on Paul's bed. "They say the Catchers are busier than ever," he begins. Paul stares. His parents have never mentioned the Catchers, those despicable Jews who help the Gestapo to save their own skins. He doesn't even remember how or when he first heard about them; they are a dark, horrible secret.

"Now that the tide is turning they are desperate, some say they're more to be feared than the Germans," Papa goes on. "They say that some are students from Frau Goldschmidt's school, so don't greet anyone, even someone you recognize. Just stare through them, then slip away as quickly and unobtrusively as possible. You've grown a lot taller since you were at Frau Goldschmidt's, thank God, so they might not recognize you."

Paul lowers his eyes and his cheeks flush with shame at the thought of some of his classmates becoming Catchers. "Thank God Frau Goldschmidt is far away and doesn't know this. That's what war does, makes people lose their minds," his father adds, gesturing towards downstairs where Aunt Sophie is jabbering uncontrollably about all the horrors she and Ernest saw. Paul can only nod.

As he pulls on the tennis shoes that will muffle his tread, he understands that this isn't a conversation, but a rite of passage. An admission on Papa's part that Paul is now old enough to witness his father's shame—not only for the Catchers, or for the real Germany, but, most of all, for his own mistakes. Paul has already turned 13, but he has not had a Bar Mitzvah; even if they weren't in hiding, Reform Jews like the Bergers don't have Bar Mitzvahs. Yet at this moment Paul understands how there can be an instantaneous transformation from boy to man. His father is speaking not only of his infinite regret for his great blunder in not leaving Germany when he could, Papa is also warning Paul that he can't protect any of them from the dangers that will inevitably come. Young as he is, Paul must be his father's equal from now on.

*   *   *

Paulie and Rose race along, two are not enough to make a human chain and these streets are more hazardous than the Grunewald or the area around the Grunewald station which swarms with Nazis sorting through the Jews held for deportation. And there will be no whistles from Hjalmar if someone is looking for trouble. Still, how wonderful it is to be out under the shimmering sky of an August night, and not be stuck in that house where apprehension hangs like fog.

His aunt and uncle have lost their wits, at least for now. Describing what they saw in such minute detail made Paul smell the fires and hear the screaming children. When Sophie started going on about pieces of flesh caught in the branches of trees, Mamma clapped her hands and hissed, "Enough! No more talk!" Mamma, who never raised her voice, finally shouting, then rushing off to find tennis shoes for Rose. Now those soft soles make a gentle thudding sound as they dart along on the pavement.

Heavy heat presses down. So bitter in winter, so hot in summer. Berlin. How they have all longed for the hills and fresh breezes to the south. They went last year, and the year before that, wearing disguises, carrying forged papers. Once they got there they were fine. The country folk can be trusted, but now, who knows? Aunt Sophie said Berlin is next. Will it be safer to stay or try to escape to the country? What will Papa and Hjalmar decree?

Although he has seen the Swedish Church and gone to an occasional service, Paul has not been here since they went into hiding. Now the building doesn't even look like a church, more like an alms-house, with people lying on mattresses and playing cards and reading while a radio bleats snatches of classical music. Only the eerie lack of conversation gives a clue to what it had become: a hiding-place for Jews because of the amazing persistence of Erik Perwe and a few resisters who pretend to be Nazi policemen. These resisters help Perwe whenever they can because they are totally repelled by the Nazis' methods.

Paul has heard talk about them, one of them is a cousin of Tante Hilda. They are Prussians, good Berliners, who believe that everything, even war, must be conducted with dignity and respect for the rights of other men, for order and justice. They are men who have no hatred for Jews or Catholics or gypsies or the maimed or handicapped. When they talk about Hitler and Himmler and Goebbels, their lips curl with scorn. Those leaders of the Nazi party are not men, they are aberrations, animals whose tricks must be foiled at every opportunity.

Pastor Perwe is not here, but as soon as Paul and Rose whisper who they are, they are shown into the rectory where a tall, beautiful woman greets them, stretching out her hand and telling them, "I am Pastor's wife." Paul cannot take his eyes off her. Even Rose is speechless.

Quickly Paul whispers the news of his aunt and uncle. He knows that Papa and Hjalmar are praying they can come here for the night. "Be sure to tell Pastor Perwe they are already disguised as workmen, that will make it easier," were Papa's last words. Mrs. Perwe nods, then bids them wait, and goes into the church. She comes back with a man in a policeman's uniform and instructs Paul to write down the address of the house.

"I wish I could drive you home, but it's too dangerous," the man says, then they watch him hurry along the side of the house into what looks like an official Nazi car, and pull away.

"Are you hungry?" Mrs. Perwe asked. Her voice is as lovely as her face, like the soughing of a clear mountain stream dappled with sunlight. How can there be evil in such a gorgeous, green world? her voice seems to ask. And her eyes are a clear, iridescent blue, as penetrating as lamps glistening in a faraway house. As if she can see things you can't. You could never lie to this woman, Paul realizes, as he shakes his head.

"Are you hungry?" she persists. What she asks everyone who appears in her home. Rose and he refuse again. Food is scarce everywhere, yet they are far from hungry. Still, he hates to leave. Within the circle of this woman's presence, Paul feels safer than he has in a long time.

But they mustn't linger. He reaches for Rose's hand and they follow Mrs. Perwe through to the door. She hands them some sealed boxes. "They are filled with old newspapers," she tells them, "if someone stops you, say you are delivering something from the church to Hjalmar Friedmann."

On their way home they are silent, except when Rose sighs, "Isn't she beautiful. How can anyone be so lovely?" and reaches again for Paul's hand. For the first time since he has known her, Paul feels a stirring in his loins. He wants to tell her that she is as pretty, in her way, as Mrs. Perwe. That her passion for books and for languages and for life, even for their proscribed existence, is one of the most beautiful things he has ever known. But he is too shy, and besides she wouldn't believe him. If Rose is convinced of nothing else, she is sure she is exactly what her mother calls her—jokingly, of course—"The Ugly Duckling."

Suddenly Paul becomes aware of a strange smell, like fruit ripening, a sickening, foul odor. He stiffens, frightened. There have been rumors of dead people found under crumpled buildings, in attics and cellars, mostly suicides. He peers into the darkness. Nothing. Again he sniffs.

"What's the matter?"

"A smell, a funny smell."

"I don't smell it."

"Well, I do!" Just as he's answering, Paul realizes that the smell is coming from Rose. Too embarrassed to tell her, he drops her hand and hangs back a little.

"Come on, Paulie, we don't have all night, you're just as bad as Grete, always sniffing and complaining. Come on." She whirls towards him, grabbing for his hand, and that's when he sees it: a dark stain spreading across the back of her print skirt.

"Now, what? You look like you've seen a ghost." Rose stares at him, then, "What the devil? . . ." and her face blanches, too, and she smiles. "I told Mama this was no ordinary stomach-ache, but she said I was too young, it couldn't possibly be, it wouldn't come for years because we aren't eating normally. She insisted that all the girls are

older when they get it now. She was so sure of herself, you know how she is." Rose cocks her head towards him with a triumphant smile.

Then she reaches around her to feel the dark stain on her skirt and brings a finger to her face. "Ugh, it really is blood, I never believed it would truly be blood, I don't know what I thought it would be like, but I wasn't prepared for something so smelly."

Then she whispers, "Paulie, now I am a woman." Joy and trepidation mingle in her voice. "But I'll never be as beautiful as Mrs. Perwe. She looks like an angel, no wonder the people hiding there never want to leave!" And soon they are running like the wind, exactly as they are not supposed to do. But they don't care. The harder they run, the worse it is for Rose. A black trickle wanders down her legs, staining her socks, and drips off her shoes. She is panting. Paul pulls her towards him. Together they look up at the meteor shower which has begun shooting through the sky.

When Paul pulls Rose close, the smell is stronger, but Paul doesn't care, as long as it's not someone dead, as long as everyone close to them is safe. "Won't Mother be surprised?" Rose asks again, and they are both concentrating so hard on what Marga's reaction will be, they miss the long black limousine crawling as cautiously as a blind man groping his way. Only the uniformed driver is visible. But crouched on its floors are two people who will insist indignantly they are workmen from Hamburg, should they have the bad luck to get stopped.

15

MOONLIGHT streamed in through the window. When he and Eve returned to the hotel all he had wanted was to escape into the oblivion of sleep. They had abandoned the idea of going to a club and had agreed to meet for a light, late supper after they napped. Now he concentrated and could hear strands of chamber music. Beethoven.

Distant music. Why did it hold such promise? Why did he love it so much? Sometimes he thought it was because of Alix, at other times it seemed to be bred into his Jewish bones. He looked at his watch. Now he could feel Eve's eyes on him as he told the story of that summer night. In the years afterwards it had begun to seem ridiculous: a young German girl getting her first period in the midst of such danger—but Eve's sympathetic reaction had validated Rose's confusion and pride. Life went on in the midst of all that deliberate killing. The absurdity of it didn't negate the reality of it. And he was grateful that she understood how it was all mixed up in his memory.

But what to do with the shame about that incident with Frankie and Claudia? He had realized that day what a devil Frankie was. And now to discover that Eve had witnessed it. The whole thing was incredible, the wonder was that she had kept silent all these years.

Yet what a relief to have it come out. He had almost convinced himself it had never happened; but hearing Eve recount it in that flat voice made him realize that not only had it happened, but so had all the other things he was now telling her. Moreover, it confirmed his ability to be cruel, to do loathsome things and would prepare her, in a strange way, for all that he still had to reveal to her.

He knew, though, that he had to stop for a while. It was exactly as the African proverb said, "Words are like strands of straw in a thatched roof. Once out you can't put them back." He first heard it at law school and had lived by it for much of his life.

Now, as he saw Eve's pale, distressed face in his mind, Paul thought: Enough words, enough of the past.

He pulled on a robe, shoved his feet into his slippers and went to knock on her door. When she opened it, her skin had the transparency that came not only with fatigue, but also with fright. Embarrassed, Paul wanted to retreat, but they stood there, flanking the threshold like chessmen.

"Come in, come in," she urged, then confessed, "I wanted to sleep, but every time I was about to drop off, those lines from Celan came back, like a hammer in my head."

"Listen, Eve, we can quit, any time you want to, I don't want to force you . . . "

"No, I don't want to quit, it's just that the reading . . . was so unexpected, then, me blabbering about you and Frankie and Claudia. I promised myself I would listen, and I broke my promise . . . " she stopped and looked out the window, hugging herself with her arms.

"There were no promises," Paul interrupted her. "You had every right to say what was on your mind."

Now it was her turn to stare. "You really believe that, don't you?"

"Yes. And I certainly don't hold it against you for speaking up. I deserved it."

"Well, I'm not going to do it again, so let's put it behind us." She pushed her hair back from her forehead, a gesture he remembered when they had been on the verge of a fight and felt it best to retreat. Relief flooded through him as they sank into the matching loveseats.

Eve continued, "The worst was that image of you and Rose racing home in such danger. My war is like something from a play, shades drawn, sitting in the halls at school during air raid drills, singing madly, a wonderful lark, pretending we were going to be bombed. While you—how you didn't die of fright is a miracle. Those years cooped up in that attic, your childhood and adolescence lost. Then telling it, you must be worn out."

"I was when we got back, then I slept, and now I feel lighter. For years before I met you, I would get this terrible heaviness and dream I was walking through the Public Garden and a shadowy woman would spit at me."

Eve brought the back of her hand to her lips. "Why would anyone spit at you?" she began, but stopped when she saw his mouth tighten. "No, no more questions," she conceded.

"And no more telling, you've had enough for one day. How about a drink?" Paul suggested.

"Good idea, and while you're making the drinks, I'm going to wash my face," she said as she slipped into the bathroom.

"Scotch or sherry?" he called.

"Scotch is fine."

As he busied himself with the drinks Paul realized that by bringing her here, by telling her his story he had transferred some of the burden to her. What he'd been afraid of when they were young, why he'd never been able to do it. But "it's exactly as Hölderlin said," Hjalmar would tell them, "danger and salvation are always braided together. The circumstances that bring danger also bring the power to save."

Then Paul thought: Although a dangerous truth can save, it can also bring more danger, like Eve becoming more jittery, or her becoming completely repelled when he told all he had to tell. The stakes were growing higher with each incident he related.

Her fundamental innocence reminded him of the eager young men in his firm, who had not yet learned that evil was part of the human condition and that laws were necessary to protect man from himself. If you learn that young, as he did, you don't expect so much, you don't hang onto those ideals about justice and dignity. So American, that innocence, so convinced it was right.

Once she had said, "I hate your cynicism, I'll always hate it." She meant not only how he led his life, but his way of regarding the world. Now as Paul stirred the Scotch, he wondered, Why had he told her so much so soon, why couldn't he have ladled it out more carefully?

Then he asked himself: How can you ladle sorrow, or cruelty?

As they sipped their drinks Paul said, "You know, we weren't frightened all the time. Sure, there were scary moments, but while Hjalmar was alive, it never occurred to me that it wouldn't all work out. Most of the time it was a fabulous adventure, exactly as he intended, and I wasn't really afraid until the end."

"I'm not sure I believe you," she said. "As a matter of fact, I'm sure I don't believe you. But I don't want that to stop you." Her eyes were calm.

He put down his drink and reached for her hand. "Let's find an American movie and forget we're in Berlin, then we'll see how we feel tomorrow. You know, we can ditch this whole thing and go see Claudia in Paris, and if I feel I need to come back, I can do it alone."

"No. We have tickets for the concert tomorrow evening, and I know you want to see the Philharmonie. So do I. Every architect I know has an opinion about it." Gently she extricated her hand. "But I'm really fine, it's just that you caught me half asleep."

And before you could put yourself on guard, Paul thought. But she was beginning to look better. Oddly, her distress had yielded to unflinching determination and a new, astonishing openness, which deepened her eyes, lit up her skin, accentuated her good bones. Now he saw reserves of emotion and stamina that he, and maybe she, too, never suspected she had.

"Right now, though, my main worry is facing another German

waiter. Let's do room service." She rose to get the room service menu on the desk.

As he watched her, Paul was intensely aware of everything about her. Her robe was of fine wool, a gorgeous greenish gray that brought out her eyes and clung to her slender figure. When the kids were growing up she had "filled out," and always blamed it on the eating out. Now she was as lean as she'd been when she was young. And still with that straight, almost regal carriage. The robe had to be a gift, Eve would never buy such an extravagance. Though Paul couldn't see Max buying it, either.

"How about some French toast and tea and fruit?" she asked.

"Fine, that sounds fine."

When his glance met hers she looked down, and her face crinkled into a smile. "Blanche gave it to me, with a nightgown to match. They're much too expensive, but she said I had a whole other life ahead of me, something like that. It's more a gift for a bride than for me..." her voice dwindled and she colored, "God knows why I'm telling you this."

"Because I'm dying of curiosity and we both know you'd never spend so much for a robe."

"I'm better than I used to be."

"I've noticed."

"I think some of that was to torture you."

"A confession at last. Well, that's something!" He smiled at her, and at last the air between them loosened.

*　　*　　*

The next day they took a long walk in the eastern part of the city, along Unter Den Linden until it became Karl Liebnecht-strasse. When they stopped for lunch Paul said, "You know, Hjalmar used to say that the Second World War started right here, when Karl Liebnecht and Rosa Luxembourg were tortured in the Eden Hotel and then killed in January 1919 for participating in the Bolshevik Revolution."

"After that Kathe Kollwitz did a large woodcut depicting Karl's untimely, brutal death. It's in the Dallas Museum of Art," Eve told him, delighted to be able to give him some miscellany for a change.

But now Paul was looking at her thoughtfully, as he muttered, "Bach, Beethoven, Brahms, and brutality." Then, abruptly, "Let's so back, we need a rest from this." So they got into a cab and retreated to their rooms for the afternoon.

Eve finished *Goodbye to Berlin,* reading the last few pages a few times, marking a few places in light pencil. Blanche had plucked the book from the shelf in Jack's study. "Take it. It meant a lot to Jack, he thought Isherwood captured beautifully the craziness of that city at that time."

Now Eve marked a passage from Isherwood's visit to a reformatory without any locked gates where he asks the director, "Don't your boys run away? . . . isn't there a kind of natural instinct for freedom?" The man answers, "Yes, you are right. But the boys soon lose it. The system helps them lose it. I think, perhaps that, in Germans, this instinct is never very strong."

A few pages later: "Herr N. is always charmingly polite, and listens gravely, and carefully to my explanations of grammatical points. Behind everything he says I am aware of an immense sadness."

And finally, describing his landlady, Fraulein Schneider who is inconsolable that he is leaving the city:

"It's no use trying to explain to her, or talking politics. Already she is adapting herself, as she will adapt herself every new regime. This morning I even heard her talking reverently about "Der Fuhrer" to the porter's wife. If anybody were to remind her that, at the elections last November she voted communist, she would probably deny it hotly, and in perfect good faith. She is merely acclimatizing herself, in accordance with a natural law, like an animal which changes its coat for the winter. Thousands of people like Frl. Schneider are acclimatizing themselves. After all, whatever government is in power, they are doomed to live in this town."

Such foreboding. How well Isherwood got it. And it is still here. Is that what comes of such brutality? Despite herself, Eve trembled. When she agreed to come she didn't really understand that such a palpable sense of melancholy would haunt them, even now. Making them afraid, filling them with that "immense sadness."

*　　*　　*

The Philharmonie is perched on the edge of the Tiergarten, its rounded surfaces like resting wings, but so forlorn, hanging in the wind, all alone, away from everything. Especially at night, Paul thought, as they approached it in a cab.

When he was young his family went to either "Hansel and Gretel" or "The Magic Flute" around New Year's. What feverish excitement there was about going to the Staatsoper, near Under den Linden. They had stood outside it this morning and he had told Eve about the last time he saw it in April, 1944, when he foraged for food on its back steps, placed there by cooks from the few remaining restaurants still open.

But those famous halls for opera and concerts were in the eastern part of the city. So after the Wall went up, the westerners built their own Philharmonie Hall in 1963. "It looks better at night," Paul said as they alighted from the taxi.

And the inside was wonderful: The lobby inviting and spacious, the auditorium airy, yet intimate, its sloping wood walls holding the audience in a honey-colored embrace. They were seated behind the orchestra, facing the conductor. "Though less expensive than those in the orchestra, these are excellent seats," the ticket agent had told him. Sizing him up as he spoke, concluding from Paul's clothes that he was used to the best of everything. For a moment Paul was offended by the man's frank appraisal, yet he had no one to blame but himself. He had always been too interested in what he looked like, and since Eve had left he'd gotten worse. What he couldn't admit to anyone was that he, who used to haunt bookstores and spend long afternoons reading, couldn't find refuge in books after she was gone and spent far too much time at Paul Stuart's or in Saks' Men's Department.

"It's grief," his psychiatrist told him, "a classic symptom of grief, it will pass." And it finally had.

Quickly Paul scanned the program. Beethoven's Sixth Symphony, Richard Strauss's "Ein Heldenleben," the Sibelius Fifth. The conductor was a young Finn. "No soloist, those concerts were sold out," he murmured.

"Doesn't matter, it's the hall that's important," Eve said. He was relieved to see her so relaxed, but not surprised. She always loved the symphony. So did Frieda and Gunther. Now he could see his young parents, dressed in their elegant clothes, rushing off to a concert. How often had Hjalmar said, "If Germany becomes *judenfrei* who will go to the concerts and opera?" It was especially true in Berlin. The Bergers went to synagogue for the High Holidays and for their parents' *yahrseits,* and had elaborate, memorable Seders, but their true religion was music. And when they came to America, there was always money for Carnegie Hall and the Metropolitan Opera. There they would shed their cares, and become, magically, their vibrant younger selves. For only music had the power to wash away the stains of the 20th century.

Eve's love of classical music became a crucial bond between her and Frieda and Gunther, and they often went to concerts together when he was nowhere to be found. By then Paul and Gunther had drifted apart, as well. Something he never would have predicted.

After the night he and Rose went to the Perwe's church, he had felt like his father's equal. Later, without Hjalmar to guide them, his parents showed their true mettle, using their great intelligence and reserves of ingenuity to get their beloved children to safety. Wandering through the German countryside, they had showed remarkable stamina and good sense.

Yet as soon as they were physically safe in New Jersey, Gunther retreated to some place Paul could not enter. All that had happened was finally taking its toll, and his father slowly became a shadow of himself when he was not in the store. Where he lived when he was in the privacy of his home, at least in his mind, was a strange, inhospitable place, which precluded frankness between father and son.

Paul supposed he could have confided his worries to his mother, but he never did. Yet his parents always seemed to know when Paul was in trouble. Still, they would never pry, perhaps because they simply didn't have the strength to hear about Paul's infidelities.

And Berthe never gave him away, even when she was furious. "We had no idea who it was when we approached, and there you were, you and Frankie Bidwell pressed against a wall of a building like horny teenagers. How could you, Paul? She's so hard, with all that flashy jewelry, like some Nazi whore," she snapped after she had seen him and Frankie one night in Manhattan. Berthe's acid voice went on, "What a liar you are, Paul, mostly to yourself, you make me sick."

Still, she never carried tales to their parents.

Nor would she forsake him. After Eve left, she said, "I'm amazed she stayed so long, but blood is thicker than water. You and I have been through too much for me to turn on you now." He was stunned.

And when he called to tell his sister about this trip, she was unexpectedly gentle. "It will be hard, Paulie, and horrible for Eve. She doesn't know from things like this, neither does Zach. She's brave to go." A pause. "You do know that it will be very hard?"

"I know."

"Wild horses couldn't drag me there, still, everyone's different. Good luck, Paulie, and for God's sake, be careful." Then, just as he was about to hang up, in her quietest voice, Berthe asked, "If it's still there, will you take a photo of the house and bring it to me?"

Which he'd forgotten until this moment.

When he turned to remind Eve they must take a photo for Berthe, her face was alive with excitement. "While you were reading the program, I've been talking to the people next to us. They're from Falkensee, in East Germany, and they are celebrating their 20th anniversary," she said and beckoned to them and Paul leaned forward. "This is my husband, Paul Bertram, and this is Ursula and Rolf Wolff." They were in their 40s, in their best clothes and greeted him with broad smiles. Their teeth were terrible.

"Rolf doesn't speak English but I do," Ursula confided. "I have a correspondent in Minneapolis, Minnesota."

"Oh, a pen pal," Eve interposed.

"Yes, that's it! I could not recall the word," Ursula sighed with happiness, and the music began.

*   *   *

The performance was superb, and at the end of the first half, Eve was struck by the tumultuous clapping. Such an enthusiastic audience, you rarely saw that in New York these days. How glad she was that she had refused Paul's offer of a movie.

When they told her how much they liked the orchestra, Ursula blushed with pleasure, then she and Rolf disappeared. Eve and Paul walked through an exhibition of photographs. "It was interesting, to see the conductor's face," Eve was saying when Ursula came up, sly as a cat, behind them.

She was beaming. "Rolf and I invite you to see a little of Berlin, in our car, after the concert," she said in a rush, but her voice was tentative, her eyes worried. Then she whispered, "It's been so long since we could do something like this, we are so . . . " she lapsed into German.

"Unschooled, awkward," Paul whispered into Eve's hair. How touching Ursula's discomfort was. Eve was relieved when Paul said, "How nice of you, and we accept, gladly, but only if you let us take you out for your anniversary."

"But we are the hosts, you are in our country," Ursula protested.

"But it's your anniversary, and anniversaries are special," Eve reminded her. "It would give us great pleasure to do this."

Shaking her head Ursula slipped away again and consulted with Rolf. When they faced the Bertrams, they were smiling. "Rolf says it is okay," Ursula reported, "we have so few chances to meet foreigners, none really, we cannot let this slip away."

Eve was filled with a sudden burst of affection for this stranger who was trying so hard to make her comfortable in her country. Quickly she tucked her arm into Ursula's and they walked back to their seats together. Suddenly, all the trepidation she had felt earlier today disappeared. As they settled again, Eve felt absolutely content for the first time since they had arrived in this baffling city.

*   *   *

Paul loved this Sibelius, he loved all Sibelius: the abrupt shifts of emotion, the throbbing tension that erupts into sheer joy, then wanes again to become something inexplicably dark and melancholy. Like life, itself. When he closed his eyes, he could picture the old composer walking down the main street of Helsinki each morning though he had not published a note of music for decades. Sibelius finished his last symphony in the mid-1920s, then wrote a few shorter things the following year, but for the last thirty years of his life, nothing. What would it be like to live for so long with nothing more to say? To know you were finished? Paul's own work was so important to him, he couldn't imagine it. Now, for the first time since he'd left New York, he envisioned sitting at his desk.

But there was still so much to tell before they returned. What would happen with him and Eve? Tonight she was so like her young self, indomitable, yet lighthearted. It was so long since he had seen her like this.

And above all, he reminded himself, be vigilant. He must not reveal his past to anyone, even to this couple she had befriended.

Once they left the hall and were bundled into the Wolff's small car, Paul realized that Rolf didn't really know his way around East Berlin. A lot of the streets had also become one way since the destruction of the Wall. Slowly, with enough hesitations that no one could possibly suspect that he knew this city with his eyes closed, Paul gave him directions to a café the concierge had suggested.

Soon they were not far from the little park where they had sat yesterday, close to the ghostly shell of the old Neue synagogue. And here were the transvestites prancing around the cars, looking for clients. "How interesting," Rolf said in English several times, then explained to Ursula that they were smack in the middle of the Red Light District. It had been moved from the trailers near the Brandenburger Tor to here. But when some of the prostitutes assured them their car would be safe, he seemed to relax.

The café was hot, smoky, filled with young people. Snatches of English, Hebrew and German drifted towards them. It was an Israeli café, even the smells were of the Middle East, and the customers mostly Jews celebrating another huge historical change. How well they had learned to do that. You could almost taste their excitement. And, unbelievably, in the far corner, was the couple from the restaurant two night ago, the rangy man and his small white-haired wife, talking vivaciously to each other, looking years younger than they had when arguing with their son.

While they waited for a table, Paul whispered as much to Eve; when she spied them her eyes grew wide. But only at the coincidence, she was so busy talking to Ursula she hadn't yet realized what this place was. As soon as they sat down, though, Rolf announced, in slow English, "This is a *Judische* café."

Anger rose in Paul's throat. Nothing had changed. He had once heard a lecture called "To Be a Jew." The gist of it was that there is no escaping one's Judaism, no such thing as true assimilation for Jews, because, " 'A Jew is like a table,' " the lecturer said. " 'That's a direct quotation from the Englishman, Isaiah Berlin,' he went on, 'it is part of your basic identity, and although you can pass for something else, a Jew is always a Jew.' "

When he was in law school Ian had tried—in vain—to convince him that Berlin was wrong, and years later, so had Eve. She's said that no one thought of Jews in America as Jews first. They were lawyers, doctors, teachers, musicians, writers, most of all Americans, and then Jews. Paul wasn't sure, he knew his parents and Berthe agreed with Isaiah Berlin, and he never discussed it with them because it would open up a hornets' nest. But he recalled telling both Ian and Eve that even if they were right about the States, in Europe a Jew was always a Jew. No one would call a café a Lutheran café, or a Catholic café, or a Mormon café. But this was "a Jewish café."

With no warning he was filled with loathing for Ursula and Rolf who seemed far more interested in their food than them. Fine. But he took almost sadistic pleasure in watching Ursula struggle to speak English after they had gotten past the amenities. Perspiration budded her upper lip each time she began, her halting speech a contrast to the pleasant burr of lively conversation around them.

Such an invigorating hum. And so much laughter, plumes of laughter, as plentiful as the smoke. People leaned towards each other, often touching. Next to them someone turned to ask, in English, "Here to see the Wall?" Paul nodded, then turned away. He couldn't chance any more questions, not with champagne flooding his brain. He could easily give himself away; each day he seemed to be thinking more and more in German, and last night he had dreamed in German.

"We will never forget this anniversary," Ursula said very slowly. "Not because of the Wall, but because we meet. It is good . . ." she frowned, turning to Rolf, said the German word for "omen," then paused while it came to her, "I think it is a fine omen."

Over coffee they explained that their business was restoration of tin objects, chandeliers, sconces, mostly in government buildings. "But now there will be competition, and we are afraid. The West Germans don't like the East, not so much the Berliners, but the rest of Germany, people in the small towns. The Russians were terrible when they invaded, and country folk have long memories. They want to punish someone. Still, it is better to be free to come and go, democracy is better."

"Absolutely." Eve's voice was firm. "You mustn't worry. Freedom will bring opportunities, why look how optimistic the papers are. And see what happened tonight. You met us. Other chances will come." Eve spoke slowly, and her delight was contagious. Ursula smiled and translated for Rolf who raised his eyebrows and said, "We'll see."

Paul agreed with Rolf's skepticism, but he didn't want to contradict Eve. Besides, he had had enough. Excusing himself, he headed for the men's room. He was passing the coat rack when he was suddenly face to face with the man from two nights ago. He stared at Paul, recognizing him, but he clearly had no idea where he'd seen him. Then he asked, in German, "Have we met?"

"Night before last, at the French place in Savigny Platz, you were with your son," Paul answered in German before he could stop himself.

"The American?" Paul nodded.

"Jewish? You do know this is a Jewish café?" Again Paul nodded. "But your German is flawless."

"I was born here," Paul confessed, and the man's face opened, and all barriers between them fell away. Then the man's wife appeared and murmured that they had to leave. She looked at her husband with concern. Talking with Paul had left him puzzled, and pale.

"Come to the Pestalozzi synagogue tomorrow," the man told Paul. "For Shabbat. I was born here, too, and never left." He laughed a rueful, bitter laugh. "You were smarter than I," he added, clapping Paul on the shoulder.

When Paul returned to the table they were agreeing that the Sibelius was more interesting than the Strauss. "But parts of it were wonderful, and *Der Rosenkavalier* is a perfect opera," Paul said.

Ursula nodded vigorously, asking, "Do they play much German music in America?"

Incredulous, they stared, but she was serious. "Of course," Eve said. "Lots of Bach and Beethoven, everyone loves Beethoven, and Brahms, Mendelssohn, Schubert and Schumann, Richard Strauss, even Wagner."

Rolf wrinkled his nose. "Too long, too . . ." he asked his wife the English for "twisted," but she didn't know it, so the conversation dwindled and he frowned, frustrated.

Ursula looked at them. "We don't have children. After the Wall went up it didn't seem a good time, and then there were terrible things, neighbors spying on neighbors, friends betraying friends, brothers and sisters turning in each other, even wives and husbands. The *Stasi.* Not a good world to bring children into." She shrugged and described their house.

When it was Eve's turn to tell the Wolffs about their life, she simply told them about their three children, then said, "The Beethoven Pastorale was beautiful." A shiver went up Paul's spine. They had heard the Pastorale for the first time together at Tanglewood, sheets of rain streaming down and people giggling because the storm section was getting so much competition from the weather. Going to the car they got drenched, and drove to the motel in dense fog. A deer passed fearsomely close. Paul swerved, cursed, and they sat, stiff and silent until he maneuvered them to safety. In their room, relief mixed with desire, and the pleasure of peeling away their wet clothes, which clung like Saran wrap to their bodies.

Did she remember? he wondered as he watched her take a pad from her pocketbook to exchange addresses as the Wolffs insisted on driving them to their hotel. Like the cabbie from the airport, they approved of their choice. By now Paul felt drained by watching Eve be nice to these people who were, deep down, still anti-Semitic. Yet they weren't stupid. When Rolf heard strains of Dvorak coming from the conservatory (didn't they ever sleep?), he said, "Getting ready for the future," to his wife in German.

When it was time to part, Paul was courteous and shook hands with them. But he was glad to see them pull away in their tiny Russian car, which sounded more like a scooter than a car.

"Walk?" Paul asked. Eve nodded. Watching her tonight, Paul knew Dozie had been right. Each time he got one of Dozie's scribbled messages, he thought she was exaggerating Eve's serenity, but now he knew he was mistaken. Passages surfaced:

"Eve no longer eating by herself at The Black Dog, now she's inviting people to dinner, and she's more than a passable cook. Sets a beautiful table, they say, although she uses stainless steel instead of silver, Oh, I do miss you, Paul . . .

"She's become a prompter for the Vineyard Opera. Max Mayer directs and is writing an article on The Mathematics of Opera, such an odd man, such swarthy Semitic looks . . .

"Eve and Max are going to India. People are taking wagers whether they'll marry. I don't think so, she's doing much better alone than I'd have dreamed, better than I did . . . "

After that one he'd called Claudia, his palms sweating. "Yes, Mom and Max are going to India, over Passover, Mom's a little sad about being away for the holiday, but she seems excited about the trip." Not a word, though, about marriage.

After getting Dozie's notes he was sometimes tempted to write back, but Dozie didn't want a correspondence, she wanted to issue report cards about Eve. When she wrote, "You know

I'm the loneliest woman in the world, perhaps we could meet, just say when and where ... " Paul knew he'd better keep his distance. So he had Noreen, his secretary, send her flowers occasionally, and once, when she asked for it, a photograph. Now he wondered: Was it a coincidence that he had met Anna the night he got Dozie's letter about India?

16

IN THE CORNER of the lobby the small bar was empty and the bartender was cleaning up, but neither of them was ready to go upstairs. Eve flopped into a chair, settling in for a nightcap, her cheeks flushed with joy. "Weren't they wonderful, do you think they knew?"

"That we're divorced, that we're Jewish, that I was born here," he began, his tone testy. He could feel himself flush. "They are disgusting Germans who still hate Jews," he lashed out. Eve's face fell. "That crack about the Jewish café. Nothing has changed, nothing will ever change."

"I think you're jumping the gun. He was just stating a fact, and they were hardly disgusting, more pathetic than anything," she began, but her voice began to dwindle.

"Have you ever heard of a Catholic café? Or a Protestant one?" His voice grew belligerent, and he could see a speck of fright beginning to settle in her eyes. Stop it, he told himself. "Oh, forget it," he said abruptly.

Her glance softened. "Gladly. Let's not fight, not now," she said, almost pleading. She was right. Tonight was the first time they had relaxed since they arrived.

Before they could go on, the bartender put goblets of wine in front of them. "On the house," he announced, regarding them benignly. They raised their glasses with a thankful "*Salut.*" Eve slipped out of the jacket of her suit. Just that small gesture drew Paul's eyes to her, to her neck, her breasts, and again he remembered the night at Tanglewood, and he was filled with desire. He looked away before she could sense it, while the bartender told them they could stay as long as they liked and finish the wine. He put the rest of the bottle on the table and announced that he was closing but they were welcome to sit as long as they liked.

"I want to hear more about Hjalmar," Eve said, her eyes eager, still radiant with pleasure at the evening. It reminded him of the time they'd ended up at El Faro in New York with some South Americans after seeing "Carmen." Tonight, though, they were in Berlin, and he had been disgusted with those Germans she liked so much. Yet it wasn't worth arguing about, and not so important. Quickly the dark walls receded and he concentrated on the light from the lone candle between them. As it cast its luminous silvery glow Paul's voice gathered strength ...

"Soon after Aunt Sophie and Uncle Ernest were spirited to sympathetic families in the country, the Allies began to bomb Berlin. All through the autumn of 1943 the city was cloaked in a haze of purplish red. People retreated to the shelters with wet towels over their heads, but there was no way to battle the torrents of fire which snaked relentlessly in the streets, rekindling themselves as they moved. Any measure was as puny as sticking your finger in a weakening dike.

"Hjalmar had become a man possessed. When he wasn't helping the wounded, he was helping Perwe. Although he and Marga went out occasionally, more to keep up her spirits, he was determined to protect us and preferred to stay home where he could stand between our family and any intrusion. Still filled with anecdotes, black humor, news. How people were flocking like sheep to plays, concerts, films. 'As if there were no tomorrow, well, maybe they're right. Live now because you will surely die later.' When he spoke you could hear the bitterness coating his words, because he had to admit that Hitler had done far more than they ever thought possible, and even though he would not win the war, he had damaged the very soul of Europe. Why else would the British and Americans be killing civilians this way?

"You woke up each morning with only one goal: To get through the day. Food was scarce, even if you had money, there was nothing to buy; even shellfish, once plentiful, was gone. The shops on the Ku'damm looked like dioramas because their windows were blown out, our family shop now had a facade of wood boards, customers were few and far between, school was often canceled, trams were unreliable, and one night, in the calmest, saddest voice we had ever heard, Tante Hilda announced that she was leaving. 'I am no good to you. I am becoming a burden,' the old woman said. We stared; never before had she begun a sentence with 'I.'

"We tried to convince her that we could not do without her, but she was determined. 'It will be better this way,' she assured us, 'and perhaps I can help you. There is more food in the country, and perhaps I can send you some.' She had clearly been planning this for some time and would not budge.

"What she didn't say, couldn't say, was that although she adored Hjalmar, she was sick of his irritating and contentious wife, she thought Grete was spoiled, and she would not save the best food for Rose and Grete as she had been instructed and which had made her so ashamed she only spoke of it once. Our family was like kin to her, Papa's parents had treated her with the utmost dignity and so had my parents, and Hjalmar, but Marga was another story. Now she was old and didn't have the strength to shield us from this woman who insisted she was our protector. The situation had become intolerable, because, like all petty people, Marga was a master at lying to herself.

"Tante's home was a tiny town not far from the farm Mamma's family, the Strassers, had owned for generations. Where we all went for the summer, even as late as last year, jumping on the train, like everyone else escaping the Berlin heat, not even taking the clothing sewn with the yellow stars. Equipped with false papers, Tante Hilda as our cover.

"Yet now she was leaving.

"The very next day, in the middle of November, Hjalmar and Marga took her to the Zoo station. Trains were packed with fleeing Berliners, people disgusted with Hitler and his gang. Clearly, the Fuhrer had gone mad. 'They'd say 'Heil Hitler,' and salute the conductors, but as soon as they were getting into their seats they began to lace into Hitler for everything, for the bombing, for Hamburg, for no food, the crowded train, not at all afraid,' Marga reported in awe.

"'Why should they be afraid, they have nothing left to lose,' Hjalmar retorted while we were listening that night to the BBC. He had stopped talking of afterwards, of the true Germans who might marshal effective resistance against Hitler. And, unbeknownst to their wives, he and Papa were exploring alternatives to this dangerous game of hide and seek. Some Jews were still getting out, with the help of Perwe and a minister named Harald Poelchau. Also involved were members of the German nobility, the "Kreisau Circle" who were steadfastly convinced of Hitler's defeat, like Helmut von Moltke. The von Moltke farm, now run by General Von Moltke's wife, served as a refuge for fleeing Jews, they told me because I was included in their private talks. And there had been talk of a conspiracy to kill Hitler by the very same German aristocracy.

"Each week the bombing got worse, and on November 23rd and 24th, central Berlin was destroyed. Carpets of bombs creating circles of fire, people dashing for shelter like beheaded chickens, covered with blood after they tried to help the wounded, then wandering, homeless, penniless, bereft. Weeping as they stepped over bleeding limbs, groveling for scraps of food. Ambulances screeched as they delivered the bodies to mass graves. Walls ripped from buildings to reveal lives utterly exposed: now all Berlin could see how people made love, beat each other up, attempted suicide.

"How pathetic were those good German burghers and *hausfrauen*, still caring if they were seen in their pajamas. Still trying to recreate behind barricades of furniture what they remembered as a normal existence. Then, finally comprehending that though they had not believed in Hitler, they lived in *his* town, which was now a major target for the Allies. That winter was the worst: The black market was gone, water was rationed, a faint odor of gas hung over us like a poisoned shroud.

"Christmas was possible because Tante Hilda somehow managed to bribe a workman bringing machine parts to the city to deliver two geese and other supplies. Bravely we donned our best clothes: Rose in green velvet that showed her new breasts, Grete and Berthe in matching blue dresses fashioned by Marga from an old suit of Mamma's, me in a new shirt and tie Marga found in a street sale. By now I was taller than Gunther and Hjalmar. And the mothers in soft flowing wools with their beautifully designed brooches and earrings, and the men in suits and ties. For once the fireplace was banked with a decent supply of wood, and we pulled the oval inlaid table close to the warmth, and there, happier than we'd been in months, savored the Christmas goose and trimmings after the Friedmanns returned from church.

"'Let us each thank God for the blessing of life, for Tante's thoughtful contribution of this food which we are about to eat in health and together,' Hjalmar said, then looked at Papa with a gaze so transparent that everyone knew what it meant: This may be our last Christmas, my friend. A surge of fear rippled up my spine.

"In seconds my thoughts ran wild. Maybe I could get a job in a bar or brothel. I'd heard that's where other Jews were hiding. If you had something the Nazis wanted, they left you alone. Because I was sick of this ridiculous charade, and, strangely, I felt angriest at Hjalmar and all his clowning. Clowns were for peacetime, didn't Hjalmar know that? All I could think of was how I hated them all, and I hated this prison of a house. I had a chance because of my Aryan looks, I told myself, now it was time for me to be on my own, with people my age. Only then, unencumbered, would I have a chance at a future.

"What would it be like to wake free of Mamma's cringing, Marga's imperiousness, Berthe and Grete's bickering, the heavy looks that passed between Hjalmar and Papa, the tension that you could cut like a knife? Heaven!

"I looked around at their smiling faces, grateful for this good meal, still so hopeful, and I was filled with shame. How could I be so selfish? How could I leave my family? I was part of a unit. To stop my mind from running away with these horrible thoughts I put out my glass for more wine. After the third, Mamma said, 'Paulie, that's enough,' but I shook my head and downed another. Within minutes I was so sick I had to make a mad dash for the bathroom. Mamma, then Papa, held my head while I vomited up that gorgeous food.

"'What a waste,' Papa muttered. 'What's got into him? So unlike him to be so rebellious, and with drink, no less!' Later, while I was sipping peppermint tea and nibbling crackers, Papa was more indulgent. 'Well you gave us something normal to think about, a teenage boy drinking too much, I remember doing that, actually at a Seder,' he admitted, 'though not so dramatically.'

"And when Mamma sighed, then said, 'Better to get drunk for the first time at home,' It was clear that no one would want to pursue the reason for my bad behavior. This was merely another guilt I would have to bear alone." Paul stopped and shrugged, then went on,

"In January 1944 von Moltke was imprisoned by the Gestapo. So were others in the Resistance. That meant more meetings with Perwe, which resulted in a plan. The Bergers would be smuggled to Sweden, how or when they didn't yet know. But for the time being we had to stay put. By then we were feeling that almost reckless euphoria of the northern countries when the days lengthen and the air grows soft and mild. Yet not even spring could drive out the odor of ash which lurked in the hair, lingered on the tongue, seeped into the bones. Still, spring cleaning must be done.

"One March morning Marga threw open the windows. A crisp, beautiful day, with a stiff wind. By afternoon she and Mamma were pounding the eiderdowns and carpets, laughing as they used to, heedless of anything but their chores.

"Suddenly, a ring at the door. Quickly Mamma slipped into the garden shed and Berthe and Papa and I slithered up the stairs to a hidden closet above the secret attic. We had been through this before, and our movements were sure, synchronized.

"It was a worker from the shop. Papa breathed easier at the sound of a familiar voice. The tension in the closet wavered, slackened. But as he was pushing open the door, a moan rose through the house, knocking against the walls, threatening to take off the roof. Never had anyone heard such a moan. All you wanted was to escape it. Papa held out his arm to stop us, and we waited. Finally we heard, 'Hjalmar's had a heart attack!'

"Our legs turned to rubber. We were stunned. Yet Papa could not appear at the top of the stairs, nor could Mamma leave the garden shed. They and we had to endure Marga's terror and panic in silence. Rose and Grete were at school. Tante Hilda was gone. Only the worker could help. We were totally powerless.

"Officially, we did not exist." Paul's voice was cold. "But there was worse to come . . .

When Hjalmar arrives home in a week Paulie cannot believe how old he looks. Yet, in a strange way, the next month is the happiest time of their peculiar exile. After the spring holiday Rose decides she and Grete don't have to go to school, and Marga doesn't have the strength to argue with her. "So," Rose announces, "Berthe and Grete and Paulie and I will cook and clean, and you," she gives her parents a long look, "and Frieda and Gunther can listen to music and play chess and read Shakespeare." She is irresistible.

Because this house is on the outskirts of the city, it is still intact. So is the garden. It seems a miracle to watch the crocus and daffodils give way to tulips and early azalea. Each morning Hjalmar and Marga walk through the garden, as the doctor prescribed, marveling at how the buds have opened so cunningly in the night. Sometimes Hjalmar makes a sketch, to use later. Promising himself to make some outstanding pin or earrings, never admitting how it rankles him to create something so beautiful for the Nazis, now his only customers.

Grete follows them, hanging on her father's words, saying over and over, how much he is improving. Rose has no such delusions. Out of her father's sight, her gestures are dogged, discouraged, when she's with him her gaiety and exuberance veer close to hysteria. Paul tries to calm her, but for the first time she has no time for him. Sometimes she is so curt he cannot believe it is the same girl. He wishes in vain for Tante Hilda's patient ear. But he knows that Rose's sorrow is too deep to share, even with her best friend, Paulie Berger.

Before long the sharp fragrance of the viburnum mingles with the heavy sweetness of the early lilies, and by late afternoon the heady fragrance in the garden temporarily triumphs over the ashy smell of war. Then Hjalmar leans back in his chaise and closes his eyes and murmurs contentedly that this is surely as close to Paradise as one can get.

If the neighborhood is quiet—no stomping boots or sniffing, panting dogs, or even soldiers starting to carouse—they sit in the garden after supper and by the light of a small oil lamp read a Shakespeare play. Hjalmar is obsessed with stuffing them with as much English as they can absorb, and if the children stumble on a word, he corrects them with an edge in his voice they have not heard before. Later Paul wonders if Hjalmar has kept himself alive only until they could get through the most important plays, but how can someone keep himself alive? If a person could do that, we would all live forever. Hjalmar wants Paul to be Prospero, but he is overruled. He must be Prospero, this man whose rough magic has kept them going, this man they all adore. He stands, the planes of his face lit by a lonely incandescent wick and he recites:

> I have bedimm'd
> The noontide sun, call'd forth the mutinous winds,
> And twixt the green sea and the azured vault

Set roaring war: to the dread rattling thunder
Have I given fire; and the strong-based promontory
Have I made shake and by the spurs pluck'd up
The pine and cedar; graves at my command
Have waked their sleepers, oped, and led them forth
By my so potent art. But this rough magic
I here abjure, and . . . when . . . I . . . have . . . required
Some heavenly music—which even now I do—

His voice tapers, threadlike, until he cannot speak. He looks at Gunther, then at Frieda and Marga, and when his glance rests on Paul, his hazel eyes seem, as always, to know the boy's thoughts. Paul stiffens, afraid Hjalmar is going to ask him to finish the speech, but now Hjalmar's eyes seem to be begging for help. As Paul steps forward, the older man shrugs and lifts his arms, as if imploring God. Then, in the blink of an eye, with not even a gasp, he spins like a slowing top to the ground. He is dead by the time Marga gathers him to her.

Paralyzed by fear, Paulie wonders, What will they do now?

*   *   *

Paul could not remember how they got from the lobby into his room. He remembered the lonely candle flickering out, then Eve's stricken face as she helped him loosen his tie and handed him his pajamas and helped him undress. He also remembered brushing his teeth and her waiting in the chair near his bed while he fell asleep. By then her face was calmer and he felt only a sense of absolute peace as, finally exhausted, he closed his eyes.

So he was astonished when he woke a few hours later and heard her even breathing in the dark next to him. By the light of the streetlamp—she had not closed the curtains, she had always hated sleeping in utter dark—he could see she was wearing a familiar flannel nightgown, frayed a little around the collar and sleeves, and that she was sleeping, as always, on her side with one hand tucked beneath her chin.

He had thought he would tell her the whole ghastly ending to his story, but after he related the details of Hjalmar's almost uncanny death and the candle went out, they were both too emotionally exhausted to go on.

Now she stirred a little, and when she opened her eyes, she smiled at him, "Feeling better?" she whispered. He nodded, too afraid to make the first move. But she held out her arms, and when they embraced it was as if they were young again. He had imagined this for months after she left and then, again, when he was making all the arrangements to come to Berlin. It had seemed impossible. Yet here they were, her touch as silky as he remembered, their bodies still wary. It reminded him of making love after childbirth, and he was about to give up, murmuring, "I'm not sure it's worth adding sex to this complicated mix, are you?" But he had not counted on her resolve and within minutes they both began to relax and it was all right. Better than all right.

Afterwards, they talked as they never really had after making love.

"It's so sad that you never talked about Hjalmar before. You deprived yourself twice, when you lost him and by not letting him live again with us. The children would have loved him."

"I know. Gunther and Frieda talked about him when we first came here, almost as if to convince themselves he had existed. I've never met anyone so sure of what was right and wrong. Still, how could I make an example of him? Look where all his high ideals landed him?"

"Oh, Paul, how can you say that? He lived as he had to live. Besides, think about the legacy he gave you"

"What legacy?"

"That one must have convictions, do what's right, that you can't knuckle under to any tyrant, even to a Hitler."

"Eve, you're so idealistic. It's not that way at all, if anything, it's the opposite. Hjalmar's legacy to us was innocence, naïveté.

He took care of everything, but the truth is that we would have been better off if Hjalmar had been more realistic," Paul went on. "The world was more vicious than he knew. Shakespeare knew it, though. I can't believe I remembered that whole Prospero speech, it was as if Hjalmar were whispering to me."

"That's just the point. You say I'm stupid . . . "

"Not stupid, never stupid, naïve."

"Okay, naïve, but it seems to me he was behind you every step of the way, and because you could never forget him and what he did, his memory made it possible for you to go on."

"Still such an incurable romantic. In these last few days I've told you terrible, unspeakable things, and you hang on to Hjalmar. It's not that simple. He was amazing, but good and right in Hitler's Germany didn't mean a goddamn thing. I'm not even sure good and right ever mean anything. "

Eve gave a small gasp at the harshness of his words, but when he looked at her he saw that she was not frightened, no, now her eyes were bold.

"You're wrong. You can't live like that. Good and right have survived, not least because of men like Hjalmar. He did the best he could, and it got you all out of there. Give him credit for that," she flung back the covers, then sat up and swiveled her legs and stood. Now she was gathering her clothes.

Paul didn't respond.

How dare she lecture him about good and right? How dare she reproach him for not sharing Hjalmar with her and the children? Hjalmar was too sacred to share, Hjalmar had kept him going for years, until he met Henry Simmons and her. Besides, she didn't know the whole story. He bristled, exactly as he had in the past when they reached an impasse because she never knew his whole story.

But that isn't her fault, it's yours. Why did you need to keep all this to yourself? Did you need to feel sorry for yourself, or to be different, superior to the rest of them? The voice in his head was Hjalmar's. Paul looked up.

Eve's voice was firm, as she sat down in the chair facing him. "Paul, you can't blame me for what you could not do. I will take some of the blame. I should have asked a lot more questions. We both know that. But it wasn't enough to plant things like that letter from the spies who found you, in the leather folder." Finally her voice was gentler and her eyes soft as they locked with his.

"Yes, I found it, and was mystified, and also afraid to approach you. The truth is, though, you were also afraid and extremely secretive, and until you tell me everything, we'll never sort it all out. You kept blaming me for things I couldn't possibly know. You still do." Now Eve was folding her shawl. She reminded him of the curator in the Kollwitz Museum gesturing: Do what you want, whatever you want, it's beyond me. Like her shawl, she had folded into herself.

He hated the resignation that came over her as suddenly, as inexorably as anger sometimes overcame him. When he watched her in the café, piling Ursula and Rolf's plates high, Paul wondered if they might sleep together tonight. And they had, against all odds. The feeling of closeness, the sense of release—it seemed a miracle. Her generosity of spirit was a miracle. But then she asked about Hjalmar, and here they were: Stiff, awkward, separated by rancor and confusion.

Primo Levi leaped to his death in the apartment house where he was born only two years ago. At his death the world had been reminded that what made the Second World War unique was that millions were killed for an accident of birth from which they could never escape. But not even survival could save him. He had killed himself because he could no longer bear to live. So had Celan. Because their lives after the War had been filled with excruciating pain.

How dare you? he had wanted to ask the rest of those writers, the ones who danced on the graves of those who had died in the Holocaust. Do you really think sitting at Yivo and visiting every memorial in the world can teach you what it was really like in those camps, or in Berlin living as a U-boat?

But he never said a word. Nor did he speak now. He watched Eve pick up her shoes and head for the door. There she turned to face him, waiting stoically, and asked, "What is the plan for today?"

"The man we saw in the restaurant and also in the café last night is Jewish, he was hidden, too, and he invited us to come to the Pestalozzi synagogue this morning," Paul said. "And then I thought we'd take a ride to the south, near where Tante Hilda lived."

Eve nodded. "Fine with me. I'll be ready in an hour." Her voice was serene, yet she was frowning and he knew she had something more to say. Trembling at first, her voice grew stronger. "I just want you to know that there is no way I will not see this through to the end." He was too surprised to do more than nod before she left to go to her own room.

Back in her room Eve flung open the door to her terrace. The singers were at it again. This time it was "The Marriage of Figaro," and here was Countess Almaviva begging Love to help her, to give her back the Count or let her die:

"Then, why, if everything for me / Is changed to tears and grief. / Has the memory of that happiness / Not faded from my breast?" The soprano was good, with wonderful diction.

Paul adored "Figaro." And now, so did she. When she'd first settled on the Vineyard, she'd gotten involved in the Vineyard Opera Company. As prompter for the Countess, Susannah, and Marcellina, she had etched the opera on her mind, ashamed she had ever thought it tinsel. This was no silly farce about infidelity, but a magical masterpiece.

When they made love in the later years of their marriage—and it was rarely—she felt dirty, ashamed, as if all his other women were not only imprinted on his body, but on her, as well. She had never dreamed they could ever be as open with each other again. But a long marriage is like a labyrinth, filled with surprises.

You are no longer legally married. Yet suddenly all the legalities of their life had no relevance. Their marriage was still very real to them both. That was why she was here. And although the simple fact that they had made love this morning was not really so important in light of all that was happening in the world and in this city which was suddenly at a crossroads in history, it mattered very much to both of them.

Of that she was sure.

Eve thought about all he had told her. What she knew as adolescence, what her children knew, were inconceivable to Paul. No friends, no classrooms, no playing fields; no dates, no parties; none of the normal to and fro of a family with connections to the outside world. Love and contentment depend profoundly on such connections. That's why people madly in love who think they need only each other are doomed.

Yet in Paul's experience, nothing was normal, not even Hjalmar's attempts at creating joy. Every act, every thought was tinged with the smell of fear. It was bad enough to be hidden in that bewitched, enchanted house, but to be the only one in the family who went out, who dealt with the wartime city, and the Nazis roaming constantly through its streets. What did that do to him? And surely it would get worse now that Hjalmar was dead.

As she stood there, hoping that the crisp air of the fall morning would give her a sense of equilibrium, she was haunted by question after question. How had he had the courage to fashion a whole new life for himself in America? That he had gone to college and law school and become a well-known lawyer and married and fathered children took her breath away. But does that kind of blind courage arise from fear, cowardice, or maybe just plain spitefulness? Was the philandering a way to allay his anger or grief or resentment?

At this moment the soprano was singing: "Ah! If only my constancy / In yearning for him always / Could bring the hope / Of changing his ungrateful heart!" For years Eve had yearned as the Countess did, and she'd gone for help, but when the psychiatrist wanted Paul to come, too, he refused. She didn't press him, and when she finally left him, she had mistaken relief for happiness.

Not even contentment is happiness.

How vulnerable Paul had looked while describing Hjalmar's death. She had longed to take him into her arms at that moment, and before the night was over she had. "Do you still love him?" she could hear Blanche's words in her head.

Yes, she thought. Hearing his story so far had made her realize how one-dimensional their life had been, and now that she knew more . . . "Yes," she would tell Blanche. "At this moment in time, I do." Then she realized that she had forgotten to wear her new nightgown. Never mind. It hadn't seemed to matter. As she went to get dressed, still listening to the Mozart aria, her heart lifted. Somewhere in the distance there might be a glimmer of joy.

17

"ARE YOU SURE this is right?" she asked as they passed one apartment house after another: Pleasant, tidy, new buildings of red or yellow brick, but nothing that faintly resembled a synagogue. Paul studied a piece of paper in his hand. "It should be on the next block, the numbers are going down."

Just then the numbers abruptly went up. Baffled, they stopped. He took her arm, murmuring, "That concierge is much too efficient for this to be wrong, it has to be here." They took a few more steps.

"Here it is," he called, peering at the number, which was, if anything, smaller than the others, on an ordinary apartment house door. Off to the side was a small brass plaque which said, *Pestalozzi Synagogue.* "I knew he couldn't be wrong," Paul said as he rang the bell.

When the heavy wooden door was pulled open from the other side, they both gasped, speechless. Before them stretched a spacious courtyard, and then, set back, a high and stately brick building with imposing arches and stained glass windows and a prominent Jewish star over the entrance. Around the main door were carefully tended laurels and the remains of a formal perennial garden. This was a dazzling magnificence they had not yet seen in Berlin—the hues of the still-blooming asters, dahlias, chrysanthemum more intense in this protected place, totally hidden from the life of the city, from the eyes of anyone inclined to do harm.

"Something there is that doesn't love a wall." Eve could hear the Australian quoting it their first night here. But something there is that needs a wall, like Paul's family when they were hiding and the Jews of Berlin in 1989.

A few people were mingling near the doorway, and when they saw Paul and Eve, they smiled and gestured to the benches, then explained in German that they were early. The meticulous concierge had finally made an error; the service started at ten-thirty, not ten, Paul told her. Eve felt the press of his body as he took her arm and led her to a bench. The wind that had plagued them since their arrival, had calmed, and here, in this blessed space the leaves were still.

"It feels like the garden on Kuhler Weg," Paul said softly, still astonished. "Quiet, safe. A far cry from Vienna."

"Or Florence, or Amsterdam, or Rome," she said. At those synagogues, which they'd seen together, policemen stood guard with guns at the ready in wait for terrorists. Here, nothing. Eve leaned back. The air around them was spun gold, the light radiant on the deep green of the bushes and the still vibrant flowers. Though she had never seen an oasis, this came closest to what she imagined.

But instead of making Paul relax, the splendor of the place unsettled him. "I don't belong here," he began, "what can I say to that man I talked to last night? I left but he stayed, it must have been terrible here the last year of the war, by then the Nazis knew they'd lost and were crazy with vengeance and hate. Caged animals who know they are going to be killed have no mercy. Even the Catchers went nuts, wanting only to save their own skin. It had to have been horrible, they were all, Germans, Jews, everyone, close to starvation."

Their eyes met. "What can I possibly say to him?"

"Maybe you don't have to say anything, maybe all you have to do is listen."

At that Paul's face finally crinkled into a smile. Now, maybe he, too, would lean back and let the sun bathe him in its gentle glow. But he wanted to talk.

"It's wonderful here, and safe, Maybe the best place to tell you about the hardest part, with Marga and what happened afterwards." He stopped with an unfamiliar catch in his voice. "The key to it all, what I've never been able tell anyone, not any of the shrinks, not even Frieda or Gunther, or Berthe."

Eve stared. She had always thought the Bergers had experienced everything together, it had actually been a source of comfort to her to know that he had never been alone once they started wandering, but now, when she looked at Paul, she understood she had been wrong.

"I thought we'd have to go south, to where we were hidden, that's why I arranged for a car this afternoon, but I think I can tell it here, right here, now," he said so urgently Eve felt a flash of fear. Yet there was no sign of the sweating and nausea she had seen before.

Paul paused, fully intending to go on, and Eve braced herself. Now, though, Paul became vaguely aware of a small figure in a print silk suit approaching them. Eve had not moved. The figure came closer, and for a second it seemed to be his mother.

He rose. It was the wife of the man who had invited them here. "My husband would like to introduce you to the Rabbi, and several of the trustees of the synagogue. And by then the service will begin. There is a luncheon afterward, very simple, but we would be honored if you would join us. My husband is helping with the service," she told them in German.

"Thank you," Paul replied. He translated for Eve. Then he added, in English, "The rest can wait." She nodded, pushing her hair from her temples, and they followed the woman.

Simple wooden pews, set off by ochre walls, and a lavish ark and *bima*. Jews who had pride in themselves, who apologized for nothing. Who are they, why are they here? How could they stay here in Berlin? A man who looked to be in his 70s handed Paul two English books, showed him the place, and he sat there alternately following the service and looking around. Some people were his age or older, others in middle age, a few quite young, one or two families with small children who could be from Morocco or Egypt.

Several of the women were staring at Eve, but she was totally unaware. In anticipation of the end of his story, she had retreated to some place deep inside her. She was never good at changing gears. He'd seen it before: those mechanical movements, the empty eyes. She needed time. Perhaps the service would help. She always went to synagogue more often than he, her family was more observant than his, and after she moved to the Vineyard she came to New York for the High Holidays. Just entering a synagogue had always comforted her. When they married she had told him she believed in God, and although they had not discussed it in the later years of their marriage, he would guess that she still did.

When the Bergers had first come to America, he knew he didn't believe in God, but after the children were born, he wasn't sure. They say you believe more as you get older, but it wasn't something they really talked about very much. Until they parted he had always gone with her when she wished because she expected them to go as a family. Now that he thought about it, he realized he had always been home for the high holidays and Passover and Chanukah.

After the divorce, he went rarely, usually only for Gunther and Frieda's *yahrseits*. Sometimes he ran into Eve's parents. Though they were always courteous, their eyes asked: How did we arrive at this unpleasant place, feeling so strange with you whom we loved, who still call us Mother and Dad but who is no longer married to our daughter? What happened? And do you understand why we can no longer be friends? He hated it. Yet he had never implored God for help. God just wasn't in the picture.

Now Paul gave Eve his prayer book, marking the place with his forefinger. After a bit she began to look around, at the building, at the people sitting beside her.

The service was a mishmash, more Conservative than Reform, with more Hebrew than he remembered from his childhood, though the melodies were the same. The sermon was about the Wall, the peculiar German obedience to the Wall, its magical hold on them these last twenty-eight years, the possible consequences of its destruction. Intelligent, eloquent, hopeful, exactly what a sermon should be. The man's German was wonderful. To hear his native tongue spoken so flawlessly gave Paul unexpected pleasure. He who used to beg his parents not to speak it, who used to feel pain when forced to hear it.

Yet, here, now, it was perfect: The language of his youth, the language of his hopes and dreams. And the Hebrew had the plaintive, comforting sound it always had. By the time they got to *Adon Olam* the color was beginning to return to Eve's face. And then people were greeting each other. Paul bent slightly and gave Eve a kiss and said, "*Gutten Shabbos*" like those around them. As they left the sanctuary he wanted to take her hand but settled for her elbow. They stood apart while people greeted each other, then the man who had invited them approached. "I am Martin Zweig, and this is my wife, Hannah," he told them in English.

"And I am Paul Berger, and this is my wife, Eve," Paul replied in German. Together they walked down a hall into a cheerful blue and white room where tables were arranged in a horseshoe and laden with salads and Challah and wine and juice. On a bridge table was a coffee maker surrounded by empty cups and pies and cakes.

Hannah's English was halting, but she and Eve were managing, helped by a young woman who had spent some time in the States. Zweig's German was easy, straightforward.

"I was young and wild," he said, "absolutely convinced nothing could happen to me. My parents were killed before the war in a bizarre auto accident, and my sister was sent by an aunt on the *Kindertransport* and landed in the Orkney Islands. She had a wonderful family, and she is still close to them and lives in Edinburgh because she married a Scot. One of the lucky ones." He smiled.

"Some of those who went out on the *Kindertransport* suffered terribly later. There are psychiatrists in the British Isles and Canada and the United States who specialize in those patients, we even have a few here in Germany. As adults some of them feel doubly abandoned by their parents, once when they were put on the trains, and again after the parents were killed." He shrugged, his eyes clouding with sadness.

"I still don't know how they did it, the parents, I mean. But ours were dead already, and my sister was fortunate—a happy marriage and children and a grandchild on the way."

Then his voice became firmer. "My sister was only twelve. I was seventeen when the war began and refused to listen to my aunt and insisted on staying here in Berlin. I worked in a sleazy bar in Wedding where Nazis came all the time. They never had a clue about who or what I was, and I was too dumb, too rash to be scared."

A sense of release flooded through Paul. What a welcome change it was to be the listener. Now Paul gave total attention to this kind stranger who made it all sound like a harum-scarum Marx Brothers movie with him leading the Nazis on the chase of the century. Until the winter of 1944, when nothing could lighten the agony. But Martin didn't dwell on that and closed with the irony that he and two friends had to drop their pants at the end of the war to convince the Russians they were Jews. "Saved by circumcision," he murmured with a chuckle.

He looked inquiringly at Paul.

"We were hidden, in our own house, by Hjalmar Friedmann, my father's designer. My father was Gunther Berger, the jeweler," Paul began, but Martin's eyes were suddenly alight with recognition.

"I knew about you! We all knew about you, that you left Berlin and were rescued in the countryside, all four of you. It was one of the success stories of the Resistance. I knew Perwe and Poelchau, too," Martin told him, but did not give him a chance to go on. "We heard you were in America."

But now there was no more talk. Hannah had sidled up to her husband with the Rabbi, who, it turned out, was the son of a man who had worked in Wedding with Martin. "Hiding during the war made them either more religious or more secular," Hannah said, more to Eve than anyone. "In our case, it worked in the secular direction."

"But you're here, in synagogue, clearly it means something to you," Eve said.

"To me, yes, to Martin almost nothing. He comes because he had good training in Hebrew and they depend on him, and it's a social thing, too. But don't get into a discussion with him about God, he absolutely refuses to believe there is such a thing." Then Hannah took Eve's arm, and it was time to sit down to lunch.

Suddenly Paul was apprehensive. He didn't want to be questioned, but when he and Martin exchanged glances, he breathed easier. As soon as they were seated, Martin introduced Paul and Eve to the rest of the table as Americans who were in Berlin because of the destruction of the Wall. Nothing more.

The meal was delicious and gave Eve a chance to catch her breath. She was still quite pale, and Paul concentrated on making sure she ate. She obliged him, although when they finished, she still looked very tired. The Zweigs were friendly and urged them to come to their home, but Paul knew it was time to go back to the hotel. He didn't even try to explain.

After exchanging addresses, Paul hesitated, searching for a graceful way to ask the question. Martin Zweig sensed what was bothering him and put his hand on Paul's shoulder. "You want to know how I could stay here, that's what everyone wants to know."

Paul nodded.

Zweig shrugged. "Why do people stay in places that have floods, or droughts, or earthquakes? This is all I know, the only country I have ever known, it is home. It is also a good place to practice medicine. I'm a physician." All Paul could do was nod. Then they promised each other—"As well as you can promise anything in this uncertain world," Zweig interjected—that they would meet again.

18

WHEN THEY RETURNED to the Crown Prince they went to Eve's room, which was a little larger, with two matching love-seats. After Paul called Avis to cancel the rental car for today and reserve it for tomorrow, Eve said, "Now you must go to the end."

In the cab, she had thought they'd talk about the service, the Zweigs, the Rabbi, the other people they had talked to. But all that would have to wait. The urgency they had felt in that beautiful garden at the Pestalozzi had returned, and when he saw her determined gray eyes, Paul knew he would have to tell the rest of the story. Now.

As she took off her jacket and sat back into the pillows, he nodded, and went to the mini-bar to get the ginger ale she'd requested. Then he shed his jacket and loosened his tie. Eve watched him in silence. He leaned back and looked around and then, almost as if he was alone, began...

Hjalmar Friedmann's funeral, performed by Erik Perwe, is attended by hundreds of people who bought his designs, who knew his puck-ish humor, who gloried in his spellbinding zest for life, who shared his political views and admired his unswerving convictions. But the person who meant the most to Hjalmar, Gunther Berger, is not present. Neither is Gunther's family. They consider going in disguise, but it is simply too dangerous. Someone might betray them, these days you don't know who is a rabid Nazi and who is not. Lives have been shattered with a few words, no one can be trusted, everyone is afraid.

So they stand in a corner of the attic while Gunther intones, "Yis kaddal, v'yis kaddash..." Paul has heard his father recite the

Hebrew words in synagogue, but never before in this house. They resonate through the attic, yet create no comfort. What they do is emphasize the inexorable fact that the Bergers are utterly alone. They have each other, but their link to the world, Hjalmar, is gone.

When they return from the funeral, Marga and the girls seem too tired to talk and actually flinch when Frieda and Gunther try to touch them. The numbness brought on by Hjalmar's sudden death has created a hardness around them, through which nothing can pass.

After his parents and Berthe go to bed Paul sits in the study, pretending to be looking something up. Marga and Rose and Grete are talking in the kitchen over one last cup of tea. He knocks a book to the floor, hoping they will ask him to join them. They don't. He feels peculiar going in there uninvited, still, it would be so much better if they could have a good cry together. To his astonishment, they don't seem aware of him at all, he might as well be invisible.

Later, he wishes he had retreated with the others. Then he would not have heard Marga say, as he headed for the back stairs, "This would never have happened if not for them." He waits for Rose's indignant voice, expressing some logic or reason, but only hears Marga, more stolidly, "I know he would still be alive. He was obsessed with them, it was this ridiculous hiding that killed him."

A pause. Finally Rose says, "What will you do?" Her voice is small, child-like, almost unrecognizable.

"I don't know." Marga sounds so sad, as if drowning in sorrow. "But one thing I do know is that we cannot sacrifice anyone else, it's enough that Pa gave his life for them."

Paul grabs the edge of a shelf to steady himself. What would Hjalmar say to that? And how he can tell his parents what he's heard? So he doesn't say a word, even though he hears, later, the unfamiliar sound of Papa's hoarse weeping, and Mamma trying to comfort him. But Paul is grateful for what he overheard. At least one of them is prepared for what is to come.

But can one ever be totally prepared? Later that week Paul has come down to the kitchen for a glass of warm milk, Tante's antidote for sleeplessness, and here is Marga sitting at the kitchen table with a Siddur opened in front of her, saying haltingly, "Yis Kaddal, v'yis kaddal . . ." Stunned, Paul stops and tries to step backwards and close the door, but she has sensed his presence and now stares at him with strangely vacant eyes.

"You're Jewish," he blurts.

She nods. "I was born Jewish, but I converted when I married Hjalmar. I had seen them burning books as early as 1931 and I knew these people were ruthless. My parents had no interest in Judaism so before Hjalmar and I married we went to the Swedish Church and I took classes and was converted, and everyone we knew later assumed I was a Gentile, as he was. A friend destroyed my records. But once a Jew, always a Jew, that's something the Nazis know, too, isn't it?"

Now she looks up at Paul and her eyes are glassy with tears. "And for whatever reason I needed to take out this Siddur from your grand-father's library and intone the Kaddish for Hjalmar."

She speaks so simply, so eloquently. Paul hardly recognizes the woman he has begun to hate. But then she nods brusquely, more the woman he knows, and says, "I wanted to leave, but Hjalmar insisted on staying, he kept saying it couldn't happen, and when it did it was too late." She closes the Siddur *and stands. He is dismissed before he can ask if Rose and Grete know the truth.*

He tells no one. What she has told him is her deepest, dark-est secret. This knowledge turns his world upside down. But what would be the point of telling his parents? Is it possible that they know? No, he doesn't think so. But he also knows that now is not the time to take the chance of angering this complicated and some-times scary woman.

A few weeks pass and nothing really changes. He goes out to forage for food which is increasingly scarce, although they rarely eat with Marga and Rose and Grete anymore. But, still, to all outward appear-ances, nothing has really changed inside the house.

The garden has become off-limits since Hjalmar died. Everyone is more afraid because the Allies are relentless; one morning it was rumored that over a thousand planes were over Berlin. The central part of the city is a vast ruin. Berthe and Paulie have also realized that it will be complicated if the Nazis surrender, and there is no assurance that it will be orderly. The Nazis, too, are becoming more ruthless and more reckless. All safety nets for Jews are disappearing.

Then one Friday night in May, an hour after Rose and Grete have left to spend the weekend in Potsdam with cousins, Marga climbs the stairs to the attic. Catching her breath as she stands before them, she announces, "You must leave. I've wrestled with myself and I wish it were different, but I am not Hjalmar. I cannot take it any longer. If you do not leave I will call the authorities. It is enough that he died for you, but I will not sacrifice my children, too. My nerves are wrecked, so is my sanity, you must leave. Now."

No one tries to dissuade her or tell her that her reasoning is fallacious, that if she tells the authorities at this late date, they will all be killed, she and her children as well as the Bergers. She is totally irrational. They don't even try to argue when she says, "Perwe will put you in touch with other U-boats. Surely someone will help you."

They stare in disbelief. Is she crazy? By then the Swedish Church has been bombed, there is no place for Jews to find shelter, besides, they cannot survive as U-boats who dart through Berlin, sleeping here, eating there, dependent on their wits and daring. They have no skills to live that way. All they know is this bulwark of a house. And Hjalmar's need to protect them.

Still, no one says a word.

"This weekend," she adds, "before Rose and Grete return." That is the hardest part, to leave without saying goodbye to the girls, especially Rose. And never to know what she told them when they came home or how they reacted. After Marga has given her decree and leaves them, Paulie cannot believe how passive his parents are, how submissively they accept this harsh verdict.

Is this what years of hiding have done to them? Or were they like this before, and was that why Hjalmar insisted that they stay put? Why didn't they try to dissuade Marga? Why didn't they absolutely refuse? It is their house, it's been their house for generations.

But when he ventures to question his father, he gets no answers. Only a stubborn: "We must pack and go tomorrow."

Paul's anger overwhelms him. How dare Marga turn them out of their home? How dare she presume to take control of them and their destiny? As soon as he can, he leaves the house, with the excuse that he heard there was food being left outside a café nearby. He goes into the Grunewald, trying to think what to do, trying to put out of his mind the puzzled faces of his parents and Berthe's low sobbing after Marga turned to go downstairs. He doesn't know what to do with all this anger, but he knows he must do something. Then the image of Marga sitting there, saying Kaddish comes to him.

When he returns empty-handed, Gunther doesn't question him, and soon he, too, is packing his belongings. Just two changes of clothes and one book and two pairs of sturdy shoes. And of course the cash and jewels and their forged papers, some bread and a few tins Marga left grudgingly on the kitchen table for them. Even the kitchen smells different now, Paul thinks, as they scoop up the bits of food into clean rags. He lingers in the library until the house is quiet. Then he takes a sheet of blank paper from his father's desk. On it he writes: There are Jews hiding at 22 Kuhler Weg. *He folds the paper and puts it into his pocket. The next night, before they board the midnight train from the Zoo station that will take them within walking distance of Tante Hilda's village, he lingers after Gunther leaves the station rest room and leaves the folded paper on the edge of a sink. Only then does his anger dissipate enough to allow him to breathe. Let her get what she deserves.*

Paul stopped, expecting to hear a gasp, but Eve's face was impassive.

"So now you know how despicable I could be. Even at fourteen I was a monster," Paul said. She remained silent, staring at him. He could see her trying to grasp what he had told her. What he had never told another soul.

She sat there, eyes cast downwards. He waited.

When she finally spoke her voice was barely more than a

whisper, and her eyes were filled with such pity that it hurt to look at her. "What you did was monstrous and cruel, because you were living in cruel times. But you were not a monster. You were a boy, a frightened, angry boy." Her voice grew stronger. "And now you must go to the end, I need to hear this to the very end."

Paul stood up and poured two Scotches. When she tried to protest, he shook his head and said, "You'll need it." They sat there silent, averting their eyes from each other, all the closeness they had achieved this morning utterly gone. Filled with a sadness he could never hope to describe, Paul continued...

On the train a sleepy young soldier finds nothing irregular with their false papers. They doze fitfully for a few hours until their destination, then continue on foot, Paul always first, scouting.

They are lucky. The country people have no time for them, and if they are questioned, they say they've been bombed out of their home. They are given scraps and shelter in a barn where they nap a little, mounding the hay around them for sleeping. When they wake daylight is seeping away towards the horizon. Quickly they start their last lap, a walk of about two hours, under a gauzy sunset of faint plum-colored light.

When they reach Tante Hilda's home that evening, they hide in the barn, then Paul slips through the back door of her house. At the sight of him she gives a sudden cry and presses him to her. "It is a miracle!" she exclaims, and when she sees the others, she becomes faint with joy. Here is all the proof she needs that there is still a God, and she promises she will keep them safe and close to her until the war ends, she is no Marga Friedmann.

They stay with Hilda and her niece and her husband for the rest of May, which is cool and wet. During the day they sleep in the barn; at night they do their exercises, eat a hot meal, bathe, change their clothes and read newspapers and books by the light of an oil lantern under a makeshift tent in the cellar of the house. Turning day into night, night into day.

At the beginning of June rumors begin. Within the next few weeks Nazi troops will be billeted in the tiny village, something to do with art, with transporting art. Whatever brought them here doesn't really matter, the point is they are here, and Hilda and her relatives will be killed if the Bergers are found.

Then there is the Allied victory at Normandy, D-Day, the radio calls it, and everything is stepped up. The rumors are truth. A special unit of the SS is coming to this sleepy village. Tante Hilda is beside herself. Gunther and Frieda make their plans. "No farewell," Gunther instructs. It would be too devastating. Yet to leave such a haven seems madness, "and the shock of finding us gone will kill her," Frieda protests. But they can't take the risk of telling anyone in which direction they will go.

Gunther stands firm. "We have no choice." Since they were turned out by Marga, his word is law. His Bible is a detailed topographic map of the area, and only he knows exactly where they are headed.

A few days later, at dawn, when Hilda returns to the house after settling them in the barn, they wait until she goes up to her room for a nap. Then they pack food they've hoarded, leave a note, and slip into the fields. Each night another barn, where, if they aren't welcomed by the startled women and children (by then most men are gone at the Front), they are not betrayed. Always moving, trudging through the magnificent smells of the stirring, black earth, to what is surely their death. Because you can't just wait for death, you have to keep moving, and if your fate is death, it will find you. How or when you don't know, but you have to keep moving. And all the while Paulie realizing with each passing day what a terrible thing he has done.

*   *   *

In Papa's canvas bag is a piece of paper on which he keeps track of the days. They have been wandering for a little more than three weeks when they come upon a large farm that belongs to a man who was crippled during the First World War and avoided the army and tends his once prosperous farm. By their reckoning it is the beginning of

July. Near the farm is a beautiful, swiftly flowing brook where they can bathe. The daughter of the house leads them there. Utterly silent. So much of the help they get is couched in silence, when what they crave most of all is speech, company, even laughter. But that is the least of it. The girl, about Paulie's age, shyly, miraculously, puts a cake of soap and a large towel on a rock and withdraws.

They swim and wash themselves and their clothes, then lay on a bed of pine needles in their underwear while everything dries and Mamma smoothes Berthe's skirt, almost ironing it on a rock, and Papa removes the topographic map from its waterproof case and marks their route to determine where, exactly, they are. While the smell of pine and cedar and the spangled sunlight floats above them. So peaceful, the stand of trees, the brook, the healing sun. Like the Strasser farm where they swam hundreds of times, never suspecting that someday such a place could feel so blessed. After their things dry, they go back to the barn where they are fed bread and potato soup, with apologies that that is all they have, then they are given instructions by the father, who hates the Nazis. He also tells them that soon this insanity will be over. There is a plot to kill the Fuhrer, within days he will be gone.

In the black of night they begin to walk. After about eight hours they come to a path lit by a dazzling sun, and at the end, several hundred yards in the distance, looms the huge Schloss. Closer, as the man said, is a summer house—half of it built into a hill, the other half a wall of glass facing south. The farmer had said he would let "Fraulein Alix" know they were coming. When Papa wanted to know who she was, he did not reply. "Just go to the summer house and let the boy go to the Schloss. Someone will be waiting for you," he instructed. His distances are precise, the place is exactly as he has described it.

What if it's a trap? They creep nearer, unable to help themselves, like animals moving towards the scent of food. Quickly Papa motions them to stop and only Paulie approaches the structure. Then he sees it: that blue dot to the right of the highest corner of the door, announcing that here is a safe place for Jews, gypsies, deserters, prisoners of war. If you don't have sharp eyes and know exactly where to look you can miss it. Breathing easier, Paulie gently pushes the door. Its creak makes him jump a mile.

It doesn't look like a trap. There is one cot in the front, and on the tables are empty terra cotta pots and folded tarpaulins, then a long bench, and in the back corner three cots, two at right angles and one against the wall. Piled on them are linen, blankets and pillows, all clean and free of lice or fleas. He signals the others to come along.

Within minutes Mamma and Berthe are snug under the blanket on one bed, too excited to sleep but happier than they have been since they left Tante Hilda's. Slowly Papa and Paulie walk up and down the tile floor, getting used to the sound of their footsteps, trying not to be frightened by the echo. They look skeptically at each other when they spy a sink, partly hidden by another tarpaulin. The faucet works. Their joy is boundless.

When he tries to lift a pane of glass that has fallen, Papa says, "Leave it as we found it, no one must see any change." Then he lies down. For a second Paul is tempted to lie down, too, and listen to them all breathe, as he used to in the attic space in Berlin. Never realizing that he could long for what he used to think of as "the Grunewald prison."

But he has a job to do. As the farmer instructed, he goes up the sunlit path towards the Schloss. She is talking to men in work clothes, and with the sun behind her, its streaks of light framing her body, she is all angles. Tall and very lean, her elbows jutting as she holds herself around the waist, as if she were suddenly cold or a little scared. Her hair is a reddish brown, lighter where the sun strikes it.

"But Fraulein Alix," one of the men is saying, "that part of the house has been closed since the beginning of the war. God knows what is there."

Her answer is a bitter chuckle. "Now you and God will know what is there."

Paul is quite close now, yet they hardly give him a glance. They probably think he is a vagrant, that's what most people think when they see him, and when he is lucky, he gets work for a day. But now *she sees him, so he waits. She is at least two inches taller than he, and wearing a long, sensible brown skirt and a man-tailored beige shirt. Her walk is graceful, though resolute, and soon the fragrance of freshly laundered clothes mixed with a bittersweet cologne drifts towards him. Her eyes dance with a rare openness. When she begins to speak he spies faint dimples which deepen, he soon learns, when she smiles.*

"What kind of work can you do?" she asks in perfect, high-born German. His heart sinks. Something must have happened to the chain of communication. She has no idea who he is, which means he is on his own. Well, if he knows one thing, it is how to get work.

"Anything, I am strong, I've worked on farms." He puts out his hands with their filthy fingernails. She nods impatiently, then searches his face, and he waits for the usual: Are you a deserter, oh, not so old as you look, your home was burned, your mother killed? Any sisters or brothers? A litany of questions before being handed a shovel, and put to work at the lowliest job. Because a lone blond, blue-eyed boy of almost fifteen wandering the German countryside has to be the son of a German soldier (who was probably killed) and must be helped. Besides, now all Germans know how it feels to be hungry.

Her reply is a surprise. "Can you speak French?"
"Yes."

"Good. Come with me." Slowly and silently they walk around the Schloss. They pass the crew of men she was instructing before. They are prying planks of wood from doors and windows along the east wing of the castle, then opening them. She explains, "Two of them have worked here for years, the other four are French prisoners of war who speak only French. It was very peaceful until last night when I learned that the Nazis have requisitioned this Schloss, the military, I mean." She pauses.

"Three soldiers are arriving in a few days, and are going to store art here, from Berlin's museums, and from other places, too. The Schloss has very thick walls, and they will guard the art." Her voice is a monotone.

"They don't care about the art and don't even realize most of it is stolen from other countries. All they're interested in is the wine from my father's famous cellar, and heavy meals. But we have almost no animals left for slaughter, we eat only vegetables, and are already feeding the Frenchmen. And now you. With the servants and the soldiers, that means fifteen people to feed." She sighs. "Somehow, we will do it, I hope you're strong."

Then she gazes at Paulie. "There is a summer house near the path you were on. Maybe you saw it. Stay there. The soldiers know about it, they saw it when they made their initial search, and I will tell them you're there, but I doubt they will bother you. A chamber pot is stored in a cupboard beneath the bench, you can empty it in the woods to the south. You will get a meal at midday and evening, and coffee, ersatz, of course, and a roll in the morning. At seven. What is your Christian name?"

He sees no reason to lie. "Paul."

"A good name, I have a brother named Paul."

Within an hour he is given a pair of farmer's overalls—too short—and a pair of rubber boots and soon he is working with the Frenchmen, who seem to have lost their sense of smell because their odor is so stifling. But they are cheerful and sensible and bear no grudge against Paul for being German. He is not sure if they realize he is Jewish, or if they would care. That evening Alix beckons him aside and leads Paul to a small stoop behind the kitchen.

"Come here after dark tonight," she whispers. That night he finds a tray of cheese and vegetables. Quickly he empties them into Papa's canvas bag and hurries back to the summer house.

It takes only another day or so to develop a code. When there is food she wears huge china earrings, painted pansies dangling from her ears. When there is nothing she wears simple pearl studs. Mamma and Papa and Berthe rarely go more than two days without food, and of course they ration whatever they have. Mostly produce from the garden. Sometimes cooked, sometimes not. Bread, now and then a tin of sardines, or a jar of jam, probably gifts from the Nazis who are supposedly cataloging the art as well as guarding it, but who do nothing all day except play cards and drink wine and grumble about all the vegetables they have to eat.

*   *   *

The summer days are hot. While Paul throws himself into the work, Mamma and Berthe retreat into the woods while Papa stands watch, hidden behind the tarpaulin. Then after they return, he goes to stretch his legs. They have rigged a frame over the beds so that at night, in the shadows, even if you point a flashlight at the low rambling house, all you can see is Paul's bed, and not far from it a tarpaulin hanging off a wide shelf, on top of which are the largest, most cumbersome flower pots. Papa has found some tools and constructed it himself, a clever disguise for the other beds, and always scrupulously used. But no one ever comes. Even when the soldiers have "Inspection," they rarely go more than 100 feet from the Schloss and are often drunk by twilight. The Frenchmen have beds in a long low potting shed connected to the kitchen and are too tired to move after supper.

When, after a week, there is fresh linen on the back step for four beds, Paul realizes that Alix knows everything. He also knows she is the one who forages in the kitchen and puts the food on the tray, always lining it with a linen towel, and placing it carefully on the stoop after everyone else has gone to bed. Sometimes she leaves a pitcher of sugared milk with the food. Yet Paul has not spoken about her to his parents and Berthe. Do you tell anyone when you've seen an angel?

As the days turn into weeks Paul considers her his special secret, and what she does and how she looks and behaves belongs only to him. What she does is run that huge farm. Where her parents and brother and sisters have gone, Paul doesn't know, though from clues dropped here and there he knows that before the War they all lived there with a full staff of servants. A few of those are left, all women, and mostly old, and the elderly gardeners and the Frenchmen and Paul. He also knows she has never been a Nazi and may even be a member of the Resistance. But she is careful. Once she muttered that the soldiers are "mad, totally mad," but most of the time she behaves as if they are all guests in her home: the Nazis, the Frenchmen, Paul and his family, whom she has never seen.

Although she is appalled by the cigarette burns in the furniture and rugs and the windows that get broken during the Nazis' drunken orgies, she keeps her temper. But beneath her calm exterior flare convictions, passions, great vitality, maybe even a streak of wildness. You can sense it when she speaks, because her voice is as expressive as music, even violent music. And you can also sense her anger even when she shrugs off the insolent soldiers who ply her with questions or insist she kowtow to them. Paul sees all this because it is his job to bring the baskets of beans and broccoli and summer squash into the kitchen at the end of the day. Some evenings she asks him to stay and help sort the vegetables, and together they sing nursery rhymes in French and German.

How can one describe her? Wonderful long bones, and the dignity and grace of the nobility, yet with not an ounce of arrogance. No, she has an inborn shyness, a gentleness that seems to ask, Why was I born lucky? And does my luck require me to do more for those not as fortunate as I am?

Of course he falls in love with her, they are all in love with her: her servants, the Frenchmen, and Paul, maybe even the soldiers. When Paul sees her in the distance he does anything to get close to her, and when she is near enough for him to catch a whiff of her fragrance, his legs melt under him. Once when she brushed by him and he could feel the tender skin of her pale forearm, he became hard, then faint with fear that someone would see.

Paul knows about sex, Rose and he talked endlessly about what men and women do together, especially after she got her period, and he'd seen starving, desperate prostitutes prowling Berlin after Hjalmar died, while he was scurrying madly through the streets searching for tidbits that might placate Marga. But Paul has had very few sexual feelings. Hunger and fear don't mix well with sex. And Rose and Grete were like sisters.

Only Mrs. Perwe awakened something in him that could be called sexual longing, or, possibly, love, but she was probably old enough to be his mother when he saw her. So this is his first experience, and Alix is as beautiful as any man, or boy, can wish. Her high breasts and lithe, narrow hips haunt him. And her face is exquisite, her features even, perfectly placed in her gorgeous, rosy complexion. She usually wears her long, wavy hair up, and when dampened with sweat a few stray hairs sometimes escape, then loop into tantalizing curls. Anyone in his right mind would have fallen in love.

Besides, they seem to be living in a cocoon. Later they hear that the plot to kill Hitler failed, but Alix refuses to listen to Nazi radio— to protect them or to protect herself, Paul never really knows.

One day the cows find a way out of the pasture and as they are rounding them up one gets loose and takes off in the direction of the summer house. With his heart in his mouth Paul chases it. Papa is standing guard and Mamma and Berthe are coming back from the woods, carrying a basket of berries, gabbing as happily as if they were at the Strasser farm. Paul starts to coax the cow to come with him, and, suddenly, Alix is there with a rope in her hand, smiling at the cow and at the four of them so absorbed in getting the cow to obey they have forgotten where they are. She gives Mamma and Papa and Berthe a little bow of greeting, then calls firmly to the cow, puts a lasso on her, and she and Paul walk with the animal back to the pasture. They don't exchange a word. She has known they were there, but what astonishes Paul is how she looked at them, that there was such enormous benevolence in her eyes.

Strangely Papa and Mamma and Berthe don't ply him with questions. It seems understood that Fraulein Alix is above anything resembling gossip, and that, in a profound way, she is not theirs to discuss.

She belongs to Paul.

Each morning he wakes up, excited at the prospect of seeing her, and filled with admiration for her willingness to help them: strange Jews about whom she knows nothing. "Why?" he longs to ask her, but, in his heart he knows the answer, "Because it is the right thing to do."

He becomes obsessed with her, she seems the one sane thing in an insane world, and they all need to know she is near. Somehow she senses this, and when they can't see her, they often hear her because she is a wonderful pianist. Each day she plays: A Bach Prelude and Fugue, then Chopin or Schubert or Mozart or Schumann or Beethoven. That summer she is learning Beethoven's Opus 26, the one that starts with variations, then goes into the Funeral March. As soon as she begins that sonata, everyone breathes easier. As if everything—the trees and grass and the phlox and hollyhock and daisies, as well as the grosbeaks and swallows and finches that swoop around them—can finally relax a little. Stop and listen, the notes command, and I will tell you what matters in this life, what can rescue us from this miserable existence we have been forced to lead.

With such music emanating from the Schloss how can the world be hurtling towards its death? How can Germany have become the inferno it now is? Is there not some higher goal which will somehow erase the horror? These are the questions they are asking during that summer of 1944. By then they know all too well that the camps are not mere waiting places until the Germans can figure out how to make the country Judenfrei, but extermination camps. The truth is, that although they have not wanted to admit it, they had known since the Wannsee declaration that the people who were marched at night to the Halensee Station holding those orange paper bags that glowed under the Nazis' flashlights—unmistakable bags filled with sandwiches made by the Jewish volunteer organizations—had an appointment with death.

Paul is asking himself other questions: What happened to the Friedmanns? Have they been picked up? If they have, can they escape? Questions that should paralyze him, but that somehow recede within the circle of Alix's radiance. When he can feel the warm earth in his hands and hear that superb sonata drifting from the castle, he isn't afraid. He can forget what he did and exult in the simple fact that he is alive.

Some days Alix begins by playing the entire piece through, other days she works on certain difficult passages. By early August she is

doing the spirited last movement, which is like a postscript, remind-
ing her listeners that joy comes after sadness. After she has practiced
that sonata she is always cheerful, and her outlandish pansy earrings
which lurch back and forth when she moves, make Paul happy, too.

For three nights in a row Alix plays the Beethoven while they eat.
As if these are dress rehearsals for some imaginary concert. After she
finishes, her face glowing with exhaustion, she stands at the end of
the long table, filled with pride that she can feed them all. Looking
at her you feel she is guarding a secret, and that she and those who
believe in her are approaching the brink of something tremendous,
something rapturous. The air around her, her gestures, her playing all
throb with an eerie splendor and excitement.

The fourth evening she asks Paul to follow her into the music
room where two grand pianos wind around each other, like a pair
of huge cats dozing, in the bow window. A magnificent room with a
gold leaf ceiling and painted wall panels. When she sees Paul look-
ing at the panels, Alix murmurs, "Ovid. The Metamorphoses. *My*
father's favorite classic." He wants her to explain them, he doesn't
know them, but she just gives them a glance, then asks, "You know
my sonata, don't you?"

He nods, looking around, afraid the soldiers might barge in, as
they so often did. "Oh, don't worry, they're gone, they've gotten bored
here, they know the art is safe, so they've gone away for a few days.
Good riddance. How do you know this piece so well?"

"My parents had a recording of it. And I know they played the
Funeral March at Beethoven's funeral. They played it at Uncle
Hjalmar's funeral, too, when he died, that's why we're here," Paul
begins, then stops, feeling his cheeks flush. For a second he imagines
telling her everything, how they were hidden, how they were turned
out, how he betrayed Marga and her children. But his thoughts get
tangled in his brain when he feels her staring so intently at him, so
he stops.

Impatiently she shakes her head. "It doesn't matter, all that is
past, but what I want to tell you is that one of these days you'll hear
it again, all of you, in a concert hall. Because soon this madness will

*be over, the Resistance is still alive, and one day soon we will be able
to live like human beings again and walk without fear in Berlin and
Dresden and Munich. Because there are people who believe in good,
not evil. German people. The true Germans, who will triumph."*

*Then her voice slides into a higher range and is filled with quiver-
ing delight. "Who knows, Paul, maybe you and I will meet someday,
on Unter den Linden, or near the Tiergarten." Dumbstruck, he stares
at her. He has never told her they are from Berlin. But she simply
tosses her hair over her shoulder, and laughs gaily and goes to the
piano and plays the sonata through. She is still playing when he
walks back to the summer house that night.*

*The next day when Paul enters the kitchen, tension fills the air.
"Come," says Jacques, one of the Frenchman, and he leads Paul into
the music room. There are the three soldiers, drunk as lords, hanging
over Alix as she now starts to play some honky-tonk cabaret songs
from music they have brought with them. Watching them are the
other Frenchmen and the gardeners.*

*When they see Paul one cries, "Ah, here he is," and he thinks it is
all over for him, that they will fall on him and tear him to pieces, as
coyotes fall on dogs. Instead the older soldier puts out his hand for
her to stop. "Get the women," he commands Jacques, motioning for
everyone to sit in the chairs arranged around the piano, him in the
middle, in front.*

*As soon as everyone is assembled they hear a click, and suddenly
the two younger soldiers are pointing their guns at them while the older
soldier stands there and says, through a clenched jaw, "Now, quiet,
and if anyone moves he is killed." Then he taps Alix on the shoulder.*

*Ah, now it will happen, now she will say something to stop this
silly sadistic game, Paul thinks. But he is wrong. As the soldier starts
to pull her towards him, kissing her neck and shoulder, placing his
hands on her breasts, Paul watches her face go blank. She doesn't
even look like herself. In speechless horror they watch her limp body
being pushed onto the carpet, then her skirt lifted with one hand
while the soldier unzips his pants with the other. The other soldiers
click their guns again in warning, and no one moves. All of them*

are transfixed, horrified. Not only by the man's coarseness, but even more by Alix's refusal to fight, by her resigned acceptance of the man's crude caresses and murmurs. She simply turns her head away.

Would that drunken soldier have eventually stopped without any encouragement from her? They will never know. Because within seconds Alix's personal maid begins to wail, and the soldiers are startled, and suddenly the Frenchmen have knocked the guns from their hands, and everyone, the servants, the French, and Paul, fall on those soldiers and Paul can feel a huge wave of relief that at last this charade of terror is over.

But it has just begun. A melee, with the older soldier still holding Alix down, and the others screaming about her collaborating with Resisters, hating Hitler, helping Jews. Shrieking that she and her fancy friends will die, that it was she and her kind who had ruined Germany, until Jacques aims and shoots the two Germans who are standing. He motions to the last soldier who lies on top of Alix to stand. Everyone stares as the man rises, raising his hands, thinking, when she doesn't move, that she is too exhausted, or frightened. But they are absolutely confident she will rise and, in her firm, no-nonsense way, tell them what to do next.

Then the Nazi says, "You stupid fools. She's dead. I broke her neck. It's one of the first things we learn, one motion, and finish."

At that Jacques shoots him between the eyes. Then the Frenchman goes closer, a sob escaping his throat. A sob so terrible Paul can hear it still. A sob that made the wails that day of the Kindertransport seem like nothing, that made Marga's cries when Hjalmar died seem restrained.

She died without a sound. "It would have been better if we had died with her, all of us," Jacques says. Then he leads Paul into the kitchen.

Paul sits, aware only of a deep sensation of cold, an iciness on his skin, in his bones; he is convinced he will never be warm again. Her silent, cold-blooded murder makes him realize what he has not been able to admit before: he has sent Hjalmar's wife and daughters to these murderers, and any fantasies he may have had that they could be safe have been shattered. These Nazis are not human. Violence runs in their veins.

Finally, Paul understands that he has delivered Marga and Grete and Rose to their deaths. He becomes desolate and stops speaking. And from then on, his betrayal of the Friedmanns is forever entangled with Alix and her death.

*   *   *

The room was utterly still. Eve could not speak, but she could see that he wasn't finished, and after a long pause, Paul went on,

"Her death was probably part of the vendetta against the aristocracy after the July 20th assassination attempt against Hitler. She was wrong about there being more resisters that summer, hundreds were executed after July 20th. Or maybe those Nazis were bored, and hated her confidence, her noble birth. Class consciousness in Germany has always been a kind of disease. Or maybe they were tired of lusting after her. Or maybe they knew their days were numbered and needed to flex their muscles, kill before you are killed.

"I never knew and never talked about it because I promised Jacques I would never tell anyone, not even my family, what had happened. I think that to him silence was a way of containing the evil we had witnessed, or perhaps he insisted on it because he was ashamed of our passiveness. Not mine, because I was the youngest there, but his and the other Frenchmen. I don't know. I have wondered about it thousands of times and I have never come up with a logical answer.

"It turned out that the Frenchmen had known all along about us, but when Jacques insisted on secrecy, all I told Mamma and Papa and Berthe was that Fraulein Alix had had a freak accident while horse back riding.

"We built a pine coffin and they said Papa could come with me to the graveside deep in the woods and they let us throw dirt on her coffin and say *Kaddish*. I think Papa suspected something when he saw the terror on everyone's face, but he never asked and I didn't tell. Were we next? That very night Jacques gave me a map marked with a star. We were to head to a village about forty kilometers away where there were people who would help us. We had to leave immediately because the Nazis would be sending others to find out what had happened to the soldiers.

"We got to the village two days later. They were expecting us, and we stayed almost a month. But I did not speak during that entire time, and all I remember is Gunther and Frieda forcing bread soaked in a weak broth into my mouth. It was as if I was committed to silence forever, it seemed to me that if I spoke I would have to tell not only what had happened with Alix but also what I had done.

"After several weeks we were given instructions to go north where we might get to Sweden. By then things had changed, the people had heard Hitler on the radio after the July 20th plot, and even the most rabid Nazis had to face the fact that he was a raving lunatic. They also knew the English and Americans were coming from one direction, and the Russians from the other. Saving a few Jews might mean their own survival. It was laughable to watch their faces when they wanted to help us, as if we were some longed-for reward.

"By then I was more dead than alive. My parents took turns staying awake at night, afraid that if they didn't watch me I would somehow slip away. While we were wandering that autumn I began to understand that the Schloss was famous, and so were Alix and her family, and there couldn't be any connection between them and us because her parents and sisters were in a camp. They had been put there when her brother Paul, who was at Cambridge, was interned in England, and Alix was studying in Switzerland. By the end of 1943 she had obtained permission to return, supposedly to run the farm and supply food for the Nazis, but really to try to free her parents. Sometimes I think she knew she was marked for death, and playing the piano kept her brave. Other times I think she was innocent and didn't have a clue and played because she wanted to give us something beautiful, something that would let us know we had a future. Maybe it was a combination.

"But I couldn't speak about her death, even to the men on the reconnaissance mission who found us. They questioned us for hours at a long refectory table in a farm kitchen and kept giving us chocolate while we told them about the Schloss and the art, but only the bare facts about Alix. As soon as they had heard those, they decided to get us out of there as soon as possible.

"We were actually taken by a car fitted out to look like a hearse north of Berlin, and then we boarded a train for Stettin. There we were taken by boat across the Baltic to Sweden, where we rested for a while, and bought new clothes. Finally, I began to say a few words and my parents knew I had not become mute from either grief or fright. They began to breathe easier, and I remember going to a Jewish house for Shabbat and realizing, at last, that we were safe and would remain safe.

"From there it was arranged for us to fly to England. Soon after we arrived, in the first week of December, we heard that a plane carrying Erik Perwe to Sweden had crashed near Falsterbo, either shot down by Germans or blown up in the air because of sabotage. Everyone was killed. Our connection to Perwe had a weird symmetry, and now the circle was closed, utterly closed."

Paul finally leaned back and closed his eyes. "Tante Hilda survived and we corresponded with her." He paused and looked directly at Eve.

"After the war I found out that the Friedmanns had been picked up and sent to Theresienstadt. That's all I have ever been able to find out.

"In England I was tutored by a wonderful man named Henry Simmons, a retired physician who sensed some of what I was hiding and never pried, but somehow conveyed to me that I could continue to live, no matter what. We read *The Iliad* and

The Odyssey to improve my English, and when it was time to go to the States, I was in better shape.

"When we got here, I was convinced that I could put my past behind me. Only when you are young can you have such a conviction. But it worked through college and law school, and then when I met you and we fell in love, I felt invincible. You and the children were my protection. But as I got older and more came out about the Holocaust I began to understand all that had happened and my anguish haunted me.

"The dawns were the worst. I would be haunted by Marga and Rose and Grete, their faces would get mixed up with Alix's face, and when I saw yours, which was the closest thing to hers, I became totally confused. The most terrible times were after you and I had made love, then I would sometimes dream of Alix, such vivid dreams that the reality of the morning seemed a trick. And I would be convinced that everything I had would be taken away from me. You'd think that that would have made me more cautious. But it didn't work that way. I think that in my heart I knew everything would eventually be taken away from me, so I became more and more reckless. I behaved badly, very badly, yet didn't seem to know what I was doing until I had done it." When Eve looked up, his eyes sought hers.

"Time didn't help, nothing helped, and although I stopped womanizing, my suffering seemed to be getting worse rather than better over time. No one should have to carry so many secrets around for so long. And contrary to what people think, they don't fade. Time doesn't really heal certain memories. Secrets grow more powerful, more oppressive over time." His eyes were so intense Eve had to look away, but she couldn't escape his voice. He stopped and looked down, ashamed.

"But when I saw the Wall being destroyed, I knew I had to do something. I could not go on like this." At last he was finished.

Eve could not make a sound. She felt disembodied, her senses plucked from her flesh. Her fingers scraped her lap but she could not feel the wool of her skirt. She had envisioned some closure from this trip, but nothing like this. What startled her most was that he had told the story so simply, so nakedly, and behind each word, was the immense sadness that Isherwood understood so well.

Why would someone have to reinvent himself? What was he trying to escape? She had known, deep inside of her, that it had to be something shocking, but the truth was that she hadn't wanted to know.

Who in her right mind would want to know?

As she saw the abject shame on his face, she felt that she could actually see into his brain. Where there was a skein of confusion and a need to punish those who had punished him. A skein so tangled that no one could even hope to unravel it.

Suddenly she understood why he had remained silent.

How could you tell inflict such a ghastly story on someone else? Who would believe you? A strange psychiatrist? A wife who loved you? No, better to remain silent and tell yourself that the memories would fade.

Yet, such memories do not fade. But by the time Paul learned that, it was too late. So you try to live with the knowledge you have gained. But how? And how is it possible to apply any moral principles to a fourteen year old under such duress, such stress? By the time they were turned out of the house on Kuhler Weg the very idea of individual will was meaningless. Marga had become crazed by her grief, and Paul had become crazed by his anger. Everyone was marked for life, whether or not they had a number on their arm.

And then, the worst question of all: How would *you* have behaved against such odds?

PART III

19

THEY LOOKED like any couple from either England or America going to see this new, much touted production of "Cabaret." They had heard about it as soon as they arrived and she had asked the concierge the first day, when he showed her the map, but he had been quick to inform her that there were absolutely no tickets, it was sold out for the entirety of its run. Then, this afternoon, within minutes of Paul describing Alix's brutal death, the phone had rung and the concierge was announcing in a triumphant voice that he had secured two tickets for tonight, last minute tickets that had just come free, and for Saturday night, when the troupe gave the best performance. "House seats, I have a friend who works on the sets," he blared into the phone. "The performance is at eight."

So, against all expectations, or reason, here they were. Just one more bizarre occurrence in a series of bizarre incidents that had happened to them since they had arrived. After they were seated, Eve looked around. Along with the many other visitors were lots of families, fathers and mothers and grandparents with young children, even though it was Saturday night.

Eve remembered seeing John van Druten's "I Am a Camera" when she was in high school and when it was turned into "Cabaret" in 1966, she and Paul had been knocked out by the production with Joel Grey and Lotte Lenya and Jack Gilford. That night they left the theater convinced they would never see anything to match it.

Yet here, before their eyes, was a "Cabaret" so unique and stunning in its frankness that they found themselves gasping for breath as they watched. All the effects had been conjoined to create the most nightmarish take on this material: The Nazis were more despicable, the story had more violent overtones, Sally Bowles was wilder, and the foreboding of all that was to come sharper, more piercing. Here was Berlin in the darkest night of its history with all its mystery, its daring, and its capacity for terror and cruelty before their eyes. Riveted by the performances, they were astonished by the edginess of the production. No one was spared—not even the audience. You've come for entertainment? We'll give you an entertainment you will never forget!

As she sat there taking it in, feeling her heart race at times, Eve noticed a family to the left of them. The grandmother was explaining to a boy and girl who looked about eight and ten what was happening on stage. Although Eve couldn't hear the words she could see how badly the older woman wanted those beautifully dressed children to understand the story.

"It seems a bit raw for the kids," she remarked as they left their seats for the first intermission.

Paul shook his head. "I could catch some of what she's saying. She's not really telling them the story, she's only pointing out the political implications." He paused. "The warnings no one paid attention to, the way the Nazis were insinuating themselves into the society. I guess she's trying to expiate her sins, she was certainly here, she's probably my age, or even a bit older."

Before Eve could answer, a well-dressed American man of about fifty approached them, saying, "Not exactly what I expected. They certainly aren't afraid to tell it like it is." Waving off anything that could be construed as a reply, he barreled on, "But you have to confess that things are better here, they're admitting what they did and taking responsibility for it, the children are all learning English in school, and anti-Semitism is a hate crime." Then he disappeared into the crowd.

What does it mean to take responsibility for those sins? Surely a night at "Cabaret" is not enough, Eve thought, as Paul said, "Now he'll go back to his church in the States and tell them everything has changed because he saw this amazingly honest production of 'Cabaret.' He'll soothe them with platitudes about the world being a better place, forgetting, of course, about Vietnam and Laos and Cambodia and Africa. Or," he hesitated, "that what's portrayed in this show is merely the tip of the iceberg."

The second act was even more effective, really a version of all Paul had related, Eve realized. And that's when she felt herself losing control. At the reprise of "Tomorrow Belongs to Me," Eve finally wept. She wept not only for what was depicted on stage, but for what she had heard these last days, for all that she knew about this horrible, unique catastrophe that had been named, for want of something more precise, The Holocaust. For the vicious things that had happened here, for the Bergers and the Friedmanns and Alix and the Frenchmen and the piles of emaciated bodies found by the Russians and the GIs and the families left haunted by fear and loathing who longed in vain for a speck of contentment as they endured the present and the future. For Celan and Levi and the others who could not continue to live. Even for the reconnaissance team who found the Bergers and didn't quite know what to make of their story.

She excused herself and went to the Ladies Room, the tears pouring out of her. She sat there, while women came and went, staring at her with fear in their eyes, curious, yet not really wanting to know why such a nicely dressed, still young woman would be so upset. Not a single person offered solace or help. They were too afraid to ask.

Finally, she collected herself, and soon they were in the cab going back to the hotel. There Eve said, "So much for Nabokov thinking Isherwood is *kitsch*."

*　　*　　*

The next morning Paul asked the concierge if the Jewish Community Center on Fasenstrasse was open. "Of course, sir, it's part of the Jewish Museum, but it's really best to go when the archivists are there, that is if you want to look up any names. Those offices are closed on Sunday." So they decided to stick to their plan of going south in the direction of the *Schloss*, so Eve could see the countryside where the Bergers had wandered.

As they walked, Paul thought: Life always intruded, that's what it means to live. They had been rescued from their extreme emotions by the performance of "Cabaret." And going to the play had brought them back to the reality of their lives: That they were tourists in Berlin with only a few days before they had to get home to celebrate the justly famous American Thanksgiving.

Now he remembered Blanche describing how, after Jack died, she would hear his key turning in the lock. "It was impossible, I knew it was impossible, yet I heard it. Until life found me again." What accurate eloquence. He's always loved Blanche and hated the mistrust in her eyes since the divorce. Like the other night. Monday night. Less than a week ago.

How can so much have happened in a week? he wondered.

And how could they begin to talk normally again?

He sighed and let Eve set the pace. After a few minutes he plunged in, telling her, in as casual a voice as he could muster, about the couple who had invited them to the Pestalozzi synagogue. "The first time we saw them, they were arguing with their son, Theodor, Ted, named for Herzl, about his marriage. He's fallen in love with a Protestant girl. So ironic, yet Martin is amazingly rational about it. A lot more tolerant than most would be in his place. He told me, 'That's the risk I took when I remained in this totally crazy city.' He met Hannah in Munich, they were both studying there, and she'd been hidden in a convent. He's a doctor," Paul reported as they turn into Budapesterstrasse.

"I'll tell you more in the car, it's fascinating, he's got real guts, and the most amazing optimism," he added.

*   *   *

Eve couldn't believe she was on her feet. When Paul had finished his story she had thought, I must sit here and let the words sink into my brain. She had wondered, How had he borne this knowledge all these years alone? But she had also wondered, How do you go on after hearing this?

Then the phone had rung and she heard the concierge's triumphant voice and they were getting dressed and sitting in the theater and she had cried—but only begun, she now realized—and they had gone back to their rooms and slept fitfully, and separately (any more intimacy between them seemed, suddenly, out of bounds) and here she was, walking to the rental car place.

How, she really didn't know.

But, finally, she had been given the gift of the truth. What if the truth is a story of horror and betrayal?

It is still a gift because it is the truth.

Yet now she understood why he had never told it; keeping it secret was completely consistent with his personality and their life. When they were courting he had been so amazed by what he called his "great good luck." She never understood what he was talking about and with time the phrase began to annoy her. When he said it, she felt as if she were in a play, and that sentence the first lie in a long string of lies.

She was wrong. He had truly believed in that great good luck, and although he had thought he would tell her everything when they married, he had convinced himself over the months and years that his luck might disappear if he did. Especially when she was not responsive after he tried, however feebly, to begin.

Again she remembered them sitting under that radiant sky in Switzerland. How much grief they might have avoided if it had all come out then? Or might it have ended their marriage? It was possible, she was younger then, saw the world more in black and white. What would have happened if they had parted then, when the children were young and still needed them?

"Damned if I do, and damned if I don't," he used to say when faced with a difficult case. But this was the most difficult case of all.

Now, though, it was all in the open. No longer a festering wound, hidden under bandages. Yet what could one do with such terrible information?

She could hear the clack of her heels on the pavement. So quiet. Sunday morning in Europe. The shops closed, a few *"Bittes"* and *"Dankes"* as people with children wove through the streets, heading for playgrounds where they would push swings, fly kites, have a cup of cocoa to warm up, then window shop with weary children pulling on their hands all the way home. Where they would feed the children lunch, read, listen to music, tidy up the house while the children napped.

Eve sighed. People living what looked like normal lives on these streets and houses that had been anything but normal. Always back to the same thing. Now the sun was behind the clouds, the sky a bleak gray. Eve wished she had her raincoat. But soon they'd be in the car. She longed to sit next to Paul in a car, cars were where they had done their best talking when they were young. Where, hopefully, she would gain some stability, some strength to go on.

Soon the neighborhood became seedier, giving way to ancient antiques shops, then pawnshops and bars. Scraps of paper rose about their heels as a faint wind began to shudder through the streets. Finally Eve spied the Avis sign. As her step quickened, she caught some English. Turning the corner was a bunch of American kids, six, she counted, probably in college, jabbering, laughing, poking each other—doing the universal dance of youth with just the right amount of American cockiness to identify them.

As they approached, Eve could feel relief when she heard their English, and she, who was usually reserved in situations like this, now pressed Paul's arm to stop. "Where are you from?" she asked the group—three boys and three girls.

"We're studying in Munich, graduate school, three of us are in linguistics and two in art," a Korean boy replied with a warm smile. "Doctoral studies. I'm Michael and originally from New Haven so I went to Yale and lived at home. But these guys are from the Midwest, went to Kenyon and Carnegie Mellon."

"You look so young," Eve said.

"We know, they keep proofing us when we want a beer. Very precise, these Germans, absolutely play by the rules," one of the girls offered. "But I'm originally from New York."

"We are, too," Paul finally joined in.

"Isn't it exciting? The Wall, I mean. Watching all this exhilaration and hope, it's amazing, especially in this place. So dreary in the east part, have you seen those depressing apartment houses?" Michael asked.

Eve nodded. Then he went on, "Are you here because of the Wall?"

Paul shrugged a little, saying, "Basically, but it's a long story, too long to go into, I lived here when I was a child. This is my first time back," he offered, surprising Eve. But these kids were too fixated on the Wall to be curious about Paul.

"Fabulous, isn't it, to see history being made before your eyes. We had to come, although our professors in Munich didn't think it was such a big deal. I can't understand why they'd think that, but we didn't listen, and here we are." There was a pause.

Then another voice, a girl's, chimed in, "The truth is they should have come, too. It's amazing to talk to students from the Eastern zone, they're so full of energy and hope. It's like the beginning of the world for them." She linked her arm through Michael's, and he looked at her with pride and affection.

Another added, "And besides the Wall and all the rubble around it, we were lucky enough to catch an amazing production of 'Cabaret,' you mustn't miss it. The agents all have tickets, but at terrifically expensive prices. But it's worth it. Really biting, with a cruel edge, much better than the movie. Even better than Joel Grey. Awesome."

"We were there last night," Paul broke in.

"So were we. Did you see all those older people and their kids and grandchildren? We talked to them, they were interesting. One woman said going to things like this is part of their repentance. She told us that even though it's upsetting, they must do it and take their grandchildren."

"Not nearly as upsetting as spending time in a concentration camp," one of the girls murmured. When Eve stared at her, she said, "I'm Jewish, I'm not finding this as much of a lark as they are." She tilted her head and the others looked abashed. "There's something barbaric about this city. You can feel it in the air. And the people are so extreme—so rigid and proper, or utterly wild. When the men have too much beer in them they scare me. I know they went through the War and then the Russians came, but this doesn't feel at all like Paris or London," the girl went on.

"No, it doesn't," Paul said and looked at her thoughtfully. "It never did."

Then one of the boys said, "Oh, Rachel, you're exaggerating. You've seen that kind of drunken horniness at fraternity parties in college. I'll bet you even saw it back in sleepy Dayton, Ohio."

Stubbornly, Rachel shook her head. "No, I didn't. This is different. This whole place is different, maybe that's why the Gestapo was here?" She looked at Paul for corroboration, but he simply shrugged.

Then Michael asked, "How long do you think it will be before the Communists will have to tell it like it is, too? We learned at college that Stalin killed far more people than Hitler."

"Oh, Michael, enough, that's just too damned depressing," one of the boys rejoined, punching him in the upper arm and said, "Come on, guys, we have a ton of things to see."

With that they started on their way, calling over their shoulders, "See you in New York," and waving carefree, easy farewells.

As they retreated, Eve said, wistfully, "Maybe we can try to get through to the kids tonight?" Seeing these young people had made her wish Claudia had met them in Berlin. But would Paul have told his story then? She doubted it.

"Of course. Good idea. It'll be easier to reach them on a Sunday afternoon." Paul took her arm and they started to walk again. From the corner of her eye she could still see the Americans scampering along, their blithe happiness making her smile for the first time in twenty-four hours.

All at once, though, Eve sensed a peculiar shift in the air, a change in the voices now floating towards her and Paul. She stopped and listened. What she thought was happy banter had become something else.

"Paul?" she said, nervously plucking at his arm and turning back into the direction from which they came. In a flash the Americans were surrounded by motorcycles, shining black motorcycles, and shiny black helmets, shiny leather jackets and pants. At first Eve thought she had reacted too quickly, that the two groups were talking, exchanging ideas, after all, what could be better?

But then, there were tentative sounds of guarded dread, then downright alarm. At first faint, then coaxing, even peremptory. Finally, one of the boys said loudly, "Come on, you guys, this isn't funny. Now let us pass, you have no right . . . please . . . don't be so ridiculous, you've got to let us get by . . . " Fright mounted in his voice.

"Paul!" Eve cried and began to run as pandemonium began to break loose. As she came closer, the voices grew louder, a nervous mix of English and German, and now the motorcyclists were focused on Michael, springing off their cycles, yelling in a mad tangle of German and English. But out of the muddle came, all too distinctly, a bully's snarl in perfect English, "Get out of here, slit-eyes, go back where you belong with the other geeks!"

With Paul at her heels, Eve began to fly. Never had she moved so fast. When they reached them the Americans were making a wall around Michael but the cyclists had begun to push through, their faces ugly. They were too impatient for any more talk and were now punching blindly, simultaneously yelling, "Fucking Americans, coming here, trying to tell us what to do."

Never had she felt such rage. Her head was about to explode. Rapidly, Eve calculated her best move, then flung herself at the one punching Michael, tackling him. A technique the twins had once made her learn when they were about twelve. Digging her elbow into the back of his knee until his leg went limp and he gave an astonished curse.

Seconds later Paul was shouting in German, and the tearing, cruel sound of the scrape of bone against the pavement, and finally, a shocked silence as they all—Americans, Germans, converging bystanders—stared speechless at the blood seeping onto the sleeve of her suit. Her wrist bone had broken through her skin and now Eve regarded it with total disbelief. It seemed disengaged from her body, and for a few seconds she felt nothing. Then, slowly falling back into Paul's arms, she could feel her legs go out from under her, as she succumbed to the pain now flaring like a prairie fire through her.

Her breath came quickly but she had lost the power of speech, so she couldn't answer when she heard Paul pleading, "Eve? Eve, please!" And in her head pulsed Celan's words, like a fugue against the confusion and noise surrounding her: "Nothing was whole, the world was in pieces . . . Once I heard him, he was washing the world."

But how, Eve thought in that long, protracted moment before the pain became unbearable and she lost consciousness, how on earth can you cleanse such a world?

20

PAUL SCOOPS her into his arms and holds her as tightly as he dares. Her arm is clearly broken, but someone has shouted that help is coming, and he knows it is better not to move. She doesn't seem afraid and smiles when he says, "You're going to be all right, it's a broken arm, but help is on the way."

Eve nods. She is probably still in shock, pumping lots of adrenaline. Then he sees the bruise on her scalp, the blood slowly spreading over his sport coat, but it seems a surface abrasion. Still, there is nothing more he can do. Gingerly he moves his arms so he has a better grasp of her, but she doesn't even wince, just looks up at him, then closes her eyes while they wait. Talking is simply too difficult.

Paul looks around.

Surrounding them are eyes startled into disbelief. The same expressions of disbelief he knew as a child. And mouths utterly still. As if only words can give reality to violence, as if by staying silent they can somehow put the chaos they just witnessed in a place where it won't intrude into their minds.

He remembers asking himself as a child: How could the sweepers and conductors in the Hauptbahnhof ignore those distraught mothers and children, how could the policemen herd those elderly Jews and the small children onto the trains at the Grunewald Station, how could the shopkeepers refuse the starving who were so wretched, so desperate in the winter of 1944?

It amazed him then, and it amazes him now. The motor cyclists—young women as well as men—and one policeman and the bystanders, who became witness to this ugly scene despite their fervent wish to go about their business in peace, are behaving as if their tongues were cut out of their mouths. They stare, stupefied, then quickly cast their eyes downwards.

His idiomatic German made them think he is someone important, and when he commanded the ruffians to remain here and take the consequences, they froze like kids playing Statue. So did everyone else. He feels totally disoriented, as if running madly in a dream to a place you can never reach.

Nothing has changed.

Whenever they are forced to see violence these passive Germans cover it up with infuriating, blind obedience. We were just following orders, no we never smelled anything near Dachau, we never wondered about all the sounds from the cattlecars, we were too busy minding our own business. What a culture, what a people, what a city! No wonder this is the place that had the first traffic light in the world.

What was he thinking when he brought her here?

Paul looks down at Eve. Now she is mouthing something. "Michael? Where is Michael?" Paul motions for Michael to stand in front of her so she can see him. He has a bloody nose, and a scratch on his hand, but when he says, "I'm okay," Eve nods, then curls into herself.

For now, he can see, the pain has kicked in, and she has to concentrate on it with fierce intensity. He's seen it twice before: when she gave birth to the twins, then to Claudia. Both times he felt horrible, but that was the irrational guilt of a husband taking part in the births of children. Birth is a natural process, with a reward. Like millions of men before and after him, he could do nothing but watch and pray that she and the babies would be all right.

But this? There is nothing natural about this kind of violence. Oh, why did he bring her to this hell? And why didn't he move faster when he realized what she was doing? It happened so fast, he was paralyzed. And awed. Where had she learned that move? And how did she calculate what she had to do and go so fast?

Then he hears himself calling to her, begging her not to pass out, but she is too weary and he is helpless as he watches her lose consciousness.

Always helpless, he thinks, as she sinks into a faint just at the moment the ambulance siren penetrates the silence. When the paramedics pass some smelling salts beneath her nose, Eve begins to stir and now his arms are empty and they are moving her onto the stretcher and asking him in German if he wants to ride with her to the hospital. Their efficiency is impressive.

Once she is no longer in his arms, Paul realizes how frightened he was. Whatever possessed her to do what she did? Someone could have had a gun, she could have been killed, they both could have been killed. Yet she gave no thought to herself and took on this gang of hoodlums in a foreign country, where she doesn't know the rules. It is astonishing, and marvelous, and as he climbs into the ambulance Paul can feel his fear and weariness give way to triumph and admiration.

*   *   *

People are arguing. Eve seems bound in some way, she cannot move easily, nor can she open her eyes though she is aware of sound. All she can remember after the ambulance came is some reassurance from Paul, then the pleasant feeling of being enveloped in a cocoon of exhaustion and peace. What she wished for on their way to the car rental place but which eluded her until she was put into the ambulance.

She recalls someone saying, "We are going to give you some Valium combined with a shot of local anesthesia," and Paul's voice saying, "It's going to be all right, Eve, it will make you numb." But it did not last very long.

Now she is still floating in a huge warm whiteness, hearing calm whispers in a mixture of English and German. She feels as if she's living in a fugue—where one line of melody goes in one direction and beneath it is another, sometimes more insistent line. Yet when will it all come together? She is too tired to pursue that line of thought.

After a time, though, her eyelashes unglue; abruptly her nose informs her she is in a recovery room. She can see beds stretching towards the door, and Paul and Michael, who are speaking softly, but urgently. When she opens her eyes they stop and stare at her.

"I was just trying to distract Mr. Berger," the boy tells her after a pause. His smile is shamefaced. "That's why we were arguing, he was so worried about you I thought the best thing to do was disagree with him." His eyes are so black, so admiring. It embarrasses her to be looked at like that. Eve moves her head, expecting the movement to produce pain, but nothing. If only the boy would stop, she wants to talk to Paul, but Michael can't seem to stop.

"You're a brave lady, Mrs. Berger. A real hero, heroine, I mean. The Police were amazed, they told us the Germans on the motorcycles are part of a gang that has its headquarters in a rough neighborhood called Neukolln, and that they meant business. They hate Asians. Somehow you stopped them." She thinks he's going to pause, but he is so wound up that he continues to speak.

"I was just telling your husband how much it's changed here, 50 years ago, who knows? I would probably have been killed. From all I've read they were in the killing business then, and foreigners were high on the list. Once you ran and tackled that guy, and Mr. Berger started to yell in German, they stopped. Where did you learn to do that? And how lucky I am that your husband can speak such good German, God knows what would have happened if he hadn't yelled like he did." He pauses and Eve would like to tell him about her twin sons, but she has the strength only to shrug and smile.

He goes on, "All I got was a bloody nose and a bruise on my hand, and some of my friends got bruises, but you got a broken arm. All because of me. I don't know how to say thank you, my friends are waiting for me, and they thank you, too, but I had to wait until you got up, to thank you myself. I hardly know what to say." He stops, finally uncomfortable, then stands, as if that will help, and shifts uneasily from foot to foot.

"They're not going to get off so quick. The Germans, I mean. One of the witnesses told us that here it's a crime against the State to attack foreigners and Jews. They may even go to jail. And the medics were terrific, weren't they, Mr. Berger?" He turns to Paul, then back to her. "So things have changed a little, haven't they? How does your arm feel?"

"Fine, Michael, they fixed me up just fine," Eve says, making a supreme effort; she can hardly stand to see him so uneasy, not able to leave. "And I hope you're right, about the changes, I mean."

"Oh, I know I'm right. I have to be right," he says, then, "Well, I'll be going now. I have your address in New York, and I want to write to you, find out how your arm is doing. You won't mind, will you?"

"Not at all, Michael, and you be careful in Munich, be careful everywhere," she says, hoping the alarm she still feels for him isn't too obvious.

"Oh, don't worry about me, Mrs. Berger, you just take care of yourself. You, too, Mr. Berger, and have a safe trip home." Finally he is shaking Paul's hand and backing towards the door at the far end of the room.

Before she can say anything Paul sits down and takes her free hand. He peers into her eyes. "It's a compound fracture of the wrist, but the break was clean, and the surgeon said there should be no complications. He seems a careful man, and the nurses say he's the best orthopedist here. The hospital is good, up-to-date. But it's a nightmare, the whole place is a nightmare. All my fault. I never should have brought you here. And the worst news is that we have to stay a few days, the doctor is very conservative and doesn't want you on a plane."

Eve shakes her head. "You're wrong," she tells him. "You were right to come back, and I'm glad we did. I had to know everything, and I had to hear it here." She stops, surprised at how tired she is.

"As for this," she looks at the cast that climbs from her fingertips to her elbow, "it's only a broken wrist, and, really, it has nothing to do with you. It has to do with me, and Michael and our kids . . . and Fraulein Alix . . . and those Frenchmen, and Hjalmar and Marga and Rose and Grete . . . besides, it will heal. We were lucky, Paul." But she is too weary to say any more.

What she wants to say is this: What she did this afternoon she did of her own free will. And only she is responsible for the consequences. She must make that clear, somehow; he has enough guilt already. But now she understands how it is possible to act on impulse, not to think about the consequences, do something that is sometimes good, and sometimes cruel and awful. To be so angry nothing matters except ridding oneself of the anger . . .

All at once she is enveloped by an enormous drowsiness and her tongue feels too thick for speech. Before she can utter another word, she is overwhelmed by sleep.

*   *   *

Paul sits in the surprisingly roomy booth for the public telephone at the end of the corridor. He is rehearsing what he will say to Blanche. Eve's words, "We were lucky, Paul," reverberate in his head. She is right, they should be thankful. But he feels terrible. He didn't even sense her anger until she was lunging for the young German, such daring, such courage, he would never have imagined her capable of it.

Again he consults his watch. Noon in New York, and Blanche is probably home, it's Sunday, but where can he begin? How? How can he explain this bizarre turn of events?

Then he consults his address book. The boys? Claudia in Paris? Eve's parents? No, not her parents, there's no point in frightening them. Ian? He doesn't even know he's here. Berthe? She'll go berserk, she was afraid of this trip before he started, and he doesn't need to hear her tell him, I told you so.

His first instinct was right. Blanche. He dials the number, tells the operator his credit card number, then listens for Blanche's low, pleasant voice. "Blanche, it's Paul, from Berlin, is everything okay there?"

"Fine. How's Eve? Eve's all right, isn't she?" Brusque, alert, wary.

"Yes, but there's been an accident. She fell and broke her wrist, she's fine, though, we got good medical care, she's in a cast, but we're stuck here for a while."

"Oh, Paul. Oh, this is horrible," Blanche interrupts, then falls silent.

"They don't want her to fly until the shock is over," Paul goes on, "so we may stay here for at least another week. Maybe even through Thanksgiving. I'm going to call Claudia in Paris and see if she can come and join us for the holiday. That's partly why I called, Eve was planning to make Thanksgiving on the Vineyard, with the usual crowd. Do you think you could call Gwen? There's no way she'll be home on time." He stops.

No response.

"Blanche, can you hear me?"

"Yes, I can hear fine. Of course I can call Gwen. Oh, this is so strange, Paul, last night I had such a frightening dream, about Eve being lost when she was a child and her parents and I were running through an enormous department store trying to find her. I woke up this morning filled with anxiety. I knew something had happened to Eve. You're sure she's all right? That you're telling me the truth?"

She sounds on the verge of tears.

"Yes, Blanche, she's more than all right. She helped some American kids who were in trouble, she fought off a neo-Nazi gang that was about to beat up an American Korean, stopped them all by herself. It was utterly incredible, she seemed to do it without thinking, just did what had to be done, and she got hurt, fell, bruised her scalp, and broke her wrist. It's her right arm, unfortunately, but they are confident that she's going to be fine. She was magnificent, Blanche, totally fearless."

"She was fearless as a child, in her quiet way, only people who knew her well understood that. It's why Jack loved her so much," Blanche begins, then she stops herself.

"Oh, Paul, I'm so glad you called, I never believed in telepathy, not even after Jack died, but I do now. I was going to call your hotel later because I was so uneasy, but please phone me tomorrow and let me know how she is. Or perhaps she'll be well enough to talk, I'd love to hear her voice." Blanche pauses to catch her breath.

"You know I was afraid something like this might happen, the newspapers have warned that everyone's on edge, that there could be random attacks of xenophobia."

For the first time in four and a half years Blanche sounds like herself when talking to him. He wishes she would talk more, especially about Eve as a child, but of course he can't press her now.

Then Blanche's voice, louder, stronger, "I'm so glad she's all right. Take care of her, Paul, and please give her my love." Yet her voice is still quivering, which only makes him feel worse.

As he hangs up he thinks, What if something had happened to Eve?

The thought is so dreadful that Paul goes into the lounge to sit for a moment and collect himself. Then he dials Claudia. In a flash he has figured out what to do. They will have a belated Thanksgiving here, just the three of them. For a second he considers the idea of calling Eric and Jeremy and Sarah to come, too, but he is afraid. It has been so long since he has been in an intimate situation with all three children. And now there is Sarah to add to the mix. No, it would be too much, the six of them walking on eggs around each other. Too much for Eve. And too much for you, he reminds himself.

"Claude? Are you okay?" he asks, and again he gets the same alert concern. Having told the story once already, he is surer of himself.

"Claude, Mom's had an accident," Paul begins, explaining as patiently and precisely as he can.

Claudia's response is "Oh, no!" over and over.

"She's really fine, the doctors have assured us she will be 'as good as new,' and she's remarkably calm and focused. Amazing, really."

"I'm coming to Berlin," Claudia says, anticipating him.

"But how, what about your papers?"

"I'll figure it out. I'm sure I can get an extension, I'll let you know tomorrow, Dad. I want to come as soon as I can. We can celebrate Thanksgiving. We'll have the holiday in Berlin, even if it's a little late." Claudia's voice is stronger now. Paul exhales in relief, the first real relief he has felt since Eve broke away from him to tackle the German boy. Then Claudia surprises him.

"What does this mean, Dad? I mean, for the two of you?"

"Oh, Claude, let's not even think about that now, too much has happened to think about that now," he says. Will the children ever know all he has shared with Eve? And what will she do when it sinks in? He's not even sure she will ever want to see him again now that she knows all there is to know about him. But all that is for the future.

"Let's take one thing at a time, darling," he says slowly. "If you can get away, we'll make Thanksgiving here. What you have to concentrate on right now is shooting a turkey, a French turkey, which I hear tell is much more canny than his American cousin, then getting it to Berlin. Think you can do that?"

Her reply is a relieved giggle. "But who will cook it?" She has always loved it when he teases.

"Don't you worry about that, that's my job. Your job is to shoot it." Now Paul sees himself in the hotel kitchen, instructing them on the intricacies of cooking a Thanksgiving meal. That's all our nervous concierge needs, he thinks with a smile.

When Paul hangs up the phone, he feels better than he could have dreamed when they were on their way to this hospital. Regret has been replaced by something close to real hope. Not the hope he felt when he got off the plane. That was a form of apprehension. What he feels now is elation.

He hardly recognizes it, it's been so long since he's felt it.

Then Paul realizes that he never considered calling Anna. He remembers them in that pretty little restaurant while Eve and Blanche were sitting across the room. How hurt Anna was when he finally confessed he was going to Berlin with his former wife. How angry!

He would never forget the sneer in her voice when she asked, "Am I going to be another one of your discards? I always prided myself that what we had was different, but I guess I was wrong?" It was a question that wanted not an answer, but reassurance. Reassurance he couldn't give. All he could do was stare at her, then rise and pay the bill. She was so furious she wouldn't let him see her home.

But now he knows that he and Anna had merely assuaged each other's loneliness. After he had seen Eve with Blanche in the restaurant, Paul understood that Anna was a stop-gap, there was no future with her, and, finally, he was through with those kinds of lies. So he left for Berlin without contacting her.

And now?

At this moment she might never have existed.

21

THEIR LITTLE DANCE with the concierge, which Paul referred to as a gavotte, and over time became something more flowing and graceful, maybe a fox trot, or even a waltz, is now something harsher, more like a jagged, exaggerated version of The Twist.

It is Tuesday and Eve has been discharged and they are back here at their hotel. Although Paul has explained to the concierge that Ms. Bertram had an accident, the man is totally shocked at the sight of her with her arm in a cast. He moves shakily towards them. When he questions them, he starts to stutter.

Eve looks at him in disbelief, but he will not get any answers from her. She can't go into it again, each time she hears the story from Paul, she is more and more embarrassed. She is no heroine, she simply acted on instinct, the way she had when her kids were small and something might hurt them.

Polite and guarded, Eve eludes the concierge, who becomes more rattled. To have an injured guest! Someone hurt by young German hoodlums! It is unthinkable, something that requires reserves of energy he hasn't had to call upon for years. His solicitude wearies them, and, finally, after Paul gives him the barest outline of what happened, telling the absolute truth because the Police will surely have some contact with this man, they go upstairs. They will rest for an hour, and after that, they promise him, they will come down to the restaurant to have something to eat.

"On the house. It must be on the house," he insists.

When they return, his watchful eye finds them, and he remains close to them as they eat their food, poached eggs, and Eve tries to drink some mint tea. It tastes like rusty water. Paul tells her about Blanche and Claudia.

She nods when he mentions Blanche's warning. "She didn't want me to come, she seemed to have a premonition of some violence."

"So did Berthe," he admits.

But when he tells her about Claudia's question, she murmurs, "Let's not even think about that, right now I'd like to feel better." Then she shrugs and pushes away the tray, while tears well uncontrollably in her eyes.

Finally she's exhausted, and they all give up. The man, still nameless (are they always nameless? Eve asks herself) insists on taking her good arm when she walks to the elevator. Paul goes to the desk to arrange for them to stay several more days and to get a room for Claudia. Only when Paul has pushed the elevator button and moved close to her does this overwrought man let go of her arm.

As he starts to help her get ready for bed, Eve takes the beautiful new nightgown and hands it to him. She doesn't know why she wants to wear it now, but somehow she needs to use this gift from Blanche. As if it will complete something, though what, she has no idea.

While he's helping her wrestle off her clothes and put on the nightgown Eve remembers them making love, the pleasure she was so surprised to feel, and then, less than twenty-fours later, his face as he told her the end of the story.

What will happen to them? She looks at Paul as he concentrates, head down, on the task at hand. She has no idea what he's thinking.

Suddenly it comes to her. With her arm jutting out in front of her, she is like a broken doll. Now she sees that dancing doll on the plaza of the museum, totally helpless, totally dependent on her partner. Wanting suddenly to tell Paul about that man and his doll, she looks at him, but he's so intent on getting her into the nightgown, she can't bring herself to interrupt him. And besides, she's so tired. Overcome with tiredness.

At last her clothes are folded in a neat pile, and she is in her nightgown, and her teeth have been brushed and her face washed, after a fashion. Paul watches her trying to get comfortable in bed. He insisted she take one round of pain-killers when they arrived, and now he says, "You have two hours before taking the pills again, you mustn't wait, because if the pain kicks in, it's harder to control." She nods. Such lavish attention, it has never been his style, and she doesn't know quite how to react.

After he's settled into an easy chair near the bed, she casts a quizzical glance at the book. He holds it up. "Keats' letters. A paperback Dozie sent a few months ago, said she was getting rid of her favorite books, told me she was trying to find good homes for them before she died. What a nut she is. I didn't even answer it, simply had Noreen send her an old photo and write her a letter saying I was away."

Everything has an explanation, Eve thinks with relief, if only you are patient enough to wait for it.

Slowly Paul begins to read and she drifts in and out of sleep, the city noise mingling with the Mendelssohn Paul found on the radio.

Coming out of a doze she says, softly, "Read to me."

"Of course." And here are the words, soothing words she has heard before:

> ... I met Mr. Green our demonstrator at Guy's in conversation with Coleridge—I joined them ... In those two Miles he broached a thousand things—let me see if I can give you a list—Nightingales, Poetry—on Poetical sensation—Metaphysics—Different genera and species of Dreams—Nightmare—a dream accompanied by a sense of touch—single and double touch—A dream

related—First and second consciousness—the difference explained between will and volition.... Monsters.... Mermaids.... A Ghost story—Good morning—I heard his voice as he came toward me—I heard it as he moved away ... He was civil enough to ask me to call on him at Highgate ...

She wants to say that she's sorry she's caused so much trouble, but the words won't come, so she closes her eyes and is back in that sparse room in their first rented house on the Vineyard, and the wind is whipping around the house and the chandelier is lurching over their heads and they are rocking the infant Claudia to sleep. His voice is strong as it comes towards her, he is reading these very letters, and they are arguing about will and volition and she realizes that what comforted her then and what comforts her now is not stretching her mind to find the meaning of the words, but the timbre of his voice, letting her know that he is here, that she is not alone.

Now Eve sees images of a young man, far too young, dying of TB, the 19th century disease, peaceful at last. And, superimposed on that, the images in the final chapter of Paul's story: his feelings of anger at Marga, the note of betrayal on the sink in the lavatory of the Zoo station, Alix lying there with her neck broken.

Violence and cruelty, the 20th century disease.

Will they talk some more? Eve wonders. How can you talk about such terrible things? And how is it possible to live after the unspeakable has been revealed? Some people say the story of the 20th century is the Holocaust, but what will be the story of the 21st century, which is only a little more than a decade away?

It is one thing to know and remember, another to live with the knowledge and the memories. How can they go on?

What about you? Where do you fit in? You fostered ignorance, then fled. Isn't that a crime? And if you multiply your blindness a hundred fold, what do you have? A world in chaos, a world almost ten years away from the Millennium that is unable to respond to its own humanity.

"Then nothing was whole, the world was in pieces . . . " Never has she felt so estranged from the world. She is in a place she has never known, and what she feels, she supposes, is a form of grief she has never known, either.

*   *   *

Light pours in through the sheer curtains. It is morning, and Paul is standing over her. "Any pain?" he asks, but surprisingly, she feels none.

"What time is it?" she wants to know, then props herself up with her good arm, expecting the movement to create some discomfort, but nothing. All she has is some swelling in her fingers.

"Almost nine-thirty. Better take a pill now, before the pain has a chance to start," Paul cautions, then goes to get a glass of water and hands her a pill. "And I've ordered you some breakfast, I've already eaten," he adds. So efficient, so thoughtful, yet he seems uneasy. Now Eve remembers that she dreamt of her children, but she can't get the outline of the dream, just their faces and bodies dashing somewhere. And a room with murals on the walls, murals of ancient figures changing into animals, monsters, mermaids, trees, flowers, God knows what else?

How she longs to see the kids, to touch them! She starts to tell Paul about the dream, but his face is troubled.

"What's wrong?"

"Blanche called back last night, after you fell asleep. She told Gwen we'll be here for Thanksgiving, in fact she told Gwen everything, our coming here, the accident, your arm. Gwen wasn't surprised, she said she knew there was more going on than just a trip to New York." He smiles.

"You're such a lousy liar, Eve. But about an hour later Gwen called Blanche back to tell her Dozie died. She's going to be cremated and there will be a memorial service next month. It's uncanny that I was reading from Keats, probably at the very moment she was dying." Paul shakes his head, but his face is clear with the relief of having told her.

Eve stares. It's hard to take in. Dozie was part of the landscape, her landscape. And now she's gone.

"I don't want to rush you, Eve," Paul's voice penetrates her thoughts, "but we have to get going. We have a doctor's appointment at noon."

"But what about the Jewish Museum archive, to look at their records?"

He ignores her, adding, "And after the doctor we have to go to the airport to get Claudia."

Eve nods. How relieved she was, how relieved they both were, when Claudia called last night to tell them she was coming to Berlin, that she'd gone to her professors and gotten extensions on her papers, and that she'd even gotten the name of a butcher in Wilmersdorf who could get a turkey. A French butcher told her that this butcher took care of all the American expats in Berlin, that he could even get Kosher turkeys. It was "so Claudia" they had laughed delightedly, and Eve had no trouble falling back to sleep. Yet not even the thrill of seeing Claudia in a few hours can erase the news of Dozie's death.

"Poor Dozie," she says as Paul helps her out of bed and into the shower, and again they wrestle with her clothes to get her dressed. She feels in a trance, a trance of docility, the doll again, waiting for her ankles to be tied. But still she doesn't tell Paul about it. The only thing that registers now is gratitude that her pants and sweater are a soft cashmere, which makes the tugging and pulling easier.

Slowly she sips her coffee and nibbles on the croissant he has broken into pieces and slathered with jam just as she likes it.

"I took a walk before breakfast, and it's cool," he tells her.

Eve catches sight of herself in the mirror. One arm of her sweater has been stretched to make room for the cast, her body looks crooked, her face is chalky because she can't put on any make-up, her hair no better than a bad wig.

"You look fine," he says.

"You're going blind," she tells him. His reply is a firm shake of his head.

But when they go downstairs to the lobby and the concierge calls Paul Mr. Bertram, Eve suddenly remembers what she wanted to ask him last night when her mind was such a blur, "Why did Michael call me Mrs. Berger?"

"Because I gave my name as Paul Berger when the Police came. It was out before I realized it, weird, isn't it, and then I had to explain, which got far too jumbled. I ended up giving them a lecture on anti-Semitism in the States in the late 1940s to make them understand why I had changed my name. Talk about surreal, it was like a piece of dialogue from Beckett." Paul chuckles.

No, Eve thinks, it's not weird. He called himself Berger when he introduced himself to Martin Zweig, but he wasn't even aware of it. She didn't remark on it then, and she's not going to remark on it now. Nor did she say anything when he called her his wife. The truth finds its way into the smallest crevices. Finally, no more lies or evasions. Even unconscious ones. From now on everything will be out in the open. Here his name was Berger and will always be Berger.

And will she always be his wife?

But the cab is here. When Eve climbs into it, she feels clumsy and uncomfortably aware of the concierge staring at them. He'd love to know their story, years in the hotel business have taught him that everyone has a story, and most are perfectly happy to tell theirs. It's the ones who guard their privacy fiercely who are most interesting. Those are the ones who have a dignity he prizes. It is all there in the concierge's eyes as he helps her into the cab.

All at once Eve is aware of a strange silence. She tilts her head towards the Conservatory, then says, "Why is it so quiet? Where are the musicians?"

Finally the man smiles, really smiles. At last someone has noticed. "They are gone, Madam. Sometimes they have a chance to perform and they go away for a few days to the small towns and villages, to bring music to the country people. It happens more in the late fall and for Christmas celebrations, and then in the spring, when Easter comes." His voice is proud. As if this can make up for the actions of hoodlums, the evidence of which is here, shockingly, before his eyes.

Then their eyes meet and the man says, "A wonderful day to fly." Eve looks up. The bleak gray sky of yesterday has yielded to a gorgeous, cobalt blue. "You have a relative coming from Paris," the man says and she nods. The buildings shimmer in the sunlight, even the dying garden next to the hotel is burnished a lustrous gold. Maybe we can take Claudia to the Pestalozzi garden, Eve thinks, then settles back in her seat. How strange her life has become in just one short week. Against all logic, she and Paul are going to see their youngest child, here, in Berlin.

And now when her questioning eyes meet Paul's, he says, "We'll go to the archive tomorrow, when Claude is writing her other paper. I promise. And then we'll celebrate Thanksgiving over the weekend." Finally the tension that has been hanging between them for the last forty-eight hours begins to lessen.

22

CLAUDIA SQUINTS, then she sees her mother's cast glowing in the glare of the airport waiting room, and within seconds, hears her father's urgent, "Claude, Claude, over here."

Incredibly, they are making a sandwich of her as they used to when she was small. She can feel her limbs go weak with bliss. Can it be? Her parents with their arms around her, actually close enough to touch? Suddenly she can hear them chuckling and teasing while she and the twins played cards on their lumpy high bed.

Everything in that old saltbox in Menemsha was worn: the furniture scarred, the dishes chipped, the quilts almost threadbare, but all of it was utterly beautiful in the gentle yet lavish light. Her vision of happiness. She knew it was illogical. How could happiness be a room, or the passing shadows and sounds of two people getting ready to go out to dinner? Yet the image persisted, a snapshot of paradise, and ultimately lost, as paradise always seemed to be, sometime when she was around thirteen.

Her mother would brush her amazing auburn hair, which none of them had gotten, and her father would be opening drawers, muttering to himself, "Shall I wear a knit shirt or a sport shirt," while she and Eric and Jeremy made it into a little song: "Knit shirt or sport shirt? What shall I wear? And what shall we eat? Penguin or bear?" And everyone laughing and her mother flushing with such pleasure it hurt to look at her.

But why is all this coming back? Claudia hasn't thought about the rental on the Vineyard for years. She doesn't even think about her mother's new house. It's simply too painful, and neither house is relevant to her now, standing in the Berlin airport, surrounded by her estranged parents. Yet they, too, seem entangled in the past, and now want nothing more than to hold her in a kind of contented silence, ignoring the harsh cacophony of the crowd around them.

After a few moments, though, her mother is wriggling free and standing back to look at her and saying, as if she can't believe Claudia is hers, "You look wonderful, it's so good to see you."

"I look terrible, and you know it. I was up all night finishing that damn paper on *Pere Goriot*. What an amazing book, you know, the better the book, the harder it is to write about it," Claudia answers, then feels a tingle go up her spine as they both laugh. It's been years since she's heard such a relaxed chuckle, from either of them.

Then she exclaims, "Oh, it's so good to see you!" as they hurry to collect her bag.

*   *   *

Her parents have separate rooms. Claudia can feel her throat fill as she retreats to her own room. How can you have three kids and not be able to share a room? Here comes another memory, of their beautiful bedroom in New York where she would wander early in the morning and find her parents strangely detached as they got dressed, silent, and sad, maybe even angry, but where the evidence of the night's activity was still on the floor near the bed: her nightgown and his pajamas. Those dispirited early mornings in New York never fit with the evenings in Menemsha.

She remembers a conversation she had once had with her brother Eric when they finally realized that Paul (he was always Paul in her mind when she thought about his messing around) was not faithful to her mother. "But how can they be unhappy when they still sleep together?" she'd asked, and Eric's answer was a puzzled shrug.

Then they were still young enough to confuse sex with happiness.

Now, layered on top of the recollection of those melancholy mornings in New York is the sight of her father and Aunt Frankie standing in Bryant Park, a few years after Frankie had disappeared from their life. A crisp, freezing day, her father with his ice skates slung over one shoulder, facing Frankie, the two of them talking urgently, while she and her eighth grade class marched to the 42nd Street branch of the New York Public Library to see some exhibition on Robert Louis Stevenson.

Frankie was wearing a fox fur hat, and from the corner of her eye Claudia spied a familiar gesture, one she had seen hundreds of times when her father tucked her mother's scarf inside the lapels of her winter coat, only this time the woman was not her mother. It was Frankie, looking absolutely marvelous, ducking playfully away from her father's touch, teasing him as her mother never did, because to tease someone like that you had to be wholly sure of his affection for you, and by now her mother wasn't sure of anything.

When Claudia came home and told her mother she had seen Frankie and her father, she didn't say anything about her father tucking in Frankie's scarf. Her mother looked at her over the reading glasses she had begun to wear and nodded. "I've heard all about it, it's nothing new."

"But what are you going to do? How can he be seeing her, when she's supposed to live out in the Midwest, or Texas?" Claudia asked, she never could remember which.

"I think she did move, but maybe she comes back for visits."

"Are you going to tell him what I told you?"

Her mother gazed thoughtfully at her and shook her head.

"I've talked to him about it, and he insists he never sees her. At this point there's nothing I can do." Her mother's voice was flat, resigned, and her eyes were tired. From that moment everything changed, and down deep Claudia knew it was merely a question of time before she and her family joined the ranks of the divorced. Although it took several more years for her mother to leave, astonishing her children who had been convinced it would be he who would leave, the fear of separation and divorce had taken hold.

And then another memory, another class trip, when she must have been a freshman or sophomore in high school. Floating through Central Park on one of those glorious late spring days on their way to the Met. And there was her father sitting on the grass, just like someone out of Manet, with a woman she could have sworn was Frankie. But the woman said she was someone from his office and her father agreed, and by then it had been so long since Claudia had seen Frankie she wasn't sure.

The twins expected their father to marry Frankie, but Claudia had never thought of Frankie in that way. About a year and a half ago, when she finally asked about that tall, high-spirited woman, referring only to the winter day so long ago, he'd said, "She was a passing fancy."

"She didn't look like a passing fancy that day."

"Oh, by then we were just friends, we hadn't been lovers for years, I never slept with her after your mother found me out. Besides, even when we were close, she was nobody for the long haul. Amusing, attractive, but never anyone I'd want to spend the rest of my life with." He was so casual, it gave her the shivers.

How many women had he slept with while he was married to her mother?

"Well, you could have fooled me," she had said. Then, "Is this Anna person for the long haul?"

"I don't know, Claude."

Still, he hadn't asked Anna to go with him to Berlin. And now he and her mother are sitting on the loveseat in her room watching her unpack, as if they were still married and had never contemplated divorce.

Her mother, who was always rather fearful about physical danger and pain, isn't in the least bothered by her broken wrist or the cast or her still swollen fingers, saying, casually, "It will heal. All it needs is time. Let's talk about what we're going to do. Today I need to nap and we'll have dinner, and we know you have to work on your papers, Claude. But what shall we do tomorrow?"

"I'd like to see the house," Claudia replies.

*   *   *

The weather changed suddenly in the night and in the now wintry air the house looks even larger than it did a few days ago. A rime of hoarfrost circles the lawn, and the greenhouse glitters wildly under a sharp blue sky. After a few days of heavy showers, the trees are almost bare and without their leaves softening its outlines, the house looks absolutely enormous.

"It's so big," Claudia says, her eyes wide.

"Yes," Paul murmurs, "bigger than I remembered. Even I was surprised."

"But usually houses from the past are small, aren't they?" Claudia persists. Eve smiles. Once she and Claudia went to see the old house in Menemsha. Claudia rang the bell and the couple who lived there let them walk through it. In the bedrooms Claudia kept saying, "It's so small, I can't believe how small it is."

Now, as if she has read Eve's mind, Claudia cries, "Let's ring the bell," and before either of them can respond, she has run up the path and done just that. Eve's heart leaps into her mouth.

A woman answers, a young woman in her late 30s or early 40s, slim, dressed in jeans and a sparkling white shirt, with that ubiquitous maroon hair, cool green eyes. Prickles rise on Eve's skin. While Eve and Paul stand back, Claudia explains that her father once lived here, and they have come from the States, and can they come in and look around?

The woman's face softens and she says, "*Wilkommen.*" She and Paul have a brief exchange in German during which she tells him she can understand English but is unsure of speaking it. Paul tells them: "She and her husband bought the house in

1980 and have four children and her mother-in-law lives with them. She's the one who keeps the greenhouse and garden. Her husband works for IBM in Berlin."

Some of the Bergers' furniture is still here, Paul is now telling them, huge pieces—the dining room table and credenza, the built-in bookcases in the library, the enchanting double desk that looks like something out of Hollywood, where Gunther and Hjalmar used to go over the accounts for the shop. The concert Bechstein, which Frieda and Berthe, and later, Hjalmar, played. Paul points out the various objects and lets his fingers graze their polished surfaces.

The woman observes him closely and steps forward to hear every word. Finally she says, in English far better than she claimed, "My name is Clara Untermann, take as much time as you like. The children are in school, and *die Shweigermutter* is shopping. I was doing the laundry."

"That's her mother-in-law," Paul interjects. Eve nods, by now overwhelmed. This house, whose details have remained in Paul's mind for so many years, which has been so vivid to him, is now becoming hers, as well. As they walk slowly through the rooms, Eve realizes: It is the linchpin of his story, as it was the linchpin of his life. And now, knowing what she knows, she is deeply affected by the sight of it.

Claudia and Paul go ahead, while she and Clara linger a little behind. Fortunately, the woman doesn't expect any conversation. Clara is a tidy housekeeper, but that isn't hard in a home with so many well-appointed cupboards and closets. Rarely has Eve seen such a comfortable, commodious house, and in such exquisite taste.

Is this why he was so obsessed with every detail when they started to fix up their apartment? Why everything mattered so much to him? Why each object was chosen with so much care? While she had watched Paul acquire all those things, she had thought, He is burying himself alive. And when he took a corner of her sunny, spare dining room and piled it high with baskets, she was furious. Those sublime icons of usefulness, woven so lovingly by women to hold their handiwork, laundry, flowers and vegetables, were now stacked up to show greed and wealth. When she suggested they use them instead of displaying them, he said, curtly, "They're too valuable."

A few months later, when he was proudly giving their provenance to a house guest, she flew out of the apartment, panting with fright until she arrived at Blanche's, knowing that she had to get out of there, or she, too, would be buried alive. That was the day she told him she was leaving him. *Forever,* she had said.

"It is a wonderful house," Clara is now saying, especially to Paul, "very easy to live in. And its very heart is this kitchen," she says as she ushers them into the large room. Bright sun bathes the whitewashed walls, lemon motes of sunlight gleam above the huge scrubbed wood table that dominates the room. Eve can picture Tante Hilda, her hairline ringed with perspiration, chopping and dicing as she stands there, and Paul and Berthe sitting there watching her as they drink hot chocolate or lemonade, depending on the season.

Old pots hang from the ceiling, and Eve observes Paul looking at them. Clara does, too, and now she says, quickly, "They were all here when we came, in wonderful condition, so we decided to use them. It is hard to find such large pots now, no one has such a big stove as this." It is an old cast-iron stove with two large ovens, like some ancient ancestor of the Aga that Paul insisted they put in the New York apartment.

A new refrigerator is the only concession to the times. This beautiful space looks so benign it is hard to imagine fear and sorrow invading it. But they did. Still, Claudia doesn't know that and neither does this woman, Clara, who is walking them again through the more formal living and dining rooms.

For a moment Eve thinks that will be all, but Clara is insisting they go upstairs. A lump rises in Eve's throat when they stand in the master bedroom before the fireplace that figured so prominently in Paul's tale. Two chairs still sit before it, and there is a small pile of logs stacked on the hearth waiting for the first cold night. Radiating from the large west-facing room, are the two bedrooms that were once Paul's and Berthe's. In the boy's room is an enormous map of the world from the beginning of the century.

"But it's totally out of date, it was out of date even when I slept here," Paul says, "they kept it simply because it was so beautiful."

"It still is," Claudia says as she peers at it. "The United States is still the same, that never changes. Or rarely," she adds, explaining to Clara that Hawaii and Alaska were recently added. Then she and Paul go across the hall while Eve lingers here, where Paul spent his first twelve years, and where Rose lived after he went upstairs to the attic.

"Mama sleeps in the other wing with the older children. Some people felt it not an advantage to have the children's rooms near, and the bathroom across the hall, but we like to have the younger children close," Clara speaks English, choosing each word very carefully.

"So did the Bergers," Eve murmurs, and finally looks directly into the woman's eyes. Clara reddens with embarrassment.

"We are sorry, it was terrible, it never should have happened, what can I say to you?" she pleads.

Eve shakes her head. "Nothing more than what you have just said. His great-grandfather built this house, and none of them imagined they would ever have to leave it. The idea was beyond their wildest dreams. But they did." And then, because the woman's eyes hold so many questions, she explains that they were hidden by the Friedmanns in the attic and that they all, mother, father, sister, and Paul, survived.

Clara gives a visible sigh of relief, then says, with a tinge of wonder, "We thought perhaps an aunt and uncle lived there at one time. It is so beautifully done." She stops.

"My parents were not Berliners,'" Clara continues, "we lived in Stuttgart, but I went to university here and that's when I met my husband. His family has lived here for generations." Then they walk a little faster to catch up with Claudia and Paul.

When they do Claudia is wandering towards a small dressing room. "Oh, look," she calls in a high excited voice, and points to marks on the walls, carefully dated, which record Paul's and Berthe's growth.

"It is so charming, we did not have the heart to paint over it, we kept it as a," she hesitates, "testament, you might say." She gives Paul an expectant look, but he shrugs.

It surprises Eve to see that he has almost no interest in this stranger who is being so kind to them—he, who always made it a point to charm strangers wherever they went. But now he is oddly aloof as he walks through the rooms, as if he is checking them off in his mind. And his eyes have that hollowness she remembers from their worst mornings together. His skin also seems suddenly parched and pale.

"Seen enough?" she says, as casually as she can when their eyes meet. He shakes his head.

"I want Claudia to see it all," he tells her.

*   *   *

Paul can see that Eve is worried. She thinks this is too much for him. But it isn't. Now that they are here, Paul realizes that the brilliant, silken span of memory which he had fondled for so many years in his mind has become, in a few minutes, a piece of drab, serviceable cotton. These rooms, so painfully alive to him for so many years, are merely four walls; even the remaining pieces of furniture whose beauty was so intertwined with his feelings for his family and the Friedmanns, are no longer precious heirlooms, but simply wood. Pretty pieces of wood, which have outlasted the people who once used them with such love and care, but which evoke nothing now that they are used by strangers.

Unlike the city whose beauty and ugliness can still summon forth some of the most searing recollections, this house no longer has any power over him. It's just a house, a big comfortable house with airy magnificent spaces, but it is no longer his. So all that yearning he once felt is gone.

As he guides his youngest child through it, Paul feels an incredible sense of relief. Through a strange turn of events, Providence has finally come over to his side. He remembers that man Rolf using the word, "twisted," in German to describe Wagner. Well, all of life is twisted in some ways.

When he told her everything, Eve was bewildered and unbearably sad. Far sadder than she was when she understood he had been unfaithful. Then they got mixed up with that neo-Nazi gang and she broke her wrist, and his past had to be put aside until they got her help. But since then he has watched her struggling with all that he has told her, trying, somehow, to figure out how they might find a way to go on.

Now Paul remembers mornings on the Vineyard, slipping out of bed at dawn while the others were sleeping and walking on the dewy grass until the hems of his pajamas pants were soaking wet, then standing there in the damp mist as that beautiful hairy fog drifted upward to reveal a more distant patch of green here, then another there, until finally the world appeared to be born before your very eyes and your view stretched as far as the sea. The day has begun, and your job is to live in the present, he told himself, day after day, year after year. But it was no solution.

And now that he has come clean? Is there a solution after that? He had thought the hardest part was over, but how will Eve react when they discover what happened to Marga and Rose and Grete? That's when he realizes that they cannot leave without seeing the attic. He turns to Clara and says, "I'd like to see the attic."

"Of course," she says.

"During the war we used a secret entrance, through the closet in the dressing room," he tells her.

She nods, and her voice is solemn. "We found it after we bought the house, I don't think the realtor realized it was there, because by the time we came someone had put in another staircase from the upstairs hall, through the small sewing room at the back. I'll show it to you. And the closet door was locked and no one could find a key." She stops, embarrassed.

"But when the contractors got the closet door open, we decided not to keep the secret staircase, so we took out the stairs and made it into a closet again. We didn't want to have to explain to the children when they grew up . . . why it was here." She bends her head, shame in her eyes.

The silence around them thickens as they all follow her into the old sewing room which now has a tasteful, wide staircase to the attic, a staircase that announces the third floor of the house with pride.

The attic space has not been divided and is still a very large room that has been left pretty much as Paul remembers it. Only a little kitchen has been added in the corner. One area is a bedroom, and high bookcases separate it from the living space where there are couches and chairs and a round table Tante Hilda had in her little apartment off the kitchen.

Clara tells Paul, "There were only two families who lived here before us, and they rented. We were told that each family had a boarder who used these quarters, but we always wondered why this attic was so well fitted out. Now I understand . . ." She shrugs, unable to go on, then she collects herself. "We should have asked, but there are things no one really wants to know. When we bought the house from Grete Meyerhoff, she had no interest in telling us anything about it."

She has more to say, but now Eve has stepped forward and is asking, urgently, "Did you say Grete?"

"Why, yes, Grete Meyerhoff. She had owned the house forever, but she no longer wanted the responsibility of being a landlord, she told us. So she sold it to us. At that time she lived somewhere in Wilmersdorf, but we've lost touch over the years." Clara shrugs apologetically. Paul can feel himself gasping for breath.

So Grete is alive!

23

"GRETE is a very common name in Germany. Every other girl is named Gretel or Margaret or Marguerite. How can you be sure it's her?" Paul wants to know after they have come back to the hotel and had lunch and Claudia is in her room working on another paper.

Although today is Thanksgiving at home, they are going to celebrate it on Saturday. It turns out that the concierge at the hotel, whose name is Joseph, has cousins in Chicago and once spent a Thanksgiving with them there. He is thrilled to be able to make all the traditional dishes, and has told them he is especially fond of the sweet potation so amiably that none of them had the heart to correct him.

"I can't," Eve says, "but I think we ought to go to those archives this afternoon, not wait until tomorrow."

"What about resting? The doctor said you should rest each afternoon."

"I can't rest, Paul. Not now."

He simply nods, his eyes cast down. Eve realizes that he's afraid. That incident with the American kids sidetracked them, made them gentler with each other, but it was only temporary. They cannot postpone this any longer.

* * *

The woman in the Archive section is courteous and attentive, and her English is good, but it is clear as she takes in their blue eyes and Eve's hair that she thinks they're Gentiles. Will these

Germans never learn? Their rigidity, their lack of imagination is laughable, Eve thinks, as she steps back and lets Paul do all the asking.

"We are Eve and Paul Bertram," Paul begins, in English. "We're American and have been asked by some friends back home to inquire about a family named Friedmann—Hjalmar and Marga Friedmann and their two daughters, Rose and Grete. I believe Hjalmar died during the war, here in Berlin."

The woman nods and goes to a file, and pulls out a folder. "Our death records of citizens of Berlin who died during the War are very complete. He died in May of 1944. He is also on our list of Righteous Gentiles, because he helped a Jewish family hide here in Berlin from 1940 until he died. But there is no mention of their names. For our purposes they didn't exist unless they or someone related to them comes here and tells us about them. If compensation has been made to them, their name is in the government file, but we are a private organization and we have no information about them." Her voice is a monotone. Then she looks up.

"I have a photograph of Mr. Friedmann, but since you didn't know him, there is no point in showing it to you," she adds as she consults more information in the folder.

After a pause, the woman goes on, "He had a Jewish wife and two *mischlinge* daughters, and while he was alive he seemed to have enough connections to keep them safe. But after his death . . . " she shrugs.

"What happened to them?"

"It's confusing," the woman replies with a frown. "The mother and children were picked up in June of 1944 and sent to Theresienstadt. The mother perished there. But there is no record of what happened to the daughters."

"Do you have any information on whether they lived, or where they are now?"

"I'm sorry. The camps kept good records, but when the war ended and people fled, it was impossible to know where they went. We have records only of those survivors who register with us and still live in Germany. You know, there were thousands of Jews hidden in Berlin during the War, but only those who want to be counted are here." She motions towards the file cabinets, then shrugs and closes the folder and puts it back into the file.

"Anyone with Jewish blood was considered Jewish," she adds. "But not everyone with Jewish blood comes here and registers with us. There is no requirement to do that anymore, thank God." Another pause. "And now, if you don't mind . . ." They are dismissed.

*　　*　　*

Paul sits on the bench with his head in his hands. "I'm not surprised," he says at last. "Without Hjalmar, Marga had no fight left in her." Eve doesn't reply.

Perished. Such a delicate euphemism, perish. Rhymes with cherish.

Eve looks at the people going in and out of the museum, mostly tourists. Many of them are crying as they leave.

Finally, Paul stands up. "I think we'd better go to Wilmersdorf. I know the address." His body is hunched as it was the first few days, and his face is gray. Now he pulls out a scarf from his pocket and wraps it around his neck. It has gotten colder, and Eve is grateful for a small wool hat she threw into her suitcase at the last minute.

In the cab he tells her, "I think I saw Grete that day at the Kollwitz Museum. I saw the back of her as she was leaving. I called to her but she didn't hear me. Or maybe she did. I don't know. At the time I thought I was crazy, I was so sure she and Rose were dead."

"They may be."

He shakes his head. "I don't think so. I have a hunch that woman was Grete."

*   *   *

They stop in front of a block of flats. "It's almost as I remember it," Paul says. "But these buildings had to be rebuilt, this street was bombed heavily just around the time Hjalmar died." Quickly he steers Eve into the lobby and consults the list of occupants.

"Don't we have to buzz first?" Eve asks.

He shakes his head, but when the elevator comes, he breathes a sigh of relief that it is empty. He pushes five.

Eve is watching him carefully. "Paul, you know we don't have to do this," she starts to say.

"You're wrong. We do," he interrupts her, and then they are standing in a hall that smells of sausage and ripening fruit and onions and now he is ringing the bell.

A tall woman wearing an apron opens the door. She is dressed in a sensible gray flannel skirt and white blouse and she holds a dish towel. As she wipes her hands, she looks at them. She wears her hair exactly like Marga, blonde braids wrapped around her head. But her face is worn and her skin pasty. She glances at them, then says, with exaggerated politeness, in German, "You must have made a mistake," and starts to close the door.

Paul raises his hand and says softly in German, "Grete, it's Paul . . ."

The woman's eyes shut down as quickly as a window slammed in a howling storm.

Now Paul knows for sure that it is Grete. He half expects her to raise her hands and cover her ears, which she did all the time as a child. But she stands there, stolid, waiting, so he repeats, in German, "Grete, it's me, Paulie Berger . . ." He steps forward.

Recognition begins to dawn. Greedily those sharp blue eyes devour his features, and she finally nods. "Yes, it is you. I can see it now. But how dare you come here?" Her voice is very low, but her English is absolutely fluent. She goes on. "We knew you went to America." For a moment, Paul thinks she will soften, but as she continues, disgust spills from her eyes as she looks at him, then at Eve.

"I came back . . . to Berlin, after all these years, we went to the house, and the woman there told us you were alive . . . "

"No thanks to you."

"Marga turned us out."

"She was mad with grief. And then she became utterly crazed with fear, all because of you, because you betrayed us. It had to be you, you were the only person in the world besides Papa and Rose and me who knew Mama was born Jewish." But there is a question in her voice.

He looks directly into her eyes, which are ravaged with pain and anger. Never has he seen such pain. Then he says, "It was me. I was filled with rage, I wanted to hurt her."

"You murdered her, and Rose, too, though Rose lived for ten years after the war. She went to France and married and had a baby and died a year after that from the after-effects of cholera, which she got in the camp. I survived because I met my husband there, also a *mischlinge*, and he wouldn't let me die. He still won't."

She stops and looks at him and Eve for a long time. She takes in Eve's cast and a flicker of curiosity registers in her eyes, but then they go completely flat and Paul knows she has reached the end of her tether.

"But you," she says firmly, and now it is the voice he remembers from his childhood: Marga's voice when she was angry, the same voice that told them they had to leave their home.

"But you . . . why you are no better than a Catcher. You are a monster. No." She stops. "There are no words, in any language, for the likes of you." She speaks slowly so there is no room for a misunderstanding. Then, as exactly, as obscenely as it has occurred in his dreams, she spits in Paul's face.

*   *   *

The echo of the slamming door reverberates around them. Saliva is dripping onto Paul's wool scarf. Eve takes out her handkerchief and approaches him. "Are you sure you want to do that?" he asks, shying away from her as if he is not worthy of being helped, or touched.

"Of course, I'm sure." Carefully she wipes his neck and scarf where the saliva wobbles on the woolen surface. She notes that the rash on his neck is still there. Time seems to have slowed down so drastically that she can feel each second.

"Thank you," he says when she is finished, looking at her so intensely that she has to look away. "I thought you'd have fled by now," he murmurs. "Anyone in her right mind would have."

"I told you I would see it through to the end."

"But you didn't think it would be this bad. Neither did I."

"No, I didn't, you're right, but now it's done . . . " she falters and shrugs, and her throat fills as she realizes that the pain she feels now will always be there, and so will the pity and the brimming sorrow. This is far worse than the sadness she felt when he got to the end of his story in her room at the hotel. This is beyond description. *Gottverlassen,* the boy said about Celan.

Godforsaken.

Now they enter the elevator and are silent until they reach the lobby. On the street a woman with two string bags filled to the brim with food and flowers passes them and gives them a curious stare. Of course, it is almost the weekend again. A lot of the American tourists have left to celebrate Thanksgiving, and the Germans are continuing to go about their business, probably glad that their city is beginning to return to normal.

But is there such a thing as normal in Berlin? Eve isn't sure. They stand there for several minutes, silent. Paul cannot meet her glance and looks up at the blind, curtained windows of the apartment house. When Eve looks up, she sees a curtain being pulled slightly away. It could be Grete, it could be someone else.

In her mind Eve sees the hatred spurting from Grete's eyes. What must it be like to live every day of your life with such hatred? She cannot imagine, but just as her heart fills with pity for Grete and Rose and even Marga, just as Eve realizes they, too, are Godforsaken, she also knows that there is nothing she can do for Grete or her husband or her children, if she has any.

What matters is Paul. When Eve turns towards him she sees him touching his face, as if he can't really take in what has happened. Now his eyes meet hers. "In my dream I never knew who that shadowy woman was. I would run through every path in the Public Garden and wake up in a sweat. Sometimes, just before I would wake up she would become Alix. Sometimes she would become you. But it never occurred to me that it would be Grete."

*   *   *

Luckily for them Claudia has to work on her paper way into the night and for most of the day on Friday. They have a late dinner together, and on Saturday take a ride to the countryside, the same ride they planned the day Eve got hurt. The sun is hard and bright as it glints off the still green fields. They discover that the *Schloss* that once belonged to Alix and her family is now an exclusive girls' boarding school. Even from the gates, though, you can see how impressive it must have been. They have lunch in a little village tavern and on their way back to Berlin, as the sun begins its descent, the landscape is bathed in that magical purple glow Paul remembers from his childhood, when the world seems touched by the hand of God. It leaves both Eve and Claudia breathless with delight.

Later, when they come down for dinner they are amazed to see their table decorated with plants and dried fruits, almost exactly as Eve does her Thanksgiving table every year. And the meal is a triumph for Joseph and the kitchen staff—there is a marvelously cooked turkey and all the trimmings. Especially good is the sweet potato dish, filled with an interesting combination of nuts and dried fruit, more savory than sweet.

After dessert, a delicious apple strudel—"We make this an international effort," Joseph explains—Claudia insists on knowing the recipe of the "sweet potation," as Joseph insists on calling it—and it is amusing, and also touching, to see the young woman chef trying to explain it to her. Unlike so many of the young, she isn't comfortable with English.

"I come from the country," she explains shyly, with a shrug. "Our schools are not so good with English, although they get better each year. But I graduate five years ago, when not so good. All I know is how to cook." She gives a little curtsy.

"Which you do very well," they reassure her with a hearty exchange of smiles and pats on the back.

*　　*　　*

The next day, before Claudia takes a plane back to Paris, she announces that she isn't leaving Berlin without seeing Gestapo headquarters.

Since Eve and Paul retreated to their own rooms after that encounter with Grete on Thursday, they have not had a moment alone with each other. Once Claudia finished her paper, she craved every minute with them, and Eve and Paul have been grateful for this reprieve with their youngest child. Claudia is so delighted to see them at ease with each other that she, too, is more relaxed than Eve has seen her since the divorce.

But Eve knows this is just a reprieve. At some point she and Paul will have to talk and face all that awaits them. Each night after she has gone to her own room and prepared for bed by herself—for now the pain in her arm has receded—she has dreamt about her and Paul and their three young children living in her present house on the Vineyard. She wakes up breathless with all that she has had to do in her dream—change beds, cook, go marketing, even get them off to school. One night she dreamt that she got a call from friends who were coming to visit and she spent the entire dream changing the beds and trying to figure out how to fit everyone in her house. It is insane, there is no way her young family could ever have lived in the house she built five years ago and there is no way they would come to live with her. They are grown and on their own. Do these crazy dreams mean she's anxious about the possibility of living with someone again, that she doesn't want to give up her privacy, the peace she has worked so hard to achieve?

But what about the loneliness, that awful loneliness she felt for more than a year after she and Paul separated, when she could barely eat alone, when she had the radio on all the time? Is that what she wants? Out of the blue Dozie looms in her mind. Old, lonely, frail, embittered. And then there is Max. It is the first time she's thought of him in almost two weeks, Eve realizes. No, Max is just a friend. Then Eve thinks about her Aunt Blanche. She manages, more than manages, alone. But Blanche is widowed and 75. Now she hears Blanche's voice in her head, "You have a lot more living to do."

Somehow she and Paul must go on. Once told, Paul's story has become a fact of their life, of their children's lives.

Suddenly Eve feels the way you do when you are recovering from a protracted illness, when you emerge from all that time in bed in a shadowy room, when, finally, you feel that life claims you again. When even the leaves on the trees look shiny, new.

Can they live together? Can they live apart? Despite that moment of clarity she just experienced, Eve realizes that there are still so many questions. And, most pressing right now, how can they begin to talk? She needs time to think.

So when Claudia wants to know if she's coming to the Gestapo museum, Eve says, "I can't, darling, I'm beat." No one protests.

Since Paul will go with Claudia to the airport from the museum, Eve says goodbye at the hotel. Holding her child in her arms, she fights back tears, and as she watches them get into the cab to go to the street that, Paul explains, was the old Prinz-Albrecht-Strasse, Eve wonders how long it will be before she sees Claudia again? And what will happen between now and then?

That's what they have to figure out. But she knows this: She doesn't need to go through this open air museum that the

East and West Germans opened two years ago and which is so graphically called The Topography of Terror.

She has heard enough terror to last her for a lifetime.

*   *   *

Although they planned to have a long leisurely dinner after Claudia left, they end up having a quick bite and going to see "Amarcord" at a movie house not far from the hotel that specialized in old foreign films. A movie they had loved when they were young and is as good as they remembered. They had every intention of talking after that, but went quickly to their separate rooms. "There will be time tomorrow," Paul murmured as he gave her a quick kiss on the cheek, then said, "Do you need any help, with your arm?" She shook her head.

Now it is Monday. Their plane leaves this afternoon. Paul sits in the lobby after they have packed reading *Frankfurter Allgemeine Zeitung* while Eve talks to Joseph. She is determined to find the old waterworks Paul described the day he almost got caught in the Grunewald. Joseph is making a map for her and as she stands next to him Eve is holding an old knit hat she bought years ago from the bargain bin after Christmas in Vineyardhaven.

When he closes his eyes he can see her and Claudia rifling through the hats, then cutting the tags off, and wearing them out of the store. Love asserts itself in countless images, he thinks as he tries to concentrate on the newsprint. But it is no good. He cannot read the paper but keeps it in front of his face while he wrestles with what he must say to her.

Somehow he has to convince her that this trip is the beginning of a second life together. That there is no way he will let her go again.

But there is hardly any time to form the argument, in seconds here she is, standing over him, telling him, "Joseph says it isn't far at all, but we have to make a sharp left at the first fork. He also says it's a lot colder than it's been." Her voice is high and lilting, as it always is when she is pleased about something.

"Are you sure you want to go?" Paul says.

"Positive. It's a gorgeous sunny day."

They stride along, the breath pluming from their mouths, each trying to begin.

Whenever she tried to rationalize to herself what happened in the past, Eve realized that somehow, somewhere along the way she and Paul had become unable to give each other what they needed. So she says just that.

They stop, and Paul stares at her intently while she continues, "The question was why. Because you weren't willing to talk and because I wasn't willing to press you, I had no answers. Which is why I decided I had to come with you on this trip." She begins to falter. This isn't going the way she had planned, it sounds as if she's the heroine because she came, and that is not at all what she wants to convey.

Paul rescues her. "That's just the point. You came, even though, I suspect, everyone you spoke to thought you were crazy. I know the kids did. They told me so. And I'm sure your parents and Blanche weren't happy. Nor Max."

"Blanche understood. My parents were more surprised than anything. And I never told Max, it's not his affair," she interrupts him, frowning. This is harder than she anticipated.

"Look," she says, "this is between us, it has nothing to do with anyone else."

He is smiling as he shakes his head. "You're right that it's between us, but you're naïve to think that that's where it ends. This trip and what you've learned here has everything to do with the children and your parents and Berthe and Blanche and the rest of our family and our friends. They, too, never understood what really went wrong. That's why your decision to come was the linchpin. And that you had the stamina, the courage to hear every last horrible detail, that you came with me to Grete's house, why it's remarkable."

Finally his voice begins to quiver, and they walk some more in silence.

Eve puts her hand on his arm. "Paul, don't. Don't make it sound so heroic."

"I'm not. I'm being as truthful as I can. You were heroic, you are . . . But, you're also right that in some profound way your heroism is beside the point. The real question is: Can you live with someone who has committed such loathsome acts?"

She stares. She can always count on Paul to get to the crux of the matter before anyone else. There is another long silence and they begin to walk again.

But then Paul seems to gather strength, and he forges ahead. "I know it's not a pretty picture, but it's my childhood, all I've ever had. And it has been a constant source of shame. So although I wanted to tell you years ago, I did everything I could to avoid it. To our peril and that of our children."

A long pause. "You say we couldn't give each other what we needed, and you're right. It was like that for years and years, too many years. Precious time wasted. But when you consented to come with me to this crazy city you gave me exactly what I needed. We walked and I talked and you listened, and finally I feel freed from that crushing shame."

Without realizing it Eve had begun to look downwards when he started to speak, so now Paul steps closer and lifts her chin with his forefinger. He is not wearing gloves, he never wears gloves, and at his touch, she can feel tears welling in her eyes.

"What will we do?" she finally asks.

"We will continue to tell each other the truth. And we'll begin by telling the children all that I've told you."

"Did you say anything to Claudia?" Eve asks.

Paul shakes his head. "She was overwhelmed when we walked through that Gestapo Museum. She'd had enough for one day. But it's a superb job of historical research and probably helped prepare her for what's to come. When I saw her reaction, I wondered if you and I shouldn't have started there. Then maybe you would have been better prepared."

"No, I don't think so," Eve interrupts him. "There really is no preparation for what you had to tell."

Now the sun, at its highest point in the sky, is shining directly on their faces. A thin sun, whose rays light up the planes of Paul's face. A face she knows as well as her own. Eve lowers her glance to meet his. His blue eyes are as clear as she has ever seen them, clearer than they were that day so long ago when she surprised him in his office. Seeing Paul's face stripped naked of all the masks he needed in order to live, seeing his brilliant blue eyes, Eve realizes that here is the husband she longed for, the man who sometimes appears in her dreams.

Although she cannot predict their future, although she knows it won't be easy, she knows that he is right. After this tumultuous trip they are bound together in ways she never could have anticipated, and at this moment it's as if she is seeing him in an entirely new way. Does she look different to him, she wonders. And then, the larger question: Is this what true forgiveness can do?

Before they begin to walk again, Eve reaches up and pulls his scarf a little tighter. Then she tucks her arm into his, and soon Paul turns and stops, "It should be right here," he says. And sure enough, they are standing in front of that old waterworks, which looks exactly as he remembers, as if untouched by time.

AUTHOR'S NOTE

How a work of fiction comes into being is always mysterious, but several books were indispensable to the telling of this story: *Before The Deluge, A Portrait of Berlin in the 1920's* by Otto Friedrich and *Last Jews in Berlin* by Edward Gross. I must also acknowledge a debt to Isherwood's *Goodbye to Berlin* which inspired a lifelong interest in that complex city.

More thanks to my colleague Ira Berkowitz for his help, especially with the plot. But most of all, great gratitude to my husband Robert Silman for his continued encouragement and support.